ALSO BY ALIX OHLIN

The Missing Person

Babylon and Other Stories

INSIDE

INSIDE

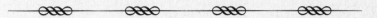

Alix Ohlin

ALFRED A. KNOPF   NEW YORK 2012

THIS IS A BORZOI BOOK
PUBLISHED BY ALFRED A. KNOPF

www.aaknopf.com

Library of Congress Cataloging-in-Publication Data
Ohlin, Alix.
  Inside / by Alix Ohlin.—1st ed.
    p. cm.
ISBN 978-0-307-59692-5
  "This is a Borzoi book."
1. Therapist and patient—Fiction. 2. Psychological fiction. I. Title.
PS3615.H57I57 2012
813'.6—dc23

                        2011050565

Jacket photograph by Simon Lee
Jacket design by Gabriele Wilson

Manufactured in the United States of America

First Edition

INSIDE

ONE

Montreal, 1996

AT FIRST GLANCE, she mistook him for something else. In the fading winter light he could have been a branch or a log, even a tire; in the many years she'd been cross-country skiing on Mount Royal, she'd found stranger debris across her path. People left behind their scarves, their shoes, their inhibitions: she'd come across lovers naked to the sky, even on cold days. In spite of these distractions, the mountain was the one place where she felt at peace, especially in winter, when tree branches stretched empty of leaves and she could see the city below her—its clusters of green-spired churches and gray skyscrapers laid out, graspable, streets rolling down to the Old Port, and in either direction the bridges extending over the pale water of the St. Lawrence. This winter had been mild, and what snow did fall first melted, then turned to ice overnight. Now, at the end of January, it had finally snowed all night and all day, at last enough to ski on. Luckily her final appointment that afternoon had canceled, leaving her free to drive up before the light was gone. She slipped around the Chalet and headed into the woods, losing the vista of Montreal below, gaining muffled silence and solitude, the trees turning the light even fainter. One skier had been here before her, leaving a path of parallel stripes. On a slight downhill slope she crouched down and picked up speed as she moved around a bend.

Turning, she saw the branch or whatever it was too late. Though she tried to slow down, she wasn't quick enough and ran right into it and was knocked out of her skis, falling sideways into the snow, realizing only when she sat up that what had tripped her was the body of a man. Her legs were on top of his, her right knee throbbing from the impact.

The air torn from her returned slowly, painfully, to her burning lungs. When she could breathe she said, "Are you all right?"

There was no answer. He was flung across the trail with his head half buried in the snow. Beyond his body the ski marks stopped. She thought he must have had an accident, but then she saw his skis propped neatly against a tree.

She got to her feet and gingerly stepped around until she could see his face. He wasn't wearing a hat. "Excuse me," she said, louder. "Are you okay?" She thought maybe he'd collapsed after a heart attack or stroke. He lay sprawled on his side, knees bent, eyes closed, one arm up above his head. *"Monsieur?"* she said. *"Ça va?"*

Kneeling down to check his pulse, she saw the rope around his neck. Thick and braided, it trailed beneath him, almost nestled under his arm, and the other end rested on a snowbank—no, was buried underneath it—and on the other side she could see that the branch it had been tied to had broken off.

She hurriedly loosened the rope and found the beating rhythm in his neck, then opened the first few snaps of his coat in the hope that this might help him to breathe. His face wasn't blue. He was around her age, thirties, his short, wavy, brown hair riddled with gray. Still his eyes wouldn't open. Should she slap him? Administer CPR? She pushed him gently onto his back. *"Monsieur?"* she said again. He didn't move.

She skied quickly back to the Chalet and called 911. In her halting French, all the more fractured because she was out of breath, she tried to describe where in the woods they were. When she returned, he was lying where she'd found him. "Sir," she said, "my name is Grace. *Je m'appelle Grace.* I called for help. Everything will be all right. *Vous êtes sauvé.*"

She put her ear next to his mouth to hear his breath. His eyes were still closed, but he heavily, unmistakably, sighed.

Later, at the Montreal General, she realized that both pairs of skis had been left behind. The emergency workers had loaded the man into the ambulance and she had followed it, weaving through the traffic along Côte-des-Neiges. She wasn't even sure why. Because the Urgences-santé men had looked at her expectantly, assuming she and the man had been skiing together? Because one of them had said, in commingled English and French, "The police—*ils vont vous poser des questions* at the 'ospital," and she had nodded obediently, like a schoolgirl?

It was partly curiosity, to know what had driven him to such an act; and partly pity, because anyone driven to hang himself would have to be suffering deeply and terribly. And it was partly that she of all people had been the one to throw herself across his path.

Maybe it was just because she wanted to know what had happened. Regardless, she was sitting in the waiting room hours later, shivering each time the glass doors slid open with an icy draft. The linoleum was streaked with gray-brown slush people had tracked in, and she could smell car exhaust and cigarette smoke from the sidewalk outside. There was no sign of any police officer wanting to ask her questions. The man had been wheeled off, with a canopy of nurses over his still-silent body. Grace waited, though she wasn't sure for what or whom. When she remembered the skis—probably long gone by now—she smacked herself on the forehead. Hers were practically brand-new. She looked at her watch; it was seven o'clock, completely dark on the mountain. She was tired and hungry and ready to go home. Before she did, though, she wanted to know that he was being taken care of. She walked over to a nurse at the reception area.

"Excuse me," she said. "Can I see him?"

The nurse didn't look up from her paperwork. *"Qui, madame?"*

"The man who was brought in earlier. The skier."

"Who?"

"I don't know his name. He was found on the mountain."

"You don't know his name?"

"I found him up there."

"So you aren't family." Her tone was hostile, weary.

"I'm a therapist," Grace said suddenly. *"Une psychologue?"* The nurse nodded, her manner softening at the French. Now she seemed to grant her a professional capacity, and Grace didn't disabuse her. "I must see him as soon as possible," she said, trying to sound authoritative.

The nurse hesitated for a moment, then shrugged and pointed to the elevator. "Three sixteen," she said.

Grace knocked before entering. The man was lying on his back, wearing a hospital gown, an IV drip attached to his arm. He was staring at the ceiling with a blank expression that didn't change when she came in. Whatever pain he'd been feeling on the mountain was absent from his face now; he might have been waiting for a train. Visible around his neck was the thick red abrasion from the rope. Clearing her throat, she sat down in a chair next to the bed.

"Do you speak English?" she said. No answer. *"Vous parlez français?"* Again, nothing. "I took a little Spanish in high school, but that's all gone, so these are pretty much your only options," she said. His clothes were folded and stacked on a bedside table. "I'm going to look through your things for your name, unless you specifically tell me not to." She went through the clothes, feeling for a wallet, and he made no move to stop her, even when she found it and pulled out his license. *John Tugwell.* English after all. She put everything back as it had been and sat down again. "John, my name is Grace," she said, "and I'm a therapist, though that's not why I'm here. I was just skiing when I found you lying on the ground. The branch you tied yourself to broke off. I called the ambulance." But for a blink, he made no sign of being conscious. She couldn't even tell if he was listening. His hands, palms down above the blanket, lay flat, unclenched.

"There usually aren't many people in that part of the park," she said, "which I guess must be why you chose it. I don't know what would've happened if I hadn't come along. Would you have tried again, after a while?"

He said nothing.

There were deep lines around his eyes, as if he spent a lot of time outdoors. His lips were unnaturally pale. Beneath the thin hospital blanket his body looked sturdy and solidly muscled. It was impossible to tell, as he lay there, whether he was handsome or not. The spirit that would have animated his face, giving it character and attitude, had receded from view. She stepped closer. Even at this little distance his body seemed to give off no heat whatsoever, as if he'd been permanently chilled.

"You're back from the dead," she said. "Maybe you don't want to be, but you are."

For the first time his eyes met hers. They were green. Then he blinked again and closed them.

"If you want to talk," Grace said, "I can listen."

They wheeled him out and then returned him to the room with his leg encased in a black boot, and the doctor came and spoke to Grace as if she had a right to be there. His ankle was sprained. There were scrapes and bruises all over his face, but they weren't serious. A nurse dropped off some crutches. The doctor, who looked exhausted and no more than twenty-five, gave him a prescription for painkillers and told him to come back in two weeks. Grace said she'd drive him home.

"Sir, we need to evaluate your situation before you go," the doctor said obliquely. When the patient said nothing, he turned to Grace. "An appointment will be made with the psychiatric department," he said, his manner very formal.

She nodded.

"Our staff will make you the appointment?" the doctor said, turning back toward him.

From the bed, the man's eyes met hers in a plea. She shrugged; he had already refused her help.

He coughed and said, "I didn't really mean to do it." His voice was hoarse and clouded with phlegm, as if the words were caught deep inside, trapped in some cave or web.

"What do you mean?" the doctor asked.

"I just wanted to see what she'd say." Tugwell jerked a thumb in Grace's direction. His voice was painfully rasped and he swallowed visibly after he spoke, but then he modulated it to a tone of playful wryness. "We were skiing together and I told her I was going to kill myself and went off in a different direction. I said I had the rope with me and was going to do it immediately. It took her *nine minutes* to decide to come after me. Nine minutes! Can you believe that? I timed her."

"You told your wife you were going to kill yourself to see how she would react, and then you timed her?" the doctor said, frowning skeptically. A francophone, possibly he thought he hadn't understood the story correctly.

"Almost ten minutes," Tugwell said. His eyes sprang back to her, and her heart twisted strangely in her chest.

The doctor looked at Grace. For a moment she hesitated: to go along with his story was so absurd that no sane person would even consider it. This man needed help, starting with the psychiatric evaluation and professional intervention. Yet something in his expression, a sense of collusion, drew her in. The spark of life in his eyes was so sudden and bright that she wanted to keep it there, to fan it from a flicker to a flame.

Maybe it was because she thought the hospital would likely give him the briefest, most cursory treatment. Or because she felt responsible for having brought him in. Or because she was happy that he'd turned to her for help.

"He's never there for me either," she said, as petulantly as she could.

The doctor sighed heavily and checked his watch. "So this is a marital squabble."

Grace nodded.

Tugwell said, "I guess things got out of hand."

The doctor, shrugging as if this weren't the strangest behavior he had ever seen, clicked the end of his pen and made a notation on the chart.

"I'll take care of him," Grace said.

Too busy to worry about it, the doctor left.

When they were alone in the room, Tugwell looked at her again. The flicker had gone from his eyes, as if the effort of that one lie had tired him beyond all reckoning. "Don't you have anywhere else to be?"

"This isn't about me," she said.

"Dodgeball."

"Excuse me?"

"Sorry, I meant dodging the question. I'm groggy."

"I'm not dodging the question," Grace said, although she was. "I just don't think it really matters. Nothing about me really matters right now, not to you. You're hurt and I'm willing to drive you home and get you settled. Or I can call someone else. Do you want me to do that? Is there somebody you want me to call?"

He closed his eyes.

"Do you need help getting dressed, John?"

"Tug," he said. "And no."

"Is this another dodgeball thing?"

"I'm called Tug."

"Okay, Tug," she said. "I'll be right outside. Call if you need me."

When she came back five minutes later he was in his gray fleece jacket and black ski pants, with one unzipped pant leg rolled up over the ankle cast. She pushed him in a wheelchair to the parking lot and helped him into her car, stowing the crutches in the backseat. Inside she cranked up the heat, and he leaned his head back and said nothing. She wondered where his family was. He wasn't wearing a wedding ring. If he didn't want her to be taking care of him, he wasn't putting up much of a fight—but the resistance could be internal. He might just be waiting for her to go away, and then he'd try again. Those were the ones who often went through with it, the cases who humored you until you finally left them alone.

"Do you live by yourself?"

"Yes. You?"

"Yes."

"Not married?"

"Divorced."

"Me too," he said. "Well, separated. Not official."

"I'm sorry," she said. "Is that why you wanted to do this?"

There was a slight pause before he said, "You don't beat around."

"No point," she said, adopting his bulleted way of speaking.

He looked out the window until she understood he wasn't going to answer the question. Which was fair enough, but then he turned back. "You're a therapist, you said."

"Yes, that's right. I have an office on Côte-des-Neiges. Grace Tomlinson. You could come by if you wanted to, or call, any time. I'm listed."

"This is how you get business? Skiing around looking for depressed people?"

"That's right, exactly," Grace said cheerfully. One of her professional skills was to remain unruffled. "It was a slow day until you turned up. Can you direct me from here?"

He nodded. They drove north along St. Laurent, through Little Italy, into a neighborhood where most of the signs were in Vietnamese. He told her to turn onto a darker side street, mainly of triplexes, the external staircases dusted with snow. Finally, in front of a yellow brick building, he asked her to pull over. Lights showed on every floor. People don't leave lights on unless they think they're coming back, she thought. "Someone waiting for you in there, Tug?"

"You're inquisitive," he said.

"Yes. You said you lived alone, so why didn't you turn off the lights?"

He sighed and rubbed his eyes. After a moment he said, "The lights are on for the dog."

"You have a dog?"

He shook his head. "It's my ex-wife's dog. My wife's. Whatever she is to me now, it's her dog. But she had to go out of town, so I'm taking care of it. This happens all the time. She's picking him up later. He would've been fine, okay? He has water, food, a chew toy. I hate that dog."

"Why do you suppose that is?" Grace said.

"Jesus, is this the therapy-mobile? Are you giving therapy to me *in your car*? I've been in therapy before." The words spilled out of him, scratchy but hectic. "You know, the most helpful thing the therapist ever said to me was, *There's never going to be a perfect time to do anything in your life.* Maybe today wasn't the perfect time to do what I did, what with the dog being there and everything, but I remembered what the therapist told me and I was consoled."

"You were consoled, really?" Grace said. This wasn't a phrase she heard every day.

"Yeah, kind of. Within limits."

"As with everything," Grace said, earning, for the first time, a nod of agreement from him.

He opened the door and hopped out, then opened the back door to retrieve his crutches. As he tried to pull them out, he lost his balance and fell to the ground, and the crutches careened away on the icy sidewalk. "Fucking hell," he said.

She turned off the engine and got out. He was hopping angrily up and down, trying to reach a crutch that had landed upside down in a snowbank. She picked it up, dusted off the snow, and held it under his right arm. He was balancing, just barely, on the other crutch. He took a step toward the front door, then fell down again.

"Look, I think you're going to have to let me help you."

He said nothing. She put her arm around his waist and braced her hip against his, forcing him to lean on her, then stepped carefully up the walk with his arm across her shoulders. He used a crutch on the other side to help them both up the stairs. It took them five minutes to reach the front door, and another two for him to fish the keys out of his pocket.

Once the door was open, without looking at her, he muttered, "Thanks."

"Can I come in?"

"Why?"

"You need help. I don't think there's anybody in there except a dog that can't help you with the crutches."

"You don't know that. He's a pretty smart dog."

"Well, he'd also have to be a tall and dexterous dog," Grace said, "which is rarer."

He shrugged. Resignation was all he had to offer. Inside, the place was nicer than she had expected: wood floors, Persian rugs, bookshelves, artwork. There were stairs off to the right; she was sure the bedroom was upstairs, which wouldn't be easy for him.

He crutched awkwardly toward the back of the apartment, and the dog came out to greet him, a tiny Dachshund that pranced around his shins and whined. Worried that Tug might lose his balance, Grace sat down on the couch and called the dog over, and he jumped up into her lap and settled down like a cat.

"Aren't you friendly?" Grace said. She heard water running in the kitchen, then it stopped.

Tug stumbled back into view. "Look, I appreciate your help and everything, but I'll be fine now."

"Do you have some friends or family we could call? You shouldn't be alone."

"In our hearts none of us are ever alone," Tug said. "The therapist told me that, too."

She decided to try a different tack. "What floor is the bathroom on?"

"There's one on each."

"And your bedroom?"

He sighed. "Upstairs. Why are you so pushy?"

"I'm not pushy. I'm *efficient*. I'll get you settled in and then I'll go. I think it makes the most sense for you to sleep down here. I can go upstairs and get some sheets and things. I'll just take them off the bed, okay? I won't snoop around or touch anything. I'll be right back."

He shrugged, as best he could with the crutches under his arms, and sat down in an armchair. The dog deserted her for him.

Though she tried to keep her pledge, she couldn't help but notice that the furnishings upstairs were equally tasteful. It didn't seem like him at all. It wasn't that she thought he wouldn't be tasteful, just that he would be neglectful of things like that. It must be the influence of the ex-wife. She stripped the bed of its duvet and sheets, carried them bundled in her arms downstairs, and made up the couch.

"What do you have in here to eat?" she said.

Now he looked not annoyed but amused, the barest quiver of a smile hovering around his lips. "Nothing."

"Let's order a pizza," she said.

"Are you serious? Come on. Who *are* you?"

"I found you in the snow," she said, "and I don't want you to kill yourself."

"So you think you control me now. You own my life."

"No, I think we should order a pizza."

And she did. The dog went outside through a pet door into the triplex's small backyard, where he tiptoed around anxiously before running back inside. Grace set plates, napkins, and glasses out on the coffee table. When the pizza came, she paid for it. It was ten o'clock already and she had patients the next morning, but she didn't care. She could tell Tug thought she was a busybody or some deeply lonely person with nothing to go home to. These things were possibly a little bit true. What was mostly true, though, was that she didn't like to fail at things, as she would if she left him and he killed himself, because it was within her power—merely with her presence—to stop it.

They ate pizza and watched a movie from the seventies starring Jane Fonda. After it ended she said, "Why don't you try to get some sleep? Do you want me to bring you some painkillers?" Thus far, she hadn't seen him take any of the prescribed drugs.

"Nightingale," he said.

"You mean Florence? Look, I just want you to be comfortable."

"I'd be more comfortable if you left," he said. "Didn't you say you'd get me settled and then leave?"

"I can't do that," Grace said. "At least not tonight."

"Why?" he said, his voice flattened to a tone of pure exasperation.

"Because if I left and you killed yourself, it would be my fault."

Prone on the couch, his head against a cushion, his bandaged ankle raised on another, he frowned at her. The color had returned to his lips, and she noticed that they were quite pink, not feminine but sensual, the lower lip full, even when straightened, as it was right now, in an angry line. "You want this to be all about you, is that it? You have a complex or something."

"Maybe," she said lightly.

"You want me to owe you."

"You don't owe me anything. I don't want anything except for you not to kill yourself."

"Why?" he said again.

"If you saw someone about to commit a murder," Grace said, "wouldn't you feel obligated to stop it?"

He shook his head. "This is different."

"Not to me."

"Maybe you're on some kind of sexual kick. You're attracted to damaged men you think you can save and therefore control."

Grace laughed. "Who's the therapist now?"

Though she would have denied this last charge to her dying breath, she did have to fight the urge to go over, sit down next to him, and hold his hand. She felt that a physical touch might ground him somehow. She wanted to put her palm on his shoulder or cheek, to communicate through her skin that he wasn't alone, that his particular self was worthy of recognition, held value and weight. She moved a little closer, though still in the armchair, not wanting to alarm him.

"My ex-wife would be very unhappy if she found you here," Tug said.

"Why is that?"

"She's very jealous."

"There's nothing here to be jealous of."

"You don't think? She comes back and finds a strange woman in my house giving me an extracurricular therapy session? *Is that what they're calling it these days?* That's what she'd say."

"You're getting divorced because you were unfaithful," Grace said.

"No," Tug said. "No." For the first time she saw his face lose its impassive hold, now twisting in the grip of emotion, with tears welling in his eyes.

She waited for him to go on, but when he didn't, she decided to change the subject. "What do you do for a living?"

Tug looked at her evenly, his eyes gone suddenly dry. "I work at a stationery store."

"Stationery as in paper."

"Wedding invitations, office letterhead, thank-you notes. Whereas you're a commando therapist, running around offering counsel to people in pain wherever you find them."

"I don't know how you feel about your work," Grace said slowly. "But for me, it doesn't necessarily make sense to pick and choose your moments. It seems inconsistent to be a therapist all day and then act completely different at night. Do you see what I mean?"

She saw him finally see her, really take her in, not as an irritant or an obstacle but as a person. She saw herself register on his mind. He was staring at her, and without knowing exactly why, she felt herself flush.

"I guess I don't feel that way about my work with paper," he said, and smiled.

"Does your ankle hurt?"

"Not so you'd notice," he said.

It was midnight, the dog sleeping in Tug's lap. There was no sign of the ex-wife. Grace watched him for a little while, in the dark of the strange living room. By half past twelve they were both asleep, she in the armchair, he on the couch, and when she woke up in the morning he was still alive.

Having quickly showered and changed, Grace was in her office before nine. Her back ached from dozing off and on in the armchair all night. She'd left Tug glowering on the couch, no happier than he'd been the night before, nor any more willing to discuss what had happened on the mountain. She was reluctant to leave him alone, but she couldn't stay and witness his life indefinitely, much as she'd been tempted. The morning passed quickly, though Tug was always there in the back of her mind, his voice coming back like a song's refrain. She kept thinking about his blank face as he lay in the snow, the angry redness on his neck, and how his eyes had suddenly, startlingly come to life when he concocted that ridiculous story in the hospital. What kind of person was he?

Again and again she pushed her curiosity away and tried to focus on the individuals in her office, the bustle and din of an ordinary day. Frank Lavallée, the fifty-five-year-old, mid-divorce recovering alcoholic. Mike and Denise Morgenstern, a married couple from Rosemount who couldn't talk to each other without arguing. Annie Hardwick, who was sixteen years old and cut herself. As they spoke, Grace narrowed her gaze on their faces. Their mouths moved constantly, their lips pressed flat in concentration, wet with spittle or foam when agitated, injury or emotion written there first. Annie's mouth showed a twinkle of braces that came and went, flashing in the soft light of the office lamp like signals from a faraway ship.

When Annie felt the urge to cut herself, Grace told her, she should visualize herself as a movie star—the girl's fantasy of a successful life—and convert the energy into a different behavior, something a star might do, like exercise or studying her lines (for which homework could stand in). This was what they were working on. Annie had a journal in which she wrote down her thoughts, and she reluctantly showed it to Grace, her neat handwriting chronicling all her dismal urges, the thirst for pain, the hunger to see her own blood. Cutting, she wrote, was the only thing she could really feel. She craved it, enjoying the building anticipation and then the secret, controlled fulfillment, the private pain she lavished upon herself like a gift. On the journal's cover was a photo of an all-boy band she'd scissored out of a magazine, and next to that was a shot of the beach house where she spent summers with her family and a strip of pictures taken with a friend in a booth at the mall. All these images were safe and sweet and innocent, while the notes inside were unhappy and violent and tortured. *I am rotten*, she wrote. *I am diseased.*

Grace had given her an assignment: to write a letter to herself from the future, a happy future in which she'd gotten everything she wanted, about what she'd been through as a teenager and how she'd survived it. Annie complained—she had enough homework to deal with already!—but Grace knew she liked the satisfaction of being given tasks she could complete, unlike the larger task she set herself every day, which was to be beautiful, smart, unassailable, and perfect.

Grace felt for Annie the particular pity that a person who had a happy childhood feels for one who didn't. An only child, she herself had grown up in a world dense with her own imagination. For three years she'd had a make-believe friend named Rollo Hartin. Her indulgent parents had set a place for Rollo at the dinner table and plumped an extra pillow for him in her bed. Grace was the kind of child who brought home injured birds and tried to nurse them back to health. When she saw cats wandering around the neighborhood, she took them home for bowls of milk. Hours or days later, their confused, angry owners would stop by to reclaim them.

This was in a leafy suburb of Toronto. Her parents were happily married. Doctors themselves, they had found in each other the ideal mate. Every evening at five o'clock they'd come home, open a bottle of white wine, and talk to each other about their day for half an hour; just the two of them, wrapped up in their own company. They believed that the foundation of a family was a strong marriage—which Grace, as an adult, also believed—and yet somehow the very strength of their marriage, the unity of the front, sometimes gave her the impression that she was an intruder in it. As soon as she went off to the University of Toronto her parents retired, sold the house, and moved to an island off the coast of British Columbia, where her father worked on a novel, her mother made ceramics, and they still observed the white-wine ritual at five o'clock every day.

Grace had spent her life attempting to recreate in her own space the perfection of her parents' lives. It hadn't helped that they always made it look so easy. There was an inherent mystery to the simplicity of it, to how well things worked out for them. They must have been the luckiest people alive.

When she was at university, she met Mitch Mitchell. His actual first name, which he considered unusable, was Francis. A graduate student in clinical psychology, he was the teaching assistant in a lab her second year. She had originally intended to study literature, because she liked analyzing the motivations of people in stories, but it turned out that the truer draw was psychology itself. Getting to the roots of human behavior, the mind laid bare in all its frailties and contradictions, fascinated her. She fell in love with the subject and Mitch at the same time, and later on she wasn't always certain that she had kept the two things separate in her mind. After they married, she followed him to Montreal, where he had a residency, and enrolled in graduate school herself.

The first few years passed quickly. They both kept very busy. On the weekends they went hiking in the Laurentians or out to eat downtown, Grace marveling, as they drove past, at the crowds lined up outside Schwartz's all day and night. Mitch taught her to love Fairmount bagels, which they ate straight from the bag and still hot from the oven, unable to wait until they got home. Sometimes they visited his mother, who was frail and lived alone in Lachine. Grace took French classes and worked at a clinic, counseling people who were addicts, or getting divorced, or failing at school or their jobs, who couldn't get out of bed in the morning. Every day she and Mitch came home and drank wine and talked about everything except their jobs, the dull weight of all those intense and brutal conversations. They talked about politics, the weather, houses they were thinking of buying. They never talked about sex, which they were having less and less of. They never talked about unhappiness, their own or other people's. In other words, they did everything they had been taught professionally was wrong.

One Saturday morning she came home from the store to find Mitch emerging, oddly red-faced, from the bedroom. At first she didn't want to say anything. She put away the groceries, and Mitch got into the shower. Then she walked into the bedroom and started looking around his side of the bed. Stuffed hastily below the mattress, its shiny spine extruding like a scab, was a porn magazine. The girls were young, with enormous fake breasts. That was the most disturbing part, she thought at first, their lack of resemblance to any real woman. But this wasn't true; the most disturbing part was that her husband was jerking off to a porn magazine while she was at the grocery store. She tried speaking to herself as if she were a client: *This kind of behavior is not uncommon, nor does it signal an automatic betrayal.* But it was bullshit. All the counsel she had ever given burned to ashes in the face of lived experience.

Mitch walked in, wearing a towel, and stopped. Seeming to read her mind, which he could still do, he said, "No. The most disturbing part is that I feel more emotionally connected to the girls in those pictures than I do to you."

Grace began to cry, tears not of anger or sadness but of sheer, straight pain. Mitch comforted her, because he was good at that. And they slept together with a kind of pathetic, slippery lust she hated even to remember, the porn magazine askew on the floor beside the bed. They didn't separate until a year later, but looking back she knew this was the day their marriage ended.

She lived alone now, in a two-bedroom apartment in Notre-Dame-de-Grâce. She'd been on some dates since the divorce, but nothing had taken. She was thirty-five and thought that maybe she just wasn't the marrying kind—a statement she would have dismissed, or at least

raised an eyebrow at, if it came from a client. The therapist's preroga-
tive was sometimes to put the blinders back on.

Most of the day's appointments were routine, until it came to
Annie Hardwick. During an earlier visit, Grace had seen the shiny
pink scars that inched up the girl's pale stomach to her rib cage;
she had lifted her shirt with a feigned reluctance that failed to
conceal her pride in the harm she'd done herself. As common as
cutting was, Grace still winced to see the evidence of it on Annie's
skin. The girl wasn't beautiful yet, but she was going to be. She
hadn't grown into herself or into her body. Her features loomed
too large on her face, and blue veins showed through her translu-
cent skin at her temples and chin. Her dirty-blond hair hung thin
and lank to her shoulders, and her forehead was covered with small
red pimples. In a few years, Grace could imagine, when Annie was
taller and learned to sit up straight, when her body grew curves to
match her face, she would look like the movie star she so desperately wanted to be.

But Annie didn't know this. All she saw was the infinite distance
between herself as she was and the perfection to which she aspired.
Her father was an orthodontist and her mother a lawyer, and they
had raised her to hold herself to a high standard. She got good grades,
participated in extracurricular activities, had friends and family who
cared for her. All this was invisible to her, or at least immaterial. Her
lack of perspective was gigantic. When she looked at herself she saw
an ugly, mean, ungainly girl, constantly failing, deservedly ignored.
She believed wholeheartedly in her own shortcomings, and nothing
Grace had told her had unsettled this conviction.

One day her mother had found her asleep on the couch. A button on her shirt gaped open, exposing her midriff, and her mother
thought she saw a rash there. Bending closer to inspect it, she saw
that it was an intricate maze of cuts, each line crossing the next,
forming a mass that looked like a star.

Hence, therapy.

Annie's after-school hours passed in appointments: the dentist, the hairdresser, the dermatologist. She was being raised and tended by a corps of professionals, to which Grace was only the latest addition. Thus far, she didn't think they had made much headway. The girl was polite, did as she was asked, and answered questions at a reasonable length, all while giving away as little as possible. Her parents believed her when she said she wasn't cutting anymore. Grace didn't.

But today was different. She came in wearing a fleece zip-up over her uniform, with her long hair swept up in a messy ponytail. Usually she sat staring at the ground with her legs crossed as Grace prodded her to get the conversation rolling. This time, though, she held the homework assignment out right away.

Taking it, Grace said, "Why don't you tell me, in your own words, what it says?"

Annie shook her head. "Please don't make me," she said. "Look, I did it. You can read it, okay?"

"This wasn't really for me. It was for you. To get you thinking when you're on your own, and to give us a basis for our discussion here."

Annie didn't say anything, just looked at her with her enormous eyes. Her face had a coltish, unfinished look, a softness in her features, as if her bones hadn't quite finished forming. Her hands played nervously with the pleats of her navy-blue kilt. Her fingernails were long and perfectly manicured; it was something she and her mother did together. As Grace watched, Annie lifted her hand and squeezed a pimple on her chin, tried to stop, then pressed it again, the look on her face pleading.

Grace waited her out for a minute, hoping she'd give in, but finally relented. "All right," she said. "I'll read it out loud—"

"No!" Annie said. "Please."

"Okay. I'll read it to myself, and then we'll talk about it. You have to promise that we'll be able to discuss it together, all right? Is that a deal?"

The girl nodded and looked down at the floor. Finally, Grace looked down at the page. The letter was extremely short, the handwriting strangely androgynous: slanted, angular, not the usual bubbled teenage-girl script.

A Letter to Myself Now From Myself
When I Am 24, by Annie Hardwick
Im sorry I couldn't focus on this assignment.
I think Im pregnant.

Grace looked up. The girl was crying, her head turned toward the corner of the room as if this made her invisible. She sniffled.

Grace held out a box of tissues. "Here, blow." Then she said, "Do your parents know?"

Annie shook her head.

"Have you taken a pregnancy test?"

She nodded.

"How late are you? When was your last period?"

"I should have gotten it almost a month ago," the girl burst out. "You have to help me."

"Of course I'll help you," Grace said calmly. Instantly Annie's face brightened, only to dim again when she added, "I'll help you tell your parents."

"Are you out of your fucking mind?" Annie said. She'd never sworn in session before. She'd stopped crying now, and her face was red and swollen. "My mom threw a fit this morning because I have a *hangnail.* 'Annie, there's no point in me buying you a twenty-dollar manicure if you can't keep it neat for more than a day. Why are you so careless?' What do you think she'd say if she found out I had a fetus inside me? How *careless* is that?"

Careless was the last thing Annie was. She was weighted with care, which was rounding her shoulders and curving her spine; it was crushing her.

"I think she'd be glad, in the end, that you could confide in her," Grace said, though truthfully, Annie's characterization of her mother seemed accurate. The girl might have been high-strung and deluded about her own failings, but she had a pretty good grasp of her parents'.

"You're crazy," Annie said, the tears falling again, "if you think she wants to hear about this."

"What about your father?"

This question made Annie cry even harder. "Oh, God," she said.

As bad as Grace felt for her, her pulse was quickening. This was the first time Annie had reached out to ask for help, or ask for anything at all. It was a major crisis that could push her over the edge, but, properly handled, it could also bring her back.

Grace let her cry for a moment, her shoulder shuddering with sobs before finally slowing. Annie blew her nose loudly once, twice, then sat fidgeting with the tissue in her lap. After a while, Grace said, "Tell me about the boy."

The girl shook her head.

"He's part of this too, you know," Grace went on. She needed Annie to say if she knew him well or just a little, whether she loved him, anything that might lead to a real discussion.

But Annie only shook her head again and smiled wryly. "He's nobody," she said, her tone weary, suddenly wise. She was a chameleon: in her school uniform, crying and begging for help, she'd seemed a child; now, crossing her legs and smiling mysteriously, she could have been five years older. Grace could feel her receding, the mask of her face closing. So for the next few minutes she gave a rote explanation of the options, of Annie's future, urging her to seriously consider all the possibilities, to talk to her doctor, to *think*, and to remember that no matter what happened, her life would not be over.

Annie nodded, acting as though she were listening, but when Grace paused, she said, "I can't trust the doctor. She's friends with my mom and I know she'd tell her even if she promised she wouldn't. I can't trust my friends, they're such total gossips I know they'd have to tell somebody and soon it'll be all over school. You're the only person I can tell."

"I'm glad you feel you can talk to me."

The girl saw an advantage and pressed it, leaning forward and locking her wide eyes on Grace's—the same posture she probably used at home when asking for some special present. "Will you promise not to tell my parents?"

Grace sat back. For the second time in as many days she felt herself being enlisted in a pretense, a story in which she ought to play no part. And again she felt that same need to take a risk, to earn the trust of someone in need, because nobody else in the world seemed to have it. But this was a child. "I can't do that," she told her.

"I should've known," Annie said. "This is such a waste of time." She stood up and stuffed her things into her bag, the zipper of her fleece singing as she pulled it up.

"Wait," Grace said, wanting to give the girl something to carry with her out of the office. "Just remember that you have options."

When Annie turned, her face was as blank as snow; anything she'd just revealed of herself was now hidden behind a gate of disbelief. Only the tinges of pink at her eyes and nose hinted at the explosions of the past hour. "Sure," she said, "options."

Grace had the sharp, sudden feeling that the girl would never come back again, or share anything of herself if she did. This wasn't the first time that she'd seen a teenage girl in trouble, but Annie had gotten under her skin—her quicksilver changes between adult and child, how hard she came down on herself, the shy glitter of her braces-thick smile. Grace wished it were permissible to tell her the simple truth: that the same thing had happened to her in high school, and that while she would never wish it on anyone else, everything had turned out fine. This was hardly appropriate therapeutic practice, and she never once had been tempted to confess it before. Something about Annie was different from other patients, and it made her want to prick the bubble of the girl's unhappiness. And the way she talked about the baby's father, her air of shielding secrecy, had touched Grace's heart, and her memory.

She bit her lip. "Okay, Annie," she said, "I won't tell."

When she closed the office at five thirty and stepped outside, it was her own life, not Annie's, that she was thinking of. Back in high school, she had been a champion downhill skier, gifted on the slopes. She had spent her weekends drowsing on overheated buses to and from Blue Mountain. Her parents' house had a wall filled with her trophies and medals and blurry photographs showing her swooping across the finish line in an aerodynamic crouch. There had been talk of recruitment, of Olympic possibilities. Her coach said he'd never seen a skier so confident, so fearless. Her connection to the sport was part instinct and part habit: she skied because she always had and because her body knew how to do it without being instructed. Even the muscle aches that sometimes woke her up at night felt like part of her, as natural as breathing. Then, the year of her sixteenth birthday, her boyfriend Kevin blew out his knee on a sharp turn in a semifinal heat.

Kevin's was the first body Grace knew as well as her own. Sinewy, olive hued, it had revealed itself to hers in the backs of buses, cars, a room at their friend Cheri's house during a parents-out-of-town party. His chest was almost hairless, his muscular calves ropy with veins. The fact that she at first had been frightened by its contours and smells, its unexpected explosions of hair, its capacity for sexual performance, made her eventual familiarity with it seem all the more important, more earned. Seeing him in the hospital bed with his right side bandaged and cast in plaster, she felt the throb and pulse of pain in her own body.

Two weeks after his accident, Grace said she just didn't feel like skiing anymore, that she was quitting. This was understood as an act of dramatic renunciation by her teammates, parents, and coaches. Taking it as a testament of her great love, Kevin burst into tears, though this might have had something to do with all the drugs he was on. Her parents encouraged her to confront her fears and get back on the horse. Grace explained calmly and maturely that she had simply decided it wasn't worth it, that there were other things in life she wanted to pursue. But she was lying. The truth was that just before Kevin's accident she had discovered she was pregnant. She knew exactly what to do, and she shot toward it as if on skis: she had an abortion. She didn't tell Kevin, or her parents, or her friends. It was all very straightforward.

Afterward, to her surprise, she in fact didn't feel like skiing, and Kevin's accident provided the perfect cover story. Originally she'd thought she might take a couple of days to recover, as if from a flu, and then, to the rousing cheers of her parents and teammates, return to the sport. But she soon discovered that the urge to race, to compete, to win, had been bled from her on the same morning. It had all been too ridiculously and awfully easy. She had a baby inside her, just like that, and she got rid of it, also just like that. Two equally momentous, symmetrical events.

Not one soul knew what she'd done, and the air of corrupt superiority this secret engendered in her changed her more than either the accidental pregnancy or its termination had. She told herself that she ought to give up something she loved—skiing—in reparation for her carelessness and ruthlessness. But even this sacrifice proved easy and false. Once she quit skiing, she was surprised to discover how little she missed it.

Kevin endured months of rehab and within a year was back on the team. Grace had no idea what had become of him, this boy whose body had once been so familiar, whose child she'd had inside her. During his recuperation she'd tended his skin with vitamin E lotion to minimize the scars. She'd thought about the thin, olive-skinned children they'd have someday, when they were ready, when it was time. As his knee healed, they swore they'd always be together. Yet when she got into U of T, she accepted without even really discussing it with him, knowing he'd already started eyeing a girl on the swim team with chlorine-bleached hair. Life carried them so fast down the slope and far away from where they'd started that they hardly noticed it happening. They broke the promises they'd made to each other so quickly and easily that they didn't even have time to feel betrayed.

TWO

∮∮∮   ∮∮∮   ∮∮∮

New York, 2002

SHE WAS NEW to the city at a time when having been there *before* meant something. She was late to the event. She didn't know any-one, hadn't lost anyone, wasn't part of the history. This was all okay with her.

It was January. She found an apartment on the Lower East Side through a guy she met in her acting class. Larry's grandmother had lived in the apartment for decades, keeping the rent low; now she was in a nursing home, adrift in an Alzheimer's haze, only occasion-ally convinced she would soon move back home. The family, having cleared the apartment of its doilied furniture and ancient knick-knacks, sublet it to Anne at what even she, new to New York, could tell was an insane bargain. This was because Larry hoped to have sex with her. She took the apartment and dropped the class.

Sometimes he came by, supposedly to pick up his grandmother's mail or check on the faucets. "I never see you anymore," he'd say, barely dampening the complaint in his voice.

"I'm so busy," she'd say, never specifying at what.

Larry worked in commercials. He was the husband strolling through the house in the real-estate ad, the man grimacing with hemorrhoid pain before exhaling in relief. In between these shoots he took classes and auditioned for plays. "Keeping busy's important," he told Anne. "An unstructured life is a terrible thing."

She politely agreed, then left as soon as possible, abandoning him in her apartment. She knew he wouldn't disturb anything or rifle through her things—he was a transparently honest person, which was one reason he wasn't a very successful actor—and also that he wouldn't find anything of interest if he did.

She was not, in fact, busy at all. If her life was unstructured, at least it was terrible in ways she enjoyed. She had saved enough money to tide her over while she looked for work, and she believed that something perfect would come along—without knowing what it might be—and that before it did she shouldn't accept substitutes. Her confidence in the universe's generosity was mystical, and no less strong for not having been confirmed. She spent her days in coffee shops on Houston Street, reading Stanislavsky and scanning ads for casting calls. People at auditions kept shaking their heads and saying, "This part isn't right for you, but trust me, it's only a matter of time," and she believed them. She heard the phrase so often that she came to see *a matter of time* as a literal, physical thing she could wrap around herself like a blanket, comforting and soft.

Finally she took a job at a temp agency in Midtown, mostly because she thought waitressing was a cliché. She did data entry in the off-hours, leaving the days free for auditions. In the waiting areas she always saw the same people, who became the closest thing to friends she had, although she knew they really weren't, that they would resent anyone who broke through. She was cast as a fairy in a *Midsummer* that, being post 9/11, obliged her to wear a turban and carry a hand grenade. Even though the production was awful, she felt the lights on her face and knew the audience in the darkness was watching her, and her blood boiled like a kettle, dying to be poured.

The play closed after ten days, and her nights were free. Larry had stopped coming around. One evening she saw him inside a bar on Avenue A, holding hands with a woman across a tiny table, his eyes

glassy with triumph. She didn't care about him, of course, but a physical ache rippled across her skin. She went to a poetry reading that
night at the New School. The reader was middle-aged and Irish, with
ghostly, blue-green eyes. Each poem concerned the dissolution of his
marriage and his resulting loss of faith in the world, which he thought
had already been lost. This was the worst part, his poems seemed to
say: you believed your cynicism would save you from hurt, only to
discover a secret, uncherished vulnerability in your soul. Anne sat in
the front row, bought his book afterward, and told him that his work
spoke to her as little else did. "You've made me feel less alone," she
said.

    They went out for a drink. The poet was rambling, sweet, and ten-
der, and wept while describing his mother, who had died when he
was a child. He didn't ask Anne any questions about her life, but she
didn't mind. Acting was about listening, one of her teachers had told
her: you focused on the other person in the scene and let them dictate
to you. You reacted. Even more than that, you let them change you. So
there was no need to decide in advance how to say your line. It was all
response. This is what she did that night; by listening, she became—or
pretended to become—the only woman in the world who understood
him. Two days' growth of salt-and-pepper beard grazed her cheek
when they kissed; on his breath was the sour smell of red wine. At her
apartment, he lay in bed and ranted about the man who was fucking
his wife. The next morning he apologized if he'd talked too much.

    "Not at all," she said. "It was exactly what I needed." What she
needed was the bruise and crash of another body against her own, a
collision that made her feel real. She'd wanted to be manhandled, not
listened to, or cared for, or even seen.

"You pretty women are such goddamn nightmares," a drunk told her
one night in a dim bar on Fiftieth Street, where she'd stopped by after
a day of temping. She had let him buy her a drink, then turned him
down for dinner because she didn't like the smell of his cologne, and
now he was mad. "You're all the same. Hollow at the core."

    "I'm not hollow," she said, smiling sweetly. Her core was molten, radioactive. She knew that beneath the surface she was diseased, rotten, incinerating herself from the inside. But that wasn't the same thing as being hollow. Not the same thing at all.

Toward the end of February, she got back to her building around six in the afternoon. She had been cast, through the intervention of the Irish poet, in a play about the potato famine. In rehearsals she had to roll around moaning in hunger in a chilly basement, and after every session she was exhausted and aching and, indeed, starving.

There was a bad smell inside the front door. The landlord, wanting to make life unpleasant for those in the rent-stabilized apartments, had suspended superintendent services. Nothing was cleaned, there were no functioning lightbulbs in the stairwell, there was no one to call in case of an emergency. In the corner, just below the mailboxes, was a pile of what Anne took to be discarded clothes until she realized, with a start, that it was a person.

Whoever it was shifted slightly beneath a brown wool blanket and a green army coat that were somehow twisted together in a kind of shelter. Outside it was damp and blustery, the kind of freezing cold that slips through zippers and buttons to get at your skin, even into your muscles. She let him be.

The next day, though, he was still there. The grandmothers in the building—almost all the apartments were rented by little old ladies— had clustered anxiously on the landings, whispering. Of course the super wouldn't answer his phone or buzzer, so one of the old ladies had called the police. "They laughed in my face, those rat bastards," she said. "Said they had more important things to do." Other tenants, probably nervous about their own status in the building or the country, slipped past without so much as a glance.

Anne, theoretically, should have done the same thing. She was living in an illegal sublet with no proof that she belonged there, and only Larry's fear of confrontation kept him from kicking her out. But she could handle him. She jumped right into the conversation.

Soon the intruder in the lobby had drawn the residents together, like survivors of a storm. For the next two days, as Anne went into and out of the building, she would meet her neighbors' eyes with a shrug and a smile, and they'd shrug and smile back.

In all this time the guy beneath the blanket didn't show his face, though the smell of urine started wafting up the stairwell. When the tenants met now, they scrunched their noses in distaste and hurried into their apartments as quickly as possible, disgusted and afraid.

Finally, Mrs. Bondarchuk, the one who had called the police, clutched Anne's arm outside her door and drew her into the kitchen. "You've got to do something."

"Me? What about the super? Or the cops?"

Mrs. Bondarchuk shot her a scornful look. "You don't think they have other things to do?"

"Sure, but what am I supposed to do?"

Mrs. Bondarchuk was a tiny Ukrainian lady, barely five feet tall, but her wrinkled face was powerfully insistent. Her short hair was dyed a lurid, unconvincing red. Until recently, she had refused to acknowledge Anne's presence, but her new friendliness came at a price. "You go talk to them," she said firmly. "You're a young person." The logic of this was self-evident to her. "*You* go talk."

"All right," Anne said. "Fine."

She went downstairs and stood next to the pile without any idea what sort of creature was hidden beneath it. "Excuse me," she finally said.

There was neither answer nor movement in the pile, and the smell was rank. It had been four days.

"I'm sorry, but you can't stay here. You have to leave."

No answer. Was he asleep? Passed out on drugs?

"I know it's cold out," she said. "But there are places, right? I mean, shelters. They'll feed you, and give you a shower and stuff. You have options."

As she said it, she remembered someone speaking those last three words to her, *You have options*, when she was very young, and the way a voice had risen up inside her, silent but stubborn, that said, *No, I don't.*

The pile, however, said nothing. Defeated, she turned on her heel and went back to her apartment.

———

What put the situation over the edge was the shit. She left for rehearsal and when she came back, three hours later, a few pages of the *New York Times* Arts section were neatly folded into quarters in the opposite corner of the entryway. The smell was unmistakable.

"Jesus Christ," she said. "Are you kidding me?"

Taking a deep breath and holding it, she grabbed one edge of the wool blanket and pulled. Whoever was underneath—both underneath and inside and twisted around, it seemed—pulled back, and for a minute it was like a tug of war. Anne wanted to give up, because holding this filthy blanket was grossing her out, but then the other person gave in and she reeled backward, almost stumbling flat on her ass, and when the blanket dropped from her hand, she saw to her shock that it was a girl. Blond, teenage, stocky, her round cheeks constellated with pimples.

"I need some food," the girl said, then burrowed into the green army coat and pulled her knees up to her chin, wrapping her arm around them. It was as if she were anchoring herself to the floor, folding herself into a packet as neat and small as the newspaper. She smelled like mold and garbage, like something discarded and left to rot.

"I'm hungry," the girl insisted. Then, as if reading Anne's mind, she added, "And I stink. Can I use your shower? I feel kind of disgusting."

She was so matter-of-fact, so unapologetic, that Anne was speechless. She had been picturing a man, older, maybe a vet, somewhat or completely out of his mind, homeless for a long time. A teenage runaway—a girl who could shit in a building and then curl up asleep next to it—had never occurred to her.

"If I bring you upstairs and let you shower," she said, "will you go to one of the shelters? I'll help you get there."

The girl gazed at her, the expression in her eyes impossible to read. "I'm starving," she said.

"I have some food," Anne said. "Okay?"

The girl struggled heavily to her feet, gathering her coat around her. She looked sleepy, and willing, if not happy, to follow her upstairs. As they passed Mrs. Bondarchuk's door, Anne knocked lightly to let her know what was happening—though she didn't doubt that the old lady was already peering through the keyhole. You owe me one, she thought.

The girl stepped into the apartment as if it were hers. She was wearing dirty jeans, sneakers, and a blue sweater, and Anne had only a moment to guess at her age—fifteen, maybe sixteen?—before she went into the bathroom and closed the door, without asking directions or permission. After a minute, Anne heard the shower running.

"Okay," she said out loud. She went into the kitchen and set out bread and peanut butter and jelly. Not caring much about food herself, she hardly ever cooked, and her cupboards held little beyond takeout menus and leftover packets of soy sauce. In the other apartments in the building, the little old ladies spent their days simmering soups and boiling potatoes, wanting to have something on hand in case their families stopped by (though they rarely did), always smelling up the hallways with their traditionally prepared recipes. Probably the girl wished one of them had taken her in.

Anne started to make a sandwich, then realized the girl would need clean clothes when she got out of the shower. She rummaged through her dresser for some rarely worn sweatpants and oversized T-shirts—the girl was much heavier than Anne. Then she went into the bathroom and said, "I'm putting some clothes on the toilet," but she got no response from the shadow behind the shower curtain. Back in the living room, she waited. All these actions were unaccustomed. She never had houseguests; when men came over, she gave them what they wanted—time with her in bed—and never thought about whether they were hungry, or thirsty, or uncomfortable. If they needed a drink of water, they could get it themselves. If the girl was planning to steal from her, too bad, since Anne didn't have anything worth stealing. There were advantages to living an unbuilt life.

A few minutes after the water stopped, the girl came out wearing the sweatpants and several T-shirts layered one over the other. Anne couldn't help noticing that her breasts were enormous, pendulous, beneath the shirts. Her body looked like a woman's, but her face was chubby, childlike, round. Eyeing the peanut butter, the girl sat down on the kitchen stool. She made herself a sandwich, ate it, then made herself another. Halfway through this one she said, "Milk?"

Anne shook her head, regret washing over her. Why had she let this person—this *animal*—into her apartment?

While the girl kept eating, Anne went into the bathroom and stuffed the reeking clothes into a plastic garbage bag, wincing when she saw that her shampoo, conditioner, exfoliating scrub, and lotion were all uncapped and messy. Those products were expensive, an investment in her looks.

"I'm going downstairs to put your stuff in the laundry," she said. When she got back upstairs, the girl was fast asleep in her bed.

She slept poorly on her uncomfortable couch. She had never been one for good deeds. She wasn't selfish—just self-contained. She liked to stay within her own borders. Yet in the morning, for some reason, she dragged herself to the deli and came back with orange juice and donuts. The girl looked like a donut eater. She sat sipping black coffee on the couch until the girl woke up around ten and wandered into the living room, apparently surprised to see Anne there.

"Don't you have to go to work?" she said. She had a slight accent, not quite midwestern but broad, the consonants slurry and soft, like she was from the country.

"Not today." Anne studied the girl's slow, lumbering slide down onto the stool, noting how her face, creased from sleep, remained inert, as if frozen during a boring dream. The closest thing to an expression Anne had yet seen washed over the girl's face at the sight of the donuts. She pulled the box toward her and started chewing on one, powdered sugar smudging the tip of her nose.

"What's your name?"

Without a word, the girl picked up a second donut.

Anne stood up, snatched the donut out of her hand, and threw it, along with the rest of the box, into the garbage, then stood there with her arms folded, playing the disapproving mother.

The girl chewed, swallowed.

Get out, Anne thought.

"Hilary."

If, at this point, the girl had said nothing more, Anne would have pinched her ear and marched her to the door, or called the police, anything to get her out of the apartment and her life.

But she said, "Are you an actress or model or something? You're, like, gorgeous."

Even while recognizing this as flattery, Anne found herself pleased. "I'm in the theater," she said.

The girl grimaced. "I could never do that," she said. "Too fat, too ugly."

"You're not," Anne said mechanically. She had this conversation with other actresses almost every day, *I'm so fat* leading to *No you're not, you're emaciated*, *I'm so ugly* to *No you're not, you're gorgeous*. It was a call-and-response pattern, rhythmic and codified, like birdsong.

The girl accepted this insincerity and moved on. "Are you in a play right now?"

"In rehearsals. I play an Irish peasant woman during the potato famine. You know about the potato famine? I wind up prostituting myself in exchange for food for my family."

"Prostituting yourself?" Hilary said, putting her elbows on the kitchen counter. Her large breasts rested on the counter like lumps of bread dough.

Anne nodded. In fact the prostitution was more implied than seen; she only had a few lines, but to make things interesting she had embroidered the character's backstory. She'd spent so much time on this that she now felt the character had the tragic richness of a starring role. She was the center of the play, its crucial beating heart, but she was the only one who knew it. "Actually, if you wanted to be helpful, you could run some lines with me," she said, feeling generous. "Then we can figure out the shelter situation."

While she fished the script out of her bag, Hilary retrieved the donuts from the trash. She inhaled another one, drank some orange juice, then held out her hand for the pages. "Ready," she said.

Hilary had a surprisingly clear voice and didn't seem to tire of reading the lines over and over again. Once they started, Anne lowered herself into the character as if into a swimming pool: the water was cold at first, uncomfortable but bracing; then gradually, as the muscles warmed, the temperature turned out to be perfect, and the laps went by in strong, sure strokes, the body now fully engaged. She forgot everything else. It was only in these moments of concentration and release that she felt she could shed her own skin and slip free.

Suddenly it was noon.

"Shit," Anne said, "I have to go. I'm supposed to meet the costume designer in fifteen minutes. Listen, Hilary." It was the first time she'd called the girl by her name, but the effect was nil, the round face as inert as ever.

Then Hilary suddenly said, "The bathroom's disgusting."

"What?"

"I can clean it, while you're at your meeting. The toilet, the bathtub, the floor. I can do all that." Her voice was urgent and quick. She would neither plead nor act desperate, Anne could tell, but she would bargain.

In the days and months to come, she'd question her decision again and again. She couldn't even remember what was going through her mind: it was as if she had blacked out and come to after the choice had been made. But the fact that she couldn't explain it to herself was maybe as good a reason to do something as she'd ever had. Sometimes you needed to surprise yourself with randomness, to prove you have depths that even you can't understand.

"Okay," she said. "I'm not giving you a key, so you have to stay here. Eat whatever you want, not that you'll find much food. I really don't have any stuff for you to steal, but you still better not take anything. If I find anything gone when I come back, I'll call the cops."

"I don't steal," Hilary said.

"Sure you don't. I'll be back at five."

When she left the apartment, she forgot about the girl completely—her name, her predicament, even her shit in the lobby. It wasn't that she was naive or trusting; only that nothing was as real to her as herself.

After the meeting with the costume designer was rehearsal, and after that she had a drink with a guy who was putting together a production of *Equus* with a female cast, to be staged in a parking garage by the Manhattan Bridge. She walked home through Chinatown. On the steps of a church a man was selling shoes he'd collected from who knows where, lined up in obedient pairs as if they belonged to some invisible congregation. She picked out a pair of black pointy-toed heels with rhinestone clips. They smelled faintly of sweat and smoke or fire and the leather was creased, but they fit perfectly. As a child she had played dress-up in her mother's clothes, dreaming of the day when she'd be a beautiful, grown-up lady, and the sensation of wearing someone else's castoffs reminded her of this childhood pleasure. She handed the man a five, and he said, "God bless you, sweet thing."

It was only as she pulled open the outer door that she remembered Hilary. She'd left a stranger alone in her apartment all day. She had to be insane.

But the apartment was quiet. Hilary was curled up on the couch beneath a blanket, her stocky body surprisingly compact, and seeing her asleep somehow changed everything. Anne had been planning to charge in and kick her out, but instead found herself slipping off her boots and setting her bag down quietly, so as not to disturb.

Then she thought, What the hell am I doing?

She turned on the lights and served herself a plate of noodles she'd picked up at Panda Kitchen, eating at the counter. When Hilary stirred, moving tectonically to an upright position, Anne wondered if she was on drugs.

"Could I have some?" Hilary said.

Anne didn't eat much; she always had leftovers. "All right."

Seeming to sense her mood, Hilary took some lo mein and carried her plate back to the couch. She was like an animal, observing unspoken, intuitive protocols of distance.

Anne, suddenly exhausted, put her plate in the sink and went into the bedroom, where the sheets had been changed. In the bathroom, the toothpaste blobs were gone from the sink, the bathtub was unstreaked, and everything smelled faintly of bleach. She crawled into bed and lay there listening for disruptive sounds—Hilary tossing or snoring or even breathing too loudly. Outside she heard traffic, horns, voices; but inside, nothing at all.

She didn't kick her out the next day, or the day after that, and gradually they became strange, unlikely roommates. The shelter was never discussed. Hilary cleaned and sometimes cooked. She fixed the bedroom window that had gotten stuck, did the laundry, even swept the stairwells and changed the lightbulbs on the landings. Mrs. Bondarchuk, who didn't realize where Hilary had come from, decided she was Anne's cousin, and they didn't correct her. The other old ladies in the building began saying hello to her and were friendlier to Anne as well, as if they had found her somehow alarming when she was on her own.

Anne went to rehearsals, to work, and out for drinks, never once asking Hilary what she did during the day besides housework. After a while, she gave Hilary a set of keys and started leaving out some cash, twenty bucks at a time, for groceries. Now when she came home there was milk and bread and fruit. She didn't know what else Hilary ate, but the girl had already grown even stockier; she was definitely getting enough food somewhere. Her complexion had cleared up; her hair, shampooed regularly, was shinier, lighter, and she sometimes wore it in two braids. She looked scrubbed and healthy, like a milk-maid, and this farmgirl impression was reinforced when Anne, backstage for an audition one day, stumbled on an unlocked wardrobe room and brought back some baggy overalls and plaid shirts that Hilary wore without complaining or even asking where they came from.

Neither of them asked the other any questions. Anne assumed Hilary had run away from home, and in her experience, kids who did that usually had good reasons. And though Hilary had marched right into Anne's apartment, she seemed to have a second sense about invading her privacy otherwise. When Anne came home from work she often went straight into the bedroom, and Hilary never bothered her. The few clothes Hilary now owned were kept in a milk crate beside the couch, with the blanket she slept under folded on top. Sometimes days would pass without them exchanging a single word.

Anne stopped bringing men home, a little hiatus that was nice at first, giving her a feeling of astringent purity and asceticism. But she soon decided that if she could trust Hilary in the apartment during the day, then she could trust her there at night. So when she wanted to be with a man or felt it would be helpful to her career—a choice she made pragmatically, having never been foolish about sex—she went to his place instead. This eliminated married men from the realm of possibility, which was probably a good thing anyway. And she could control when the evening ended, just by leaving.

One night, she walked home along St. Mark's Place through the throngs of kids who flocked to the city to buy T-shirts and records and festoon themselves with nose rings and tattoos. Two teenagers, blond Rastas, with a mangy, half-starved golden retriever on a leash, sat on a Mexican blanket on the sidewalk like they were having a picnic. Anne made the mistake of looking the thin, dirty girl in the eye. She was wearing a hooded sweatshirt, her fingernails painted green, and though her hair was greasy, her teeth were pearly and perfect; Anne guessed she hadn't been gone from home for long. Somewhere people were looking for her, wondering why she'd left and where she'd gone.

"Hey," the thin girl said, "can you give us some change? Please?"

Anne shook her head.

"Our dog's really hungry."

Anne kept walking as the girl kept talking, her voice rising to an angry squawk.

"What about a dollar?" she said. "What about fifty fucking cents?"

Anne didn't look back. You couldn't help everybody.

"I'm glad I don't have a sister," Hilary said.

She and Anne were sitting on the couch on a Thursday night, eating spaghetti and watching reality TV. Their latest routine, whenever Anne wasn't rehearsing, was to have dinner together in the living room. Hilary herself had provided the television, which she claimed to have found on the street. After a month in the apartment, she was cleaner, calmer, and fatter. Anne sometimes thought of her as *the cow*, but not pejoratively; it had to do with the girl's quietness, her large brown eyes, her shifting, bovine way of settling herself on the couch.

They were watching a show in which two sisters exchanged lives, each one now having to deal with the other's annoying husband and children, thus learning to appreciate her own annoying husband and children.

"I have a brother," Hilary said. "He's twelve. He likes video games. I send him postcards sometimes."

It might have been the longest Anne had ever heard her speak. "What's his name?"

"Joshua."

"Not Josh?"

Hilary shook her head. "We always use his full name. My parents are real religious. I'm from the country—well, not the country, exactly, just a small town. We live right in town, but there's not much town there. Joshua wants to leave too. I write him postcards, like I said, but I don't send them from here. I give them to people in the train station and ask them to mail them from wherever they're going. That way nobody knows where I am."

"You give them to strangers at the train station?"

"Older women, ones that are alone. They're the nicest. I just say that I couldn't find a mailbox, and would they mind dropping this postcard in the mail whenever they have time? They always say yes and don't ask any questions."

"You're good at figuring people out," Anne said.

The girl gave her a measured look. "Yeah, I guess I am."

Through these casual Thursday-night disclosures, Anne learned that Hilary liked bananas and was allergic to coconut. That there wasn't anything for her and her hometown friends to do at night except go to Walmart. That her father was dead and she'd grown up with her mother and stepfather, and that Joshua was actually her stepbrother. But beyond these random, basic facts, she didn't share much. No sentence ever blossomed into anecdote, and she showed so little emotion, positive or negative, that Anne started to wonder if she was repressing some intense trauma. If she were a movie character, this would eventually burst loose in a flood of bad behavior. But life was longer than movies and a person never knew when the flood would finally come, or sometimes even how to recognize it when it did.

As they spent more time together, Anne began to feel not like a mother—because she thought of mothers as old and asexual—but like an older sister. It made her sad that Hilary was all alone in the world. She was alone too, but that was different; she was twenty-two, attractive, an actress in New York. A runaway who slept in doorways was vulnerable, pathetic. She brooded about Hilary's weight, burgeoning day by day. Somewhere she had found a shapeless, navy-blue sweatsuit; she wore it constantly, and it made her look like an aging football player gone to fat. Anne didn't buy her any more donuts, and stocked the fridge with fruit and vegetables. When she got home at night, she often made a salad and forced Hilary to eat it. Not that there was much forcing involved; she only had to say, "Here," and the girl would eat whatever was put in front of her.

Sometimes, after dinner, Anne would suggest going for a walk, and they'd put on their coats and window-shop around the East Village for an hour or two. They'd stop at Café Mogador for a cup of tea, eavesdropping on people flirting or breaking up or arguing about the war, then resume their walk. None of this activity seemed to take any of the weight off, though.

Anne also started thinking about the girl's future, wondering about school, or jobs, or friends. She didn't put much trust in convention, but she did believe in self-actualization—a word she had picked up from other actors. For her it meant that you alone decided what your true self should be. But Hilary never mentioned wanting to do anything or be anything. She never read a book, listened to music, or even talked about dreams. She seemed to live in an eternal present, never worrying about what came next.

In the middle of March, Anne was cast in a great part in a new play. She wasn't the leading lady but the catalyst, the unhinged and sexualized stranger whose energy makes all the normal people disintegrate. "You're so perfect for this I want to die," the director said. Everything he loved made him want to die. But when she read the script, she knew exactly how he felt. She wanted to die too, preferably onstage.

It was a long play, with commensurately long rehearsals in Long Island City that started almost immediately. So Anne was suddenly home a lot less. When she returned late at night, she sometimes saw no more of Hilary than her blanketed, sleeping form on the couch.

Another thing: there was a man, a member of the crew and a friend of the director's, a soft-spoken, scruffy carpenter. He was earnest and cute, with dark eyes and a surprisingly white, toothy smile. She often went home with him after rehearsals, and when she came back to her apartment after a day or two away it almost felt like she was entering a stranger's home, where she was now the guest.

One weekend, the director got food poisoning and canceled the rehearsals. Anne had fallen so in love with her character, and the extra dimension it gave her own personality, that she felt almost jilted. Grumpily, she decided to spend the empty days catching up on the few basic tasks of her streamlined life: laundry, bills, nails. On Saturday morning Hilary wasn't at home, and Anne wondered if she had followed her advice and found some kind of job. Anne came and went throughout the day, and when the girl still hadn't reappeared she was unaccountably freaked out. She'd held a certain image of the apartment in her mind all those days and nights when she'd been gone, with Hilary there and the apartment somehow *tended*, waiting for her to come back. Realizing now that she had no idea of Hilary's movements or whereabouts made her feel strangely unmoored.

Once her laundry was finished, she went to the bodega for milk. She was pulling a carton out of the fridge when she heard a familiar voice say, "I'm dying for some ice cream."

Hilary was standing on the other side of the store, her blond braids snaking down her shoulder blades. There was a crowded aisle between them, and the girl had no idea she was there. Anne couldn't see the guy she was talking to—a stack of cereal and toilet paper was blocking her view—but she heard him say, "You always want ice cream. You're, like, obsessed with ice cream."

"I'm not obsessed."

"Are too."

"Am not. Which do you want? I want chocolate chunk, cookie dough, or cherry cheesecake."

"Three flavors, but you're not obsessed?"

"Shut up!"

Hilary's tone was gauzy and flirty, lithe with laughter. It sounded like a voice that belonged to a girl who moved quickly, showed some skin, fell in love. Not like the Hilary Anne knew at all.

She took a step closer, peering through the dry goods while staying hidden. The guy looked even younger than Hilary and was very thin, with pocked skin that contrasted sharply with his full, dark lips. His hair was sculpted into a miniature Mohawk, and his eyebrow and nose were pierced. His red hoodie was slipping off his slouched shoulders, and his jeans were sliding off his hips. There was barely enough of him to hang clothes on. She could crush him, Anne thought. He didn't look like much, but neither did Hilary, in her shapeless blue sweatsuit. In this, they were a matched pair.

They finally settled on chocolate, and Anne followed them, leaving her own purchase behind, back to the apartment. She waited five minutes, then went inside.

Hilary glanced up, her expression blinkered, unrepentant. "This is Alan," she said.

"Hey," he said.

Anne said nothing, just sat down on the couch and watched them. She hoped this would make them so uncomfortable that the guy would leave, but it didn't seem to. They stood at the counter eating ice cream and teasing each other, and Anne's presence didn't even seem to have registered. Their dialogue was like the worst play she'd ever seen.

"You're a messy eater."

"I am not."

"You have chocolate on your chin."

"So do you."

"Where?"

"Right there."

And so on and so on. She was the audience, which she hated being. After a while she went into the bedroom and closed the door, her emotions feeding on themselves: she was upset because she was mad, and that made her even angrier. She took deep breaths and counted to a hundred, then left the apartment without a word and spent two hours at yoga. They were gone when she got back, their bowls washed and drying by the sink.

Even by herself, her apartment felt different, the air contaminated by someone else's sexual energies, someone else's flirt. What was happening?

She slept uneasily that night, waiting for Hilary to come back. Somehow she missed her reentry, but when she woke up at three in the morning, they were both in the living room—Hilary on the couch, Alan on the floor. He was sleeping on a pad made of blankets they must have scavenged, and his pillow was a bundled square of clothes.

She stood in the doorway watching them. The shadows were tinted blue from a neon sign across the street. Hilary turned over on the couch, her movements slow, labored, her body huge. She opened her eyes and looked right at Anne with no expression at all. Vacancy didn't begin to describe it. Standing there in her tank top and pajama pants, the hair rising on her arms, Anne felt sticklike, insubstantial, and for the first time she could remember she wished she were bigger, stronger, heavier. Now she felt like the one who could be crushed. Without saying anything, Hilary closed her eyes and seemed to fall back asleep.

What would you say to the police? There's someone in my apartment—no, it wasn't a break-in, more of a slow slide-in. Or, I'm under attack by a fat teenage girl and her pimple-faced boyfriend? What was the crime here, exactly? She stewed over these questions in the night, cooked them to an angry boil. She decided that in the morning she'd tell Hilary the boy had to go, or else she'd call the police. A runaway is a runaway. Maybe Hilary's face was on a milk carton somewhere. Maybe her parents would be thankful.

In the morning, in fact, the boy *was* gone. Anne made coffee and waited for Hilary to wake up, wondering what she was going to say. They had no language, the two of them, for the kind of conversation she needed to have. They'd never exchanged any confidences, romantic or otherwise, and it was too late now to establish that kind of base. She couldn't ask Hilary who the boy was, because she'd never asked who *Hilary* was.

When Hilary finally woke up and saw Anne watching her, she didn't look startled. Even in her sleep she seemed to have been preparing for the confrontation. Her languid cow's eyes were ready. "Listen," she said, "thanks for letting us stay."

"Us?" Anne said.

"Me and Alan. We were desperate before. You're really saving our asses."

"I didn't realize I was saving both your asses."

"Yeah, well, for a while Alan was up in Syracuse working construction. But now he's back."

For the life of her, Anne couldn't picture that scrawny punk lifting a hammer or a two-by-four. Surely he'd snag the tools on his eyebrow rings. As these thoughts piled up, she realized she had become just like her mother, and she could also blame Hilary for putting her on the wrong side of a generational divide. "You can't both stay here," she said.

Hilary nodded as if she'd been expecting this. "Okay, I figured. But can we stay until the baby comes?"

Until the baby comes. Anne had to repeat the words in her mind several times before they made any sense. "Jesus," she said. "You're pregnant."

The looks passing across Hilary's face—understanding, disgust, slight amusement—were subtle, brief, and controlled. "I'm not due for three months," she said. "Alan's going to get us a place by then. He knows some people squatting in Jersey City."

Anne couldn't think of what to say, despite knowing that her silence would be taken for acquiescence. She felt like an idiot.

"Don't worry," Hilary added kindly, as if to a child. "It'll be okay."

For the first time in ages, Anne didn't know what to do; she wished she had a friend to ask for advice. She'd left home when she wasn't much older than Hilary, and since then had kept herself aloof, especially from women, who tended to dive into confidences as if they were salvation. Being alone and being aloof were the same as being superior. But maybe this wasn't the best system.

Out of respect or, more likely, a calculated desire not to provoke her, Alan didn't return that morning. After breakfast, Anne said, "Let's go for a walk," and Hilary nodded.

They headed toward Tompkins Square Park, the spring wind lashing their faces, and Anne pulled her hat down over her ears. Despite the cool weather, all around the park people were having brunch, shopping, walking dogs. The girls wore frayed cords, the boys plaid shirts. From an open window came the smell of pot. In the park kids were playing kickball, and under an enormous elm tree Hare Krishnas were chanting and singing.

Hilary walked along beside her, matching her stride like a dog on a leash.

Now that Anne recognized the girl's bulk for what it was, her every bodily sign seemed to broadcast pregnancy: hands resting on her stomach, her cheeks even broader, her calm eyes hoarding all internal energy. Things Anne hadn't even realized were confusing suddenly made sense, which maddened and embarrassed her because actresses were supposed to be observant. So as they walked she asked Hilary every question she could think of. Where was she from, exactly? Why had she left home? Did her parents know where she was? Did they know she was pregnant? Was Alan from her hometown? When exactly was the baby due? How long had she been living on the street before ending up downstairs? What were her *plans*?

Unruffled, undefensive, Hilary answered each question in turn. She was from a small town between Binghamton and Syracuse. Her mother worked in a grocery store. Her stepfather had sexually abused her and she had run away twice before. She went back because of Alan, who'd promised to protect her, and did. They'd come down to the city just before Christmas and stayed with Alan's cousin in Brooklyn, where he had a one-bedroom apartment with two roommates, but he'd kicked them out after they had a fight. Then she found an NYU ID and key card on the street and managed to get inside a dorm, where she set up a bed in an unused storage room and passed through the hallways without any trouble, everybody assuming she was a student. Once she was settled, Alan went up to Syracuse to make some money so that when the baby came they'd be ready with an apartment and "stuff like that." From that melting phrase Anne could tell Hilary was both sentimental about the baby and clueless about what it would involve. During Alan's absence, Hilary got evicted from the room and had to stay out of shelters, because the security guard was probably calling out a description and "with that Amber alert and everything, it was such a drag," which is why she'd ended up downstairs. She was sick and tired and just needed to, you know, lie down inside and be warm for a few days. By the time Alan got back she was at Anne's.

"I told him I'd be all right, and I was," she finished. "I can take care of myself, but he worries a lot about me."

"You should've told me," Anne said.

"About what?"

"Everything."

The girl stared at her. "You didn't ask," she pointed out.

"Didn't ask what? 'Oh, by the way, are you pregnant?' 'Oh, are you on the lam from the police?' 'Oh, will some snotty punk kid show up in my kitchen one day?'"

The Hare Krishnas turned around at the sound of Anne's raised voice, and she glared at them until they went back to their routine.

Hilary shook her head angrily. "Alan's not snotty. Look, we're both real clean. We don't make a mess. I keep the place okay, right? I know you've done a lot. You didn't have to let me stay. But, I swear, eventually we'll have a place and money and stuff, and I'll pay you back, whatever you want." For the first time, she sounded like a teenager. And once again, she had the knack of saying the right thing at the right time. "Anyway, Anne? Aren't you a runaway too?"

And of course she was right. But there was no way she could have known it. She was a magician, a diviner. Anne was so freaked out that she shut up and let them stay.

<hr>

In the weeks to come, Anne told Hilary her own story, how she'd left her home in Montreal at the age of sixteen. She'd met a guy who drove her to Burlington, Vermont, where she got a job waiting tables at a coffee shop and rented a room from the guy's sister, who thought she was a college student. From Burlington she went to Vancouver; she didn't like it, but while she was there she fell in with some theater people and decided she wanted to act. She stayed for a year before moving on: Las Vegas, Denver, Chicago. She lived for a year with a guy she'd met in a park, where he was feeding the ducks. He offered her a room if she'd cook his meals, and after six months he told her he loved her, and she believed him. He was a gentleman, and he said he knew she'd been through hard times, that he wanted to treat her with the respect and delicacy she deserved. This was how he talked, using words like *delicacy*. In all the time she lived with him he never touched her. At the end of the year he proposed, and she said she didn't think she was ready for marriage yet. He nodded and said he understood, but at midnight he came into her room, got into her bed, and ran his hands up and down her bare back. She sat up and said, "Please don't do that," trying to keep her voice high and childish, frail with youth.

"I know your real self," he said. "I know what you want."

She ran from the house in her pajamas. It was the first night since she left home that she stayed in a shelter, and she vowed it would be the only one. From then on she never lived with a man. She used them for food, jobs, and transportation, but wouldn't live with them. When she got to New York, she paid cash for a room at a hostel until the apartment deal with Larry came through. She never counted on anyone but herself.

In the six years she'd been gone, she'd written to her parents three times. The first was to tell them she was fine and not to try to find her. The second was a Christmas card she'd sent from Las Vegas, a drunken, sentimental mistake. The third was just last year. She had woken up in the middle of the night with the eeriest feeling about her mother; it was like having a scary dream that you couldn't really remember. She was shaking and sweating. She didn't believe in premonitions or portents, but she was rattled enough to write. She didn't give a return address, and wasn't thinking about going home.

Too much time had passed and she was a different person now, an adult of her own making. She simply wrote, *Mom. I love you. Annie.* It wasn't what any mother would have wanted, but it was something, and it would have to be enough.

"So how come you left?" Hilary said. "I mean, in the first place."

Anne shrugged.

"Did you ever go back?"

"No."

The girl sat in the silence, patting her belly. Her eyes were drowsy, implacable.

"How did you know that I ran away?" Anne said.

Hilary lifted her hand and gestured around the apartment. "It's empty," she said. "On purpose empty."

"I guess," Anne said.

Hilary looked at her, and suddenly her eyes were sharp, gleaming. "Girls who look like you can have whatever they want," she said. "You chose this."

Anne held her gaze. "So did you," she said.

THREE

Iqaluit, 2006

MARTINE, OF COURSE, didn't want him to go. When he told her about the contract, she stood in the living room with her arms crossed, looking, with her thick-framed glasses and disapproving frown, more like a librarian than the lawyer she was. When she was hurt or vulnerable, she reacted with stern anger, and Mitch loved her for the transparency of this posture, almost as much as he loved the quiet, resigned way in which later, in bed, crying a little, she would set it aside.

"I don't understand," she said then. Her curly hair was a tangle of silver blond on the pillow. Her French accent, as always when she was upset, grew stronger. "It's so far away."

"The rotation's only a few months," he told her. "And the money's great."

"It's depressing up there. You said so yourself."

"That's because the people are depressed."

"So why do you need to go to a place like that?"

"They don't have enough health care up there to serve the native population," he said. "They need help. They need me."

Martine raised herself up on one elbow, holding the palm of her hand against her ear as if to block out this statement. *"C'est assez, là,"* she muttered to the pillow, and he didn't ask what, specifically, she'd had enough of—this trip, or his arguments on behalf of it. In the apartment's other bedroom, Mathieu thrashed around restlessly, as he always did for hours before falling asleep. Once on the other side, though, he slept as if dead, and in the mornings, while Martine made breakfast, it was Mitch's job to guide him back to consciousness from his faraway state. He wouldn't ever have admitted to her how much he hated doing this, how often he crouched by the boy's bed, looking at his chest to make sure he was still breathing—always certain that this time, this morning, he wasn't—or how violently he sometimes had to shake Mathieu's shoulder before he finally, reluctantly, awoke. *Rousing the bear,* is how Mitch thought of it, as if the child were some gigantic, threatening animal instead of a scrawny, thin-limbed faun. Most mornings, he would scrunch himself into a ball and mutter angrily, *"Non, non"*—to consciousness, to Mitch, to the world. Then Mitch would try to pick him up and carry him to the kitchen, but Mathieu didn't like to be touched and would hammer his fists against Mitch's chest until he left him alone. This war was a daily ritual.

Unspoken between Martine and Mitch now was the accusation that he was leaving to escape the burden of her son; that he might be needed by the people in Nunavut, sure, but that most of all he needed to get away.

He'd met Martine on the day her divorce became final, a moment of sorrow and vulnerability that he wasn't too scrupulous to take advantage of. Had he met her even a day later, he believed, she wouldn't have had anything to do with him. Forty-five, sexy, and brilliantly smart, Martine took care of her job and her son with determined energy, and she dispatched her husband once he proved unequal to the task of having a difficult child and rebelled by having affairs. Only at night did cracks show in her independent daytime self; but even then she rarely reverted back to the crying woman he had first seen smoking a cigarette outside the Palais de Justice, choking and sobbing through the gray storm of her own exhale. Mitch had mostly been single since his own marriage had fallen apart, and what few relationships he'd had arose when he was pursued. But this woman was so clearly in need of help—a kind gesture, a tissue—that he stopped and fished a Kleenex packet out of his coat pocket. The day was cold, and her eyes were red and pinched. Her curly hair was piled on her head in a messy, complicated arrangement, strands escaping here and there. She thanked him in French, and he responded in kind. Delicately, she transferred her cigarette to her left hand and blew her nose goose-honkingly hard with her right. That a woman could look so beautiful in the midst of an operation like this made Mitch's heart turn over. He had always been a romantic, but divorce and middle age had squeezed it out of him, or so he'd thought until now.

"Are you all right?" he said.

The woman looked at him with an undisguised scorn that had a kind of desire glimmering around the edges of it. What she wanted, he thought, was for a better candidate to come along, but she'd take what she could get.

"I need a drink," she answered, switching to English.

"Could I buy you one?"

She nodded and led him, pretty aggressively, he thought, to a bar on Saint-Paul—but it was just that Martine, he figured out later, saw no need to pretend not to know what she wanted. He ordered a martini for her and a beer for himself. She kept smoking, lighting one du Maurier off the flaming stub of the last, as they exchanged bare-bones information: names, professions, the neighborhoods in which they lived and worked. Her hair continued to slip free from its moorings, half of it now hanging down.

"Were you married a long time?" he asked.

"It felt like a very long time," she said. "But the last few years we were living apart anyway. *Fait que*, this isn't really a very big change."

"But it is."

She nodded. "Yes."

He bought her another drink, and another. By ten o'clock they were in bed in her apartment off Pie-IX, her eyes closed, his T-shirt still on.

"*J'ai besoin*," she murmured against his neck. "*J'ai besoin de toi.*" She made it clear she needed a very specific part of him. He pressed himself against her in response, and she guided him inside. At eleven o'clock she thanked him, as sweetly and impersonally as you might thank a waiter for good service, and asked him to leave. Afterward he stood shaking his head in the icy street. The road was deserted, dark. Above the cluster of apartment buildings to the east, the tower of the Olympic Stadium seemed to be saluting him. His heart sang. He wondered if any of it had really happened. Wanted fervently to make it happen again.

He left for Iqaluit two weeks after breaking the news. From his window seat, the land was obscured by a thick layer of clouds, and he tried to imagine the rock and ice beneath, hoping to feel loose, set free. He had been happy there once before, during the summer he had separated from Grace, when the Arctic had been a refuge, a clean slate. After failing so miserably at marriage he had been determined to succeed at his job, and he'd thrown himself into it with wild energy, working twelve to fourteen hours a day. The worst thing about the divorce was that he had lost any sense of himself as a decent person. After all, he loved everything about Grace—her values, her personality, her dreams. He just didn't love *her*. Confronting this fact was humiliating, disastrous. Mitch had always been the nice guy who wryly accepted that nice guys finish last, and now he discovered that he wasn't all that nice, and that he was finishing last anyway, with only himself to blame. To make up for all of this he turned to his job and to the Arctic. When he wasn't working he founded and coached a boys' basketball league. It was the most exhausting, industrious, and ultimately rewarding time in his life. For a while, after returning to Montreal, he'd kept in touch with a couple of the kids, but gradually—and naturally enough—correspondence on both sides fell off. The invitation to return had come so suddenly, and he'd been so consumed over the last couple of weeks by his arguments with Martine, that he hadn't had much time to think about the place itself.

It was June, still light when they landed after ten o'clock. The buildings of Iqaluit lay scattered like pebbles dropped from a casual hand, inconsequential to the vast expanse around them. Here and there in the landscape rose gray slabs of rock, half covered with moss, that looked like the backs of whales rising up from a choppy sea. The sky was a brilliant blue, untouched by clouds, and the air felt clear and thin. The other passengers, most of whom looked like they were coming home, filed silently across the tarmac into the small terminal.

He'd arranged for a taxi, and the drive was his first clue that he didn't remember as much as he thought he did. It wasn't that the place looked better or worse—the same prefab buildings balanced on their stilts, some of the rocky yards neat, others strewn with snowmobiles and assorted debris—but that his sense of direction and layout had diminished over a decade. Only the rough, bruise-colored expanse of Frobisher Bay oriented him, its white-crested waves crashing against the stubborn ice. The city had grown, and there were new neighborhoods he didn't know. The taxi driver, an immigrant from Bosnia via Winnipeg, greeted his few questions with grunts. As the car drove slowly through the twisting gravel streets, children gazed at him with naked curiosity. The boys he had coached in basketball would be adults now, with families of their own, and Mitch knew he wouldn't recognize them. He had made friends here, but most of them were whites like him, from Quebec and Ontario, here to work for a short duration and doubtless gone back south by now.

The taxi pulled up to the apartment that had been leased for him. They had said only that it was a duplex, but as he was paying the driver the front door opened and a tall, thin man with a shock of red hair stepped out.

"You must be the new man, then," he said, extending a hand. "I'm Johnny."

"Mitch."

"We're sharing quarters," Johnny said, "but it's a large house by local standards, so have no fear. You know how tight housing is up here." His voice held the lilting, musical cadence of a Maritimer. He grabbed one of Mitch's bags and waved cheerfully at the taxi driver, who ignored them both and drove away. Johnny looked to be in his thirties, ruddy-cheeked and leather-skinned, whether from liquor or exposure to the elements Mitch couldn't tell. He led Mitch up to a bedroom with a bed and a desk, dumped the bag on it, then gestured down the hall.

"My room's back there, then. Come by any time you need anything,

I'm always up. Can't sleep at all in the summer here. I get this nervous energy. In the winter I sleep fourteen hours a night and watch TV all afternoon if I can. That's what this place does to you. Let's have a drink. You've been here before, I heard."

"It's been over ten years," Mitch said once they were in the kitchen, where Johnny poured him two fingers of whiskey in a smudged glass. He'd heard nothing about a roommate, but he actually didn't mind. With someone to talk to, he'd be less likely to sit around brooding.

"I'm an engineer myself," Johnny said. "From St. John's, originally, but more than happy to be away from it. Here consulting on a new sewage plant. Got my hands in the shit, as they say."

"Do they say that?"

"I say it," Johnny said. "Cheers."

They drank, sitting on red plastic-seated chairs around a Formica table, furniture that looked like it had been brought in forty years ago. At one end of the counter was a microwave splattered with sauces and grease, at the other a crowd of liquor bottles. Through the window Mitch could hear kids kicking a soccer ball around. It should've been past their bedtime, but it still felt like noon, and the Inuit weren't big on nighttime rituals anyway, he remembered, believing their children would wind down naturally on their own. He drank the whiskey slowly, holding each sip for a moment on his tongue before swallowing; the combination of flying, the brightness, and the alcohol made him feel pleasantly light-headed and numb and far from home.

Johnny topped up his whiskey. When he'd introduced himself, Mitch was sure he was younger, but up close his face was deeply lined, with dark brown splotches on his cheeks and forehead, and his teeth were stained brown. It could be he was in his forties or fifties and maybe his rangy thinness was less a product of fitness than of a diet of whiskey and cigarettes, one of which he lit right now, exhaling the smoke in a broad stream. "So you're a shrink, they say."

"A therapist, actually," Mitch said, remembering how quickly news traveled in a small place like this one. "I specialize in addict—"

"So no drugs, then. No prescriptions," Johnny said, clearly disappointed.

"No."

"No Xanax? No little helpers?"

"Cognitive behavioral therapy," Mitch said, enunciating each syllable with slow annoyance.

Johnny made a flapping gesture with his left hand. "Talk, talk, talk. Give me the drugs, is what I say. In fact, if you want to see my behavior change, shoot me straight in the vein."

Mitch stood up. "I guess I'll hit the sack."

Instantly Johnny sprang up and clapped his hand on Mitch's bicep, the long ash of his cigarette falling on the table between them. "Christ on a stick," he said, "I didn't mean to insult your line of work or nothing like that. I just hoped to score a little extra in the way of supplies, eh? Had my hopes up for the medicine cabinet here." He smiled at Mitch ingratiatingly, as if this were a natural explanation between friends. When Mitch didn't say anything, he flushed, looking suddenly youthful again. "Forgive me," he said. "I been up here too long."

"Forget it," Mitch said.

"Anyway, I've got other sources," Johnny said philosophically, "so no harm done."

Mitch left him lighting another cigarette, went to his room, and lay down on the single bed, the flimsy pink curtain doing nothing to block the sunlight. The smoky smell on his clothes reminded him of Martine, and he thought he should call to say he'd arrived safely; but as he was thinking it, his head swimming with whiskey, he closed his eyes and fell asleep.

After his first date with Martine, he should have let it go. Clearly this was what she expected; he was a prospect too lame to be considered for the long term, redeemed only by being just smart enough to recognize it. But he didn't want to. For years he had occasionally gone out with some divorced woman, usually sticking with her long enough to have sex a couple of times, to be reminded of the existence and practice of sex, after which he would let things drop. He became the guy who didn't call. The guy who met your kid and played catch with him one weekend, then never came around again. It wasn't heartlessness so much as apathy, and if Grace, at one time, would have reminded him that one could easily arise from the other, well, she wasn't around to do so now.

But with Martine he felt like he'd met a movie star. He didn't have her phone number, and he'd forgotten, after their cursory introductions at the bar, her last name. But he remembered her small charming apartment building off a little allée in Hochelaga-Maisonneuve and took a chance, showing up there on a Friday night at six thirty with a bottle of wine and a cooler filled with food. One thing Mitch had going for him: he could cook. He figured he might as well play to his strengths.

The child who answered the door was lithe, blond, storybook cute, maybe seven years old. In French, Mitch asked him if his mother was home. The kid just stared at him, rhythmically biting his lower lip and then releasing it. Mitch asked what his name was and still got no response. Finally he crouched down and introduced himself, which accomplished nothing. The boy was rubbing his right toe against the hallway carpet in exactly the same rhythm as the lip biting. In his right hand, for some reason, was a twenty-dollar bill. He dropped it on the floor and ran away.

Mitch stood up, not sure what to do now. From the back of the apartment, Martine was yelling about cold air coming in and she came down the hall to investigate, smelling of perfume and cigarettes, her hair in a bun at the base of her neck. When she saw Mitch, she stopped short.

"I'm sorry," she said. "I thought you were the pizza man. That was probably confusing for Mathieu." It was impossible to miss the tone of reproach.

"I apologize," Mitch said. "I didn't know you had a son." He wondered where the child had been the other night.

She looked at him blankly, her hands twisting in whatever task she'd just been performing—folding clothes, maybe, or washing dishes. Her glasses were slipping down her nose.

"I brought you some dinner," he said.

"Excuse me?"

"I guess you have pizza coming, but . . . well, I brought a roasted lamb shank, new potatoes, and salad. And a bottle of wine." He gestured at the cooler at his feet. "I thought, it's Friday night, and you might not feel like cooking . . . "

It seemed she wasn't going to say anything. No wonder her kid didn't talk. She was even biting her lip just as he had.

From some back corner of the apartment came an unholy shriek and the angry tumble of furniture falling over. Martine turned and ran back down the hall, and after a moment he could hear her murmuring and her son's outbursts calming, finally quieting, like waves diminishing as they lapped against the shore.

He stood in the hallway, winter's cold hands grabbing his back, feeling like more of a jackass than he had in his entire life. After a few minutes he wrote his phone number on a piece of paper, wedged it under the lid of the cooler, and called out, "Well, I'll be going now. Good-bye!"

There was no answer.

When he woke up, in Iqaluit, he called home, but there was no answer. It was Saturday, and Martine was probably out with Mathieu at the zoo or the museum. She had a mania for activities. She wanted Mathieu to be well rounded and hoped that if she constantly exposed him to a variety of events he might pick up something new instead of remaining the lightly autistic, science-obsessed boy he was. No advice on this matter would be tolerated. He left a message, and went to find the clinic. It was cool and windy, the sky a range of grays from charcoal to steel to pearl. But it was also summer, and on the hardscrabble soil were the miniature blooms of dwarf daisies and Arctic poppies, with light-green lichen spreading delicately over the rocks. He felt the gorgeous pleasure of being *away*. No matter what happened here, for good or bad, it wasn't home, and there was a luxurious freedom in that.

At the clinic, after introducing himself to the nurse on duty, he was shown to his desk and given a roster of appointments that began immediately. People had been backed up for weeks while they waited for his rotation to start—the last person, apparently, had had some kind of meltdown and returned to Toronto with a full month on the clock—and they were scheduled thickly, one every twenty minutes. In the nurse's brief description of this last counselor, Mitch heard a clear contempt for fragile southerners, but as she spoke he only nodded, feeling confident and ready to get to work and prove himself. He knew from experience that at least half of these patients wouldn't show up. They'd forget, or change their minds, or had never intended to come in the first place; they'd gone along with the idea to be polite, because a judge or doctor had recommended it, but that didn't mean they truly consented. They just didn't want to be rude and say no.

So he had some free time. He looked out his office window at the parking lot, where a few birds were pecking at trash that had spilled from a garbage can's overflow, and at something that looked suspiciously like a pool of vomit. Behind him there was a knock, and he turned around to see a young man, seventeen or so, standing in the doorway. He was very skinny, with dark eyes, floppy black hair, and lips so dark they looked painted. His red windbreaker was streaked with dirt.

"Hey," Mitch said. "Can I help you?"

The kid licked his chapped lips. "They sent me here," he said.

"Who sent you?"

"The people down the hall," the kid said.

"Which people?"

The boy's answer to this was an inconclusive shrug. Mitch gestured toward a chair and asked what his name was.

"Thomasie."

The boy sat down. With his round face and high cheekbones he was handsome, the hair falling over his eyes giving him a movie-idol look.

"Thomasie what?"

"Reeves. That was my dad's name. He's down in Sarnia. That's where he's at."

"And your mom?"

"Yeah," the kid said, giving him a weird, furtive look.

While they were talking, Mitch flipped through his files and his calendar, but there was nothing under "Reeves." The boy sat opposite him, balancing his elbows on his knees, his expression either hooded or blank. Glancing out the window at the parking lot, he began gnawing on a fingernail, pulling it off gently, bit by bit, then examining it and flicking it to the floor.

"So tell me what brings you here," Mitch said.

Thomasie smiled without humor or gratitude; he seemed shrunk beneath the protective hull of his jacket. Mitch had the feeling he was being judged, that if he said the wrong thing the kid might jump up and sprint out of there. So he waited. The silence between them grew thick, and neither appeared willing to break it.

Thomasie shook a cigarette out of a pack in his pocket, tapped it against the palm of his hand, stuck it behind his ear, then cleared his throat. When he finally looked at Mitch, his expression was strangely sincere and earnest, guileless. "You're new," he said.

"That's right. I just got here. Although I was here once before."

Thomasie nodded. "Yeah, my dad remembered you from when you were here before. He played in the basketball thing you did. We don't have basketball right now. We got a guy doing like an adventure club or something? But mostly kids stay home and play video games."

Another silence. Mitch tried to remember a kid named Reeves, but he hadn't known most of their last names—they were a mass of adolescent energy and short attention spans, and he'd spent each session trying to incite enough enthusiasm that they'd care about the game but not so much they'd get into fights. He was dismayed to realize, now, that he probably didn't remember many first names, either.

"So what can I do for you?" he finally said.

Thomasie smiled again, and the bland, empty secrecy of those smiles was starting to get on Mitch's nerves. He rubbed his temples, telling himself to be patient. He was feeling last night's whiskey a bit.

"Everybody around here knows about it," the kid said. "I thought maybe you did too."

He paused expectantly, but Mitch had no file and hadn't been following the news from up here. He shook his head slightly, and Thomasie looked down at the floor. Clearly he'd hoped to be spared having to tell the whole story.

"My mom, she's in the hospital," he said. "Been there a while now."

"I'm sorry to hear that," Mitch said. When the kid didn't go on, he added, "What happened?"

"She was out partying one night and she was walking home from her friend's house with my little sister. Anyway, there was a storm, and she didn't make it home."

"What do you mean, she didn't make it home?"

Thomasie bit off another shred of fingernail before answering. His right knee was jiggling, practically jack-hammering. "She passed out in the snow," he said, in the quiet, almost affectless manner common to many Inuit, his intonation so flat that it took Mitch a moment to grasp the horror of where this was going. "When she woke up the world was white. That's what she said. My little sister died. They might send my mum to jail, but right now she's still in the hospital. She lost most of her eyesight, that's why the world was so white. They don't know what happened to her eyes. She also lost some fingers and toes, but that don't bother her as much as the eyes. The world was white. It's weird she says that, because it was dark when she woke up. It was still winter, and anyways, she was blind."

"I'm so sorry," Mitch said, and the kid nodded. He had spoken calmly, without tears or anger, his fidgeting and nail-biting the only signs of emotion. The office door was still open, and Mitch could hear steps and voices outside. Someone with a scheduled appointment was waiting in the hallway.

Thomasie leaned back, as if spent, and sucked on his bloody fingernail. He didn't seem inclined to say anything more.

"What was your sister's name?" Mitch said.

The boy's attention strayed to his shoes, which he examined closely for some time. "Karen," he finally said. Another pause. Then, still looking at his shoes: "I dream about her sometimes. She's alone in the snow. It's like she's in heaven—except not really, 'cause she's cold and uncomfortable. She keeps asking me to come see her, and I try, but I can't get to her. Then I wake up."

Mitch nodded. "You wish you could have helped her and your mom."

Thomasie shrugged. "I been at the hospital so much, with my mom, they told me to come see you."

"I'm glad you did," Mitch said. "So let's set up some appointments."

"You got any drugs?" the boy said. "I don't sleep good."

Mitch flushed. "I'm not that kind of doctor."

"My friend got some pills when his dad died."

Mitch sat back. "I'd like to help you," he said, and Thomasie looked up. "We can work with a psychiatrist on some treatment options. But mainly, you and me, we'll just be talking, working through some of the stuff that's happened."

The boy was already standing. "Okay," he said, in a monotone that implied neither agreement nor refusal. Before Mitch could ask him to wait, he loped out, his sneakers squeaking against the linoleum. Then a middle-aged man came in complaining that he shouldn't have to be here just because he and his wife had "one goddamn fight." Mitch had to focus on calming him down, and soon grew absorbed by this new story, this new crisis. But his eye caught a flash of red out of the window—Thomasie Reeves's windbreaker, bright against the drab gray parking lot as he strode quickly away, his head down against the wind.

The rest of the day passed normally, with addiction counseling, unemployment sagas, eviction nightmares. These he was used to. He knew how to help people break such stories down into their composite elements and start to reconfigure them. He saw his job as gently prying their fingers from their own throats. A long time ago, as a young man, he had thought of himself as a savior, and this was the fervor he had passed on to Grace. Now he believed in small, specific steps and broad-based statistical results. He wasn't as enthused about his work as he once was, but he was more confident in his ability to execute, and he slept better at night.

At six he finished up and walked through the clinic toward the exit. It was a quiet, dark place, with green corridors and an overworked, lethargic-looking staff that paid him no attention, but he didn't mind. Nor did it bother him to step out into a bright June evening so brisk that he shivered. He had gotten away.

After his disastrous visit to her apartment, he thought he'd never see Martine again. The bachelor life he had grown used to now seemed pathetic, and a sense of futility draped itself over him, wrapping its suffocating arms around his neck. From now on he would be alone.

Then she called.

This time, they met in the middle of the day and took Mathieu to a movie and then to the park. An unexpected thing happened. Mitch had liked Martine—in the fizzy, hopelessly insecure way you like someone who's out of your league, and clearly slumming in your league for just one night—but he fell in love with her son. And it was reciprocated. The kid had Asperger's, it seemed; he was a dinosaur expert and could recite encyclopedia entries about them from memory. He told Mitch all about the *T. rex* and "the land before time," apparently the dinosaur era. And as Mitch listened to this beautiful, robotic child, he felt his heart cracking like ice cubes in warm water. By the end of the afternoon, Mathieu was holding his hand and lecturing him about velociraptors.

Martine, for her part, was amazed. "This never happens," she said, sounding almost offended.

"Can we take him home?" Mitch heard Mathieu say to her in French. "I want to play with him."

Martine said, "He's not a toy, my love."

The kid just looked at her blankly. Other than dinosaurs, it was hard to know what he thought about anything. Mitch could only imagine the heartbreak of this for Martine, who constantly threw him lines, hoping their hooks would catch and she could reel him in. Mitch wanted to say that of course he'd go home with them, but the memory of his first encounter with the boy prevented him from speaking.

"Ask him yourself," Martine finally said.

"You come with me?" Mathieu said to him instantly. He had yet to call Mitch by name or to acknowledge that he was an adult. He treated him like a cross between an audience and a companion.

"Yes, I'd like to come with you," Mitch said, then glanced over at Martine, expecting to see gratitude and appreciation on her face. Instead, she looked irritated and a little concerned. She held out her hand to her son, who ignored it and took Mitch's. Thus unified, thus fractured, they went home.

Over the next few months, Mitch's relationship with the boy deepened into ferocious, passionate intensity. They spent every weekend together. He took Mathieu to Parc Lafontaine, to the planetarium, played with him, read *Tintin* to him. Martine wasn't keen on school-night visits, so midweek he'd find himself in a reverie of longing, wondering what Mathieu was doing at that very moment, picturing his blond head asleep on his red flannel pillow.

Things with Martine were, understandably, a little strange. They hardly spent any time alone. They never went out to dinner or a movie, and he didn't meet any of her friends. But he stepped into her home life, drawing himself inside the bubble of her apartment, her weekends, her kitchen table. After Mathieu went to bed, the two of them would talk—mostly about the child—while doing the dishes or drinking a glass of wine. They went to bed together, but a lot of the time they just went to sleep, Martine curled up against him with a hand on his shoulder or hip. Tired from a long week, she wanted to be held and comforted as she drifted off. When they did have sex, it was ritualized, purposeful, and quick—which was not the same as unsatisfying. There was a deep comfort in the dullness of it that he could never have anticipated. Sometimes she asked him to stay with Mathieu while she took a bath and read a magazine. It was as if they had skipped dating and gone straight to the long-married stage.

This went on for a year, then another. He didn't meet the rest of Martine's family, though her parents lived in Montreal North and her sister not five streets away. Somehow, without any conversation, certain rules had been established. Weekends only, even in summer—except in August, when they went on vacation together in Maine, where Mitch and Mathieu played Frisbee on the beach and jumped in the waves.

He wondered, every so often, why he tolerated these conditions, and always reached the same conclusions. First, as strange as the situation was, there was no doubt that it was better—a thousand times better—than living on his own had been. Second, he believed, though he never articulated this to Martine, that if he hung on and stuck around, eventually he would be more than her son's companion and her weekend comfort. He would be indispensable. He was counting on that.

⊗∞⊗

Thomasie Reeves came back a week later. In the interim, Mitch had been settling into the duplex; he had bought groceries and stocked the kitchen, and gone for walks around town to let people know who he was and how long he'd be staying. He was welcomed with uncommon grace, tinged with reserve; it was clear that they were used to seeing people like him come and go.

Johnny, he learned, was prone to long absences and sudden reappearances. Mitch would go three days without seeing him, only to wake up one morning and find him frying eggs in the kitchen, asking Mitch to join him, talking a mile a minute about some woman he'd been with the night before. Sometimes he brought the woman back home, and in the morning Mitch would see her sleepily pulling on her shoes in the living room, acknowledging him with an awkward, hungover wave. He hadn't had a roommate since he was nineteen, but in fact he was glad for some activity in the house, a sense of life going on around him. A couple of times he stayed up late with Johnny, who told hilarious anecdotes about his relatives in Newfoundland, so long and involved that Mitch couldn't remember them very well the next day. Johnny was a performer, a teller of tales, and the fact that he had no interest in other people, and never asked him what his life back in Montreal was like, suited Mitch perfectly.

He still hadn't talked to Martine. He'd left several messages, and she'd called once—at a time when she must have known he'd be tied up in appointments—saying that everything was fine, she was glad he had made it safely, and there was nothing to worry about. But things were unraveling—that much was obvious. Less so was how he felt about it. Mainly he was glad to have this much distance between himself and the difficulties of home. He tried not to worry too much about Mathieu; he was opinionated, aggressive, and in his own way emotional, but not much given to abstractions. Which is to say that while he was attached to Mitch, he wouldn't miss him when he wasn't around. At least, Mitch didn't think he would.

He asked around at the clinic about Thomasie Reeves, and everyone shook their heads and talked about how sad that case was but didn't say anything more. Every conversation about it trailed off into silence. One free afternoon, he went to the library and asked a librarian about the incident. She sighed and said, "Gloria Reeves," directing him to the newspaper accounts. The little girl, Karen, had been three years old, and they'd found her curled up inside her mother's coat, pressed against her chest. The paper ran a photo of the family lined up on a couch, with Karen sitting in her mother's lap and Thomasie beside them, all three of them wearing white turtlenecks and wool sweaters, a Christmas tree in the background.

A few days later, Thomasie appeared in Mitch's doorway. He was wearing the same outfit as last time, and his lips were just as chapped.

"Come in, sit down," Mitch said calmly. "How's it going?"

"My mom's worse," the boy said. "She's like in a coma or something. I think she doesn't want to wake up."

"I don't know if that's how it works," Mitch said.

"It seems that way to me," the kid said.

"What do the doctors say?"

Thomasie seemed not to register the question, intent instead on telling Mitch what he'd come to say. "They said I should stop visiting her so much. That maybe I should go stay with my dad."

Mitch wasn't sure why anybody would tell a kid to stop coming to the hospital, but maybe getting out of town for a while wasn't such a terrible idea. "What about that?" he said. "Going down south for a little bit."

Thomasie rolled up the sleeve of his windbreaker and held out his forearm, where there was a whorl of white scar tissue, raised and bumpy, in the crook of his elbow. "My father," he said.

Mitch's heart sank. "Did you tell any—"

The boy was shaking his head. "That's family business," he said.

Mitch sat there gathering his thoughts. When he was here last time, Thomasie must have been one of those little kids he'd seen running around, apparently joyful. And his father, whom Mitch didn't remember, would've been a teenager with a family, playing basketball in the local league before going home to take out his anger on the children he'd had too soon. Mitch had been inside a number of homes in Iqaluit, and met people who'd drawn close together despite having no jobs or money, who cared for their families and sheltered relatives in need of help, who scraped together enough to buy school supplies for their kids. He'd also seen homes that weren't so lucky, where things had gotten out of control. All it took was one haywire generation and sometimes there was no coming back from that—especially for the kids. Thomasie's home must have been one of those, but it was pretty rare to come out of a place like that as well spoken and personable as he was, and rarer still to appeal to someone like Mitch for help. To have the wherewithal, or the desperation.

"Could you tell the doctors I don't have to go?" Thomasie was saying. "Maybe you could talk to them."

"Why?" Mitch said. The question came out sounding unkind, even cruel, but he just didn't know what the boy hoped he could accomplish. He instantly felt ashamed, with Thomasie's bright black eyes searching his face for a response. "All right," he said.

The boy nodded, then abruptly ran out of the room, maybe afraid that if he stayed too long Mitch might change his mind.

There was a lull before Mitch's next appointment, and he looked out the window, thinking, his gaze fixed on nothing. There was a febrile quality to the boy, a stoppered intensity no doubt born of grief. Mitch knew he was walking into an explosive situation, something almost impossible to handle easily or well, and it gave him the same sense of excitement and danger another person might find in hang gliding or drugs. In falling in love with the wrong person. In falling in love with the right person.

He sat daydreaming of Martine and Mathieu in happier times, the long weekends of dinosaur trivia and Frisbee playing. He missed them, but his longing had less to do with geography than with his demonstrated ability, in spite of all his best intentions, to fuck things up. They still hadn't spoken. She was punishing him for leaving, and for everything that had happened before he left. It was like they were having a conversation. His leaving and her not calling when he was reachable were *remarks*, just as surely as if they'd been talking it through. In this back-and-forth, it was only a question of who would budge first—and he had a feeling that it wouldn't be Martine.

Mitch had been with them for over two years when it happened. It was March, with winter still holding on tight and squeezing out one snowstorm after another, as if trying to build to some grand finale. Mitch's coworkers took turns going on vacation to Florida or the Bahamas, returning five days later with sunburns and airs of grim disappointment that winter hadn't given up and vanished while they were out of town. But Mathieu loved snow and playing in the park and never seemed to feel the cold, even when his lips were turning blue and his teeth were chattering. When Martine told him it was time to come in, he would tremble with rage, as if she were robbing him of his most precious possession, then slip loose and run away. And when she finally caught up with him he'd flail his fists, hitting her wherever he could, and Mitch could tell that it hurt her both emotionally and physically. Afterward, when she finally got him home and in bed, she would be exhausted. Mitch brought her tea and stroked her hair, and sometimes held her while she cried.

With him, Mathieu was calmer. He had moved on from dinosaurs to particle physics, and to Mitch he seemed like a genius. He could explain the principles of nuclear fission for an hour, describing its various complexities, and it didn't matter whether Mitch responded or not. If, however, he left the room, Mathieu would get upset, so he took to reading the newspaper in the boy's room while these lectures were delivered.

This wasn't a perfect life; he knew it wasn't what Martine had once imagined; but it had its own warmth and pulse and pleasures.

Then, one Saturday, the three of them went to the Biodome, an indoor zoo that featured four different habitats, with corresponding flora and fauna, and visitors could walk from one to the next, trading tropical humidity for frigid Arctic air. As ever, Martine was hoping that this new experience might open Mathieu up, move him beyond physics. And at first, things went well. After the cold outside, the warm, wet air made them feel like they were on holiday. They walked through the rain forest, glimpsing birds high above in the trees and enormous capybaras in the streams below. Mathieu held Martine's hand without complaint. Then he spotted something in the thick leaves overhead—a tamarin monkey, scampering, just barely visible, its golden-brown fur flashing against the trunk of a tree. Mathieu wanted to touch it, to play with it, for his mother to buy it for him and take it home with them. Martine patiently explained that the monkey wasn't a pet or for sale, that it was happy in this rain forest but wouldn't be in their apartment, which was too cold and didn't have any trees.

None of these arguments made sense to him. *"Singe! Singe!"* he screamed, and Mitch wondered if Mathieu not only wanted the monkey but somehow identified with it, seeing himself up there, loose and wild and uncontained.

Around them families scurried away, eager to distance themselves from the howling boy, lest his behavior prove contagious. Mitch tried to distract him by talking about the snakes in the next room, but that didn't work. Then he made the worst mistake of all, a gesture he replayed in his mind for weeks to come: he took hold of his shoulder, hoping to steer him toward a new attraction and change the scene. But Mathieu screamed even louder, wrenched himself free, and darted away. When Martine reached out to catch him, he pushed back—in a fit like this he was curiously strong—and knocked her right over the railing behind them, onto a steep, rocky slope. Unable to break her fall, she slipped and then rolled on her side, her hands grasping at air, down to the bottom. People were yelling and pointing, and Mitch instinctively grabbed Mathieu. When the boy tried to pull away, Mitch yanked his arm and heard—over the commotion of the crowd and the upset chattering of the monkeys—the soft pop of his shoulder dislocating.

Mathieu's pretty face went white with shock and pain, and then he fainted.

Later, in the hospital, they popped Mathieu's arm back into joint and bandaged Martine's sprained ankle. Despite the relatively minor injuries, all of this took hours, and Martine refused to leave Mathieu alone with Mitch, who told her, over and over, "I'm so sorry, it was an accident."

Each time she just shook her head, as if trying to clear her ears, without saying a word. She didn't tell him to go, and by the end of the night he realized why. Because of her sprained right ankle, she needed him to drive them home. She was very practical, Martine.

When they reached the apartment, she said, "I think we need to be alone tonight," and he walked back to his place in what turned into an ice storm, the freezing rain pelting his coat.

Though he called Martine the next day to apologize yet again, and swore he wouldn't let the incident dislodge him from their lives, things did change; cracks soon filtered across the surface of a situation that had been delicate to begin with. But they weren't the cracks he'd anticipated.

The next weekend, he went over to cook them dinner. He hadn't seen Martine, but they had spoken on the phone, their conversations scattered and filled with pauses that she blamed on the pain relievers she was taking for her ankle. When he showed up, it was Mathieu who came to the door. In Mitch's thoughts the boy had loomed larger, stronger, and more demonic, and it was a shock to see how fragile he was, so clearly a child.

"Hey," he said.

"*Je peux faire un ruban de Möbius. Venez voir,*" Mathieu said, turning around and walking back to his room as if nothing had ever happened. Mitch watched him twist the strip of paper for a while, the accompanying recitation high-pitched and breathless, and then said, "I'm going to say hi to your mother for a minute." Mathieu didn't respond, though he stopped talking, his small hands still turning the paper around.

In the kitchen Martine was drinking what looked to be, given her violet smile, a third or fourth glass of wine. She waved at him sloppily, hopping around to set the table. As he leaned over to kiss her cheek, she banged her hip against a chair and said, "Ow. Shit."

That was their hello.

He told her to sit down while he made the pasta Bolognese, and she sat there chattering about their follow-up visits to the doctors and funny things Mathieu had said about her sprained ankle—a performance so untypical that it filled him with dread, and he sank into silence when she called Mathieu to the table. She kept it up all during dinner, joking with Mathieu and tousling his hair until he solemnly told her to stop. After five bites he asked to be excused, and she let him go. She didn't eat much either.

Mitch washed the dishes and prepared to leave, the sorrow of endings pressing down on his heart. He felt sure he would never see any of it again: the tiny, cozy kitchen with its tomato-red walls, Martine's handwriting on refrigerator-hung lists, Mathieu's science books stacked on the counter.

Martine was in the bedroom, and when he went in to say good night she kissed him with her wine-dark mouth. He tasted the salt of tears. She dragged him to the bed and down on top of her, her hands under his sweater scratching his back, her good leg slipping over the back of his jeans. In all the time they'd spent together, she'd rarely initiated anything, and never had she shown such pulsing lust and desperation. She had his sweater and shirt off now and was trying to remove her own, but her elbow got snagged in the sleeve of her cardigan and caught him squarely in the face, knocking off his glasses.

"Fuck me," she said. She was still crying.

"Martine, my love," Mitch said, kissing her wet, crinkled cheek.

He was slipping in and out of her without rhythm or traction, trying and failing to match the jerking, spastic motion of her hips. She was crying harder now, practically choking, so Mitch slipped out and put his arms around her. He didn't know what else to do. It was as if the Martine he knew was dissolving. She shifted until her back was to him, then curled into herself, her knees meeting her chin. He was shushing and comforting her, muttering gentle and meaningless sounds, when he heard a small noise behind him, lifted his head to look, and saw Mathieu silhouetted in the doorway.

The boy stared at him, his blue eyes open and frightened. Mitch watched anxiously, waiting for him to explode, but he just stood there, his gaze never once moving from Mitch's face, even to examine his mother's hidden, shuddering figure. Then he padded back down the hallway to his room.

Martine was whispering to her knees. He bent closer, curling himself around her protectively, bark on her tree. Only when he pressed his cheek against hers could he make out what she was saying. He'd thought she was talking to herself, but she was speaking in English and, therefore, to him.

"Please don't leave me," she said.

It was the last thing he'd expected her to say. What could he do? As her tears dried, he curled even closer. He didn't leave. He told her he never would.

If only he could have stayed right there with her forever, inside that moment of calm. But life wasn't like that; it was work and cooking and mothering and chores, and Martine went back to all these things, soldiering through. He did his best to help her, but something had shifted between them. A dam had broken and he understood only now that she had kept him at bay for so long because behind that dam was a raging torrent of water that could swamp them both. She needed him. She started calling him every night at ten, after Mathieu had gone to sleep, to talk about her day. This he loved, but she never wanted to get off the phone. What she wanted, he finally realized, was to drift into sleep with the phone against her cheek, with him murmuring reassurances. Before long he was spending Wednesday nights, and then Thursday nights, at her apartment, where he would murmur those same reassurances in person.

That crying fit was never repeated, but he sometimes woke up in the middle of the night to go to the washroom, and when he came back he'd notice, in the bedroom's dim light, the glint of tears on her face. The idea that she was crying in her sleep broke his heart.

Soon he was spending all his time at their place, his own apartment gathering dust.

They talked about everything, constantly hashing things out. They discussed what had happened in the zoo, how angry she had been at him and Mathieu and how oppressive that anger was, how much he regretted what he'd done, how sorry he still felt. She said she forgave him. All he had to do to stay in her good graces, it seemed, was to listen. Martine could talk about the stress of raising Mathieu for hours, could dissect the minutiae of his sentences and gestures and bowel movements. After the first of these sessions, she put her arms around his neck and thanked him.

"For what?" he said.

"For listening. For being here. I need you so much."

These were exactly the words he'd been aching to hear for so long; but now that he heard them, the effect wasn't what he expected. This had to do with Mathieu. Mitch couldn't get over—and would never admit to Martine—how, that afternoon in the zoo, he had been so blinded with rage and protectiveness that in another second he would've knocked Mathieu to the ground. He'd thought he loved the child, but in that instant recognized the truth: he only put up with him, for her sake.

He was so disappointed in himself, so ashamed, that he began to crave escape. All through April and into May, nestling into the apartment while spring came, taking Mathieu to the park on weekends, attending the year-end concert at his school, lying in bed with this lovely, heartbreakingly vulnerable woman in his arms, he thought constantly about getting away.

He told Martine that the call to come north came out of the blue, and this was true enough—but only after weeks of dropping subtle hints and sending friendly e-mails to acquaintances he hadn't spoken to in ages, just to keep his name in their minds. And when he told Martine he was thinking of going but wanted to talk it over with her first, even as he said it he knew that he'd already made up his mind.

On a gloomy Thursday morning he met Thomasie Reeves outside the hospital where his mother lay in a coma. They had arranged this over the phone, the boy's voice slow and stilted, as if it were coming from another continent. He seemed to think that Mitch could convince the doctors of what he couldn't, and that everything would change once Mitch had seen his mother for himself. As he approached that morning, sidling up the street in the same sideways, loping stride Mitch had noted from his office window, the smell of marijuana was almost overwhelming. Thomasie seemed bathed in it, his eyes red, his expression muted, his whole personality turned down a notch. Mitch's heart went out to him; if this were his mother, he would've wanted to numb himself too.

He reached out his hand and Thomasie stared at it for a second, in confusion or fascination, before shaking it; then they went inside.

The nurses walking past smelled the pot, and one of them grimaced in disapproval. Mitch shot her a look, and she rolled her eyes. In the waiting room, a father sat cradling a sick girl maybe two or three years old; his face was impassive, the child's cheeks flushed a dark, unhealthy red. Opposite them, an old woman had fallen asleep with her round face dropped against her chest.

Thomasie, his face intent, led Mitch down a dim linoleum hall-way without saying anything. He was wearing the same windbreaker, over which he'd slung a blue backpack. Beneath the pot was another, gamy odor, and his hair hung limp and thin. Mitch wondered if any-one was taking care of him—telling him to bathe, making sure he got something to eat. Every time Mitch had seen him there were dark circles under his eyes.

Thomasie stopped at a closed door, then opened it. Inside there were two beds, one of them empty, and the woman in the other had to be the boy's mother. According to the newspaper, Gloria Reeves was only thirty-nine, but she looked much older, her face mottled and creased. Mitch glanced at Thomasie, who had wanted so desperately to come; he was standing uncertainly at the foot of the bed.

His mother's eyes were closed, and she was hooked up to an IV and a monitor that indicated her heartbeat. It took Mitch a moment to register that the index and third fingers of her right hand and a chunk of her ear were missing, lost to frostbite. The tip of her nose was black. Though her breathing was labored, she seemed composed and too still, like a wax figure someone had arranged into position.

Mitch saw a doctor passing by outside and, after nodding to Thomasie, stepped out in the hall. He had met him a few days ago, a genial, outdoorsy young man from Victoria who was just out of medi-cal school and on a year's rotation in the Arctic.

"Bobby," Mitch said, "how are you?"

In response, the doctor not only shook his hand but also grasped his upper arm, his eyes flickering with concern. "I see you're here with Thomasie," he said. "You know, we asked him not to come by so much."

"Why would you tell a kid not to visit his mother?"

"He's disruptive," Bobby said. "He comes here stoned, even gets in bed with her. Sometimes he's drunk and yelling at the doctors. It upsets the other patients. And God knows it's not helping his mother, no matter how out of it she is."

"What's her condition?"

"Bad," Bobby said flatly. "I mean, of course there's a one-in-a-million chance. But her brain was probably damaged irreparably by those hours in the snow."

"So she'll stay in that bed forever?"

"I wouldn't go that far. She's deteriorating, and I don't think there's much functioning neural activity. Thomasie gets excited because her eyes open sometimes, but that's just muscle reflex. It doesn't indicate anything significant."

When Mitch nodded, Bobby clapped him on the arm and strode off down the hall, whistling a little, young and vigorous.

When he stepped back inside he was surprised by what he saw in the dim light. Thomasie was half lying on the bed, with his legs on the floor and his upper body pressed against his mother's, his head buried in the crook of her neck. Then, sensing Mitch's return, he got up, keeping his eyes averted, and tucked something under her pillow—a small bottle of rye he must have had in his backpack. He glanced over at Mitch but didn't say anything, and they left the room.

Once they were outside, Mitch said, "Maybe you shouldn't visit quite so often, Thomasie. I'm not sure it's helping her."

The boy shrugged bashfully, as if he'd been complimented. "I don't mind," he said, "I don't have much else to do." He finally looked Mitch in the eye. "Talk to them," he said. "Tell them I like coming here." Then he walked away, his shoulders hunched against the wind.

A few days passed in which he didn't see or hear from Thomasie. Then, one windy Friday afternoon, in between appointments, he got a call from the doctor.

"Just thought you should know," Bobby said, "that Gloria Reeves died this morning. Her organs finally shut down. Thomasie was with her."

"Thanks for telling me," Mitch said. "How'd Thomasie seem?"

"He took it very quietly. Didn't say much. Maybe he'll do better now that she's not just hanging on."

"Maybe," Mitch said, and hung up, finding the doctor's optimism so misplaced as to be offensive. He sat there alone in his office thinking about the woman asleep in the snow, her tiny daughter shivering against her cold skin. *The world was white.* It made him ache for Martine and Mathieu, but when he called, there was no answer in Montreal. She was probably just screening his calls.

The next day he decided to find out where Thomasie lived, which wasn't hard. Iqaluit was small, and almost everyone was related or connected somehow. One of the night nurses turned out to be Thomasie's father's cousin, but when Mitch told her he'd heard he was down in Sarnia, she pressed her lips together and shook her head. She was a smart, competent nurse who'd earned a degree at McGill before returning to the north, and they'd talked about her time in Montreal. She'd been chatty about life in the city, but her family was a different story.

"Thomasie's been to see me a couple of times," Mitch said, as casually as he could.

She looked up at him. She was short but strong, with long black hair kept off her forehead by a headband that made her look incongruously girlish. "He lived with me for a while growing up," she said. "George and Gloria, they always drank too much, so we had Thomasie sometimes. And three of my sister's, after she took off with her second husband. But the kids grow up and they have to learn to take care of themselves."

Mitch flushed, not wanting her to feel that she was being accused. "Of course," he said, "I didn't mean—"

"He's a sweet boy," she said, her eyes softening, and gave him the address before picking up a stack of charts and moving quietly down the hall.

So on his day off Mitch set out carrying a bag of cookies. He couldn't think what else to bring. Like most houses in Iqaluit, Thomasie's was tiny, and scattered in the front yard were dolls, a beach ball, a white tricycle with pink ribbons hanging limply from the handlebars, all smudged with dirt and bleached from exposure. In the constant sunlight it was impossible to tell whether anybody was home. He knocked on the door but heard nothing inside. There wasn't a car parked on the street, but he didn't know if Thomasie's family even had one. He knocked again, and this time heard what sounded like something being dragged across the floor. He knocked a third time, and finally, a minute later, Thomasie opened the door.

He was wearing sweatpants, a long-sleeved shirt, and, draped over his shoulders, a blanket he'd apparently pulled off the bed. Mitch, never having seen him without his red windbreaker, was shocked at how thin he was. He stared at Mitch without a trace of recognition, his eyes not even seeming to focus, his hair a riot of tangles around his head. He was enormously stoned.

From behind him came a girl's voice. "Who is it? Who's out there?"

"I heard about your mom. I came to see how you're doing," Mitch said. When he didn't get any response to this, he held out the cookies, which Thomasie took without a word. Still clutching the blanket around himself, he opened the bag and started eating, crumbs falling to the floor.

"I said who is it?" the girl called again, impatient and stern. "Don't just stand there with the door open." Mitch heard footsteps, then she pushed Thomasie aside and stood there looking at him. "Oh," she said, evidently knowing who he was. She was a teenager, around Thomasie's age, wearing jeans and a hooded sweatshirt, her hair neatly combed back into a ponytail.

"This my girlfriend," Thomasie said. "Fiona."

"Hi," Mitch said stupidly, and she nodded at him.

"He brought cookies," Thomasie said.

"Invite him in," Fiona said. *"God."*

She pulled Thomasie back by the blanket and gestured for Mitch to come inside, pointing him to the couch and Thomasie to the facing chair. Her movements were strong and martial, somehow all the more convincing for her thinness and youth. She was in charge here. Mitch had been expecting a chaotic mess, but the house was clean and well cared for. All around them was the evidence of the missing mother and daughter: finger paintings tacked up on kitchen walls, a calendar with days circled on it next to the door, above a pile of little shoes and boots.

"What do you want?" Fiona asked him, sounding more curious than confrontational.

"I came to offer my condolences," Mitch said, but she looked at him as if he hadn't spoken in English. Or maybe she just couldn't imagine why he'd thought this would be helpful. When, after a long pause, she still didn't speak, Mitch tried again. "Do you live here?"

She glanced at Thomasie, who was looking down at his lap, fixated on the cookies. Her expression was equal parts disappointment, concern, and affection. "I'm his cousin," she said, then registered the look on Mitch's face. "Second cousin. My parents live down by the hospital. After his mom got hurt I came over to help take care of him."

"Fiona takes care of everybody," the boy said.

"Be quiet, Thomasie," she told him, but fondly.

"She's got the best grades at school. She's going to be a lawyer."

Fiona sighed; it was a sigh of having heard all this before, of wishing he had the expectations for himself that he had for her.

"That's great," Mitch said. "I was worried about you," he said to Thomasie. "I wanted to make sure you were all right."

Fiona kept looking at him, a straight, direct gaze he couldn't quite interpret. He wasn't sure if she was blaming him for not doing more before or asking him to do less now. Maybe both.

"He's not alone here," she finally said.

Mitch could tell she felt reproached. He seemed to make everybody feel bad, all these women doing their best to hold the lives around them together. "He's very lucky," he told her, also the wrong thing to say, because she frowned and Thomasie snorted.

Fiona stood up and, with an air of weary responsibility, offered him some tea, then went into the cramped kitchen to prepare it. Thomasie had put the cookie bag on the floor but was chewing contemplatively, looking up at the ceiling. His condition had deteriorated rapidly, and it wasn't just that he was high, more that he had given up on communicating—given up, it seemed, on everything.

Mitch sat forward, wanting somehow to break through. "I'm so sorry about your mother," he said. "What was she like?"

Slowly and with evident effort Thomasie lowered his gaze to Mitch, his eyes unfocused, red-tinged, and made a vague gesture with his hands, as if holding a watermelon. "She was small," he said.

Fiona came back into the room carrying two mugs. She gave one to Mitch and the other, after shaking him none too gently by the shoulder, to Thomasie, seeming as much his mother as his girlfriend. As he faded in and out, Fiona and Mitch managed to have a conversation. He learned she'd worked since she was thirteen at a general store in Iqaluit and was an honors student who planned to earn a bachelor of laws degree at Akitsiraq Law School. Her mother worked at the general store too, and her father mostly helped around the house. She presented these facts directly, assuming they were what Mitch had come for, sounding neither shamed nor boasting.

Thomasie fell asleep in his chair.

After twenty minutes or so, Fiona looked at her watch and said, "You should go now."

Mitch nodded, thanked her for the tea, and paused at the door to shake her hand.

As she held his hand in her cool, dry palm, Fiona's eyes suddenly glistened. "He's not doing too good," she said, and at last she seemed like a teenager, her body slight beneath her hulking hooded sweatshirt, her shoulders curved. "Maybe you can help him?"

"Of course," Mitch said, automatically. He was walking down the street before it sank in that no measures he took would bring back Thomasie's sister, or his mother, or the life he should have had. He hadn't meant to lie to the girl; he just wanted her, for that one moment, not to feel so alone.

That evening, he called Martine. They had finally spoken a couple of times over the past week, but she'd been in a hurry, eager to get off the phone. There was too much to talk about, or too little. He had already filled the air between them with explanations, and now there was no room for anything else. He talked, as he had before, about the people of Iqaluit, how much they needed him, how fulfilled he felt, all lies or at the very least exaggerations.

"I'm happy for you, Mitch," she said wearily.

They'd stopped calling each other by their first names long ago, using nicknames and endearments instead, and his name falling from her lips now sounded strangely formal, distancing, even bruising. He sighed. "How's Mathieu?"

"He's made a friend."

"Really? How did that happen?" Friendship wasn't a social need Mathieu understood.

"At camp. His name is Luc. He comes over and plays on his PlayStation while Mathieu plays on his Xbox. They never talk. But they like sitting there together. Mathieu even asks me to invite Luc over."

"Martine, that's great. Really amazing."

There was a pause on the other end. It could have been that she didn't believe him, or that hearing him say "Martine" instead of "sweetheart" was as jarring to her as it had been to him. And possibly she was thinking, You should be here to see it.

"I have to go," Martine said. "I need to get dinner."

"Okay," he said. "I can't wait to see you—just three more weeks." He was sticking to the fiction that theirs was a difficult but necessary separation, enforced by external circumstances over which he had no control, to be followed by a romantic reunion at the end of his rotation.

"I have to tell you," she said, "I'm seeing someone else."

"No," he said without even thinking. He couldn't imagine this. "I don't believe you."

She laughed. "You don't have to. It's true whether you believe it or not."

"Is it that guy Michel at your office? Because you know he's an asshole, Martine."

"It's not Michel. It's Dr. Vendetti, actually."

This was a name he'd never heard. "Who?"

"He's my gynecologist."

This information silenced him. There was so much to take in, all of it bad. That he had never once thought, in all their time together, about Martine even having a gynecologist made him dizzy with remorse. There was so much in her life he hadn't paid attention to.

And then there was the image, undesired but fully resolved, of Martine with her legs spread in stirrups, leaning back while this man put his hand inside her. He would have done anything, in that moment, to have her back, to have never left her—and this, he knew, is why she had told him.

"I have to go now," she said. "Dinner, like I said. Take care."

He was formulating exactly what to say next when he realized she'd hung up.

Mitch was a man of moderate habits. He didn't smoke, rarely overate, walked as much as he could. So it took very little, when the need arose, to obliterate him.

To accomplish this goal, he bought two bottles of whiskey and invited Johnny to play cards. A short hour later he was twenty dollars down and felt the room temperature rising, so he took off his sweater. Seated across the table, Johnny smiled enigmatically, his freckled cheeks flushed red, the smoke from his continual cigarettes wreathing him cloudily, so that he looked like a magician or a wizard.

"You don't drink much, do you?"

"I drink a regular amount."

"You're drunk now, and you've only had one drink."

"Didn't I have two?"

"And it isn't easy to lose twenty bucks at gin rummy."

"You," Mitch said drunkenly, "are a damn card shark."

Johnny shrugged and poured him another drink.

Mitch fought the urge to weep and tell him that he was his only friend. But it was true; in this place, right now, he was. Johnny won another twenty dollars before Mitch passed out.

It had been so long since he was hungover that he didn't recognize the terrible commotion in his bloodstream. He thought he had food poisoning, then remembered he hadn't eaten dinner. There was a terrible smell in the room, and when he opened his eyes he saw he'd thrown up into a bucket that Johnny must have left by his bed for just that purpose. Aching from his neck to his knees, he felt like he had a fever, so physically terrible that he couldn't even think about

Martine. Disgust—with himself, his body, and his behavior—was the closest thing to an emotion that he could summon.

Which was to say that things had worked out perfectly.

He had the day off and thought he might lie around in bed all morning, go for a walk in the afternoon, then see if Johnny was up for another night of drinking. If he could drink himself into oblivion for a couple of nights, his mind and heart might start healing, and he could sober up feeling better about Martine and Mathieu and himself. Or feeling nothing at all.

The light streaming through the thin white curtains hurt his head, and he thought about turning over, then decided this was too drastic a course of action, with potentially awful consequences. His stomach wavered unhappily, and he closed his eyes.

"You did a number on yourself," a voice said.

He looked up to see Johnny standing next to the bed, silhouetted in the window, whose curtains he'd just thrown open.

"Get up," he said. He seemed towering, mountainous. He left the room—for good, Mitch hoped—but was back all too soon with a can of Pepsi and several pills, which Mitch swallowed without asking what they were.

"You'll feel better soon," Johnny said.

"Thanks." He was sitting up in bed now, pillows propped behind his back, feeling a sense of accomplishment for having made it halfway horizontal. Johnny sat by him for a while in silence. Every few minutes he handed him the can of Pepsi and told him to take a sip, more solicitous than Mitch would have imagined possible. As his headache slowly ebbed, Mitch realized that Johnny was waiting for the pills to take effect.

The can was half empty when Johnny said, "Heard the news this morning. About the kid you were telling me about last night. Thomasie."

Mitch opened his mouth to speak, but nothing came out. He closed it again, tasting on his tongue the sick trace of whiskey, the sugary bite of Pepsi. It was too early for him to feel anything yet, and he let this moment linger, knowing that soon he would feel altogether too many things. "What has he done?"

"He drank a pint of vodka and stepped onto the highway in front of a truck in the middle of the night. The trucker's in the hospital. No note or anything."

And there it was. Another terrible thing in a world already sick to death of terrible things. I should kill myself too, Mitch thought. His shoulders shook, and he welcomed the coming sobs—but what happened instead was a shudder of his stomach, and the Pepsi and pills lurched back out, strands of spittle webbing the bucket and his sleeves.

"I know you tried to help him," Johnny said, putting a hand on his shoulder.

"I didn't do any good."

Johnny took him by the hand, as if he wanted to hold it, but then curled his palm around the still-cold Pepsi can and said, "I'll let you get dressed," and left the room.

At the clinic, for the first time, everyone wanted to talk to him. To know what Thomasie had been thinking, what he had told Mitch about his mother. A helicopter had flown in reporters from as far away as Montreal, eager to report on Inuit problems and the crises of addiction, poverty, and fractured families. Mitch was supposed to be an expert on these issues, and his phone rang so incessantly that he finally pulled the cord out of the wall. He had nothing to say.

They held a combined service for Thomasie and his mother at the community center, where an elder delivered the eulogy and no one from the family spoke. A friend of Thomasie's from high school played the guitar and sang a John Denver song. There was no sign of Thomasie's father. The nurse from the clinic was there, and so was Fiona, with her parents, but when Mitch expressed his condolences she looked right through him and said nothing. He pressed his card into her palm and told her to call if she needed anything, and she crumpled it into her pocket like some useless receipt.

When he asked to be released from his rotation, the request was granted immediately. What he wanted most was to get away from all the understanding looks and forgiving glances. Another fragile southerner, the community seemed to think. They'd never expected him to last long, and didn't condemn him for wanting to leave. If only someone had blamed him, he might have been able to stay.

He returned to Montreal in August, and the city was turgid with heat, empty of people. His apartment felt like it belonged to someone else. Several times he picked up the phone to call Martine but always put it down again. Though he was due a vacation, he reported to work anyway, knowing how much he needed that structure and company to get through the days. He'd always been like this in difficult times, working weekends even when he didn't have to, sculpting his hours to make everything else fit neatly into place.

On Sunday evening he went for a long run on the mountain, the familiar, muffled beat of the tam-tam drums by the Cartier monument matching the rhythm of his pulse. After the cold nights of Iqaluit the dense, humid air felt good against his skin, his muscles unclenching as he sweated out the poisons inside.

He'd thought he wouldn't be able to sleep, but he fell into a dreamless, blanketing state and woke at dawn feeling like he'd been deep underwater. At six thirty the phone rang, and he raced to answer it.

"You're nothing," a woman's voice said on the other line. It wasn't Martine.

"Who is this?"

She was crying in rhythmic sobs and wheezes. "You were supposed to help."

"Please, who is this?"

"I hope you lose somebody you love."

"Fiona," he said.

"You're nothing," she said again, and hung up.

He stood in the living room in his underwear, still holding the phone in his hand, the early-morning sun bright behind the curtains, birds chirping outside. He thought of nothing except Thomasie Reeves: his chapped lips, his red windbreaker, his face as it must have looked when he stepped out onto the highway, firm and unblinking, into the brilliance of those headlights, massive as planets, barreling toward him in the pale Arctic night.

The dial tone sang, then switched to a higher beep. Mitch was happy. He was satisfied that someone hated him as much as he deserved, and was willing to tell him so. At least there was one person in the world who told the truth.

FOUR

Montreal, 1996

GRACE HAD JUST come back from work when the buzzer to her apartment rang. For a second her pulse quickened; she had the brief, impossible thought that it was Tug. Maybe he had come to explain what had happened. To thank her. She'd told him her last name, so it wouldn't have been hard to track her down. She tucked her hair behind her ears, straightened her sweater, felt herself flush. All this in the few seconds before a crackling sound came through the speaker, and she realized it wasn't him.

"Dr. Tomlinson," said a female voice, "it's Annie. I'm coming up."

There were footsteps on the stairs and Grace watched Annie Hardwick climb the last few steps unsteadily, clutching the rail, her pale face turned upward. Wearing a puffy ski jacket that dwarfed her thin frame, she was hunched under the weight of her backpack.

"I took a cab here," she said, panting, when she reached the top step. "I didn't know where else to go. I need to lie down for a few hours. I can't go home, my mom will see the bleeding and she knows it's not my usual time."

"Jesus," Grace said, letting her in.

The girl was shivering. Underneath the ski jacket she wore her school uniform, a short skirt and tights and a cotton sweater over a button-down shirt. Her long hair was pulled back in a wide navy headband. Grace took her coat, led her to the couch—where she lay down, obedient, fragile—and spread a blanket over her.

"All the women in my family are very regular, my mom says," Annie said. "Set a clock by them. And the two of us cycle together because we live together, so she'll definitely notice that something's up."

"What happened?"

"I went to the doctor," she said. "Your address is listed, so I came here. I told my mom I was eating dinner at a friend's house and I'd be home by nine."

Her legs contracted under the blanket, her knees moving up toward her chin, and she started to cry, without moving to wipe her tears away. "It's too bad because I sort of wish I could just go to bed," she said in a soft, distant undertone. "I mean, I wish I had my mom."

Grace sat down on the couch and put the girl's head in her lap and stroked her long hair until she quieted, then slept.

An hour later, Annie woke up and seemed more alert. She went into the bathroom and came out a few minutes later and asked if there was anything to eat. Grace made her a bowl of soup and she sat on the couch and ate it, slurping like a child. Then she handed Grace her empty bowl, smiled, and readjusted her headband. "I like your apartment," she said. "It's small, but it's nice."

"Are you feeling better?"

"A little."

"Do you want me to call your parents to come pick you up?"

"No. I'll take a cab in a little while, okay? Listen, I'm really sorry I just showed up here, but I didn't know where else to go. I can pay you, like, for an extra session or something."

Her parents had taught her to pave her way with money. When Grace said nothing, she blushed. "I'm sorry."

She lay back down on the couch, more languorously this time, and began to ramble, talking more freely than she ever had in Grace's office about her parents, their financial problems and arguments, their general cluelessness about anything to do with her life. She said

she felt sorry for them, for how stressed out they were about everything, and that they deserved a better daughter.

"It's like with Ollie," she said. "Some of my friends, they don't
understand how I could be with him, because he's not always that
nice to me. He always acts really nice around teachers and parents, so
they all think he's like the perfect kid even though it's just an act. And
he flirts with other girls and maybe even hooks up with them for all
I know. My friends think I'm like this victim, or whatever. But what
they don't understand is that I *need* to be with somebody like that,
somebody who's like me. Ollie and I have to be together because we
can't go around hurting nice, normal people. I haven't told him about
the other stuff, but I don't have to feel as bad about that as I would
with a nice guy."

"What other stuff?"

"Oh, just stuff," Annie said dreamily. "Sometimes I meet people."

"It sounds to me like you might be putting yourself in danger,"
Grace said. "Which is a bad idea."

"No kidding," Annie said. "I mean, obviously."

She fell asleep again, and when Grace woke her at eight thirty she
sat up immediately, her forehead crinkled in worry. "Am I late?" she
said. "Shit."

Using the phone in the kitchen, she called a cab. Then she said,
"Thank you for your help," her tone blatantly impersonal, her eyes
fixed on a spot just over Grace's left shoulder. For a moment, she
seemed to consider shaking her hand, but then she turned abruptly
and left, her steps tumbling heavily down the stairs.

Grace poured herself a glass of wine and told herself she had just
made a terrible mistake. Now, even more than before, she was collud-
ing with Annie, part of her secret. She thought about calling Annie's
parents right away, but something stopped her. The girl had cried
and rambled so openly, had shown such trust in her. In trouble and
pain, she came to her door, and what could Grace do but let her in?

In her first year of practice, Grace had a patient named Morris Tinker-
ton, an American who had come to Montreal to work for a telecommunications company. He spent the entire first session explaining

his job in elaborate, technical detail, and Grace had waited for all this information to lead into whatever issue had brought him to her, before realizing it was simply an avoidance technique and irrelevant to any problem he might have. In the second session he began talking about his wife, Suzanne, a college professor who had chosen to remain behind in Minneapolis. Her field was the sociology of health care—who got what kind of medical treatment and why—and Morris spoke as knowledgeably and thoroughly of her work as he did of his own. Starting to feel like she was being held hostage at a boring dinner party, Grace took notes on a yellow legal pad. She decided that professional commitments had forced the two apart geographically and, most likely, emotionally as well.

Morris was thirty-five but looked ten years older, his face settling into the slack paunch of middle age, and his outfits, strangely childlike polo shirts and khaki pants, made him seem, paradoxically, even older. He spoke with a lilting, almost Scandinavian accent and settled himself on her couch with his palms resting on his knees and his posture rigid, as if he'd been belted into a ride. When he first mentioned the dog, he referred to her simply as Molly, and Grace thought that in her boredom she'd failed to make note of this third important person in their family.

"So when Molly and I were out walking the other day," Morris said, "I was thinking about Suzanne and certain concepts in her dissertation." And: "I've been working such long hours lately that I've hardly had any time to spend with Molly, and I resent that." These statements sent Grace scrambling back through her notes. Was there a child she hadn't registered? A sister or some relative who lived with them? Or was Morris having an affair? She had a sleepless night after that session, contemplating what a poor and inattentive therapist she was.

But then she realized Morris was doing it on purpose, that behind his rigid bearing and studied calmness was a mind restlessly circling around pain that couldn't be referred to directly and had to be approached sidelong. Pain that was occasioned—she understood in the third session, when he mentioned a leash and a park—by a dog named Molly.

"Tell me more about her, then," Grace said. "What's she like?"

At first Morris looked like he'd been punched in the stomach. He chewed the inside of his cheek, his breath labored. Then he looked across the room, staring at the poster over her head as if it were a distant horizon, and his eyes grew soft, almost wet. "When we got her, she was just a pup, just this little ball of fur. Like a pincushion or something. Really, you've never seen anything like it. Now she weighs as much as Suzanne does, practically. Almost a hundred pounds. Of course, a lot of that's fur. If she were shaved she'd probably lose at least ten." He laughed about this, low and fond, as if he'd given it a lot of thought.

"So you're the dog's primary caretaker," Grace said.

"Primary caretaker?" Morris repeated. He seemed offended by the language, and his normally static hands fluttered up in the air before resettling on his lap like large, pale moths. "I guess. I feel more like she takes care of me. When I come home at night, we'll go out to the park and she'll run and fetch, and then we go back and sit on the couch—and when she lies next to me, I feel like she's what I'm coming home to."

"And what about Suzanne?" Grace said.

"She doesn't get Molly," he declared with sudden ferocity. "She doesn't *understand* her. She'll sit there and say, in this baby voice, 'What do you want, sweetie? Come here, sweetie!' When any person with a brain in their head could tell that she wants to go out and pee, or get up on the couch. I mean, it couldn't be more obvious if Molly was using a diagram or a neon sign." He shook his head. "It drives me crazy."

They spent the rest of the session discussing his expectations, and why it mattered, in terms of their marriage, that Suzanne "get" the dog. Morris grew so exercised that the hair around his temples was matted and wet, and more than ever he looked like a little boy. Grace suspected that Molly was a stand-in for his own feelings of abandonment and betrayal, since Suzanne hadn't come along to Montreal. By the end of the hour she believed they'd made some real progress, and Morris, too, seemed tired but happy.

She was so convinced of this that she could barely speak when he showed up for their next appointment with the dog on a leash.

"Since we were talking about her, I thought you should meet the famous Molly in person," he said, and Grace felt a pricking in her temples. The dog sat at Morris's feet with her back pressed against his shins, then rested her chin on his lap. She was enormous, and her shaggy black hair obscured her eyes. Morris reached down and rubbed her chest, making an affectionate, growling sound. It so startled Grace that she sat up straight and coughed.

"Everything's changed since Molly came into my life," he said. "She makes me feel like a better person, and we understand each other. I feel *calm*."

"There's a lot of evidence that pets help soothe anxiety and depression," Grace said. "But do you think your marriage—"

"Tell me," Morris interrupted, resting his large hand on Molly's shaggy head, a gesture like a benediction, "do you think it's weird to feel more love for your dog than you do for your wife?"

Grace examined him carefully. "I think we often wish all our relationships were as full of unconditional acceptance as those we have with animals."

Morris shook his head. "I don't just mean acceptance. I mean I *love* her. I think she's beautiful and noble. I think her existence on earth is a great thing, and I'd do anything to make her happy. I never felt like that about Suzanne, not even on our honeymoon."

Grace had the feeling she should tread lightly. "I'm sure you must've felt more"—she was going to say *romantic*, but thought better of it—"optimistic about Suzanne in the early days, didn't you?"

"Optimistic? That's not what I mean," Morris said impatiently. "I love everything about this dog—her eyes, her body, the way she's leaning against me right now. She's my *home*. This dog is my home."

Grace put down her pen. It was imperative, she knew, not to judge. But passing judgment is how we navigate the world, go left instead of right, do right instead of wrong. "Don't you think, Morris," she said softly, "that dogs are easier to love because they don't talk back?"

In front of her this large, childlike man began to cry, with the creaking, stunted tears of someone who rarely sheds them. "Sometimes," he said, "I wish it were just me and Molly. That Suzanne would leave us alone. You don't have to tell me it's stupid, I know it's ridiculous." He let out a low, ravaged moan, and the dog leapt up on the couch and licked his face and squirmed into his lap, and he smiled through his tears. "I love her," he said.

To love a dog not as a pet, but as you would a person, is impossible. It's like asking a child to be an adult, or expecting your partner to always give love and never receive, or always receive and never give. A fantasy, a refusal to negotiate the complicated, muddy emotional needs that define any relationship. All this Grace tried to explain to Morris while he cradled a hundred-pound dog in his lap. He listened and nodded and dried his cheeks. Then he said, "Thank you very much," and left her office. She never heard from him again.

It was Morris she thought of when she saw John Tugwell again. Because she knew there was no good reason she should be so intensely interested in him; that he was a troubled person, one more likely to suck her into his trouble than to be drawn out of it. But when she saw him, the rush of gladness made her catch her breath. And none of the commonsense warnings she gave herself could counter that gladness and drag her back to earth.

Until that moment, she had told herself she was just looking for a birthday present for her friend Azra. That stopping into this stationery store in Westmount had nothing to do with the incident on the mountain. Then she saw him. He stood at the back of the store behind a counter, flipping through a book of wedding invitations with a couple. When she walked in, he glanced at her, but neither of them smiled or even nodded. Turning away, her heart thrumming, Grace browsed through some clothbound journals. In the background she could hear his voice patiently listing paper brands and prices.

Another clerk, a woman with bleached-blond hair, said, *"Est-ce que je peux vous aider?"* and Grace shook her head. She must have uncapped a hundred pens and flipped through every birthday card before she finally picked one out and bought a journal as her gift. He was still waiting on the bridal couple, the woman unable to make up her mind.

"I think I should ask my mom what she thinks," she was saying.

"She'll like whatever you like," her fiancé said.

"But she usually helps me figure out what I like," she said.

The blond woman, who was ringing up Grace's purchase, met her eyes and smirked. "I give them a year," she muttered.

Grace nodded mechanically, taking the bag. As she was turning to go, the couple thanked Tug for his time and left.

"I'm not totally dependent or anything," the woman said. "I just trust her judgment. It's good to get a second opinion."

"*I'm* your second opinion," her fiancé said.

Tug was smiling wryly, absently, as Grace walked toward him, trying to arrange her face in some semblance of casualness. She put her plastic bag on the counter and said, "I'm interested in some invitations."

"Are you getting married?"

"No."

"So what kind of event, then?"

"I'm just kind of interested," she said, glancing over her shoulder at the other clerk. "In general."

"Hypothetical invitations, right," he said, and flipped open an album.

Leaning over it, their heads close together, she could feel the heat coming off him. "I was just wondering," she said, "how you were."

"I'm fine."

"I don't see any crutches."

"I'm a quick healer," he said. He saw her looking at his throat, whose redness might have been mistaken for a rash, and flushed.

"And otherwise?" she said.

"I'm great," he said. "Never better."

"You don't have to be flip with me," she said evenly. "I'm not judging you or asking you for anything. I'm just concerned."

"Why?" he said, sounding more curious than angry. "It's not every day that I meet someone so . . . *invested* in my well-being."

Grace looked up, holding his gaze. "It's not every day that I meet someone the way I met you."

"I'm sorry about dragging you into my life," he said. "It's not what I meant to have happen."

"I don't mind it," she said.

She slipped a sample of expensive bonded paper out of the album he held. With one of the store's fancy pens she wrote down her name, address, and phone number. "This is who I am," she said. "You can call me, if you want to."

"What if I don't want to?" he said. "Will you leave me alone?"

Grace was taken aback. "I don't know," she said.

Another smile broke over him then, composed of equal parts surprise, cynicism, and amusement, and he looked like a different person, younger, sweeter. She realized he was handsome. He had a beautiful smile, with even white teeth and a dimple on the left side. "You're something else," he said. "I'm just not sure what."

She smiled back, and then the blond clerk cleared her throat, indicating the presence of other customers, so she gathered her purchases and left.

Of course he didn't call. She didn't expect him to. They were strangers. So she tried her best to forget about him, the day on the mountain, the unexpected sweetness of his smile. But in still moments, when she was driving home, or folding laundry, or in the shower, images would flicker in her mind. Not memories, but images of what she hadn't seen: Tug skiing by himself into the woods. Tying the rope around his neck. His body falling, heavy but soundless, into the snow. Waiting for her to come skiing down from the Chalet. Waiting to be found.

An idea came to her with the weather. She woke up on a Saturday morning to find the world softened with snow. Outside people were shoveling out their cars, the trucks rumbling through the streets, plowing and salting. Her neighbor, Mr. Diallou, cleared a path around his Honda only to see a truck banking snow around it, obstructing him again. He raised his fist and cursed the driver. Grace smiled, knowing what to do.

She called the stationery store and asked for him. When the manager said he wasn't working, she cleared her car, loaded it up, and drove to his apartment. It wasn't yet ten o'clock. He came to the door wearing a thick gray sweater and jeans, apparently still half asleep, his eyes heavy-lidded, his clothes rumpled.

"Let's go skiing," she said.

Tug looked at her with no trace of the cynical distance she'd seen in him before. Maybe she had caught him at an unguarded moment. "Do you want some coffee?" he said.

She followed him inside and took off her boots in the hall, wondering if he hadn't heard what she said. She unzipped her ski jacket as he poured her a cup of coffee from a full pot. On the table was his own cup, the newspaper, a plate with crumbs. He was rubbing his hair absentmindedly, the loose curls spreading around his head, the lines around his eyes deeper than usual.

"Milk? Sugar?"

She shook her head. He gestured at the chair across from his, and she sat down. With what she understood to be a welcoming gesture, he pushed a section of the newspaper in her direction. It was the Business section, and she read through it carefully while sipping the coffee, as if she might be tested on it later. Laurentian Bank's revenues had increased. Four people had died in an accident in a diamond mine in Botswana. Tug yawned, flipping the pages and shaking his head over some article or another.

Fifteen minutes passed. There was no sign of the dog, and she wondered if his ex-wife had come by to pick it up. If he'd told her what he had done on the mountain, or had tried to do.

He rubbed his hair again, tousling it even further. Then he said, "I'm never much good before coffee. When I used to travel a lot, I always took a coffee kit with me. People would make fun of me, and it used to drive Marcie crazy. She'd sit across from me and tell me all her dreams, and then the entire plan for the day, and think everything was settled. Half an hour later I'd go, 'Were you saying something?'"

It was his first unprompted confidence, and she didn't speak, not wanting to startle or interrupt him. She only nodded.

"No wonder she left me," he said, without apparent rancor.

She smiled at him, encouraging him to go on, and his eyes focused on her face, then on her clothes.

"Were *you* saying something?"

"I thought we could go skiing."

As if this were the first he'd heard of it, he looked out the living-room window at the snow. "I never pay attention to the weather," he said softly, seemingly to himself. "What's wrong with me?"

Grace kept quiet. It seemed like a rhetorical question, and anyway she didn't yet know the answer.

"I'd love to go," he said after a pause, "but I don't have skis." He looked at her, shrugged, and the memory of the day they met registered between them.

"I brought you some," Grace said. When he frowned, she explained, "They belonged to my ex-husband. He was around your height. Close enough to make do, anyway. You still have the boots, right? His might fit you, but I'm not sure."

Tug puffed his cheeks comically, then let the air slowly drift out. She could tell he was relieved that she hadn't actually *bought* him a new pair of skis.

"The social lives of divorced people," he said. "All the old equipment still around."

Grace leaned across the table and touched his wrist, so suddenly that the movement was upon her even before she'd decided to do it. She could feel his warm skin and the butterfly beat of his pulse. His eyes met hers, steady and green, and she knew that the electric charge between them wasn't just on her side. He was flushing too.

"Let's just go," she said, "before you change your mind."

Instead of heading to the mountain she took the Trans-Canada to a nature preserve on the West Island. In the early years of their marriage she and Mitch had often skied there. She had looked at the families around them, romping with their kids and dogs, and thought she was seeing her own future. But she hadn't seen this: herself and Tug, almost strangers, unloading skis and poles after a car ride during which neither of them had had much to say. Yet she didn't feel unhappy. She was pleased he'd agreed to go, and she was happy to be skiing, too.

They set off into the woods, Tug ahead of her moving swiftly, rhythmically. Mitch's skis seemed to suit him well enough. Fresh snow had fallen on old tracks, and they could feel both the satisfying crunch of new powder and the underlying structure of the trail. Her breath rose ahead of her. On either side pine needles confettied the snow. She could hear Tug panting a little as they pushed up a hill. The sun was shining. Looking at his back, Grace thought, before she could stop herself, You'd have to be crazy to want to leave this world.

Half an hour later they came to a clearing and stopped to catch their breath. A few winter birds were picking at the bare, desiccated trees. When she offered him some water and he turned around, his cheeks were red, his eyes bright. He looked happy.

"When I lived in Geneva," he said, "I skied all the time. Even trained to do a biathlon. But I left before I could actually compete."

"What were you doing in Geneva?" Grace asked.

He handed the bottle back and bent down to adjust his boot. "Exchange student," he said without looking up.

She assumed from his evasive tone that he was lying, but thought better of calling him out. "Must have been spectacular," she said lightly. "But this isn't bad."

"No," he said, and she hoped his look meant he was grateful she hadn't pressed him. "It's not."

They started up again, Grace in front this time. They met a middle-aged couple on the trail with two large dogs. Tug stopped and chatted with them briefly about the weather, the snow conditions, how much exercise pets need, much friendlier than he had ever been with her. With his face reddened by the wind he looked younger and healthier, a casual smile transforming his face.

By now it was noon, and the preserve was bustling with newcomers, children, and dogs. Snow was falling again, a soft, lush drift. The day was warming, the trail slick with melt, and without discussing it they quickened their pace. Grace unzipped her jacket and put her hat in her pocket, and it occurred to her that she had never seen Tug wearing one. She was already thinking like that, as if she'd been around him so many times.

The last part of the trail was uphill, back to the lodge, and they herringboned this stretch madly in a kind of crazy, splay-legged sprint. She could hear the staccato rhythm of his breath behind her, and whenever she lagged he gained, so she picked up speed, not wanting to seem anything but strong. By the crest of the hill her thighs were burning. They skied to the finish as if in a race, each taking longer and longer strides until the trail was broken up by footprints, choppy ice mixing with gravel, their skis crunching, and it was time—too soon, she thought—to stop.

Tug smiled at her. "Well," he said, "you gave me a run for my money."

"I used to race."

He raised an eyebrow. "I can picture that. You in a ski uniform with a number pinned on front. Intent on winning unless somebody was injured or in trouble. Then you'd veer off course."

She couldn't tell if he was joking, and she narrowed her eyes at him. "I was a laser beam of competitive focus," she said, and he laughed.

They loaded up the skis and she drove back east, the highway's gray-brown slush ruffled with tire marks. The car smelled of sweat and wet wool. With the heat on, she felt sleepy, almost dangerously so. How Tug felt she had no idea. He was leaning, either lethargic or relaxed, against the passenger-side door.

She double-parked in front of his apartment and waited.

"That was nice," Tug said. He sounded surprised. "It was good we went."

"I'm glad. I was hoping it would be."

"I liked seeing all those people out there, just having a good time. I sometimes forget people actually do that."

"Have a good time?"

He frowned impatiently. "No, that people ski in groups, or where other people are around, and it's still fun. For me it's always been a solitary activity. Something you do to be alone."

She nodded; this was how it usually was for her on the mountain, away from the hours and days of conversation and chatter, with end-less problems haltingly and passionately delivered.

"In Switzerland I always went to the quietest place. But maybe if I'd gone somewhere crowded I would've had a better time."

"When you were an exchange student."

She thought she'd kept her tone even, but Tug took it as a challenge. He was shaking his head. "All right, fine, I wasn't a student."

"I didn't mean to say you were lying."

"Well, I was. I'm a liar."

"Okay," she said.

There was a pause in which he must have expected her to ask him for the truth, but she didn't. She thought of the animals she'd rescued in childhood, the stray kittens and lost dogs. You didn't cajole or chase them, she'd learned; you crouched down and waited for them to come to you.

Tug opened the door and cold air rushed into the car. With one foot on the pavement outside, he smiled glancingly at her and said, "It was another life."

She nodded. "I've had one of those myself," she said.

That night she went to bed tired, with the bone-deep, gravity-flattened exhaustion of muscles that had done their part. She thought she would dream about him; but if she did, it was lost in the inky darkness of her sleep, and gone by morning.

It was the following night that she had trouble sleeping. As she lay in bed, her mind paced ahead of her into the week to come, feeling for its coming trouble spots and few expected pleasures. She'd have to figure out, for example, what to do about Annie and her parents. So she was awake, or at least not fully asleep, when the phone rang at three in the morning.

"What are you doing?" Tug's voice was garbled and slushy. He'd been drinking.

"I was trying to sleep, but not succeeding." She sat up, cradling the phone to her ear. From outside came distant sounds of traffic, and she could make out, through the curtains, the lightness of a winter night in the city when snow is on the ground.

There was a long pause before he said, "Well, I'm glad I didn't wake you up." It was clear from the pause that he hadn't, actually, given it much thought.

"What are you doing?" she said.

"I'm having a dark night of the soul. You seemed like the person to call."

"I'm glad to hear it," Grace said, trying to picture him alone in his dark apartment, in his bed, his hands agitating his curly hair. "Not that you're having a dark night of the soul, I mean. I'm not glad about that part."

"Oh, I am," Tug said. "I'm positively thrilled."

She chose not to encourage this sarcasm. Instead she concentrated on the near-silence between them on the line, the cadence of his breath. "What would you say is keeping you up?" she asked after a while.

"At this point I'd have to say it's the drinking," Tug said.

"And before that?"

"I feel bad about lying to you," he said, not an answer to her question but a separate tack. "And you knew it, too. That's probably why people don't like to spend time with you, Grace. Because you can tell when they're lying and you call them on it."

This stung her. "Who says people don't like to spend time with me?"

"You don't seem to have much of a social life. And you're pouring a lot of energy into being friends with me, God knows why. And you're divorced."

"So are you."

"My point," he said, "exactly."

Tug was wrong, Grace thought: she had friends. But she had to admit there was some truth to what he said. With men, she was curious enough to pay attention to them, but they either recoiled as if she were too intense or else unraveled, told her everything, then wound up saying, "You're a great listener, Grace," and dating somebody else. Lately she'd sort of given up on meeting anyone. As her friends got older, busy with their marriages and children, she was starting to feel isolated, marooned on her own private island, and sometimes weeks passed without her making any plans at all.

But she was still curious about Tug. "So what did you lie about?" she said.

He lowered his voice to a whisper so unfocused that she had trouble making out the words. "I was never an exchange student in Switzerland. Also, I haven't exactly worked at the store forever. I was headquartered in Geneva for a time, then Central America, then Africa, then back here. I've been restless for most of my life, and maybe that's my problem—that I came home."

"Are you a spy?" Grace said.

"I was. But not anymore."

She let the silence stretch between them again, a joint project, loose and home-fashioned, like a string between two tin cans.

"That was a lie. The spy thing, not the geography." He was barely audible now, his mouth far from the phone, and she could picture him clearly, head on the pillow, the phone next to him like a companion, a pet.

"Ah," she said.

There was a scuffle on the other end of the line as he started to say something, but then he hung up—whether accidentally or on purpose, she didn't know. He didn't call again.

The next day she was back at work. Never had she been more grateful for how the hour-long sessions broke the day down, and she poured her attention and focus into each one. Only in a few off moments did the memory of his slurred, confiding tone return to her, the intimacy of his middle-of-the-night voice. She resisted the temptation to give in to it. She wanted to be fair to the people who sought her help, without distraction, and she promised herself that she could think about him all she wanted some other time.

As if in reward for this promise, he called her that evening at seven thirty, and his voice was articulate and dry, haltingly sober. "I want to apologize," he said, "for last night."

"You don't have to."

"Maybe you don't think so," he said. "Though it's a mystery why."

"I was glad you called."

"There's something weird about a person like you," he said, "who's so intent on helping a fuck-up."

"I don't actually think you're a fuck-up," Grace said mildly. She was standing in her kitchen, holding a half-eaten sandwich. "And anyway, maybe there's something weird about a person like you, who thinks he doesn't deserve anybody's help."

"Maybe," he said, not sounding very convinced. "I shouldn't be drunk-dialing at my age. I'm sorry."

"Are you all right?"

"My hangover's more psychological than physical, if that's what you mean."

"It wasn't, but okay."

"Did you ask me if I was a spy?" he said. "I vaguely remember that."

"You were talking about a life spent in far-flung locations. It seemed like a logical question at three in the morning. I'm not sure I was thinking clearly." In the ensuing silence she could imagine him wearily rubbing his eyes.

"I was employed for a time by an international NGO working to provide basic supplies for refugees in famine areas," he said. "I handled logistics. I organized the importation of rice. Coordinated food drops and set up camps."

"Okay," she said.

"And now I coordinate paper supplies. As you can see, it was a logical step."

"What happened to you?"

"I had enough. It happens to a lot of people. Anyway, I felt I owed you an explanation. Sorry about calling in the middle of the night. It won't happen again."

"Hold on," she said, but he was gone.

In spite of his confession, she felt that they'd taken a step backward. He'd offered her bits of his past, yes, but mostly to keep her at a distance. There is a difference between the facts of a person and the truth of him, and Tug knew it. Grace wasn't so far gone that she didn't notice how little he asked about her, and she wanted to be acknowledged as someone with whom he might develop a connection. It would be a way of feeling her own weight in the world. She wondered if in all their time together she'd made any impression on him at all.

Then a couple days later she stepped out of the office and there he was in the parking lot, leaning against her car on a freezing afternoon.

His cheeks were red, his hands stuffed into the pockets of a navy-blue pea coat. She wondered how long he'd been waiting. "You look cold," she said, and smiled.

He didn't smile back, his expression so serious that he almost seemed angry. "I don't really know why I'm here."

"I'm glad to see you," she said.

"Oh," he said. "Good." For the first time, he seemed unsure of what to do next.

Grace said, "Seriously, you really do look cold."

"Do you think—" he said, then stopped. "Look, can we go somewhere?"

Grace nodded, unlocked the car, and, not knowing what else to do, drove them to her apartment. Once inside, Tug took off his coat, accepted a drink, and sat on the couch. He didn't look around the place or make any small talk. She sat down next to him, acutely conscious of his closeness. He was wearing a collared shirt and a V-neck sweater, and she could see that his throat had completely healed.

"So, how are you?" she said.

"I'm better." Looking at her, he took a sip of his wine.

"Your whole situation—it's a little confusing to me, Tug."

At the sound of his name, he smiled. "Do you wish you'd never stopped when you saw me there on the mountain?"

"No."

He nodded slowly. "You really don't care, do you? About what I did. What I almost did."

"Of course I care," she said. "It just doesn't discourage me."

His lips were dark pink, almost red, and she wondered if they were chapped or raw from cold. But they weren't. They were soft, and he was kissing her. Barely able to make any sense of it, she put her hand on his arm and felt the knit of his sweater, telling herself, This is real. I'm touching him. His other arm went around her waist, and her leg was on top of his. She stopped kissing him, almost sick to her stomach with an excess of wanting.

"Are you all right?" he said, his mouth against her ear.

"I need to stop."

"Okay." He sat back and watched her.

She took a breath, trying to calm down. Her nerves were singing, plucked like too-tight strings. It had been a long time since she'd been with anyone.

"Should I leave?" he said. "You can tell me to."

"No."

"No, you can't tell me, or no, I shouldn't leave?"

"You know which," Grace said. She went to the kitchen, drank some water, then came back to this person she hardly knew, this dark and difficult person, and kissed him. Some things were too intense to do slowly.

Afterward, they got dressed. It had happened very fast, the two of them panting and desperate and not especially well coordinated, and when it was over they still felt like strangers. Tug lounged on the couch, looking a little drowsy. Grace still felt off-kilter, feverish, her cheeks burning from his unshaven face. She poured them each more wine and wondered what she had gotten herself into. If she were her own patient, she'd tell herself to put an end to this situation as quickly as possible. Instead, she pulled her legs up beneath her and watched him. She didn't want him to go.

"So," she said, "how've you been?"

This made him laugh and he set down his glass, giving her the first real sense of accomplishment she'd felt in quite some time.

"Grace," he said, "do we have to talk?"

She couldn't imagine what else, in fact, to do.

Sensing her confusion, Tug patted the couch next to him. She felt summoned and, obscurely, condescended to. But she moved over and laid her head on his shoulder, waiting for him to say something. Then she heard a faint whistling sound. He was snoring.

With his head resting on the back of the couch, he had fallen asleep and left her just sitting there. She tried to curl gently into him, and his arm pulled her closer. She was uncomfortable but didn't want to move—he always looked so tired, so beaten down—though after ten minutes, her right leg was tingling and she desperately wanted to scratch her nose. Tug's snoring was light and sibilant, like a faraway train. Slowly, hoping not to wake him up, she straightened out her leg. In response Tug shifted, suddenly jerking his head forward, and, with the hand wrapped around her shoulder, slapped her in the face.

"Jesus!" she said. "What the hell?"

"What happened? Did I *hit* you?" He was still half asleep and confused. "Are you okay? My God, I'm sorry." He touched her cheek gently. "It's all red."

"That's not from your hand. It's from your face."

"My face?"

"Your beard. I mean, your stubble."

"Oh, Grace," he said, and kissed her sore, mottled cheek. "I'm so sorry."

"It's all right," she said. "I'm glad you slept."

"I didn't know how tired I was." He kissed her again, this time on the lips, and soon they were together again, more slowly, in the bedroom, without any awkwardness or rush, more like she'd wanted. And when they finished, she was the one who fell asleep.

Over the next two weeks, he'd show up at her apartment or invite her to his, usually late at night. They rarely went out to dinner; they just drank wine and talked before heading to bed. Mornings, over coffee, were silent. She might have considered herself tangential to his life, except that in the middle of the night she'd wake to find him twined around her, his leg over her hip, his arm over her shoulder, the heat of his chest pressed against her back; or, as they lay side by side, he'd clutch her hand in his sleep; or he'd pull her to him, her head against his chest, and as she nestled there, he'd sigh.

Grace moved through these days in a fog, shrouded in secret emotion. With her patients she was kind and warm, trying to make up for her wandering attention, and if anything they seemed grateful when she dived back into the conversation sympathetically, probing the intricacies of their situations with inexhaustible thought and care. The only one who seemed to notice a change was Annie. Since the night she'd shown up at the apartment, she'd treated Grace with a familiarity that implied both trust and condescension. It was the ease of someone used to having hired help, the scornful confidence of a girl in her housekeeper. More open and less respectful, she knew now that she could get away with things, and it bothered Grace.

When she tried to get her to talk about how she was feeling about the decision she'd made, Annie asked her, "Are you pregnant?"

"Me? No," Grace said, too surprised to say anything else. "Why do you ask that?"

"You look different," Annie said, sprawled across a chair—she even sat differently now—with her legs flung over the side. "It's like you gained weight, but in a good way."

"And the first thing you associate with that is pregnancy," Grace said, "rather than just plain good health. Why do you think that is?"

"God," Annie said. "Take a compliment."

"I wasn't sure it *was* a compliment, at first."

"Or maybe you're in *love*." She said this snidely, like a twelve-year-old boy.

"That's beneath you, Annie," Grace said.

This seemed to get her attention. She swiveled in her chair, sat up straight, and said, "I'm sorry."

"You don't have to apologize."

"Right. Therapy means never having to say you're sorry."

"You might have to, actually, maybe even a lot. But mostly you have to figure out why you did whatever you're sorry about."

"I know," Annie said. "It makes me tired."

Grace's evenings with Tug continued steadily, and soon they were going out for dinner or to see a movie. They bought him new skis and went skiing, and on lazy Sunday afternoons they would lie together in bed and read the newspaper. She forgot they had ever had a strange beginning or that there were uneasy questions hovering over them that might occasion an ending to their relationship. They were caught up in the middle, and it felt like it was going to go on forever.

One morning there was a sharp knock on the office door, and a couple walked in before Grace could respond. She couldn't place them, though she knew they had met, and as she stared at them blankly without rising from her seat, she saw them go from mad to madder.

"We need to talk to you," the man said.

"Please, sit down," Grace said, her mind coursing through unlikely scenarios before she realized they were Annie's parents.

They sat together on the couch but as far away from each other as possible. Annie's mother wore a dark-blue suit and her hair in a blond bun, her stiletto-heeled boots tapping with rage. Her husband's suit was the same color. They were a matched pair, expensive and well maintained.

"What can I do for you?" Grace said. She still couldn't remember their first names.

"What can you do? What have you *done*?" Annie's mother said. She wasn't crying, but her eyes instantly reddened, and Grace's heart turned over.

"I assume this is about Annie," she prompted.

"This is about the end of your career," the man said.

She could tell he was accustomed to making threats, and she remembered something Annie had told her: "They always get what they want, so they don't understand why I can't too."

"We know what you did for Annie," he said. "Taking her to the hospital. Encouraging her to get an abortion."

"What?" Grace said. "That did not happen."

"We heard all about it from Annie," his wife said. "You said that telling us would just complicate things. You're a monster. This was our daughter."

"Your daughter *is* very troubled," Grace said. "Perhaps more troubled than any of us realize."

"You shouldn't be allowed to muck around in people's lives," the man said.

"I just want to be clear about this," Grace said. "Is your objection to the procedure itself, or that Annie kept it a secret from you?"

"So you know all about it," the father said. "I can't believe this. I'm going to have your license revoked. I'm going to ruin you."

"You could do that," Grace said calmly, "or instead we could actually talk about your daughter."

He glared at her and stood up, livid, but his wife, Grace could tell, wanted to stay. She stroked his arm and smiled up at him pleadingly. He sat down and said, "Tell me what you know."

Grace looked at him for a long moment, choosing her words carefully. "When Annie first came to me," she said, "I believed she was on a path of self-destruction that came out of her putting too much pressure on herself. And I still think that's true." She paused.

Annie's mother tucked a strand of hair behind her ear, and despite her tailored clothing she looked very much like Annie: pretty, blond, vulnerable. The father was sitting stoically upright, allowing her to hold his hand, waiting grimly.

"I think Annie's in so far over her head," Grace said, "that she doesn't even know it. She thinks she can manipulate all the adults around her in order to get what she wants, which is to continue inflicting pain on herself and prove to everyone—and herself—just how worthless she is. Needless to say, it's a very dangerous place to be."

Annie's father's face was flushed, but he didn't say a word. Grace let the silence invade the room, waiting for the explosion she sensed was coming. Finally, Annie's mother let out a sob.

"I came home and Annie was in bed," she said. "She said she had the flu. I didn't suspect a thing. She didn't even miss any school, did you know that? She took her algebra test and then went to the hospital for a four o'clock appointment. She's that responsible. That organized. She arranged it all so we wouldn't know anything."

Grace said nothing and waited.

"We would never have known," the mother said, crying openly now.

"So how did you find out?" Grace said.

"It was after yesterday's appointment with you," the father said.

"We didn't have an appointment yesterday."

"Of course you did. Like always, the twice-a-week schedule you recommended six months ago."

Grace sighed. "And what did she say?"

"She was very upset last night and couldn't stop crying. She said she didn't want to come see you anymore. When we asked why, the whole story came out. About what you'd helped her do, and how she had doubts about it."

"She was a little girl again," the mother said, "with a boo-boo on her knee. Crying in my arms."

Grace thought, Boo-boo? "I don't know what she's been doing on Thursday afternoons," she said, "but she hasn't been coming to see me. Your statements from my office would reflect one weekly session."

"We never even have time to look at them, as Annie well knows," the father said. "Where the hell has she been?"

The mother was almost hysterical now. She couldn't speak for sobbing, just shook her head apologetically. Her husband handed her a tissue from Grace's box but made no move to comfort her.

"We called the hospital," he said, "and they won't give us any information. We can't get a straight answer from anybody. You have to tell us what you know."

Grace again said nothing for a moment, calculating how little trust these people had in her. "What Annie and I discuss is confidential," she finally said.

His eyes were glowing with rage as he leaned forward, his expensive white shirt puffing out from his chest. "Who's the father?"

"I don't know."

"Is it that Oliver kid? I'm going to kill him."

"I honestly don't know," Grace told him. "But I do know that Annie needs all of our help to get through this."

"Like helping her get an abortion without her parents' knowledge?"

"I didn't do that."

"I don't know why we should believe you." He stood up again. "You and Annie—you're both liars. No wonder you get along so well. That's why she talks to you instead of us. You just build on each other's lies."

"Please, wait. Sit down and let's talk this through."

But to sit down would be to concede defeat. "This is your fault," he said, biting off each word. "You were supposed to help her. That was your job, and you're accountable." He spoke slowly and precisely. He had located a target for his anger and was, however subconsciously, pleased. "We *will* hold you accountable. You'll lose your position. Along with the right to inflict damage on other families."

Grace stood up and faced him. "I understand how awful this is," she said. "I really do."

"I don't care what you understand."

"I care about Annie," Grace said. "I'd like to keep helping her."

"When I'm done with you," the father said, "you'll be the one who needs help. Starting with a good lawyer."

He opened the door and strode from her office. And without hesitating his wife followed him, her face full of gratitude that he'd found a place to lay the blame.

FIVE

New York, 2002

THE CHILD EXISTED for the three of them in many ways—as a bone of contention, a zone of negotiation, a locus of arguments, a reminder of sex, a sore spot, a tender spot, a sweet spot—before it existed in the world.

Hilary's body encased both the baby and herself in flesh and placidity; she could not be touched. At times, Anne couldn't stop looking at her. What was it like to grow so massive, to be a container so uncontained? Huge and getting huger, she put on pounds every day, eating gallons of ice cream and boxes of saltine crackers and even T-bone steaks that Anne, who in all her time in New York had never even noticed a butcher shop, brought home for her.

Meanwhile her boyfriend, too, bulked up. He spent several hours a day doing pushups and weights—he'd found a set of barbells on the street—in a corner of the living room he claimed as his own, a masculine realm marked by fitness magazines, the barbells, a pair of stinky running shoes. He was working as a framer on some construction site in Queens, and between that work and the lifting his skinny body was broadening; there was a rope of muscle along his neck and shoulders, also nascent biceps and thicker forearms. It was as if he thought that when it came to fatherhood, muscles were what would be required.

At least he was working, and Anne hoped he was putting money away. She had no idea what would become of them once the baby came and they moved out of her apartment. Or she assumed they would move out. When she tried to talk to Hilary about all this, her mask of placidity would break and she'd start to cry, her pale, milky face blotchy and streaked. "We're going to figure it out," she'd say weepily, which sounded less like a promise than a pallid, inadequate reassurance to herself and her unborn child. Feeling guilty, Anne would drop the subject. Nobody likes to make a pregnant woman cry.

One day she came home to find Alan by himself, lifting weights in the corner. "Where's Hilary?" she said.

He grunted and ignored her, his thin face straining with effort.

She couldn't think of another time when the two of them had ever been alone together. Hilary was always there, her body a buffer between them. Alan reached down and picked up a heavier barbell. They were his prized possessions, these weights, and they gleamed in the light. He faced the window, curling his biceps and panting with every lift. She stepped closer to him—he smelled sweaty and gross—and tried to catch his eye, but he wouldn't look away from his muscles.

"Listen," she said. "You know you guys can't stay here forever. I hope you're saving some money. Once the baby comes, you're going to have to support them. You're going to have to grow up."

But once she'd delivered these lines she felt ridiculous. What did she know about supporting a family? She had been in Hilary's position once, and had made the opposite choice. She'd left her parents behind too, getting as far away as she could from any kind of family. Thinking back on it, she could barely remember what thoughts had guided her decisions, or if she had had any thoughts at all. That time in her life was a blur of hate: her father was awful, her mother pathetic, both of them so self-absorbed they barely noticed anything she did. Anything she had made of herself, she'd accomplished without them. The one person who'd been kind to her back then was her therapist, and that was only because it was Grace's job. Thinking about this made her angry all over again, and the anger flowed onto Alan, whose only reaction to her statement had been to shift the barbell from one hand to the other. She could see his lips moving as he counted repetitions.

"Have you even thought about where you're going to live?"

With a groan, he set the weight down. He was wearing a dirty tank top and his white skin shimmered with sweat. When he straightened up, his face was flushed with blood. "Why don't you shut up?" he said.

Anne felt a physical ripple across her face, as if he'd slapped her. "Excuse me?"

"You act like you know everything. But you don't. Just mind your own business."

"Hard to do when *you're* living in *my* apartment."

"So you think you can boss us around? Act like you're better than us?"

"I don't even know what you're talking about."

"You're just some stuck-up bitch," he said, turning away.

Flashing with anger, sparks in her veins, she grabbed his arm and yanked it. She could tell he was surprised by how strong she was. "You shut the fuck up," she said. "You're nothing. *Nothing*. You owe me."

Her fingernails scraped his clammy skin as he pulled his arm away, and she liked what she saw in his eyes. He was scared.

May came to the city, the bloom of trees a wistful pink against a pale sky. In the parks the memorials were fading, the pictures of the missing now gray and tearing around the edges. Old dried flowers bobbed their stiff heads in the wind; jars that had once held candles lay empty on their sides. The streets seemed ribboned with litter. And yet the weather was pretty, and people gathered at tables outside restaurants, glad to feel the sun on their faces again.

Anne's play opened, and she was good in it; she knew she was. The audiences were tiny, mostly hipsters and college-theater nerds who went to see everything, but it was enough. There were reviews in two weeklies, and one called her performance "compelling." She cut the reviews out and pasted them in a scrapbook next to the playbill, something she hadn't done since high school.

She gave Hilary and Alan tickets for a Friday-night show, and when they didn't turn up she was angrier than she would've expected. She had sacrificed her apartment to these runaways, and they couldn't even get it together to sit through two hours of theater? And the worst part was that she couldn't get mad at them, because the whole deal, the basis of the relationship, was that they needed her, not the other way around. To tell them she was disappointed would have been to lose whatever thin emotional edge she still possessed. She assumed Alan had told Hilary about their confrontation, and that was why they hadn't come.

When she got home that night, though, they weren't there. This was more than unusual—they spent every night in front of the TV. Maybe they'd gotten lost on the subway? They were just two teen-agers from the country. But they had left their families, without a word of explanation, and probably their parents had stood silent and gape-mouthed in their homes, just like she was now, wondering where they were.

At three in the morning, sleepless, she heard the door open. She went to the living room and saw Alan leading Hilary to the couch.

"What happened? Is everything okay?"

"She had a fever and kept throwing up." Alan's voice was gentle. "We went to the emergency room. We were worried it was going to hurt the baby."

"And what did they say?" Anne turned on the fluorescent light in the kitchen, and in its blue glow Hilary looked wan, her face an uneasy gray.

"It was food poisoning, they told us. We think from Panda Kitchen."

"What are we supposed to do? Does she need some water? I could get some ginger ale."

Alan shook his head. "They put her on an IV for a while, so right now it's okay. She probably just wants to sleep."

In other words, she understood, go back to bed and leave us alone. "What about the baby? Is the baby going to be all right?"

"Doc said no problem," Alan said. "Young healthy mom, should be a young healthy baby."

"Okay." At the bedroom door she turned around and said, "I'm sorry." She waited for him to say it was all right, but he didn't.

In the morning Hilary's face still looked bad, as waxy as fake fruit. She kept pawing at the blanket around her and shifting her massive weight around the tiny couch.

"I'm cold," she said. "I'm hot. I don't feel good. My skin hurts. I have a fever." She threw these statements into the air, expecting someone to catch them. Alan wanted to stay home from work, but Anne told him he should go; she'd be home all day and could take care of her.

"I'm sweaty," Hilary said. "My clothes stink. I'm dizzy."

Feeling at once guilty and pitying, Anne said, "Maybe you should sleep in my bed instead. It's probably more comfortable."

Which is how she came to give up her bedroom and live on the couch herself.

It made more sense, really. Hilary spent her days beached on the bed, reminding Anne of her mother, who in the difficult time before Anne left home had passed most weekends this way. Her mother stole into her mind more and more often these days—her voice, her smell, her small, pleading smile, the childhood games they'd played. Anne would never have admitted she missed her; these thoughts were probably just from being around Hilary, wondering what kind of mother she was going to be.

Once Hilary was settled on the bed she treated it as her unassailable kingdom, her lily pad, her island. Every time Anne came back to the apartment, even before closing the door, she would hear Hilary calling her name from the bedroom. Then she would glance through the doorway and see her propped up on cushions, a *National Enquirer* open beside her, its pages crumpled from where she'd napped on them, a plate of half-eaten food on the nightstand, the bed dotted with candy wrappers and tissues.

"Anne? Could you bring me some ice cream?"

For her entertainment the television had been moved into the bedroom. Alan had moved in there too, but he still slept on a pallet on the floor beside her. Day by day Hilary was becoming more childlike, unable to do anything for herself, but she was also growing more demanding and physically imposing, a capricious giant whose whims must be appeased.

Anne would deliver a bowl of her favorite flavor, chocolate, with sprinkles on top. If someone had told her a year earlier that she'd be serving ice cream to a strange girl in her apartment, she wouldn't even have laughed. But now this stranger took it without thanking her and pointed at the screen, where a sitcom family was hashing out their differences over the kitchen table, the laughs ceding to a heart-to-heart talk, the teenage kids expressing contrition and shame.

"God, I'm glad I don't live *there*," Hilary said.

Anne nodded. "Me too."

Success came when she was least interested in it, much less desperate for it. This gave her a nonchalant confidence, an ability to take risks, that made her a better actress. The director loved her performances so much he wanted to die every single night. He also floated the idea of sleeping with her, which Anne previously would have considered the cost of doing business. But now she turned him down and he didn't seem to hold it against her, just renewed his efforts every once in a while, as did others in the cast and crew, confirming that she'd become a valuable commodity.

Her phone rang with offers to audition, to join workshops, to pose for photographs. Apparently what she'd heard about one break was true, how momentum starts and picks up speed. Three agents contacted her; two took her out for expensive lunches. She had new head shots made. The run on the current play was extended. Anne basked in all of it, and each night she stretched herself out, emotionally naked, unafraid, in front of the audience. Once it came to her, the attention she'd been fighting for during these months of struggle (now that they were past, she could admit that's what they'd been) felt destined, nothing less than her due.

The guy she'd been seeing, Magnus, only got sweeter in the face of this success. He took her out to dinner to celebrate; he brought flowers to every Saturday-night performance; he made all his friends come see the play and then stay for drinks with Anne afterward. On off nights, he had her over to his place and cooked dinner. The only problem was that he asked questions she wasn't inclined to answer. In New York people seemed to take intense pleasure in laying out their romantic and family histories to one another. You were supposed to be open about everything—even your neuroses; *especially* your neuroses—and chart a map of your interior life.

Anne couldn't do it. She didn't like to talk about her family and said only that she had left home at a young age and wasn't in touch with them. She might have been able to get away with this, because Magnus was falling in love with her and she could tell he was constructing his own version of her life story in his mind. Her reticence must have been rooted in a tragic past, and the details of her survival would be coaxed out of her only by the right person at the right time. He was willing to wait and prove to her that he was that person, the long-awaited prince who could wake her with a kiss.

The other problem, though, was her apartment. He had walked her to the building several times, but she never let him come up. Anne could see why this bothered him, but she couldn't let him know about Hilary and Alan. That was just too hard to explain. She wasn't even sure she could explain it to herself. So she'd say, "Maybe later. I'm tired tonight. Soon."

At first they joked about it. Magnus asked if she was extremely messy, or had a pet tiger, or—and she could hear the edge in his voice—if she was married, and she always laughed and denied everything.

What he said was, "I don't want to make this a condition. I'm not into demands or anything, but I just think it's a little weird. If this is how you want it, Anne, okay, but . . ." The final word was always *but*. It was probably the last word he ever said to her. Things between them didn't so much end as slip away. He stopped coming to every show, then stopped coming at all, and she let him go with more regret than she'd anticipated. He would have been the perfect man for some other, better version of herself.

It was Anne who found a doctor for Hilary, because as far as she could tell the girl had made no effort to do so. She was so strong-willed most of the time that Anne tended to forget that she didn't have much common sense. She treated pregnancy like a bad cold, something that called for a lot of bed rest and fluids. When Anne started asking about ultrasounds and tests, Hilary shook her head.

"I don't have insurance," she said.

"There are places you can go," Anne pointed out.

"Not that I'd want to go to."

"I don't think you have a choice."

Lying propped on pillows, Hilary gestured vaguely at her belly. "Women have been doing this, like, forever," she said. "I'm young. I'm built for this."

"Women have been dying in childbirth forever too," Anne said.

From the other room, Alan called, "Hey! Don't be scaring her and shit! She's scared enough already."

"*Are* you?" Anne said.

The girl gazed back at her, blank-eyed, and shrugged. This was her apparent defense: to go blank. Whatever fear or anger was lurking inside that house, nobody would get to see.

But some things you can't let slide. So Anne spent an afternoon calling around until she found a clinic on the Lower East Side that could offer them an appointment the next day, then told Hilary that she'd take her.

"Hey, what about me?" Alan said.

"Don't you have to work?" Anne said, sounding more unfriendly than she'd meant to.

"I'll take a day off."

"What about the money?"

"It's just money," Alan said, looking at her like she was the one with messed-up priorities. "This is about the *baby*."

"If you're so into the *baby*, how come you didn't make her go to the doctor?"

In response to this the boy flushed darkly. He was a weird kid, by turns watchful and wary, and often he seemed more like Hilary's servant than her boyfriend. He'd flare with anger and dip into sulks, and there were days when he didn't speak at all. Yet Anne saw clearly how her question pained him, how bad he felt, how confused and unprepared. How determined to do what was right. How helpless to do it.

He did take the day off, but Anne insisted on going too, feeling they needed adult supervision. So the three of them got on the subway together, Alan finding Hilary a seat and standing in front of her like a bodyguard. In the waiting room, Anne gathered up every available pamphlet and stuffed them in her purse. The clinic was run by a women's health organization and staffed by earnest young college graduates wearing handwoven sweaters and political buttons. On the walls were peeling posters that seemed to have been there since the seventies. *Yo amo la leche,* said a happy, smiling baby. Most of the patients sat with their hands folded in their laps, staring down at their bodies as if expecting them to explain how they'd gotten into this mess.

When the nurse called Hilary's name Anne and Alan jumped to attention, but she barely looked up, just nodded sleepily and slowly got to her feet.

They were shepherded into the tiny examination room, which was painted a dingy color between tea and coffee and didn't seem especially clean. Anne felt a pang of panic. What if something terrible happened? What would she do? The answer came to her instantly, from her darkest, truest recesses: Run.

Alan stood next to Hilary, who was lying on the table, and held her hand. Anne knew he wouldn't run. He might not know what to do, but he wouldn't run. She pushed aside some dog-eared copies of *Good Housekeeping* and *Redbook,* magazines no teenage mother would want to read, and sat down in a chair.

The doctor came in and said cheerfully, "Little crowded in here!" She looked about Anne's age, a crunchy type with a pencil in her hair, wearing clogs.

"Can we all stay?" Anne said.

"Why don't we ask the pregnant lady?" the doctor said. Hilary nodded her assent. "Okay, then! Let's get started."

It was the kind of place where they didn't scold you for not having come in sooner; they were more about making sure you came back. So Hilary was lavished with praise for being so healthy, for making the appointment, practically for brushing her teeth and eating ice cream. She didn't say much in response, just submitted to the examination with her legs open and her eyes focused on a spot on the wall. The doctor peeled off her latex gloves with an audible snap and said, "Looks great!" and then set up the ultrasound. And there it was, a black-and-white shadow puppet swimming in its dark pool. "Organs look good. Fingers and toes all there," the doctor reported. "Do you want to know the sex of the baby?"

"Yes," Hilary said.

"It's a little girl."

Anne, who was still gazing at the screen, heard a strange sound and saw that Hilary was crying. "I wanted a girl," she said.

That night, there was an appreciative crowd at the small theater in Long Island City, holding its breath, taut with attention. Anne's dialogue and gestures had by now become a part of her, as deep in her body as her muscles and bones. She had moved beyond conscious thought, beyond having to remember lines, toward a state of pure energy and flow. She *was* Mariska, and there was no boundary between where she left off and her character began. It didn't feel like acting, more like *being*. It was the happiest she'd ever felt, those two hours in front of the audience, but after it was over she was deflated. It was like having a dream about flying that seems so true and possible, then waking up to understand it wasn't real and never would be.

The subway trip home was long, but she didn't want to waste money on cabs or car services. She had started saving money for the baby, wanting to give her something she could rely on later, when and if other people let her down. Back at the apartment, she undressed in the dark with a minimum of noise or fuss and crawled between blankets on the couch. The place smelled of leftover pizza. She sighed. Sometime soon this phase would be over, and she would understand what it was all about, how Hilary and Alan fit into the story of her life.

Lying there strangely keyed up, she heard a moaning sound and sat up to listen. Another moan, the bed creaking, Alan making a choking sound. She squashed the pillow over her head, trying not to hear them, the runaways, the interlopers, the children about to become parents. Making love in her bed.

A month passed, and the summer grew brutal and steaming. Anne's play closed and she was temping again, trying to put aside more money. Out of all the offers that had coursed around her during the run of the play, only a few had distilled to anything concrete. She picked the one with a well-regarded experimental director whose trademark was deadpan dialogue and sacklike clothing, the actors' bodies virtually irrelevant in his productions. She hoped the play would stretch her capacities and prove her artistic mettle. So she stood on stage in scratchy burlap and muttered lines she didn't understand to an audience of bored hipsters in a church basement. Without her body to work with, she had no idea what to do. Too afraid to admit she didn't understand the aesthetic agenda, she bumbled her part, alienated the director, and got terrible reviews. Just like that, she felt like she was back to where she started.

"You're a pretty girl," the agent she had decided on said over a drink. "Let me get you into commercials. There's a detergent call that would be *perfect* for you."

"I don't want to do commercials," Anne told her.

The agent shrugged. "I guess I can try for *Law & Order*."

"Okay, but I also want something serious. Something important."

The agent raised her eyebrows. "You're a pretty girl," she repeated. "Work with your strengths."

A week later, the agent called to say she'd gotten her into summer theater in Southampton. "It isn't Williamstown, but you can hit the beach."

The play was okay. The people who came to see it were a little buzzed, on vacation, ready to be entertained, complimenting Anne extravagantly and buying her drinks afterward in the bar. She had rented a room from a group of hard-partying young lawyers and slept wearing earplugs. Early in the mornings she ran on the beach and saw herself, in these moments, as if from a great distance: a beautiful young woman, hair streaming behind her, the Atlantic crashing its gentle, gray waves. She enjoyed imagining herself like this, from the point of view of some infinitely knowledgeable and enamored stranger, someone who could tell even from afar just how special she was.

On a sweltering Sunday afternoon in July she returned to the city and found the apartment surprisingly cool; air-conditioning units had been installed in both rooms. The shades were drawn and the lights were off. "Hello?" she said, dropping her bags. "You guys home?"

No one was in the bedroom, and the food in the refrigerator was spoiling. There was an air of dust and abandonment that somehow felt new.

Then a key turned in the lock, and a middle-aged man she'd never seen before walked in.

"Get out of here," she said instinctively. "I'm calling the police."

Holding his hands up in deference, he looked afraid, even though he was well built and no doubt stronger than she was. He was wearing khaki pants and a short-sleeved plaid shirt. "Hey, now," he said. "You must be Anne."

"Who are you?"

"I'm Ned Halverson." He paused, apparently expecting some reaction, then exhaled and lowered his hands. "Hilary's uncle."

Anne frowned. Hilary's last name was Benson; she'd never mentioned an uncle. "Where is she?"

The man sighed. "Do you mind if I sit down for a second?" he said. "Those stairs just about kill me, in this heat."

He moved to the couch, where she noticed a small brown suitcase on the floor and a folded set of sheets on the cushions. He sat with his hands on his knees, back perfectly straight, a military pose. Then, reaching into his rear pocket, he pulled out a handkerchief and wiped off his forehead.

"Hilary told me about everything you've done for her," he said. "I mean to say, she didn't. She always makes out like she did it all herself, but it's clear to me that you've done a lot. Letting her stay here. And then Alan." From the way he said his name, it was obvious there was no love lost between them.

"Where are they?" Anne said.

Halverson raised an eyebrow. "She was supposed to leave you a note," he said, "but she didn't, did she? That girl was never any too good at following instructions."

Anne glanced around. "I just got here," she said.

Halverson seemed perfectly at ease on the couch and uninterested in clearing up her confusion. She walked over to the kitchen counter, then glanced into the bedroom, which was unusually tidy and free of clutter. The bed was made. Somehow this seemed more ominous than anything else.

Back in the living room, she said, "No note. Why don't you tell me what's going on? Did you make Hilary go home?"

"Well, now, of course I did," he said. "My wife took them straight away, and I'm here for the rest of their things. I'm sure you understand. We been worried sick to death. She's just a kid herself, you know. We can take care of her, and once the baby comes . . . " He spread his hands out wide. With his ramrod posture and slow, deliberate delivery, the gesture reminded her of the old men who practiced tai chi in Tompkins Square Park. Anne couldn't quite grasp what he was saying but felt irritated, then enraged, that circumstances had changed without her consent. There must have been plenty of drama—Hilary never would have left willingly—and she had missed all of it. If she had been here, would things have been different? Would they have fought harder to stay?

"You know my son means well," he said. "I mean, I think he does, anyway, but it's hard to say what's going on in that pinhead of his. Sometimes I just lose patience. It's like he's got no common sense at all. And the worst part is that he can't see around his own ideas, he's built them up so big. He's bullheaded. My wife says I am too and that's why we don't get along. I tell her, that's just what you say so we can keep loving him when he acts like an idiot."

He seemed prepared to ramble on like this indefinitely. Anne sat down on the chest in front of the couch. "What are you talking about?"

Halverson rested his palms on his knees again. "My son Alan, of course."

It turned out, as she should have guessed, that everything Hilary had said about her family was a lie. Halverson told her the whole story without ever relaxing his military bearing, and she believed him not because he seemed more credible but because she knew Hilary and had once been just like her, and therefore understood how fluidly lies come, how easily they spill from you once you get into the habit of telling them.

There was no abuse at home, according to Halverson, and Hilary, his sister's daughter, had been a good kid. Her parents ran a small farm, and she grew up tending to the cows and the chickens, more at ease with them, it seemed, than she was with people. But both her parents were killed in a car accident when she was ten, and she moved in with Halverson and his family.

"It was weird how it didn't seem to affect her," he said. "She didn't cry, or even talk about them much. We had a counselor over in Hawkington that we were taking her to for a while, but she seemed to be okay. There's something about her that's just . . . steely, you know what I mean?"

Anne nodded. Unconsciously she had mirrored Halverson's pose, sitting across from him on the chest with her hands on her knees. Noticing this, she shifted her weight and crossed her legs.

Halverson didn't need much encouragement to keep talking. He seemed to think it was his duty; in exchange for having housed Hilary, Anne would get this story from him. "She lived with us till she was around fourteen, then things went all haywire. I guess it's the hormones that set in around that age. I don't know. The kids in our town are like wildcats. One minute they're normal and the next thing you know, you can't contain them. Out of control."

He sighed. This, she could tell, was the hard part of the story. "What happened?" she said.

"Oh." Halverson made another slow, vague wave, as if she could surmise from this what he was going to tell her. When Anne said nothing, he sighed again. Still she said nothing. She could wait him out, she knew, because most men—most people—can't stand silence. Less than a minute passed before he broke down, speaking faster than he had before.

"Comes to pass that my wife gets home one day and finds Alan and

Hilary together in her little pink bedroom. The stuffed animals flung around. Bunnies on the floor. It horrified her. She was so upset by it that she threw them all away. I think she just couldn't stand the idea, you know, of those little-girl things being in the room with Hilary and Alan. You understand it wasn't just that they were cousins, or so young. It was both things together. And somehow—sure, they were still children—there was something about it that wasn't innocent. You know?"

Anne nodded, knowing exactly what he meant. Hilary and Alan, in her experience, were clueless and vague and not quite with it, but she would never have described them as innocent. They were too carnal. Too tough.

"I wanted to take the kids over to Hawkington, back to that counselor, to sort things out. They sure didn't want to, and my wife was so upset she couldn't even talk about it. The stuffed-animals thing made Hilary so mad she ran away. And she's kept running away, off and on, ever since." He kept looking over at the kitchen counter, avoiding her eyes, which she took to be a show of emotion until he cleared his throat and said, "I wouldn't mind some water."

She guessed this was where Hilary had learned her manners. But as she got him a glass, she thought of a question she wanted to ask. It wasn't about Alan; she could picture his side of things pretty clearly, and anyway he'd never interested her that much. She looked at Halverson and said, "What can you tell me about Joshua?"

The silence following this question grew so long that it was as if he might not have heard it. He just sat there staring into space, the glass, now empty, balanced on his right knee. He had Hilary's same intransigence, or she had his.

"Joshua," he finally said.

Anne was getting annoyed. "She writes to him," she prompted. "Postcards. She gives them to women at train stations and asks them to mail them."

Again he was mute. To stop herself from drumming her fingers, she looked down and clasped her hands together. Glancing back up, she saw tears shimmering in his eyes. "What?" she said.

Halverson swallowed, his jaw clenched. "He was in the car too. Six he was, at the time. I guess he'd be around twelve now. I didn't know that, about the postcards. Is that true? It breaks my heart."

She believed him.

After a while, he composed himself and went into the bedroom to pack up Hilary's and Alan's belongings. Anne sat in the living room, not sure what to do.

Finally he emerged, listing to the left with a duffel bag. He set it on the floor by the door and held out his hand. "On behalf of my family," he said, "I thank you for everything you've done."

"Wait a minute," Anne said. "Can I have your contact information?"

He looked at her blankly.

"Your address and phone number," she said. "So I can get in touch with Hilary."

His eyes skidded away from hers, around the apartment, then at the door, weighing his options. For the first time, his ordinary-guyness—plaid shirt, khaki pants, tidy haircut—started to look ominous in its very neatness. "I don't know about that, miss," he said. "You see, it would just encourage Hilary to think about coming back here. And she's got to give up on that. She's got to accept that being with her family is the right thing. It's not just about her and Alan. It's about that little baby."

That bit about the baby was, Anne thought, what a certain kind of person would consider a trump card in an argument. She moved between him and the door. "They lived here for almost six months," she said, and stopped herself from adding, *they're my family too*. She hadn't realized until the words nearly came out that she felt this way, and she was momentarily shocked into silence. But it was true.

Instead she—what else?—acted a part. She moved into his territory by making herself a substitute parent, a concerned citizen, older and more tired and folksy than she really was. "I did a lot for those kids," she said. "I fed them and gave them a roof over their heads. I gave up my own bed. I don't think it's a lot to ask, Mr. Halverson, considering everything I've done."

He put his hands on his hips, appraising her, then relented. "All righty," he said. "You got a pen?"

She watched him write down the address—a rural route upstate—and phone number. It occurred to her that he could be making it all up, like she gave out fake numbers to guys in bars. Hilary was his niece, after all; lying probably ran in the family, as it did in her own.

She took the piece of paper out of his hand. "I'll be calling to check in," she said.

Halverson's eyes grew steely. "I'd rather you didn't," he said.

He had taken all their clothes and shoes, Alan's barbells, Hilary's magazines, and the tiny apartment yawned with emptiness. She paced for a while in her living room, distracted and confused, until an image came to her—as vivid as a visitation—of her mother sitting hunched in a white-carpeted living room, picking at her nails. Crying in powerless grief.

This thought ought to have softened and saddened her, but instead it made her hard. For the rest of the day, her mission was to remove all traces of the past six months. She rearranged the furniture, cleaned out the refrigerator, changed the sheets, moved the bed against the far wall, filled three enormous Hefty bags with garbage and lugged them down to the street. By then it was nine o'clock and she was so tired that she tripped on the stairs going back up to the apartment. She sat there on the dirty landing and shuddered with tears. She let herself cry to the count of ten, then stood up and went inside.

So this was how it ended, she thought. It wasn't what she'd expected.

She could have gone up there to make sure they were all right. It wasn't out of the realm of possibility. But she didn't. She was sure that Halverson, notwithstanding his air of domination and control, would take good care of the baby-to-be. She pictured a nursery—Hilary's old room?—with a crib, pastel wallpaper, teddy bears. She doubted Hilary would get in touch when the baby was born. Anne wouldn't have, if she were Hilary.

Anne didn't believe in fate or the universe sending you signals and signs. She believed in making your own luck. So the day after Halverson's visit, she put on a low-cut top, had a date with a director, and left with the names of three theater companies that were about to go on the road. And systematically she made dates with men in those companies until she had an offer to travel to Scotland on a festival tour. By Friday she was packed and at the airport, proud of herself for having taken charge. Of Alan and Hilary, she would have said, had there been anyone in her life to ask, that she could barely remember their names.

It was the first time she'd ever been to Europe, and she hadn't been on a plane in over a decade. The security arrangements astounded her; she remembered as a child breezing through airports only minutes before departure, but that was over now. On board, she sat next to a sophisticated, sarcastic actress named Elizabeth who spent the whole flight gossiping about other members of the troupe, explaining which was a sex addict, an anorexic, an adulterer. Anne found all this helpful in terms of navigating the vipers' nest that a group of actors often amounted to, and she had no problem with the calculating, temporary alliance being offered to her. But she wasn't interested in sharing stories of her own. So when her seatmate began to press her, at first gently, then more forcefully, for details of her life, she held back. To win her confidence Elizabeth told a long story, maybe true, maybe false, about her affair with a married man, followed by depression, alcohol abuse, heroin, rehab, and "a current infatuation with coke and my nicotine patch." It was all designed to bring out Anne's own confession. In this kind of conversation, you had to give up something.

"Where did you grow up?" Elizabeth persisted, digging.

"On a farm," Anne said. "In upstate New York."

"*You* on a farm? I can't even picture it."

Anne nodded, gazing through the part in the curtain that showed a slice of first class. "I looked after the chickens."

"Now I'm imagining you in pigtails, collecting eggs and putting them in a straw basket."

"I used to gather the chickens for slaughter," Anne said, calling up stories Hilary and Alan had told her. "I picked them up and held them in my arms to calm them down. I could feel their little hearts beating like crazy. They'd run away when they saw me coming. But I always caught them. I'd grab them by the legs and turn them upside down so the blood drained to their heads and they'd go limp. Then we killed them."

"I could never do that," Elizabeth said.

Anne shrugged. "You get used to it."

Edinburgh was gray, gothic, and awash with actors. She'd had no idea of the scope of the festival, which thickened the streets with hordes of people handing out leaflets for performances and plastering posters on walls. There were Norwegian dancers, Japanese mimes, performances in churches and street corners; it was a planet of actors, and God only knew if there were enough people around to actually attend the hundreds of shows. In the evening the sound of the crowds outside filtered through the walls of their hotel, and between the noise and her excitement Anne barely slept.

In the morning they held a quick dress rehearsal in the back room of the pub where they'd be performing. Though it was August, the weather was cold and the room unheated, and she shivered throughout the warm-up. Most of the others had performed the play for a solid month in Soho and she felt she wasn't fitting in, a discordant note in the song they'd learned to sing without her. The awkwardness made her nervous, and the nervousness made her even more awkward.

She thought she saw them raising an eyebrow at the director, and Elizabeth abandoned her when it came time for lunch, briskly walking off with the male lead, Tony. Anne went back to the hotel, where they were sharing a room, for a short, furious cry. Then she wiped her tears and worked on her lines for an hour.

Though it was only early afternoon, it already felt like evening; not having slept the night before, she could feel dryness and exhaustion creasing her face, and regretted having come. Her nerves were jangled, raw. She blamed the director for not giving her enough time and guidance, and Elizabeth, that snake, for rattling her even before the first show. She'd done them a favor by stepping in at the last minute, and in return she was getting absolutely no gratitude whatsoever.

Working up this anger comforted her and helped her concentration, but she was still upset. She needed to calm down before the performance. She walked through the crowded streets looking for a day spa or a yoga center, but couldn't find either one and settled for her third choice, a bar. She sat down and ordered a Scotch, on the when-in-Rome principle. The bartender asked her what kind she wanted, and she shrugged helplessly. "You tell me," she said.

He smiled and poured her a glass. She took a dark, smoky sip. At the far end of the bar, a bunch of young Americans was tossing back pints and taking no notice of her. Anne sighed and took another sip as a man slid onto the stool next to her and ordered a drink. A few more people filtered in, and when she went to the bathroom and came back, she saw a few heads turning to watch her.

"Buy you another?" the man next to her said. He was slender and dark-haired, wearing a lot of rings. His accent sounded Spanish or Portuguese.

"Okay," she said. "Just one."

When it came, she raised it in a gesture of thanks, and he smiled and pointed at his chest. "Sergio."

"Millicent," she said.

"Milly? What a sweet name."

"Yeah, whatever," she said, rolling her eyes. Already, she was close to having what she wanted and needed—a fleeting moment of attention, her presence in the world affirmed. She slid off the stool and stood.

Sergio touched her hand gently. "I'm sorry if I have offended you," he said, knitting his eyebrows together charmingly. "I am a goofball at times."

"A goofball?" It was such an unexpected word that she laughed, and he did too, showing large, white teeth. There was a mole on the side of his mouth, light brown and slightly raised, like a bread crumb stuck there.

"This is what my friends tell me, yes."

"And where are these friends of yours? Spain?"

"I am from Lisbon originally, but right now I live in London. I work in telecommunications. I am here on business for a few days. Now you know everything about me. And you, Millicent?"

"I'm a teacher," she said. "Taking some drama students on a field trip."

"And where are your students now, Millicent?"

She shrugged. "I didn't say I was a *good* teacher," she said.

He laughed, shaking his head. "You are very intriguing."

"No, I'm not, but thank you anyway. I should go. Thank you for the drink." She turned away, only to feel his hand on her wrist, more forcefully this time.

"Can I persuade you to stay a little longer? I am sure your students are having a good time, wherever they are."

"Sorry," she said. "I have to go."

She grabbed her bag and walked out with a surge of adrenaline that was buoyant, clarifying. When he caught up with her outside and tugged on her arm, she wasn't surprised; she just sped up to try to evade him. He kept alongside her, edging her to the left, and within a few steps they were in a cobblestoned alley, her back against the wall, his weight pressed against her shoulder. Though the streets were crowded, the alley was narrow and shaded and the tourists too distracted, she knew, to glance sideways. His hand was under her sweater, his rings cold against her skin. His mouth was on her neck. She let him lean close, tilting back her neck and nudging his legs open with her knee, then slammed it against his crotch, hard.

"Fucking bitch," he said, staggering backward, with a certain admiration in his rage. They faced each other and there was a moment when she could have run but didn't want to. She was ready. When she reached out as if to brush that crumb off his face, he slapped her hard across the cheek and her ears rang and blood poured hot and thin from her nose. The taste of warm metal. He came up to her again and she hooked her ankle around his, tripping him onto the cobblestones, then pulled pepper spray out of her pocket and gave him a dose in the eyes. As he moaned and writhed on the ground, she ran away.

Back at the hotel she took a long, hot shower and studied the red-ness on her right cheek. Toweling off, she threw up her drinks. There were scratches on her neck and back.

When she got to the pub everybody stared, and Elizabeth immedi-ately cornered her in the restroom. "Are you okay? What happened?"

"I don't want to talk about it," she said.

That evening she was brilliant. She could feel the group's energy shifting as everyone responded to this new Anne, completely differ-ent from the stiff, insecure outsider at the dress rehearsal. During those two weeks in Edinburgh, she never once faltered. The other actors praised her, befriended her, and bought her drinks. Every once in a while someone would ask her to explain what had happened that afternoon—especially once the bruises started showing—but she just shook her head.

What fueled her wasn't the injury but the ownership of a story that was a mystery to everyone else. The refusal to explain. The secret high that came from thinking none of them knew her at all.

SIX

⚬⚬⚬   ⚬⚬⚬   ⚬⚬⚬

Montreal, 2006

MITCH HAD BEEN back in Montreal for two weeks when he saw his ex-wife for the first time in years. It was September, and fall was coming on strong. The Labor Day weekend passed stormy and breezy, warning everyone to put the follies of summer behind them. Kids walked the streets with their heads down, bent under backpacks, listless in their new school clothes. September had always been Martine's favorite time of year: she said it felt like promises. Whenever the phone rang, he thought it might be her. Even knowing it wasn't, he'd pick up on the first ring, alert and vulnerable to the telemarketers on the other end or his brother calling from Mississauga.

He didn't call her himself, because he didn't know what to say.

He was crossing the hospital parking lot late one afternoon when a middle-aged woman called his name. He stared at her blankly, a half smile frozen on his face. She put her hand on her chest and said, "Azra."

"My God," he said, "I'm sorry," and gave her a hug. She was Grace's best friend, or had been back when they were married. She had gained weight and her hair was different—now sleek and straight, with a red tint, not long and black and curly—but her eyes were still wry and kind, reflecting the same surprise at how he had aged as his must have about her. She had always been vibrant and wiry, a churn of energy fired by some personal electricity. She and Grace used to talk in the kitchen for hours, exchanging confidences about their futures, husbands, jobs, sex lives, problems with their parents. It always amazed him how quickly they would plunge into the depths of conversation, as if the surface held no tension at all.

"How *are* you?" he said now.

"Oh, you know," she said, and they both laughed. She held on to his elbows briefly—they'd always liked each other—before letting go. "Have you seen her?"

He followed her quick glance at the building behind him. "Is Grace here?" he said. "What happened?"

Azra grimaced, as if weighing whether or not to tell him whatever it was, but surely there was no reason not to. He and Grace had worked hard to forgive each other, and if the process was necessarily incomplete, it had been undertaken in what they both acknowledged was good faith. They'd kept in touch for the first years after the divorce, then gradually moved on with their lives.

"She was in a car accident last week," Azra said. "I thought maybe you'd heard. She was stopped at a light on Jean-Talon when a car rammed straight into her. She has a broken leg and a broken pelvis and I don't even know what else."

"That's awful," Mitch said. "Are you heading in now? I'll go with you."

She hesitated for a second, then shrugged and nodded, and they walked inside together, catching up on each other's news. Azra and Mike had two children, and Mitch heard their names and ages with the usual small pang of having let a stage of life pass him by. Outside Grace's room, he stopped and touched Azra's arm. "Why don't you go in first and make sure she doesn't mind if I say hi?"

He waited in the hallway after Azra disappeared inside. He worked on a different floor and knew few of the doctors here; it occurred to him now how circumscribed his routine really was. Then the door opened, and Azra gestured him in.

"Grace," he said.

Nobody could look their best when lying in a hospital bed after a car accident, and Grace was no exception. Her face was etched with wrinkles, her skin weathered. Threads of silver shot through her limp brown hair. Her broken leg, on top of the covers, was frozen in its white trunk. Below it, a fuzzy red sock seemed the only brightness in the room. Surrounded by machines and hooked up to an IV drip, she seemed fractured and frail. Mitch couldn't help thinking about Gloria and Thomasie Reeves, about Mathieu's shoulder and Martine's ankle. Feeling like the world had broken everyone he knew, he took one of Grace's small, dry palms in his. "You look like you got hit by a truck."

"It was a Honda, actually," she said. Her facial expression held the dreamy vagueness of sedation. Behind him, Azra cleared her throat. She had taken off her coat and was setting things on a counter by the window: books, a pillow, a stuffed animal. Watching her friend's movements, Grace seemed to have trouble turning her head.

"Sarah thought you should have the bear," Azra said, waving it at Grace. "She said he'd keep you company."

Grace licked her lips, which were chapped and feathery. "How is she?" Her voice cracked, and Mitch poured her a cup of water from a bedside pitcher and handed it to her.

"She's doing great. She really wanted to come today, but I told her you wouldn't want her to miss her swimming lesson. I'll bring her tomorrow."

"I don't even know how to thank you."

"Oh, shut up," Azra said fondly.

"Who's Sarah?" Mitch said.

Grace's eyes met his. "My daughter."

Mitch swallowed, surprised he hadn't heard that she'd gotten married and started a family. On the other hand, after the divorce they'd migrated into separate social circles and never ran into each other. He'd been the one who stopped seeing their mutual friends, who'd switched neighborhoods and haunts. It was easier that way.

"She's staying with Azra and Mike while I'm here," Grace went on. "It sounds like she's having a great time. I don't think she'll want to come home."

"It's fun for all of us, having her," Azra said lightly.

"She's always hated being an only child," Grace said. Though her words were wistful, her voice was calm.

There was no mention of the father; Mitch guessed he was out of the picture. He realized that both women were looking at him expectantly. "Is there anything I can do?" he said, more to Azra than to Grace.

"You know, there is," Azra said. "Maybe it's weird to ask, but Mike and I are both working, and with the kids and all their activities . . . Well, is there any way you could go over to Grace's and do the mail and the plants?"

"Of course. You don't mind, Grace?"

When she looked at him, her expression was dazed. She couldn't be bothered to mind right now, that much was clear.

"She lives on Monkland, I'll write down the address," Azra said. "Here, I have an extra set of keys. This really helps, Mitch. Thanks."

He felt dismissed. He squeezed Grace's hand again—cold against his own—then walked down the green hallway with her keys in his pocket.

He drove west along Sherbrooke, past the dark red turrets of the Westmount Library, the setting sun piercing the windshield. All along the street people were hurrying home from work, leaning forward against the wind that was whipping leaves off trees and whirling them around. He knew a lot of people who lived in this part of town but rarely socialized here, having peeled away this layer of his life a long time ago.

Outside Grace's building the trees were a riot of green and early, creeping yellow. He walked up the steps, remembering the apartment they had moved into as a young married couple so long ago. They had been so thrilled to buy their first things together, furniture and dishes, all of domestic life a novelty. It was hard to believe they'd ever been so young. He left the mail on a table in the hallway and went into the kitchen, looking for a watering can. There were dirty plates in the sink, and cereal boxes and granola bars and fruit scattered across the counter. But it was a homey kitchen, a child's smeared finger paintings tacked on the fridge. On the counter was a school photo of a blond girl with a gapped smile and clear, wide-set green eyes. She didn't look much like Grace, who had had dark hair even as a child.

He couldn't find anything to water with until, rummaging through the cupboards, he found a teapot that he recognized, queasily, as his mother's. God knows when she'd given it to them. She'd been dead for seven years.

He filled the teapot with water and wandered from plant to plant. Toward the back of the apartment was Grace's bedroom, and he peered in for a second and then, seeing no plants, stepped back with a feeling of relief. The other bedroom was a riot of pink sheets and stuffed animals and books and toys. No plants there, either.

Five minutes later he was done, and he put the teapot back exactly where he'd found it, which seemed stupid given how messy the kitchen was, but still. It felt like the right thing to do.

Back at his own apartment, he thought about Grace as he made dinner. When they met, he was halfway through his PhD program, the teaching assistant for a course Grace took called Personality. Later in their relationship, she confessed to having an encyclopedic memory of that time—what they'd said, where they'd been, what each of them had been wearing. He smiled and nodded, but truthfully he remembered little of those early encounters. What stuck in his mind was Grace's work, her professional, detailed lab reports, so superior to those of her peers that halfway through the term he stopped reading them and gave her an automatic A. The sophistication of her performance was in dire contrast to the handwriting on her quizzes, which was round and bubbly. She didn't dot her *i*'s with hearts or flowers, but she seemed like the kind of girl who had, and not that long ago. She pressed down so hard that sometimes the pen broke through the paper. It was the penmanship of a very young, very determined person.

Although he'd thought then that he was depressed, in retrospect his time as a grad student was, in fact, the happiest of his life. The worries that had so nagged at him now seemed like luxuries. Was psychology *important*? Was it *effective*? Did it *matter*? He stayed up at night chewing over its various intellectual and emotional bankrupt-cies, and these anxieties functioned as ballast, distracting him from his suspicion that it was himself, not the profession, that was unwor-thy. Eventually, as he started working, the worries dissipated, and at night he thought about the people he worked with and their prob-lems, not his own.

After that class was finished, he started seeing Grace around the department, meeting with her professors, working in a lab. They would run into each other late at night at the vending machine, or reach for the same milk container at the coffee shop at eight in the morning. Neither of them had a life, so they made one together.

He couldn't recall a single thing Grace had said to them when they were dating. What he did remember was how *he* felt, things *he'd* said that made her laugh or nod at his wisdom. Over candlelit dinners she sometimes looked like she wished she had a notebook handy. At first this was great; then it was uncomfortable. He wanted her to figure out that he wasn't all that wonderful.

But after he really got to know her, he understood that this was just her nature. She brought the full force of her attention to bear on you, made you drunk with that and with yourself. She wasn't being manipulative; she was genuinely interested. Once he realized this, though, he began to resent her for *not* thinking he was uniquely gifted. It was unfair, but he couldn't help it. He stopped calling, stopped inviting her out. In response, she asked him over, cooked dinner, and started telling him all about herself, her family, stories from her child-hood. Then she calmly engineered him into bed, and there, without exactly being the aggressor, she let him know that he had been ignor-ing her, that it was his turn to pay attention. And he did.

A year later they were married. They were in their early twenties, and the only married people they knew were their parents' age. Everyone seemed to think it was cute—or reckless. "You'll be divorced before you're thirty-five," his mother muttered darkly when he gave her the news. And she was right, as she was about most things. She had loved

Grace, though. He wondered if she still thought they'd get divorced when she handed over the teapot. She was a materialist, his mother, stroking her favorite blanket and cardigan sweater in her last days at the hospital, long after she'd forgotten his name.

He had never wanted to admit it, but he mourned the loss of Grace the student, the adoring undergrad. When she got her own degree and they became peers, the tectonic plates beneath them shifted, resettled. They stopped having sex. They were buddies. What this said about him, his loss of desire, his need to dominate, was so profoundly unflattering—and so unutterably, unchangeably true—that he couldn't even think about it.

Grace was perfect for him. She was trustworthy, caring, loyal, and smart; she understood both him and his work. So their divorce was, for a time, the great failure of his life—until he went on to other failures.

He discovered the truth about his marriage when he almost slept with a patient. An unhappily married forty-year-old banker whose husband was sick with pancreatic cancer, Marisa was rumpled and bosomy, with a messy tangle of upswept brown hair and lipstick that was always smudged; her perfume was unpleasantly spicy and overpowering. Every time she came in he thought she looked like she'd just gotten laid, although he knew from their sessions that this wasn't true. Lonely, bereft, she wanted someone to hold her hand; she loved talking to Mitch, and there soon developed an unspoken tension that he allowed to build. He even grew to rely on it, the excitement of it feeling, at times, like the only thing that got him through the week.

At home he and Grace were sleeping in the same bed but on different schedules; she went to bed early and he stayed up well past midnight, so they overlapped as little as possible. Then Marisa's husband died, and the day after the funeral she came into the office sobbing, dissolving, and admitted that despite her pain she was flooded with relief. Mitch patted her hand, understanding that she had chosen him for this confession instead of a priest, and that to violate her trust would be profane.

Years later he saw her at the Jean-Talon Market, and she looked great. She had lost weight, and her hair and clothes were less rumpled, though she still couldn't keep her lipstick on. She was standing fifteen feet away, choosing an eggplant, and when she looked up and saw him, the expression on her face was horrified. He nodded noncommittally and drifted away, realizing that she hadn't looked at all sexual during that terrible time in her life, of which she had just been reminded. She'd just been a mess. Only someone as lonely and narcissistic as Mitch could have interpreted it otherwise. He walked quickly to his car, half his grocery list abandoned, thanking his lucky stars that the damage hadn't been worse.

A couple of days later, he stopped by Grace's room again, during visiting hours, showing up empty-handed; bringing flowers to your ex-wife seemed like a weird thing to do, no matter what the circumstances were. There was another patient in the room, the wall-mounted television was blaring a French *téléroman*, and his heart went out to Grace. She hated television, which gave her headaches when she was tired. Now she was staring up at the ceiling, slack-jawed, her expression vacant, her hands by her sides. When he knocked, her eyes jumped to life, and she looked so happy that he flushed. He should have come back sooner.

"How are you feeling?" he said, pulling up a chair next to her.

"Fantastic." She smiled, in spite of her evident pain. She had lost the glassy-eyed look, though she was still pale and the planes of her face were shadowed. Somebody had braided her hair. "Azra says you helped out at my place. Thank you."

"It was nothing." He had brought back the key to her apartment and set it on the bedside table, on top of what looked like a drawing her daughter had done.

In the other bed, a middle-aged woman moaned, seemingly agitated by the TV as well, so Mitch turned around to look. The soap opera was taking place in a hospital too, where a young woman wearing a lot of makeup was hooked up to a life-support machine while a handsome doctor looked down at her in consternation.

"*Mais non, mais non,*" the other patient mumbled, though Mitch couldn't tell what exactly she was objecting to. A detergent commercial came on with a raucous jingle, and Grace winced. Noises carried into the room from the hallway, too: doctors being called to stations, the bright chatter of nurses, the hum and beep of distant machines. He was so used to being in a hospital that he rarely thought about it from the patient's point of view, how difficult it must be to get well in the midst of the chaos and noise. He wished now that he had brought Grace something, a magazine or a book. "Is there anything else I can do?"

"I don't know. Tell me what's new. I haven't seen you in ages."

He shrugged, not knowing where to start.

"I heard you were with someone, a lawyer or something."

This gave him pause. "Where did you hear that?"

Grace's eyes sparkled at him. "It's a small city. Somebody met her at a party." She was right, of course—it *was* a small city—and it was no big deal. Nonetheless he felt at some obscure disadvantage. "It didn't work out," he said.

Grace reached for his hand and squeezed it. "Sorry."

She was watching him intently, waiting to see if he had anything more to say about it, which was so typical of her, and so different from Martine, who simply would have changed the subject, that he smiled. He realized, now that his initial shock had passed, that Grace still looked good. She had stayed trim, probably still ran and skied. For a second he couldn't help picturing her in those early months, splayed on their bed and whispering to him urgently, "Come inside." She never put it any other way, and when he did she'd say his name, as if his identity had been a bit of mystery to her but was now, at this crucial moment, confirmed. This was the Grace he would always think of: young and smart and so fiercely competent that it took him years to discover just how vulnerable she was. She smiled at him now, wistfully, as if she were tracking his thoughts.

"It's okay," he finally said. "What about you?"

"Oh, no. Between work and Sarah, I don't have time to meet anybody."

"Where's your practice now, anyway? Are you still on Côte-des-Neiges?"

She shook her head, wincing as if it hurt to do so. "I quit. I'm a teacher now. Grade six, on the West Island."

"What? Seriously?" He was shocked by this. Plenty of therapists burned out, tired of hearing about intransigent life problems day after day, but Grace's passion for her work had always seemed inexhaustible, her curiosity about other people such an entrenched part of her personality. She was the one everybody cornered at parties, the recipient of her friends' troubled late-night phone calls. Strangers poured out their hearts to her in airports and grocery stores, and she never complained or seemed frustrated or bored. Her profession suited her better than anyone he knew, including himself.

"It's a long story," she said, clearly not intending to tell it.

Then her eyes shifted behind him, and he turned and saw a little blond girl trooping into the room—scissoring her legs in giant steps, swinging her arms like a tiny soldier—with Azra trailing her. Then she saw Mitch, stopped short, and cocked her head to the side. He guessed she was about nine.

"Come here, you," Grace said fondly.

Mitch stepped back as the girl approached her mother and gently ran her fingers along her arm, as if afraid she might break.

Grace smiled at her. "That tickles," she said.

Sarah smiled and kept doing it, her fingers scurrying up and down Grace's arm like mice.

"Stop, kiddo," Grace said. "Say hello to my friend Mitch."

"Hi," the girl said, without looking at him.

"Hi, Sarah. How are you?" This wasn't the sort of question you asked children, who didn't go in for small talk, and the girl ignored it. She didn't seem bothered by his presence. It was just one more thing that had happened—her mother in this strange place, the doctors, staying with Azra.

"What's the best thing that happened to you today?" Grace asked her.

"Azra gave me a Snickers," Sarah said.

Behind her, Azra laughed guiltily. "Sorry, Grace. I know you don't usually give her chocolate."

"It's okay," Grace said, unconvincingly.

The patient in the other bed seemed to have fallen asleep, and Mitch reached up and turned off the television. In the sudden quiet, Sarah's high voice rang brightly as she stood at her mother's bedside and talked about her day. Playtime, a story about elephants, a boy who had pulled her hair, something the teacher said, a bug at recess—he could tell Grace loved hearing all these details, her eyes fixed on Sarah. After a while, the girl ran down like a battery losing its charge. Her attention shifted to the window, and she started over to it, explaining something she'd just learned about Canada geese.

Azra took some crayons and paper out of her bag and suggested that she draw a goose for her mother.

"Okay," Sarah said, then sat down in a chair, balanced the paper on her knees, and started to draw, her tongue sticking out of the corner of her mouth in a caricature of concentration.

Leaning against the wall, Azra let out a long breath, obviously exhausted. Mitch wondered where Grace's parents were, or the rest of her support network. She had always had plenty of friends.

Azra excused herself to go to the restroom, nodding at Mitch to indicate that he should keep an eye on Sarah.

He returned to Grace's side and said softly, "She's really cute."

"Thanks."

"She looks like you."

"No she doesn't. She looks like her father."

"Does she?" Mitch said, but Grace didn't respond. The subject was clearly off-limits. "Is there anything I can do to help?" he said.

Grace looked at him with a small, quick smile, her eyes flickering. He realized—still able to read her after all these years—that she was in enormous pain, and scared, certainly not in any condition to tell him what he could do to help. He had a sudden, intense urge to hold her in his arms or, equally powerful, to walk out the door and never come back. He glanced down, afraid that his face might betray these thoughts, and when he looked up she was still smiling, as if that tight-lipped expression were holding her entire face together. He touched her hand and made his voice strong and calm. "Don't worry," he said. "Everything's going to be fine."

She barely nodded. "It's weird, isn't it?" she said. "Seeing each other again."

When he was at work, he tried to act as though his confidence hadn't been shattered. Everything there—his office, his coworkers, the nurses—felt not familiar, as it should have, but strange, his days all out of rhythm. He wondered if his chair had always seemed a little too low for the desk in his office, or if he had called the secretary on the third floor by the right name. He wasn't sure, in general, of anything. Showing up each morning in his sports jacket and khaki pants, takeout coffee in hand, he felt he was faking it even more than he ever had when, as a student and intern, he actually was. His own voice seemed to stand at a remove. Time passed stickily, each minute clinging to him as though not wanting to let go.

His coworkers had heard about what happened during his rotation in Nunavut, and their response was to avoid him, expressing their sympathy with distant nods and grimacing smiles when passing in the hallways, everyone's eyes focused on a spot just over his shoulder. Mitch understood this fear of contagion. Failing a patient as he had was every therapist's worst fear, and it was far better to steer clear of it, even for those whose profession advocated understanding. He only wished that he could steer clear of it himself.

Commencing a new group-therapy session on substance abuse, he tried to pare away self-doubt and cleave to the core of his work. There were ten patients, ranging in age from twenty-one to sixty, united by their reek of cigarette smoke. They sat in a circle, downcast, jittery, each one's chair at a calibrated distance from the next; no one wanted to touch another person, even by accident, in this room of misery and anger. Thank God for other people's problems, he thought.

"Well," he said. "Let's start."

He laid down the ground rules in a lecture he'd memorized so long ago that he didn't even mark the words as they left his mouth. Then came the introductions, and he tried to listen carefully and note every detail, but time and again he felt himself drifting away, untethered to the moment, and had to reel himself back in again.

An hour and a half later he was alone, uncomfortably, with his thoughts. The session had gone reasonably well, and they all had left with their "homework" for the next week, nodding as he'd told them what to do. He knew from experience that there would be a serious drop-off in attendance, and he usually made bets with himself about who would stay and who would go. This time, though, he couldn't bring himself to do it. Thomasie's face kept passing through his mind.

He threw his pencil across his desk, and sighed.

At five o'clock, he left work and headed to Martine's apartment. He didn't want to call in advance. He wasn't sure that what he had to say could be blurted out over the phone, in the few moments her politeness would afford him, and he wouldn't be able to say it without being able to read her face as he spoke.

He rehearsed a speech over and over in his mind, knowing he had only a few seconds in which to win her over. He was so preoccupied with the wording of his plea that he didn't even see her coming down the street until she was almost in front of him—her cheeks chafed red by the autumn wind, a blue scarf bunched beneath her chin. She was carrying grocery bags and he reached out to help her with them, but she shook her head. Her hair was twisted into one of her usual chaotic arrangements, strands escaping everywhere. They stood in the street, afternoon traffic inching by, horns blasting. She was beautiful.

"Martine," he said. "Please."

Her short, humorless laugh hung between them like smoke. All the lines he had practiced dissolved in the frigid air. Instead he said, "Will you marry me?"

He had no plan, no ring. Martine cocked her head to one side, her expression neutral, examining, as if he were some new piece of evidence brought before her in court. He had no idea what she was thinking.

"So, you're back," she said at last.

"I know I should've come by earlier. Much earlier. I just—I'm sorry. But please, I love you. I love Mathieu."

Martine set the grocery bags down, then fished around in her pocket for a cigarette, lit it, and drew on it deeply. Finally she said, "I know you're attached to him."

"It's so much more than that," he said impatiently. "I should never have gone away. I shouldn't have let us drift apart. I should have told you how much you mean to me, I should've *insisted*. I never should've let you let me go."

Almost involuntarily, it seemed, she was nodding in agreement. "That's right," she said. "You shouldn't have."

Then she glanced up at her apartment. Since the windows of both Mathieu's room and the living room faced the street, he thought she was checking to see if her son was watching, to incorporate him into the decision. This gave him the confidence to think that she might invite him in. Five more minutes, and he'd be inside.

He was buoyed by this thought, and by the idea of seeing the child again, playing with him, hearing his high, tinny voice. He had missed those cozy weekends, the family dinners, even the science lectures.

Martine was looking at him steadily, waiting for him to say more.

He wondered why she hadn't picked up Mathieu from day care, as she usually did, but maybe she had a sitter for him. Surely he wouldn't be in the apartment alone. This might explain her hesitation, when of course she ought to be inviting Mitch in so they could have this conversation in comfort rather than on the street.

"Martine," he said.

She threw her cigarette down and stubbed it out with the pointy toe of her boot, rubbing the black stain of ash into the sidewalk. When she finally met his eyes again, she just shrugged. Mitch knew, then, that Mathieu was with a man, not a sitter, and that this man had, in a matter of weeks, already gotten further with her than he ever had.

"That doctor?" he said. "Vendetti?"

"It's going well," she said. "Mathieu likes him too. You taught him to be friendlier with people. I'm grateful to you for that."

She was speaking with grave formality. He felt like he was being presented with a plaque at some awards banquet. It made him angry, and he couldn't restrain the sad, inevitable sentiments, so stale until you had to inhabit them yourself, when suddenly they glowed freshly with truth. "He's not the one for you," he said. "You and I belong together."

With a distant, constrained smile, Martine picked up her grocery bags, one in each arm, balanced, self-sufficient. "You should go," she said, and she walked away up the stairs.

And that was it. He had felt so unmoored the past few weeks that this latest blow hardly sent him into a tailspin, just dropped him deeper down the same dark well. The next morning he was back at work, greeting his coworkers and drinking coffee from his regular mug. He was sitting at his desk, feeling moody and nauseous, when he remembered someone who had it a lot worse. So when he had a break in his schedule, he took the elevator downstairs and knocked gently on Grace's door.

She was alone, staring at the ceiling, her expression pinched, the braid in her hair loose and tangled. She was still wearing the fuzzy red sock on her foot below the cast.

"Hey there," he said softly.

She turned her head slowly, as if her neck pained her, but when she saw him her eyes again lit up, giving him the first good feeling of the day and, possibly, the week. "Mitch. I wasn't expecting you."

"I hope you don't mind. I'm on a break."

"I don't mind at all. I'm just lying here in a drugged-out fog." She patted the bed beside her, her hand flopping jerkily in the air, and said, "Come over here."

He pulled up a chair and sat down.

Over her hospital gown she was wearing a pink bed jacket that looked like it belonged in an old lady's closet. The other patient had apparently been discharged, so she had the room to herself.

"How are you feeling?"

"Not bad," she said.

From her stiff posture, her hands quieted at her sides, her head leaning heavily on the thin pillow, he knew she felt a lot worse than she was letting on.

"Can I ask you a favor?" she said.

"Shoot."

"Can you get me a pen?"

He cocked his head. "You planning to write your memoirs in here?"

Instead of laughing at this admittedly pitiful joke, she was holding out her hand expectantly, her expression dire. He took a pen from his jacket pocket and handed it over. Immediately she stuck it down inside her cast, using the end of it to scratch. She let out a loud, involuntary groan of satisfaction, and Mitch, embarrassed, looked away.

She kept digging for a couple minutes, feverishly, then stopped and held the pen out to him. "Thanks."

"Keep it," he said.

She grimaced. "You have no idea how itchy a cast is. It's almost worse than the pain."

"It sounds awful, Grace."

"Oh, it's not," she said lamely. "They think I'll be able to go home soon. I don't know about going back to work."

"What kind of teacher are you, again?"

She closed her eyes, her voice faint and distant. "Grade six. In Beaconsfield."

"What happened to your practice?"

"It's a long story," she said. It was the second time she'd used the shopworn phrase about this, and he didn't know what to say. He wasn't even sure why he was here. Of course he was worried about her, as he would be about anyone he knew in this condition. But maybe there was something else, too. These days he felt disconnected from everything, even his own past, and seeing Grace again after so many years seemed to offer him something: a thread, a hope of stitching himself back together.

"How about you?" she said. "How's your work?"

That was the last question he wanted to answer. But he could see she was tired of talking, so he told her about his group this morning. The young man who was already forming a crush on the thirty-year-old management consultant next to him (Grace nodded very slightly at this), the older bus driver whose only contribution to the discussion was to say, "My wife made me come." The mousy, brown-haired woman who didn't say anything after she introduced herself and then, halfway through, burst into tears. The bus driver, with an immediate, fatherly instinct, patted her shoulder as she buried her head in her hands. And everyone else relaxed, because each of them knew that at least one other person in the room felt just as desperate and injured as they did. Grace listened to all this with her eyes closed; except for that initial nod, she didn't move at all. Her breathing was soft, and he wasn't sure if she was awake, if he was keeping her company or simply filling the room with noise. After a while, he ran out of substance-abuse anecdotes. They were quiet together, and he felt strangely peaceful. Between the slatted blinds a ray of late-afternoon winter sun shot into the room, thin but brilliant, streaking across Grace's face, and she squinted. When he realized she couldn't move away from it, he got up and closed the blinds.

"Well," he said, "I guess I'd better leave you alone. Sorry I talked your ear off."

Grace smiled at him, but her eyes looked tired. "It was nice," she said, "but you don't have to keep coming here, you know. It was kind of you to help with the apartment and everything, but you've done enough."

Mitch snorted—the idea that he'd ever done enough seemed ridiculous, given the recent truths of his life—but then nodded. "I don't mean to intrude."

"You're not intruding," she said. "You've been great. But you've done so much already."

This was as direct a request to leave as Grace would ever utter. Yet something bound him there in the room—her wan eyes, or his need to be of help. "Where are your parents?" he said.

She sighed. "My father died a few years ago. My mother isn't well enough to travel."

"I'm sorry."

Her head moved slightly in a gesture that was meant to be a shrug. She was exhausted now, her eyes fluttering open and closed, her hands splayed out beside her, palms up. He moved closer, wanting to touch her arm, to somehow lend her some of his physical strength, because she needed it.

"Look," he said. "I don't have a lot going on, so let me help you out. For old times' sake."

"That's not a good reason," she said, and the dryness of her voice was a reminder that all was not simple between them.

But she must have changed her mind, because a week or so later the phone rang one evening, and it was her, sounding quiet but determined.

"It's me, Grace. I'm out of the hospital."

"Congratulations! How are you doing?"

"I'll live," she said. "Listen, I decided I'd like to take you up on your offer."

"I'm glad," he said, and he was.

"Azra's overextended, and a couple of my other friends have flaked out on me. Do you think you could help me with some errands and getting Sarah to and from school?"

"Of course I can."

There was a pause. "That's, well, it's good of you," she said awkwardly.

"It's not a big deal, Grace. I'm happy to do it."

The next day he went over. He found her on the couch wearing a gray sweater, the bottom half of her body swaddled in a thick wool blanket, her cast a raised lump beneath it. She looked better than she had in the hospital, but not by much. A small end table was set up with essentials: a glass of water, a box of tissues, a cluster of yellow pill vials.

"Thanks again for doing this," she said.

"Stop thanking me," Mitch said. "Please."

She grimaced a little, as if her pride hurt as much as her injuries. Looking at the place more closely than he had the first time, he noticed that the furniture was slipcovered in her favorite colors, blues and pale greens, and he recognized several of the watercolors hanging on the walls. At a cruel moment late in their marriage, he had told her that her taste was bland; now it struck him as soothing, and he felt peculiarly at home. It was a quiet place, still as a pond.

"Sarah's over at a friend's," Grace said. "Here, I have a list."

On a yellow legal pad—and Mitch remembered now that she had always used one as a student—she had written down a succession of chores. Laundry. Groceries, with each item detailed down to the brand. Sarah's schedule, when to drop her off and when to bring her back. The things Sarah liked for lunch. A manual of parenting, with everything explained, in Grace's round, neat handwriting.

Her voice was all business. "I'll tell you where the laundry baskets and the machines are," she said. "Are you sure you don't mind doing this?"

"Please," he said. "I'm glad to have something to do."

It sounded more pathetic than he intended, as if he didn't have anything else to do, which wasn't exactly true. Or possibly it was a little bit true. But he busied himself around the place for an hour or so, then went out to Loblaws and came back to unload the groceries into the fridge and cupboards. All the while Grace lay on the couch, drifting in and out of consciousness. At first she seemed to make an effort to raise her head when he came into the living room, but when he told her to rest she closed her eyes gratefully.

He did laundry in the basement, nodding at a neighbor who glanced at him curiously, and ran a few errands off Grace's list during the washing and drying cycles. When the clothes were dry, he brought them back up to the apartment and put her things away in her dresser, trying not to look too closely at the underwear. Sarah's impossibly small clothes went into the white dresser in her room. When he came back into the living room, Grace's eyes were open, but her expression was even more strained.

"Are you okay?" he blurted. "Is the pain worse?"

"I have to ask you to do something," she said. "I am so, so sorry about this."

Right away he knew what it was, and oddly enough felt no hesitation. It was a relief to have another specific, physical task that needed to be accomplished. "It's all right. Remember when you got food poisoning in India? I've already been through the worst."

"Thanks for bringing that up," she said, but then she smiled.

He crouched near her. She smelled both gamy and chemical, like a specimen left unattended too long in some dusty lab. An unwashed scent mixed with the must of bandages and ointment. She pointed at the bedpan under the end table, and when he arranged it beneath her, tears glistened in her eyes from the pain of the jostling. "I'm sorry," he whispered.

"It's not your fault."

He left her alone for a few minutes, then collected and emptied the bedpan. When he came back again, Grace had cleaned herself and he disposed of the trash she'd left in a container by the couch. Her eyes had a burning, febrile expression, part humiliation, part pain.

"Worse than India?" he said.

"Much worse," she said.

He squeezed her hand and put his arm around her as gently as he could, and her head collapsed against his chest, her body buckling with a sob. For a few minutes they sat like that, then she shook her head and wiped her eyes. The most awful moment, he understood, had passed.

At five o'clock Sarah's friend's mother brought her home, and Sarah approached the couch with the same fearful care that Mitch had noted in the hospital. He microwaved some pizza, poured juice, and set up a video for her to watch on the TV. She was very quiet and sat beside her mother on the couch with her knees curled up to her chin, leaning timidly into the corner cushions.

An hour later, when a friend of Grace's stopped by to help them get ready for bed, Mitch said it was time he left.

"Thank you," Grace said, her eyes again filling with tears.

"Please," he said. "It's all right."

So he slipped into her life through the side door. He didn't think that much about it, or wonder if it was right or wrong. What he'd told her was the truth: he was grateful to have something to do.

Over the next two weeks, he stopped by Grace's every few days. He stocked the apartment with food. He drove Sarah to school and back home. He did laundry.

When he mentioned to his brother on the phone what was happening, Malcolm laughed. "I never pictured *you* as Mr. Mom," he said.

Mitch was annoyed. "That's not it," he said, and explained that other friends of Grace's were also taking turns in the rotation. But it was true that he never much bothered with these domestic tasks in his own life, where he had only himself to look after.

"Okay," Malcolm said good-naturedly. "Isn't it weird, though, hanging out with Grace and her kid?"

"No," Mitch said. "Not after such a long time, anyway."

But parts of it were, in fact, a little weird. Sarah, for example, was totally different from Mathieu. If he lived in a universe boundaried by his own mind, a planet of dinosaur facts and physics equations, she craved constant interaction with other people. She always ran to the door to let Mitch in, less out of any particular affection for him than a burning desire to talk to someone. She told him stories, put on costumes and danced for him, held his hand and asked him to play. Her need for attention was infinite. He wondered if she had been like this with Grace before the accident or if her clinginess came from knowing that her only parent was fragile and could disappear. He often came home exhausted, not from doing chores but from playing with Sarah.

As for Grace, she sometimes had bad days when her pelvis was hurting—she was trying hard to cut down on her pain medication—and would snap at him or barely register his presence. Other days, desperate for company after lying alone by herself in the apartment all day, she wanted to talk almost as much as her daughter.

One night the three of them played Sorry!, a game Mitch hadn't seen since he was a child and was amazed still existed. Sarah clasped her hands together in feverish concentration as she bent her head over the pieces. She knew all the rules, about bumping and sliding and the safety zone, and explained them to him carefully, condescendingly, as if he were the nine-year-old. But he kept messing up—doing things with his pawn that he wasn't supposed to—at first because he didn't remember how to play and later just to get a rise out of Sarah, who rolled her eyes, stuck out her palms with exaggerated irritation, and exclaimed, "Mitch! How many times do I have to tell you about this!"

"Sorry, Sarah. I'm old and slow."

She nodded. "I know that. You can't help it."

Across the table, Grace's eyes met his, sparkling with suppressed laughter, and he smiled. He was having a good time. And it was peculiar to find himself once again in the company of a single woman and her child. Not that they were replacements for Martine and Mathieu. The time he spent with them was at once less stressful, with no element of romance, and more uncomfortable, because his role was less defined. Sarah was less extreme in her behavior than Mathieu, and Grace was far less tempestuous than Martine. It felt not like a repetition of the previous triangle but a new version of it, from another angle. A pattern stretching across the recent years of his life.

They let Sarah win, and Grace read her a story, and then the two of them helped her change into her pajamas. Mitch took her into the bathroom and helped her brush her teeth, gently guiding the toothbrush around her small mouth, afraid of hurting her. She bared all her teeth in the mirror, a crazy person's smile, and said, "All clean."

She climbed into bed, muttering some story, her room dark except for the blue glow of the nightlight. She was whispering herself to sleep, casting a spell, and didn't seem to notice when he left.

Back in the living room, Grace was sitting on the couch. As he walked in, she examined him so openly, so curiously, that he felt self-conscious. "My friends think you're a saint," she said. "They say no other guy would do what you're doing."

He shrugged, blushing a little.

"I said you're just feeling guilty about something," she went on. "So what is it?"

This was Grace all over. She didn't let you get away with anything. He shrugged again. "I let people down," he said.

"Do you want to talk about it?"

"No."

"Would you like a glass of wine? I think there's a bottle of Bordeaux in the cupboard."

Mitch was touched by this. When they were married he drank Bordeaux almost exclusively, the most expensive he could afford, afraid of seeming unsophisticated. These days he drank whatever was offered or on hand. In the kitchen, he uncorked the bottle and poured himself a glass, then went back to the living room and sat down in an armchair kitty-corner to Grace. The color was back in her face, and Azra had come by the day before and helped her take a bath and wash her hair. She no longer had a wince of constant pain. She raised her mug of tea in a toast.

"You're looking a lot better," he said.

"No I'm not," she said firmly. "I look like forty miles of rough road. As my grandmother used to say."

He laughed, and they sat in silence over their drinks. Without a specific task to do, being with her did feel odd; the familiarity, combined with the distance between them, set him on edge. It was like seeing yourself in a funhouse mirror, with your features distorted and your body torqued yet insistently, regrettably, your own. Only now, sitting in her living room, did he realize what a good job he'd done of burying the painful aspects of their divorce, and how violently they still pulsed beneath the layers of the intervening years.

Stymied, he said, "Why aren't you practicing anymore?"

"Oh, I'm *practicing*," she said. It was a long-standing joke between them, so old he was surprised she even remembered it. "I'm just not very good."

"Elementary school teacher," Mitch said. "Tell me how *that* happened."

Something flitted across her face—pain, of course, but other things too, maybe memory, even humor, in some elusive combination he couldn't decipher. She was older and less beautiful, his ex-wife, and he wasn't in love with her anymore; but seeing her pain was like feeling his own, because for so long he had had a part in it.

"It was the usual, I guess. Burnout."

He didn't believe her but didn't think it was his right to press. "I never pegged you for that, somehow. I thought your energy was endless."

Grace looked at him thoughtfully. "Maybe the problem was that I had too much. That I thought you can accomplish things you really can't."

He waited.

"I had some patients," she said slowly, and then stopped.

"You realized you couldn't do as much for them as you'd hoped."

She shrugged. "I guess," she said, tears brightening her eyes.

"But sometimes we can do too much," he said. "We almost have too much power, don't you think?"

She shook her head. "I think people do whatever they want, no matter what we say."

"Maybe so," he said.

"Anyway, so I closed my practice and went back to school and became a teacher. It works well with Sarah, too, because we have the summers together. And what about you, Mitch? You still like your job? It seems like you're doing well, from what I hear at the hospital."

"Oh, there's not much to report," he said.

Grace's smile was tight. "Lucky you."

Afterward he walked out into the breezy night and strolled around the neighboring park before getting back in his car. He was a little tipsy from the wine, and the cool air felt good on his face. Plenty of others—dog walkers, hacky sack players, groups of teenagers—were in the park, reluctant to give up on the long nights of summer, with fall looming dark before them.

He walked along Monkland, on a route they might've taken together a long time ago. People were sipping drinks on the outside terraces, laughing and chatting. The door to the Old Orchard pub was open, the high, quick notes of a Celtic fiddler embroidering the air. Then he left the bustling avenue and drifted back to the side street where he was parked, the noise dampened by the leafy trees.

The windows of Grace's apartment were dark. Before leaving, he had asked how she thought Sarah was doing, and from the small nod that greeted the question he understood this was the first thing he should have said.

"She seems good. Her teacher says she's doing great. I don't know, though. I worry that she'll be affected by seeing me like this. I feel like I should talk to her about it, but everybody says I should just let it go."

"Is that what you're going to do? Let it go?"

Grace met his eyes. "No," she said.

In the lamplight her face was burnished and sallow. She looked both hopeful and sad, so much like she had when they were younger, and he drew closer to her, drawn by memory or habit or some instinct that would never die in him as long they both lived.

She put her hand on his arm. "It isn't going to be like that," she said firmly.

He nodded, and kissed her cheek like a brother or a friend, then arranged a blanket over her on the couch and left.

⌖

He woke up the next morning feeling better, if not about himself then about the world. Lying in bed, the phrase *old flame* came to him, and he considered how little it described the truth of the situation. Between him and Grace there was nothing burning, which his gesture last night had only confirmed. But there was something else, solid and enduring, that was more like *old furniture*, with the steady reassurance of lasting objects.

Since returning to Montreal he had sprung out of bed most mornings and gone for an hour-long run, hoping to purge his body of unwanted and disturbing thoughts. It was both discipline and penitence. But today he stayed in the apartment, drinking tea and reading the newspaper.

"Are you having a slow burn?" his mother used to say, trying for the second or third time to wake him up for school. As a special treat, every few weekends they'd have a slow-burn morning as a family, and she would let Malcolm and Mitch hang around the kitchen while she made pancakes and bacon.

His mother was an ample, competent woman who had raised them on her own. She worked as a secretary at CN Rail, and every morning after they left for school she'd take a bus downtown. Mitch could still remember the perfume she wore, and the hideous orange lipstick she seemed to consider a professional necessity. She had left school at sixteen to work in her family's restaurant, but never expressed any sadness at having missed out. Nor did she complain about coming home after a full day's work to cook dinner, do the laundry, help with homework. "You're my good boys," she'd say, tucking them into bed.

And they were. They both did well in school, and in this she said they took after their father. Mitch was five when he died. Malcolm, who was two years older, claimed to have memories of him, and at night after the lights were out, Mitch would sometimes beg to hear them; but these stories shifted and changed so much, often borrowing from whatever TV show or comic book Malcolm was into at the time, that Mitch was doubtful even as he hoped to believe them. What they knew of him was this: he'd been born in 1921, in Winnipeg, and served in the Canadian infantry during World War II. He'd become an engineer, also working at CN, met Rosemary in the family restaurant where she'd been waitressing, and whisked her off to Montreal and marriage. He was smart as a whip (another of their mother's favorite sayings); and he died, much too young, of a heart attack, which was why they should listen to her and never, ever start smoking.

All this Mitch accepted as gospel throughout his childhood and adolescence, as Malcolm, too, became an engineer and moved to Toronto. Not finding himself inclined to engineering, Mitch took a degree in psychology. But at Christmas one year, when he told his mother his plans to pursue this in graduate school, she burst into tears.

They were sitting at their tiny kitchen table, and he stared at her, dumbfounded. He wasn't used to disappointing her, and had expected she'd be pleased; she was always proud of his success in school. "It's almost like a doctor," he said, pathetically.

Rosemary was shaking her head. "This is because of your father, isn't it?"

Mitch had no idea what she was talking about, and by now he rarely even thought about his father.

Tears poured down his mother's face. "I knew it," she said. "I kept watching you, knowing it would come out. And here it is."

He stood up and put his arm around her. "This is just what I'm interested in," he told her. "What I care about."

She took his arm and guided him back into his chair, then held his hands and looked into his eyes. "This fascination you have with people's minds, all your curiosity. It's because you want to understand what made him do a thing like that. But you aren't like him. You know that, don't you? And some things can't ever be understood."

In that moment he felt something tilt inside him, as if a picture that had been hung upside down was suddenly righted, and he saw clearly what it showed.

Heart attack was what they told the neighbors, because Rosemary didn't want their pity, didn't want stories to surround her boys. Protecting them was always her first and overriding instinct. But the truth now came back to him with the shock of recognition: his father in the basement, on a sleeping bag, with an empty bottle of pills on the floor next to an empty bottle. He remembered a rancid stench that was mixed with the odor of bleach, because his mother had cleaned everything up before calling the doctor and asking him what to do.

Rosemary dried her tears, carefully and quickly; she never indulged herself in anything, even crying. "He was a sweet man, really," she said. "But he had such a darkness in him. His parents told me he was never the same after he came back from fighting. It weighed on him, the things he saw in France."

Mitch squeezed her hands.

"I always hated that he left us," she said. "I knew I wasn't enough for you boys."

"That's not true," he said. He would have liked to say, You've given me everything I need. He would have liked to say, Feel how much you are loved. Instead he sat with her, and let her talk about his father.

His mother wasn't sure about Grace at first. She was so young, so excited about psychology. She had no idea how to cook and no immediate plans for a family.

"That's just fine," Mitch's mother said. "You take your time."

But it was clear she was reserving judgment. Partly this had to do with psychology, which she had always distrusted; she didn't truly believe anything could be achieved by all this *talking*. Compared to Malcolm's work—he consulted on bridges and roads, projects their mother would have liked to put plaques on—Mitch's was invisible, intangible, and, quite possibly, nonsensical. Usually, when he came home to visit, he'd give her the briefest possible update and then change the subject to the news or the weather.

Snow was the great equalizer of their family. They all hated it, the three of them having shared the task of shoveling for years. They could talk about it for hours—when it would start, how much was coming, when it would end. Nothing bonded them so completely as snow.

But Grace. The first time she heard them ranting about snow, she said, "You just have to get out in it!"

Rosemary smiled at her and lit a cigarette; for all she had warned the children against smoking, she herself was never able to quit. "Now why would I want to do that, dear?"

"You have to embrace the snow. Have fun with it. Go skiing, build a snowman, throw snowballs. That's what you should do," Grace told her, her eyes shining. "I promise you, it'll change your life."

"Ah, well," Rosemary said. "I suppose I like my life the way it is."

In the brief pause that followed, Grace's cheeks turned red and she looked down at the table until Malcolm's wife, Cindy, who was good-hearted, changed the subject by telling Rosemary that she was going to start selling Avon.

"We have such pretty lipsticks. I'll bring you some."

Rosemary's orange lipstick was a running joke among Cindy, Malcolm, and Mitch.

"Well, that would be nice, dear," Rosemary said. "I'm having such a hard time finding my shade. I believe that they've stopped making it. Last time I went to Cumberland's, the girl there said they hadn't seen it for months."

So the conversation moved on, and Grace recovered. She always did, and never gave up. Her persistence, in the end, was what won Mitch's mother over—that, and the first Christmas they all spent together. Grace had been quiet for most of the day, and Mitch could tell she was nervous. She was stepping back, listening, trying to figure out how to slip into this already-formed family without disturbing its contours. They opened presents together on Christmas morning, after a breakfast of pancakes. When Rosemary opened her gift from Grace, she was silent for a long time. Mitch braced himself, wondering what was wrong. Then he saw, to his horror, that she was crying, his mother who hardly ever cried.

He stared at Grace, who didn't notice his concern. She was looking at Rosemary, waiting.

It was a box of orange lipsticks. She must have gone to every drug store in Montreal, buying up their entire supply of Rosemary's favorite shade. There was enough ugly lipstick in that box to last a lifetime.

His mother said, 'This might be the nicest thing I've ever seen."

―∞―

As she got older, Rosemary grew freer with her tears. She cried at Mitch and Grace's wedding; she cried when her grandchildren were born; and she cried, well and truly sobbed, when Mitch had to tell her that he and Grace were getting divorced.

"Now you'll never have a family," she managed to say.

For a fleeting instant, and for the first time in his life, he hated her. How could she say something so awful to someone who already felt like a failure? And what was she talking about? He was still young, and maybe he'd remarry; if he wanted a family, he could still have one.

But she was right, of course. He never did.

Five years after his divorce, Rosemary was diagnosed with stomach cancer.

"I always thought it would be my lungs," she said with typical dryness. "Now I'm glad I never gave up smoking."

It was winter, and Mitch had driven her to the hospital. They were sitting now in his parked car, and he breathed in her familiar smell of cigarettes and Jean Naté perfume.

"I don't know about that," he said.

They had been given a timeline, and it was short. Malcolm was flying in from Mississauga. Cindy and the kids would come later, by car, for one last visit. They had discussed all this calmly in the lounge over coffee, his mother orchestrating the next few months, knowing exactly what had to be done. Her knack for organization was outrageous. She should, he thought, be put in charge of the world.

At the time Mitch had a girlfriend named Mira, a nurse he'd met at work. Short and jolly, she cooked delicious Indian meals she had learned from her mother, and supported him through Rosemary's entire illness. She came along to the hospital whenever he wanted her to and stayed home when he didn't. She met Malcolm and Cindy but didn't try to ingratiate herself with them. At night, when he cried, she held him.

Within weeks it was close to the end. Malcolm had taken a leave from work and was staying in their mother's house, and Mitch often spent the night there too, the two of them staying up late drinking whiskey, sitting there silently with nothing much to say but unable to leave the comfort of each other's company. On one of the last nights, Malcolm asked him about Mira.

"I'm not sure," Mitch said. "She's been great about all this, that's for sure."

"It would make Mom happy," Malcolm said. "She always worries about you being alone so much."

Mitch remembered. *Now you'll never have a family.* And he began to think about a time in the future when maybe he could begin to pay Mira back, offer her some of the same comfort she'd given him throughout this ordeal.

The following afternoon, he brought Mira to the hospital. She hadn't seen his mother in a couple of weeks, and by now Rosemary was breathing heavily, her thin cheeks laboring, her eyes fluttering. But she looked up at Mira and smiled.

"Oh, Gracie," she said. "I knew you'd be back."

Mira patted her hand, unfazed. A nurse, she of course didn't need his explanation about how the drugs were shuttling his mother back and forth through time, how sometimes she thought he was five years old and asked him what he'd like for breakfast. But something changed between them in that moment, and after his mother died they stopped spending every night together, gradually disentangling, and finally Mira met someone else and moved to Ottawa.

Long after his mother's death, he thought about her remark. It was one of many moments in which he realized, not with shock but nonetheless with horror, how much his private pain, the decision to divorce, had stubbornly refused to remain confined to his own life. It made him feel more guilty than ever.

But gradually he began to change his mind about what she'd said. Rosemary had been capable, doting, self-sacrificing, but also bossy and desirous of control. She had made up her mind to love Grace, and the divorce made her angry because she had to undo that relationship, and not of her own choosing. She didn't let go of things easily. Or people. He remembered something she'd said about his father when they finally discussed the suicide. "He wouldn't let me in," she said, "and I refused to stay out."

Even in her last days, as her body withered and her confusion grew, she didn't fabricate events that hadn't happened or see people who weren't there. Calling Mira by Grace's name was the only time she got something like that wrong. Maybe it was intentional, a way of reminding him of what she'd said after the divorce, less a moment of sorrow than a curse. *You will never have a family.*

He understood, finally, that he would never know how to interpret her remark, because the only person he could have asked to clear it up was gone.

He missed her still, not all the time but with occasional pangs of clarity so intense they made him dizzy. He felt that now. He would have liked to tell her he'd seen Grace again, that he was trying to help her. He would have liked to present this to his mother not as a trophy or a prize but as a scar, something tough but healed, ridged with the passage of time. Because if anyone understood what it meant to lose and go on, it was her.

Or maybe it was as simple as this. He would have liked to hear that voice from his childhood, from his slow-burn mornings, the voice of orange lipstick and Craven A cigarettes, speak again; to hear her say, "Oh, Gracie. I knew you'd be back."

SEVEN

Montreal, 1996

GRACE WASN'T USED TO having a patient's parents threaten her, and she couldn't stop thinking about what Annie Hardwick's father had said. *You shouldn't be allowed to muck around in people's lives.* She hadn't been mucking around; she had only listened to the girl and offered her the best advice she could—which, after all, was the service these people were paying her for. She carried on this argument with Mr. Hardwick inside her head, because he wasn't there to listen. He did leave a brief message on her office voice mail at ten o'clock one evening, sounding like he'd been drinking. "You'll be hearing from our lawyer," he'd said.

But she hadn't heard anything at all, from any lawyer or even from Annie, who had missed three appointments in a row.

Meanwhile, things with Tug were getting serious. The distant, reserved man she'd first met was changing under her gaze. He smiled often, and there was one particular laugh that came out only when the two of them were alone; it made her laugh too, in a burst of happiness all the more intense for being private, a language they had invented and spoke only together.

On her birthday, he took her to a dark, noisy Greek restaurant in the north end, where they sat cramped in a back corner and drank harsh red wine and ate grilled octopus and lamb. His cheeks flushed, Tug told her a long story about a childhood friend of his who'd been a jumper—off tree branches, then train trestles and buildings—and never got injured, no matter the height. "It was impossible," Tug said, shaking his head, "but he always survived."

"Crazy," Grace said, smiling.

His hand was on hers across the table. He had also survived.

Every once in a while she tried to get him to talk about that day on the mountain, and he wasn't evasive so much as shallow. He'd say, "I was unhappy, Grace," and leave it at that. She'd ask a few more questions, trying to edge deeper, and he met each of them with a one-sentence answer.

The longer he refused to discuss it, the more she wondered about it, picking at the mysterious scab. Of course she wanted to know just what, exactly, had brought him to such a dark place. He was relatively forthcoming about his divorce. His ex-wife was living in Hudson with her parents. They had been together four years, but were very different people, and though it was sad, it was no huge surprise that things hadn't worked out. It didn't sound like a lie, only a flat, simple version of the truth. As for his professional life, he talked about working in Switzerland for UNESCO, which he made sound boring and bureaucratic. He had had enough of it. He wouldn't work in the stationery store forever, of course; he was just taking a little time off to decide what came next.

He had similarly specific yet terse answers for her questions about his financial situation, his time in treatment, his relationship with his family. Trying to find out more, she felt like she was hammering endlessly on the same reluctant nail.

Tug, however, had few questions for her. She suspected this wasn't because he didn't care, but because he knew it would make their conversations lopsided. If he didn't ask very many, then she would seem like an inquisitor. It worked; she stopped asking.

But the questions didn't disappear; they just lodged deeper in her consciousness. She knew, in fact, only the broadest outlines of his life: where he'd gone to school, that he'd married and worked abroad. His inner life was hidden behind a curtain, on a secret stage. The gap between what he said and what she didn't know swelled between them like a bubble that kept expanding; sometimes, when she reached out her arms to hold him, the bubble felt like all she could touch.

On a Thursday afternoon, during what had been Annie Hardwick's reserved slot, Grace was catching up on some paperwork. She hadn't yet granted this appointed time to someone else, but the next week she would. This was one of the papers she was looking at—the schedule. Then, to her surprise, there was a knock on the door, and Annie stepped inside.

"Hi," she said, and smiled.

She looked prettier, less coltish, and her braces had been removed. She took off her winter coat and threw it on the couch, revealing a low-cut sweater and jeans instead of her usual school uniform. Her posture was straight and confident, and clearly she had no plans to apologize for getting Grace in trouble with her parents.

"How are you?" Grace said.

"I'm *terrible*," she declared, then sat down with a flounce of blond hair. "I'm sure you've heard about *the catastrophe*. I've been grounded for weeks. No Ollie, no friends, no mall. My mom found my journal and just *flipped*. And the whole pregnancy thing? My God."

"And how are you feeling about the whole pregnancy thing?"

"I'm feeling glad," Annie said emphatically, "that it's over."

"Okay." Grace felt like she was dealing with an entirely new creature, one who'd molted her previous adolescent skin and had become a shinier, wilder animal.

They talked for a few minutes—about schoolwork, friends, the braces coming off—before circling back to her parents and the turbulence of the past few weeks.

"So I told my teacher, Ms. Van den Berg, that I had the flu. And then I felt, like, ashamed, because lying was so easy. That's what I never realized before, that you don't lie, because you don't think you can get away with it. But you're really the only person who knows the difference."

"That's true, I suppose," Grace said slowly. "Does this mean you're not going to lie to your parents anymore?"

Annie laughed. "My parents," she said, then sighed, shaking her head a little, as if they were her errant children and not the other way around. Something in her face softened then, and her expression grew sincere and sad. She folded her hands in her lap almost piously. "My father has a girlfriend who lives in Saint-Lambert," she said, her voice quiet, resigned, its timbre altogether different from the bright prattle of the past minutes. "We know all about her. She used to be his secretary but now she just hangs out and he supports her. My parents were arguing about her the other night. They still think I fall asleep early, but at midnight I was just lying there listening. It sounds like she's pregnant and having his baby. Wouldn't that have been, like, *hilarious*, if she and I had had babies at the same time? What would that relationship even be?"

"I don't know," Grace said.

"Maybe I'd be my own aunt or something. And my mom's threatening to have her own affair, as revenge. She'll never leave my dad, we all know that. She's too weak. I don't think she'll even have an affair. She'll just get new prescriptions instead."

She looked down at her hands as if in prayer. She was crying, a quick slipstream of tears that fell silently down her cheeks.

"It's not your fault," Grace said gently. "You can't control any of it."

"He used to—" she said, then stopped.

Grace waited.

"He used to come lie down with me at night and say I was his special girl. He doesn't do it anymore." Now she was crying harder, her shoulders shaking, snot cresting at her nose.

Grace gave her a tissue. "Tell me more about that."

"No," Annie said. "No." When she lifted her face and wiped her eyes, she looked calmer and harder, and her facade reassembled itself like a sliding door closing across her features. The fact that there were cracks in her self-presentation, that she evidently had to work so hard to construct a mask of indifference, made her success at it that much more pitiable to Grace. She was practicing the skill of keeping others at a distance, and the older she got the more proficient she would likely become, at a cost borne mainly by herself.

"Annie," Grace said firmly, "you're sixteen. Soon you'll be an adult."

"Meaning what?" the girl demanded.

"You can be anything you want to be," Grace said. "You don't have to be like them."

To her surprise, Annie smiled. She wiped her cheeks clean, smearing snot and makeup on the sleeve of her sweater. She seemed more immediately comforted by this thought than Grace had expected. "You know what, you're right," she said, suddenly standing up. "You're totally and completely right."

Grace's stomach turned over. When a patient agreed so quickly, it was rarely a good sign. "Let's talk about what this would mean for you, specifically," she said.

"No, I think I'm good," Annie said. Still smiling, she picked up her coat, and indeed she was radiant, her cheeks flushed and her eyes bright. At the door she turned around and said, "Thank you, Grace. You've been a huge help."

It was the first time she had ever expressed anything like gratitude. Then she was gone. Grace sat with her head in her hands. Something had just gone badly wrong, but she wasn't sure exactly what. The session had slipped through her fingers. She had let the girl go, and now, she felt sure, she'd never get her back.

That night Tug came over, and after she cooked dinner, they ate in silence. Grace couldn't stop replaying her session with Annie, wondering how truthful her remarks about her father were, what had made her smile so brightly at the end, what Grace could have said or done differently. It had been like she was talking to a brand-new patient, someone she'd never even met before.

If Tug noticed her distraction, he didn't show it. After they finished dinner, he washed the dishes while she read a magazine in the living room. It was only when he came in half an hour later and asked what was wrong that she realized she was crying.

She put the magazine down. "I can't do this," she said.

"What?"

He stood there, his face impassive, and she knew that he held himself apart from her just as the girl had. She couldn't live with this in two places, at work and at home. It was too much. "I need to know," she told him.

Tug made an exasperated sound, shrugged his shoulders, and glanced away. "It won't change anything," he said, still standing above her, refusing to sit down.

Still crying, she swallowed and said, as calmly as possible, "I disagree."

"I'm not your patient, Grace," he said, and his voice was rough. "You can't fix me. I know this is all some big savior thing for you, but that's not quite how I see it."

Grace's tears were falling freely now. She stood up and faced him, each of them hovering there, poised to leave the room, trembling a little. Whatever delicate balance they'd established between them was breaking down, careening away.

"I have no idea how you see it," she said, "and until you can tell me, I don't want to see you anymore."

"Oh, Gracie," he said. "We've been having a good time."

He put his arms around her and she closed her eyes, allowing herself to feel the warmth of his body, the scratch of his stubble against her cheek. Then she stepped away. "You should go," she said.

She lay in bed waiting for him to call, or come back, but he had left without a word of dissent. Her thoughts drifted restlessly to Annie, who seemed to have been freed in some way that Grace had never intended. What had she said to give the girl that smile, so radiant and strange? After a while she started thinking about Tug and the dinner they'd had at the Greek restaurant. What she remembered was his story about the childhood friend who leapt off buildings, the tree climber, the trestle jumper. At the time she'd interpreted it as a story about someone you could only shake your head at, so incomprehensible were his choices. Now she realized that the story meant something different to Tug. To him it was a marvel. A wonder.

Even though he came back at five in the morning, apologized, crawled into bed, and promised to tell her everything, she understood that he wasn't scornful of his friend, just envious of how little he cared about survival. If he had been able to join his friend, she thought, he would have. He wanted to be the one to jump into the air without worrying whether he'd land dead or alive.

The next night, after she got home from work, he poured them each a large glass of wine and started talking. He talked until midnight, hardly stopping except to refill their glasses and open new bottles. He seemed to require the wine to keep going; other than that, he needed no encouragement from Grace, no murmurs of attention. She sat there, and listened.

EIGHT

Kigali, 1994

WHEN TUG FIRST set eyes on the country, he thought it was the most beautiful place he'd ever seen. And he wasn't someone who had dreamt of Africa in childhood and pictured himself exploring it in a safari jacket and jungle gear—though plenty of the North Americans and Europeans around him harbored precisely such fantasies. Some, to conceal their infatuation, spoke of Africa in carefully jaded tones. Others talked openly about their fascination with its rich, complicated history and their long-held desire to experience it in person (for men, this usually meant its women). Aid workers were romantics who pretended not to be, their personalities swinging like pendulums between idealism and pragmatism.

Months later, a woman working for the Red Cross asked him to spend the night, both of them sweating, drunk, and sloppy with loneliness. At three in the morning, her thigh sticking to his, she confided that as a child she'd been obsessed with Dian Fossey.

"I wanted to see the gorillas in the mist," she said wryly. "I saw them the first week. Now I've been here two years." A stocky, muscular former field hockey player, she turned surprisingly clingy and weepy in the night; she said she realized she had never cared about anything as much as she had about those gorillas. Tug felt, perhaps unfairly, that this was just something she said after sex, a bit of extra drama to keep the attention coming. Although he actually would have liked to hear more about the gorillas and what seeing them was like, he didn't want to indulge her. No doubt sensing his skepticism, the gorilla woman—as he always thought of her afterward—ignored him in the morning, pretending nothing had happened between them.

To Tug, Rwanda was a surprise. He'd last been stationed in Guatemala, where he spent six months ferrying food and medicine to families in the department of Suchitepéquez after floods and landslides devastated the towns there. He had grown used to the country, liked the people, and his Spanish was pretty damn good. He hadn't necessarily wanted to leave, but his father was seriously ill and he needed to get back home. He stayed for two years while his father went in and out of hospitals. His mother was frail and his sister, who lived in Toronto with her two children and a salesman husband who spent half his life out of town, had made it clear that she couldn't or wouldn't take care of their parents on her own.

This was when he met Marcie, who worked as a paralegal for his parents' lawyer. She was blond, attractive, and extraordinarily capable in what he considered domestic matters. Tug knew how to rig tents and set up a basic medical facility, where in a given terrain the latrines should be dug, and that when you hand out rice you give it to the women first, never to men and especially never to young men. Around children with their hands outstretched he crackled with energy, thriving on their need. He could go weeks without sleeping more than three or four hours a night. At home in Canada, by contrast, he froze up. Faced with insurance companies, with the routine upkeep of his parents' house, with his mother's small talk about the neighbors, he barely had enough energy to get through the day.

But Marcie, thank God, was good at all of that. She didn't mind paperwork, didn't freak out when put on hold, listened to his mother solicitously. She wasn't a traveler; she came from a large, close-knit family and hated to leave home. They spent every weekend together, and either she cooked or they had dinner with her parents in their sprawling farmhouse in Hudson. She always brought a casserole or cookies to his mother, who protested weakly, insincerely, and loved being fussed over. In almost no time at all, his family and hers were entwined; her parents often visited his father in the hospital, and they all spent Christmas together. After a year, he proposed to Marcie while they were on vacation in Florida, and they were married two months later in a small ceremony in Hudson. As he slipped the ring on her finger, she cried a little, tears crinkling her cheeks, and he thought, This is it. This is the shape my life will have.

When his father's condition improved—at least, as much as a seventy-year-old man's can—he contacted the NGO for a new posting. Marcie wasn't thrilled with the separation but understood that he was itching to get back in the field. She admired his drive to help other people, and he basked in that, never wanting to admit that the exigency of it was like a drug, or how much adrenaline was involved. This was the first gap between them, and he told himself it wouldn't matter, years on, when he was through with international aid and they were living a settled life together somewhere.

Rwanda was where they sent him. He was assigned the same tasks—assistance, medicine, infrastructure—but for different reasons, not natural disaster but civil conflicts that put the displaced in camps and the country on edge.

He knew little about the country, but when he looked out the plane window, he felt that he had seen it before, in films or on television or maybe—this was hokey, but also his actual thought—in dreams. The landscape was hilly, green, wreathed in clouds, incomparably beautiful, somehow both severe and lush. It looked otherworldly, somewhere you'd go after exhausting your time in the earth's ordinary places. His heart lifted as it always did when he saw somewhere new: there was so much to see and do, and he felt the old energy returning, the sense of clear-eyed purpose that would help sculpt his days.

I wish Marcie could see this, he thought, and took a blurry photograph.

He had a room in a ramshackle, single-story housing complex along with some Belgian and Swiss workers. In the evenings they drank beer together in a hotel bar surrounded by other foreigners, mostly journalists, nurses, and UNAMIR personnel. In December of 1993, there was either nervous tension in the air or else everybody knew what was coming, he couldn't say which. He had only just arrived, and as far as he knew maybe every day in Rwanda was like this. He had no perspective on the situation, and the others at the bar were of little help. Their attitude was that you should figure things out for yourself rather than be instructed; everybody considered this hard-won knowledge a mark of toughness. Laughing at the newcomers and their mistakes was a tradition that built morale among the ones who had been there longer.

At first the days were long, hot, and pleasantly full. The coordination of supplies in the camps was an endless task, and the supplies were inadequate to the enormity of the need. Reddish mud from the dirt roads coated his boots and clothes, and the boxes themselves, then dried to dust that ended up in his mouth and nose and ears. He worked under a bilingual Quebecois named Philippe who gave quick, clear orders in English and French. Tug set up dispensation stations for medicine and water and walked the camp, checking on conditions. He saw what appeared to be a dying woman, her sunken cheeks spotted with flies, and next to her a boy was nestled calmly against her bony knee. He checked her pulse—she was gone—and then asked around, but couldn't find any relatives to claim the child.

Philippe told him that a group of nuns running an orphanage would take him, and added, "AIDS, most likely. Won't be long." He meant before the boy died. Tug took him over to the nuns, and he went along placidly. Probably he didn't have enough calories in his system to make a fuss.

The housing complex was supervised by a resident manager, Etienne, and his wife, son, and daughter. In the late afternoon, when Tug returned home, the son would be kicking around a soccer ball made of banana-tree leaves with his friends in the courtyard, while his sister watched. Etienne was friendly and genial, and the collared shirts and brown pants he wore every day looked elegant on his tall, thin frame. His brother-in-law had studied at the University of Laval, he said, and told many stories of his life there. At one time Etienne and his wife had wanted to visit him in Quebec, perhaps studying there themselves.

"But," he said, his voice trailing off, his delicate fingers making a vague wave, signaling, Tug supposed, a vast array of circumstance, economics, the pull and problems of home. "I am here instead," he finished, and offered Tug a beer. Often they would spend an hour together like this, drinking beer in the late afternoons as the boys played around them. He asked Tug about Marcie, his family, and his education. And he explained that his wife's family were Hutus, and that his own relatives had left Kigali and gone to the south.

"We stay here," he said firmly, gesturing at the complex, where he swept the courtyard and greeted the residents regally, as if it were his kingdom.

He had heard from his brother-in-law about hockey, and especially about the Montreal Canadiens. He asked Tug about the Stanley Cup and his favorite players, and this—of all their discussions—captured his son's attention. Yozefu was eleven years old and found this new sport intriguing. He demanded to know the rules and the names of the teams, how the game was played and for how long, and Tug was soon explaining the minutiae of penalty shots, sudden-death overtime, and off-sides. The boy and his friends clamored for more information. Tug, laughing, used a long, sturdy branch to maneuver their soccer ball around the courtyard, showing them the basics of stick handling.

Yozefu caught on quickly, moving the ball from side to side, imitating Tug's lunging motions and kicks. Tug taught him to say, "He shoots, he scores!" and the boy ran around repeating this over and over, laughing like it was the funniest thing he'd ever heard.

In the doorway of the family's apartment his sister stood in the shadows, staring fiercely, a half smile curtaining the whiteness of her teeth.

Then the boy stopped and asked Tug why the shoes with blades in them didn't get stuck. Machete shoes, he called them, because that was the only kind of blade he could picture. And Tug started to answer, before realizing just how impossible it would be to explain. There was no way that Yozefu could understand the idea of a game played on ice, that he could imagine a rink or any part of winter at all.

So he just said the ground in Canada was different. The boy shrugged, and he and his friends played stickball for a while longer until they reverted back to soccer, sometimes shouting "He shoots, he scores!" for no reason, whenever they felt like it.

In Kigali, despite the tension in the air, Tug was happy at first. In times of trouble you put your head down. You set your own worries aside. When people are talking of war and famine, of an army massing to the north, of civilians arming themselves with machetes, of children dying in camps, your only choice is to get through each day. People need help, so you give out water and rice, bring sick children to the hospital, and talk to their parents. Every single day is triage, a blur of urgent activity, a sprint. You don't worry about your mortgage or the last time you went to the dentist. You don't have time to think about any of that, and it feels like freedom.

He and Etienne listened to the radio in the courtyard, under the shade of a banana tree. Radio was everything here, and new songs were playing that had shocking lyrics, rippling with hate. In the evening, at the hotel bar, he discussed the songs with his Swiss counterparts, who shrugged them off, telling him he didn't understand the history here. Tug agreed that he didn't; he didn't understand why the Belgians were here in such small numbers when the war was a result of systems they'd instituted. He didn't understand why the Canadians had sent sufficient forces to seem involved but not enough to actually do anything.

But the big picture wasn't his area of expertise, and never had been. He was good at logistics, at surveying the topography and figuring out where to put the food tents and the field hospitals. He had always been like this, ever since Boy Scouts, taking refuge in practical problems. These were the universals, and beyond them were moral issues and cultural complexities that you could spend a lifetime trying to decipher without getting anywhere at all.

His fellow aid workers called him the Silent Canadian. Except on the subject of hockey, he would rarely be drawn out much. He didn't mean to be evasive; he just wasn't a talker by nature. As a child, he and his father would sit together in the garage working on a Meccano kit or a woodworking project; his mother and sister would be in the kitchen cooking or cleaning, chatting all the while. What his father liked most was to get away from that—he called it the hen party. "Silence is golden," he told his son, and the worst thing was to talk a lot without having anything to say. He had impressed upon Tug the integrity of saying only what you mean, and the emptiness of words without action backing them up.

At Christmas there was a party at the hotel. Though no one wanted to admit it, this was the hardest season for people far from home: the weather, the food, the company, it all felt wrong. On their way to church, Etienne and his family stopped by to wish him a merry Christmas. They were all dressed in their finest, and Etienne's wife and daughter were more beautiful than Tug had ever realized, their skin glowing against matching pale yellow dresses. Esmeralda, the girl, shyly stepped forward and handed him a doily she'd stitched. It reminded him of his mother, who also stitched and embroidered; when he told the family about this, they all nodded, evidently not surprised. It only made sense that women were the same everywhere.

Marcie had sent him a care package of thoughtful gifts. Foot powder, medicated lotion, propylene socks. And, of course, fruitcake. On a dim, crackling line he called her at her parents' house, and in the background heard Christmas carols, cocktail chatter, her nephews yelling.

"I miss you," Marcie said. "I wish you were here."

"Me too," Tug said. It was true when he said it, but by the time he got off the phone and went home to bed, it wasn't. He longed for certain things: a hot shower, Marcie's body, a hamburger. But longing was part of life here, and it made him happy to feel his lack of these things, as sharp as hunger. He was addicted to want. He didn't know how this had happened, whether it was because of his childhood or some quirk of his personality or genes, but somehow he had become a person who needed to do without in order to appreciate what he had.

———<>———

Between Christmas and Easter the situation worsened. Battles were raging to the west of Kigali; there was talk of full-blown civil war. On the streets of the city he saw gangs of teenage boys dressed in clownish outfits—the Interahamwe. They looked like garden-variety delinquents, driven to vandalism by boredom, but in their eyes was a frightening flatness. They didn't react to his presence and seemed, in fact, not to see him at all.

Etienne shook his head. "It's going to be bad," he said.

"Why don't you leave?" Tug asked.

Etienne again made that sweeping gesture with his hand, encompassing the complex, his family, their extended relatives, maybe even the country itself. Tug couldn't tell if this was obstinacy or pride. "This is where we are," he said.

Meanwhile, Marcie wanted to know how much longer he would be there. He thought he'd be back by August, he told her. "August," she echoed, her voice tinny with distance, but in it he could hear all the unsaid, freighted things. Soon, he knew, she wanted to start having children. Their life was waiting for them just over the horizon, and she was in a hurry to get there. To think of her putting her dreams on hold was a weight on his heart.

It was not awkward, apparently, for him to tell Grace about this. He spoke as if these words, these emotions, belonged to another person.

"Certain facts are known," he said. They had been reported, brought to light, so he didn't need to relate them all over again, did he? The story had already been told. How the gunshots and mortar blasts increased as the army moved closer, how the Interahamwe responded, how the radio blared. Everybody knows this happened. Even in the camps people weren't safe, and now they had to worry about bombings on top of starvation and disease. Those who could leave did, and there was an epochal movement to the south.

Tug stopped sleeping. The nights were bright with smoke. Then the president was killed, and the murders began in earnest. Children with hatchets. Blood in the streets. Relating this, his voice grew not hoarse with emotion but clipped, the words whittled to precise points. "There was a river," he said. "You must have seen the pictures.

It was piled with bodies. There were always screams in the distance, and sometimes they were close. There were dead children, and live children looking for their dead mothers."

Within hours most of the white people were evacuated. That's what happened: they left the country to its murders. He found himself in a hotel room in Nairobi, sitting cross-legged in the bathtub, and couldn't remember how he had gotten there or how long he was supposed to stay.

In Nairobi people spoke of phone calls in which their friends said good-bye just before they were murdered. Some were calm and resigned; others screamed for help until the very last second of their lives. All of this via telephone. Technology existed to hear murders, but not to stop them.

Tug shared a hotel room with two other aid workers, and they were cramped but had clean sheets and towels. They couldn't stand this, or one another, and lacking an outlet for their rage they fought among themselves instead. Tug went down to the bar, and this was when he found the gorilla woman, and spent the night with her, listening without sympathy to the story of her life. Later, one of his roommates spent the night with her too, and said she had brought out a knife, wanting him to hold it to her throat. "She loves danger," the guy said, raising his eyebrows in sexual implication.

Some people went to Goma to work in the refugee camps. That these refugees were murderers was discussed as little as possible; such were the ethics of aid. Then, when a cholera epidemic spread through the camps, the world finally began to pay attention. When the murderers died.

Tug and his roommates were sent to Entebbe to coordinate a field office. Grateful for work, they bent themselves to the task.

And Marcie, so relieved that he'd been evacuated, begged for him to come home.

"Who are these people?" she said angrily, meaning not the murderers but his supervisors at the NGO. "How can they expect you to do this, to stay on, just to fulfill your contract? This is sadistic. They need to let you come home." She was crying into the phone.

Tug said nothing. Truthfully she didn't feel real to him just then—just a voice on the phone, a crackle of sobs.

"I love you," she said. "Come home to me."

He stayed as long as he could in Entebbe, and four months later they were allowed back in. Of the spectacular green country he'd first seen, virtually no trace was left. What remained was a place that no one could fall in love with. Every farm had been left untended or destroyed. Kigali stank of rotten bodies, a riot of flies everywhere, and packs of dogs grown so aggressive and fat on human flesh that people were shooting them on sight. Here and there the first exiles were streaming into empty houses, and to see them sweeping the floors was surreal, an act of domestic normalcy patently inadequate to the task of cleaning up what had happened here.

At the complex, everything he'd left behind had been taken, not that there was much besides a few clothes and magazines. There were bullet holes in the wall.

Inside Etienne's apartment there was no trace of anyone, just a bad smell he couldn't locate the source of. He stood there sweating, thinking only that he would soon go back to work doling out medicine, salt and sugar solution, water-purification tablets. Then he heard a shuffling noise and braced himself, expecting one of the huge rats he'd seen poking through the piles of garbage. Instead, a bloody heap he had thought was trash shifted itself and came toward him. He took a backward step, then he heard his name.

It was the boy, Yozefu, and Tug was so happy that he embraced him. The boy tried to hug him back, but couldn't. He smelled terrible, wrapped in torn, dirty blankets, and the light in the room was so dim that it wasn't until they were outside in the sunny courtyard that Tug realized Yozefu had only one arm.

He had seen a doctor, and a family down the road had been feeding him occasional scraps, but his bandages were dirty and his skin red hot to the touch. Tug took him straight to the hospital for antibiotics. He was due at the camps but stayed on as a doctor cleaned the boy's wounds and put him on an IV drip. As the fever came down, Yozefu told him what had happened.

His own uncle, his mother's brother, had come in the night. He said he would hide them in his own house, but this was a lie to get his squad of three into their house. They killed his parents, then raped his sister. Yozefu didn't use that word, just said they had stuck things into her, including a branch, a bottle. When he yelled at them to stop, they said, "Then you kill her." Esmeralda looked at him, crying, begging. So he did. He used the machete they'd given him. Then his uncle took it back, hacked off his arm at the elbow, and left him to die.

He stayed in the house with the bodies of his family until another uncle found him and brought him to the doctor. But they had to move the medical facility because of the bombing and he was on his own again, so he went back to the house. In the time he'd been gone the bodies had been dragged into the courtyard and burned. He cleaned the house and courtyard and hid himself away.

He never once told Tug how he felt, or used a single emotional word. He spoke only of actions and facts.

Tug spent two days and nights at the hospital with Yozefu, but the boy had a septic infection that the doctors couldn't stop. It was three in the morning when he died. He was eleven years old.

And that was it. Tug became a zombie, useless in the field, and his supervisors ordered him first to Nairobi, then to Entebbe, then to London, and finally he landed in Montreal. At the airport, Marcie crushed him in her arms. Once at home, he took a shower and changed into his clean old clothes. It was August and children were playing on the street outside, shouting and laughing. His sister and her children came to see him, as did various friends. At night, in bed, Marcie caressed his shoulder with the tips of her fingers, a touch that didn't ask for anything, that only sought to assure him that he wasn't alone.

He went to therapy, which was what you were supposed to do when something bad happened. Everybody said so. His therapist was a professorial type, bearded, cardigan wearing, with an office full of books. In the first session, Tug told him a little bit about what he'd seen, what brought him here, and they talked about control—what he could have done then, what he could do now. The therapist suggested he keep a journal, or write a book, or a song. He was a big believer in making things.

Tug didn't mention Yozefu, but a couple of sessions later he told him about the bodies in the river, the wailing of babies. He explained how you treat a corpse infected with cholera, stuffing wadding down its throat and into its anus, then disinfecting it with chlorine and wrapping it in plastic, to keep the disease from spreading, whereas in Kigali the bodies had been left to putrefy in the streets, and only eventually got burned. He didn't mean to be graphic or shocking. He was simply trying to make a point about the importance of dealing with the dead. But he found that he was drawn to concrete details, and after talking for forty-five minutes without interruption, he felt marginally better. Emptier. Afterward he went down the hall to the washroom and sat in a stall, not thinking about anything at all. He heard the door open and someone came in; from the professorial shoes, he knew it was the therapist. The man hurried into the stall next to him and threw up in the toilet.

Tug canceled the next appointment, wanting to give the therapist a respite from the terrible details; then he decided to cancel the next one too, and after that it was just easier not to go anymore.

Marcie encouraged him to stay home and relax—no one deserved a vacation more than he did, she said—but it made him feel fidgety, restless. She had holiday time coming up herself and wanted to go somewhere, maybe the beach, but he told her he didn't want to travel. No planes, no highways, no vistas, no sensation of touching down somewhere new. He wanted the opposite of adrenaline, with none of the energy that had so animated his days in the field. He was most comfortable tiring himself out by walking around the city, appreciating the wide-open streets, the uncrowded avenues, the scentless air. Even the most hectic neighborhoods felt blanketed with calm.

The therapist had told him to write down his nightmares when he couldn't sleep. So one day he was in a stationery store, browsing for a notebook, when the clerk and the manager got into an escalating argument about scheduling and overtime. Suddenly the clerk pushed a pen display off the counter, announced she was quitting, and stormed out. The pens scattered everywhere, rattling like pebbles. Tug spent the next ten minutes helping the manager clean up the mess and listening to her complain about her flighty help, and before he knew it he had a job.

He liked working at the paper store. There was always something that needed to be arranged, inventory to be checked, questions to answer, money to handle, all joyfully inessential tasks. If someone didn't like their notebook, they could exchange it. It made him laugh to think that anyone would spend three hundred dollars on a pen. He learned more than he thought there was to know about acid-free paper. Eight hours would pass without his noticing, and by the time he walked home that was almost an entire day that he could live with.

Marcie didn't really understand the stationery-store thing, but she was supportive. That was her nature. She wanted to be there, always offering hugs and solicitude. She tried to pay attention to him when he needed her and not to bother him when he didn't. In other words, she was trying to do the impossible, and therefore she failed.

Upon his return, Tug took up drinking. It seemed like the best way to get through the hours between leaving the store and going to bed; otherwise, there was just too much time. Marcie stopped inviting friends over, for fear he would pass out at the table or throw up in the sink. Once, he took her sister's hand, raised it to his mouth, and licked her fingers, an act for which he later had no explanation. In fact, he could hardly remember it happening. When they talked about the things he did while drinking, it seemed to him that they were discussing someone else entirely; he shared Marcie's concern and disgust, and he shook his head right along with her, wishing that this man, this other Tug, would shape up and get his act together.

As things got worse, he stopped talking to Marcie without noticing that he had. Indeed he rarely thought about her at all, even when she was in the same room. Late one night, he was watching hockey and drinking Canadian Club when she came downstairs to ask him to lower the volume. He didn't ignore her on purpose; he just didn't register her presence until she picked up the remote and turned off the television.

"I need to sleep," she said, her voice trembling. "I have a huge meeting at eight. Can you please just turn it down?"

He kept looking at the television, wondering where the picture had gone. So Marcie positioned herself in front of him, still talking to him, bending over with her face close to his. She was in his line of sight, and he tried to nudge her aside, but he wasn't very gentle and she fell over the coffee table, landing hard on the floor, rubbing her elbow and crying.

"I know you're an asshole right now because of Africa," she said. "But you're also just being an asshole. Don't you get it?"

He did. He knew this darkness inside him wasn't Africa's doing. It had always been there inside his deepest self, and all his time abroad had done was to wear off the veneer, revealing the truth at his core. Or maybe it had given him permission to acknowledge that most of life just didn't matter.

Months passed, more of the same. In the winter he took to walking for hours after he got off work, letting the cold air pinch his nose and ears. He spent as little time as possible at home, hoping this might make things better for Marcie. He was standing in the park one evening watching some boys play hockey, the rink a pool of light in the darkness, their skates clashing and whistling in rhythm, when Yozefu came to him unbidden, unwanted. He saw the boy not as he'd been in the days before his death but as he'd looked when Tug first met him.

He saw him laughing as he kicked the banana-leaf puck around the dusty courtyard, yelling, "He shoots, he scores!"

He started to cry, pulling his hair with both hands. Sobbing, choking on his snot, he curled into a ball next to the rink and tried to huddle there for warmth. Probably he would have spent the night there, but one of the hockey fathers came up to him and said he had to leave, that he was scaring the children.

———✦———

This was the end of one part of his life. Afterward, he was calmer. He stopped drinking so much. He went to work, came home, was well behaved.

But he still wasn't sleeping, and he spent his nights on the couch, hollow-eyed, watching TV with headphones on, so as not to keep Marcie up. They went out to dinner with friends and he would sit quietly at the table, a pleasant smile on his face, rarely saying anything at all. He was like a well-trained dog, patiently attending his master, observing human behavior that had nothing to do with him. Many of these people complimented him on how well he was doing, and he couldn't tell if this was sarcastic, encouraging, or ripe with condescension, like telling a child how good he is at checkers. After a while he understood all they meant was that compared to the alcoholic rages, the quiet calm looked more like normalcy, and perhaps this was enough. So he tried to adopt the contours of a regular life, molding himself to it as if his personality were made of clay.

He got a promotion at the stationery store, to evening supervisor, and his hours changed. By the time he left, the parks were quiet and there were no boys to remind him of Yozefu.

Christmas came, then went.

In January there was an ice storm, and the store lost its electricity. He called the manager, who told him to close up early and go home, so he walked home with the sting of sleet against his face. The city was stippled with light and dark, some buildings still sparkling, others black, a pattern of blankness and power.

When he got home, the lights were off, and Marcie was startled to see him. He explained what happened, and she burst into tears.

"It's just a storm," he said, puzzled. "The electricity will come back on."

She was sitting on the living-room couch, and candles flickered on the coffee table in front of her. There were two glasses of wine there, sedimented with red.

"I'm sorry," she said, now crying hard.

He had no idea what she was talking about. "It's okay," he said.

"No it's not," she said. She was curling into herself, her head down.

"I know I should be more patient, but I just needed somebody. I've been so lonely. I'm so alone."

Tug had trouble focusing his attention on the scene before him, this woman and her tears. With some difficulty he realized she was still talking.

"I guess you want to know who it is," she was saying. "It's Jake. I know, I know, it's terrible, but he and Joanne are having trouble and he and I were just, well, comforting each other, I guess. That old story."

"Who's Jake?" Tug said.

Marcie raised her head, tucked her blond hair behind her ears, and drew a deep breath. When she spoke, her tone was acidic. "Jake and Joanne Herschfeld," she said, very slowly, "are our friends. We had dinner with them last weekend."

"Oh," he said. "Right."

"You're not even here," she said. Then the anger passed and she started sobbing again. "I'm sorry, I'm sorry," she said. "I'm messing them up, I'm messing us up. I should be supporting you. I'm evil, I'm terrible, I'm the worst."

Feeling sorry for her, he put his hand on her knee. (She told him later that it was the first time he had touched her in months.) He wanted to say something to make her feel better. He looked down at his fingers and thought of a child running through the streets carrying his own severed hand in the one he still had.

"This," he said, looking at her. "This is nothing."

By the time the power came back on she was living with her parents. Over the next week she emptied the apartment of her possessions, and was gone.

Should he have felt sad? Probably; but he didn't. He was enormously relieved. And best of all, he was freed from the obligation to think about the future, in which he no longer had any interest. He was released.

Of that day on the mountain he wouldn't say much, only that the idea of not having to sit in front of the television at three a.m. waiting for the night to end, of not having to pretend to be happy for the sake of other people, was perilously tempting. It was luxurious, almost a reward. He never said that he wanted to die.

He did say, "I wish I'd stayed in Africa."

When Grace thanked him for telling her all this, he shrugged. "You can tell people your story," he said, "or any terrible story, and it doesn't make any difference. Things just keep happening, over and over again."

NINE

❀❀❀ ❀❀❀ ❀❀❀

Montreal, 1996

AFTER SHE LEARNED the truth about Tug, Grace thought every-thing would be different; it seemed as though she had broken through a barrier and found herself in Tug's own country, closer to the heart of things. Tug himself acted differently—glad that he'd told her, glad that she'd understood why he hadn't wanted to talk about it earlier. Reliving it was something he had already done, and now he wanted to move beyond it and live somewhere else.

"I'm not that person anymore," he said. "I need to get used to life in the comfortable nations."

"Comfortable nations?" Grace asked.

"I heard an aid worker say that once. He said the hardest part wasn't being over there but coming back. Supermarkets. Cars every-where. Too many choices. That kind of thing."

"It's not that bad to have supermarkets and choices, is it?"

"No," he said, "it isn't."

In this comfortable nation, it was a cold spring. Grace and Tug went skiing every chance they could. She loved seeing him up ahead of her, striding hard, his shoulders broad against the gray sky; some-times he would turn around to see where she was, and she loved that he checked.

They spent their weekends together, except for Tug's Saturday shift at the stationery store. They went to movies or, more often, stayed at Grace's place and cooked. While the stews simmered or the meat roasted, they read or napped or talked. He asked her tons of questions, and she asked as many in return. Now there was no limit to their conversation. He wanted to know everything about her childhood, her family, her life with Mitch; she even told him about Kevin and the child she'd chosen not to keep. She heard all about his adolescence, his first girlfriend, his family's summer house in Muskoka, his sister in Toronto and her two spoiled children.

Tug seemed fine most of the time, but occasionally he erupted into fits of anger over things she considered trivial. He couldn't sit through a movie he found stupid and would retreat to the lobby and pace there, while the ushers looked at him worriedly. Gradually she understood that he often didn't sleep, because his mind was at a simmering boil, his muscles clenched with its heat. He brought the same explosiveness to bed, covering her body with his, kissing her neck, her shoulders, and everywhere else, murmuring in her ear. Afterward, as they held each other, he gave off so much warmth that his chest grew slippery with sweat.

This didn't trouble Grace all that much, and he did seem to be getting better. What did bother her was that he didn't want to hear about her patients. He never once asked about her sessions, and when she offered anecdotes he would change the subject as quickly and politely as he could, visibly shutting down. But she came to understand that he'd been through enough trauma and didn't need to be reminded of how much of it surrounded him. In a way it was also good for her, because it enabled her to draw a firm line between work and home. Work ended the second she left the office, and by not speaking to him about it, she found she thought about it less. During the day she concentrated on her patients, clear-minded, sharp with perspective, then later she focused on Tug.

When she made him laugh, the pulse of satisfaction was so powerful it was almost physical. Getting to know him, to understand the depths of him, felt like her vocation, a task set to her specific parameters. He was difficult, and the terms of their relationship complicated, yet being with him was somehow perfect. She'd been waiting to feel like this for years.

One Sunday they had planned to go shopping. She needed a new coffeemaker and a few other kitchen things, and wanted to take him to a store she liked in Little Italy. They were apart the night before; Tug had explained that he didn't feel well and wanted to go to bed early. In the morning he didn't come over, which was unlike him; she had never once known him not to show up where and when he said he would. And he didn't answer the phone.

Thinking he might've come down with something, she drove over to his apartment and rang the bell. The lights were off, and she heard nothing inside. He hadn't given her a key. But when she turned the handle, the door was unlocked. She walked in and said, "Tug?"

They spent almost all their time at her place, and she'd been here very little since the first weeks they'd known each other. Not much had changed. It was still very neat: no dust, no disarray, not even any mail. Wondering where he put everything, she called his name again.

Getting no response, she climbed the stairs. The apartment was so quiet that she thought he must be out. She walked into his bedroom, and stopped short.

He was lying on the bed, on top of the covers, staring up at the ceiling, his mouth open. His lips were rimmed with white flecks. Then she was on top of him, shaking him, her hands gripping his shirtsleeves, her own heart flopping and seizing, and she said, "What did you take, Tug? What did you take?"

He seemed to be looking at her through the wrong end of a telescope, and it took him a full minute to resolve her into something he recognized. "I didn't take anything," he said. "What are you doing here?"

Kneeling next to him on the bed, she wanted to wipe away the flecks from his mouth—spittle, she realized, from the hours he'd been lying there—but she could sense, as if there were an actual barricade, how little he wanted to be touched.

"We were supposed to go out," she said softly. "Did you forget?"

"Oh." He looked up back up at the ceiling, then at her. "I'm sorry," he said, the words sounding hollow, void of content or color.

"Hey," she said. "Talk to me. Are you okay?"

He swallowed. "A little sick, I guess."

"Let me get you something," she said, touching his hand as lightly as she could, knowing he wasn't physically sick. "Water?"

He nodded. She left the room to fetch it, shaken by the look in his eyes. It wasn't sadness or numbness, regret or remorse. He knew she wanted to take care of him, and he was looking at her with pity.

When she came back with the glass, though, he was sitting propped up on pillows like an actual invalid. As he drank she opened the curtains, letting the watery March day filter into the room with a lusterless, cloudy, blue-gray light.

He had licked his lips and his mouth was clear. "I'm sorry," he said again.

"You don't have to apologize to me," she said.

"I felt bad last night, and I couldn't sleep. And then the hours just kind of blended together. I lost track of things."

"I figured it was something like that."

There were things she could have said, but she didn't because she knew he had heard them before. She herself had said them. So instead she sat with him silently, and after a while the clouds seemed to clear and the light grew a little less pale.

Afterward, they didn't talk about it much.

Tug had gotten up and taken a shower, and they went off to Little Italy. At first he acted vague, distant, like a child who'd just woken from a nap and was still half submerged in the dream world. But soon he was helping her pick out the coffeemaker, and bought her a set of espresso cups, and by the time they were having lunch he was back to his normal self—asking questions, making her laugh. They went back to her place and went to bed, and it was like the conversation they should have had: tentative, then opening, finally finding their rhythm together. For the rest of the day it was as if nothing strange had ever happened.

But the incident had rattled her. She caught herself staring at him, wondering what had set it off. A child he'd seen in the street? A call from his ex-wife? She wanted to ask, but also not to, because she hoped that not asking would bring him to her of his own volition. Whenever he saw her looking at him quizzically, he would shake his head—knowing exactly what she was thinking, and asking her to let it go.

But she couldn't. Two days later, they were making dinner when she poured him a glass of wine and said, "Can we talk about it?"

"Of course we can," he said, in a tone that implied just the opposite. He was looking down at a clove of garlic, slicing it carefully. "What do you want to know?"

"Anything," she said. "Does it happen often?"

"Does *what* happen often?"

"You know what I mean."

He sighed heavily and wiped his forehead with the knife still clutched in his hand, seeming more irritated than anything else. "No," he said, "not often." Then he grabbed a tomato and started chopping it, round pieces collapsing into their own juice on the plastic board.

"So was it something I said?"

She had meant this as a joke but he flared with annoyance. "Yes, Grace, it was something you said. It was how you ask questions in that special therapist voice that's supposed to make people tell you everything."

Take a minute, she told herself. Breathe. She slowly poured herself a glass of wine, watching the liquid rise up in the crystal, a small dark sea. "Why does it upset you so much for me to ask questions?" she said.

"Oh, for fuck's sake. If you don't know, then I can't tell you."

"Yes, you can," she said softly. "You just don't want to."

"You're right," Tug said. "I don't want to talk to you at all." He put down the knife and walked out of the kitchen and out of the apartment.

Grace stood there with the half-chopped food, the still-full glasses. Nothing like this had ever happened to her before. Even in their darkest hours—especially then—she and Mitch had never stalked out of a conversation before it was finished. However estranged they

had been, or angry, or terribly sad, they had remained almost mad-
deningly communicative. And since then she hadn't really gotten to
know anybody well enough to feel stricken by an argument, or by a
departure, the way she did now.

She felt bereft. She put the food away in plastic containers, drank
the wine, and went to bed without eating. She lay there on her back,
adopting Tug's favorite position, as if by imitating him physically she
could enter his mental space too. But of course he was still far away,
and she only felt more alone.

At midnight the buzzer rang. When she opened the door, his
coat was wet from freezing rain, his curls dark and damp, his eyes
exhausted.

"I'm sorry," he said.

She would have carried him inside if she could have. Instead she
opened the door wider and stepped back. He walked toward the
bedroom, shedding his coat and sweater, rubbing his wet curly hair,
explaining that he was testy and tired, that he'd be able to talk about
it later but just couldn't right now, and he led her by this trail of
words to the bed and they crawled in together. She could feel his
pulse racing like a frantic animal's. He kissed her hair.

He looked tired in the morning, his creases and wrinkles pronounced,
his cheeks ruddy. Even his hands were rough and scaly. He had been
weathered by the world. She wanted to pour all the energy she had
into him, to siphon it into his bloodstream and organs, to blow the
air from her lungs into his.

They lay in bed holding each other, Tug's chest to her back, and she
was crying. She didn't want to be, but she was, her face resting on his
elbow, the hair on his arm scratchy against her skin.

"I'm sorry," he said. "Please don't cry."

She nodded, though she could hardly move her head, he was holding
her so tightly. "You need a doctor," she said. "The right medication . . . "

"You're going to be late for work," he said softly, kissing her cheek.
"Don't worry. I'll be fine. Just being with you helps a lot."

A few weeks passed and Tug seemed better. He began talking more about his time in Rwanda, the other aid workers, the rolling landscape, the people. He talked about Marcie, too, how he had failed her every time they were together, yet didn't want to stop failing—because failure was where he lived now, it was his comfortable new home. Stories would come to him at inconvenient, even bizarre times. Once they were in the supermarket, and he turned to her at the butcher counter and told her about a man he'd seen by the side of the road, his body dotted with open sores, flies perched on him, waiting for him to hurry up and die. Grace stood there listening and nodding until he said, "Anyway," and he was done. He turned to the butcher and bought their rack of lamb and only when they walked away did she notice the looks other customers were giving them, wary and aghast.

Another time they had dinner with her friends Azra and Mike at a Portuguese restaurant on Duluth. The first half of the meal was fine. They drank two bottles of wine and made small talk about the food, the cold weather, Azra's job. Grace's oldest friend, since high school, she had a dental practice in Côte St.-Luc and always joked that the two of them should set up an office together, a suite where they could each have an office and hang out together between appointments.

"I'll drill the teeth and you drill the minds," she said, laughing, as the dessert came.

"You're drunk," Mike said affectionately.

"What do you think, Tug?" Azra said.

He didn't answer, and Grace glanced at him. His cheeks were red, his forehead sweaty. She put her hand on his leg, but she could tell it didn't soothe him, that he didn't even register it was there.

"I think it's a pile of crap," he said.

Azra raised her eyebrows. "Excuse me?"

"You glory in the pain you inflict. Grace doesn't do that. People whose bodies are suffering can't think clearly about their lives. You're a fool if you think otherwise."

"It was really just a funny idea," Azra told him.

"Tug," Grace said softly.

He stood up suddenly and left the restaurant.

Her mouth hanging open, Azra looked at her, and Grace shook her head. She wouldn't follow him; he'd only be angry if she did. "It's not about you," she said to Azra.

"What's it about, then? My God."

"He's been through a lot. It's good, actually, for his emotions to come out like this. It means he's not suppressing them."

Azra reached across the table and touched her arm. "Watch yourself," she said.

When she got back to her apartment, he wasn't there. But in the morning she woke to find his legs wrapped around hers, their fingers interwoven. She turned and made love to him gently, as if he were injured or ill, and when they were done he was still pressed up against her.

That's how it went: one day lovely, the next flawed. In this respect, was it so much different from anybody else's life?

She wasn't expecting anything out of the ordinary on the Tuesday morning in April when her session with Roch Messier was interrupted by a knock on the door. She thought it was likely her previous patient, who maybe had left an umbrella or something else behind. But when she saw the two blue-uniformed Sûreté du Québec officers in the hallway, she felt the dread she'd long nursed within herself, the sense that she'd known this would happen.

One officer was male, the other female.

"Madame," said the woman, "are you Grace Tomlinson?"

She nodded and led them to the reception area. They refused her invitation to sit down and stood uncomfortably, like early party guests, in the middle of the room.

The woman asked, "You are an acquaintance of John Tugwell?"

"Yes," she said. Her chest felt frozen, as if a block of ice were lodged there.

From the pocket of her heavy uniform coat the woman withdrew a note, unfolded it, and held it out to Grace. She didn't take it, just read it in the officer's hand. It had only her name and the words *I'm sorry*.

"We found him on the mountain," the officer said.

She knew it was cowardly to faint, but she recognized in herself the need to exit the situation as quickly as possible. She couldn't afford to be brave, to be composed, to be *alive*. Not right now. She let herself do it, and fell.

Azra came to her apartment and sat with her through endless, empty hours. Everything had flown out of Grace's hands: it wasn't her place to identify the body, to make funeral arrangements, to call his sister or his ex-wife or friends she'd never even heard of. Her roots in his ground were shallow, and now the ground itself was gone.

By eleven that night Azra was asleep on the couch and Grace was alone, awake, in her bed. She wanted desperately to talk to someone, and almost woke Azra up; but she didn't, because the only person she wanted to talk to was Tug.

The funeral was held in Toronto, where his sister lived, and Azra drove Grace there and back. They sat in the back and didn't speak to anyone. Grace didn't feel comfortable introducing herself to his family, since Tug had made no introductions himself. Ordinarily not a pill taker, she downed enough Valium to get her through the day, then the next, and the whole following week.

She discovered that she longed to go back to work, to lose herself in the world of other people. Her patients were her only relief, their sessions the only time she was able to withstand her own thoughts, and she felt overwhelmed with gratitude. She needed them as much as they needed her, maybe even more.

But each evening she was trapped at home, hopelessly angry at him, and she couldn't stop crying, the tears fat and hot on her cheeks, her shoulders heaving, immobilized by grief. Pinioned in place on the toilet, in the shower. On the floor of the living room.

Her mind veered constantly back to that day on the mountain, remembering that she'd nearly taken a different path entirely, that for an infinitesimally brief moment she'd considered just leaving him there—choices that would have saved her from having to endure this pain.

None of which—the crying, the questions, the choices, her memories, her body's memories—changed the fact that he was gone.

Every morning her eyes were swollen, deformed, and her throat cracked and salty. One Friday she woke to find the world blanketed in snow—the last storm of the year, surely. In the pale early light she called her answering service and asked them to cancel all her appointments for the day. Then she put her skis in the car and headed west to Gatineau Park. Snow was falling lightly as she sped along the highway. She used to go to Gatineau with Mitch, so long ago it seemed like another life. She had never been there with Tug.

Her goal was to wear herself out in an enormous swath of white, blank calm. She started off fast, making long strides, her quads tight, her breath coming fast, her heart galloping in her chest. Though she was exhausted from lack of sleep her body felt strong, rich with stamina. She always felt like this right before her period, though it was late this month, probably due to stress. A suspicion blinked in her mind like a distant neon sign, then went out, then came back on again. It was possible; it wasn't impossible. She wasn't a teenager. She was always careful. Of course, as her mother had always told her, every method has its percentages.

Thinking about this, she messed up a turn and almost crashed into a tree, correcting wildly at the last minute, her right pole flying up beside her. She found herself skiing hard down an incline into a grove of skinny birches, and then she was through them and into a clearing, all by herself in a pocket of space and snow.

She stood there to catch her breath, leg muscles twitching, nose running. Twenty yards away, a fox raced to safety. She turned to Tug, to point it out to him, as if he were there. In that moment, she believed he would always be next to her, always the first person she wanted to tell about any miraculous or ordinary event, always the one whose reactions she sought, always the voice in her ear.

"Tug," she said out loud. Then she knelt down and washed her face in the snow.

Two weeks later she was standing in the bathroom with a pregnancy test in her hand—the stick's plus-sign result only confirming the changes she had already detected in her body—when the phone rang. She let it go, not caring. She hardly knew how to react. She'd always planned on it in some general sense; at the start of their marriage, before things went wrong, she and Mitch had discussed it, and once, on a trip out west to see her parents, she couldn't resist buying, in an upscale craft shop, a tiny, hand-knit purple baby cap. With the divorce and its aftermath any thoughts of parenthood had lost their immediacy, but now added to this month's turbulence was the idea that she could have a child.

Whoever was calling wouldn't stop. The phone kept ringing. She put the stick down and went into the living room to answer it.

It was Annie's mother, hysterical, her voice blurring the words, asking, "How could this be? Where did she go?"

Grace listened, barely able to make sense of what she was saying. Annie had run away, apparently, and left a note saying she was leaving and never coming back, that they shouldn't try to find her.

"How could she do this?" Annie's mother demanded.

Grace murmured some vague response, such consolation as she could muster. She was so distracted that she could hardly concentrate.

"I just don't understand," Annie's mother was saying. "People don't just do this. People don't just disappear."

Grace spoke the right words, the comforting words, and they were on the phone for an hour. But throughout the call she was thinking, Yes, they do. People disappear all the time.

TEN

Los Angeles, 2003

WHEN ANNE RETURNED from Edinburgh, there were five voice-mail messages from her agent, Julia, each more frantic than the last.

"Darling," the last message went, "this is big. Call me today or else, I swear to God."

Anne stood in the hot, dusty apartment, her unpacked bag on the couch. Though most signs of Hilary and Alan had been removed, the place still didn't feel like hers again. She walked around opening windows, glanced inside the empty fridge, and found a dead potted plant in the bedroom, tucked behind a curtain on the windowsill. Hilary must have bought it.

Besides Julia, she had no one to call to say she was home.

In the early morning, she ran five miles and was back at the apartment, showered and staring at the clock, by seven thirty. Since Julia never got in before ten, she went for a walk around the neighborhood, bought some groceries, and had a manicure. It was a beautiful late-August day, warm but not humid. Tributes were starting to go up, flowers and photographs, notices of ceremonies, everyone seeming a little teary and brave and on edge, the anniversary bearing down. Anne noticed these things only insofar as she wanted to disassociate herself from them. If she could have managed not to register the date at all, she would have. But as it was, she thought about Hilary's due date and knew that it had passed.

Back at the apartment, she called Julia, whose assistant put her through right away, an unprecedented act.

"Darling girl," Julia said, "where the fuck have you been?"

"I told you. Scotland, in a play."

"You and your plays," Julia said, trying to sound fond, though her disgust was obvious. Julia was about toothpaste commercials, modeling if necessary. She was about getting your face out there. "Fortunately for you, they waited. You must've really done a number on that guy."

The first guy who came to Anne's mind was Sergio, sprawled on the unforgiving cobblestones, his eyes flashing when he rose up again to hit her, his anger laid bare. Then she refocused and said, "What guy?"

"Michael Linker," Julia said, as if everybody knew who this was. "He saw you in that godforsaken thing on Long Island." At the time, Julia had called the godforsaken thing a masterpiece of contemporary drama.

"Whatever," Anne said.

"Not whatever! He just got promoted to a new studio-exec position and wants you to audition for this pilot that sounds *amazing*. Gritty family drama, lots of sex. It's a cable show. You need to be on a plane to Los Angeles *today*. Call me back with your flight info and I'll get you a car on both ends."

Anne had been telling Julia for months that she didn't want to leave New York, that she wasn't interested in television, that independent films were the only projects for which she wanted to be considered. Standing in her apartment, the air conditioner wheezing asthmatically, she realized that nobody cared what she wanted.

"Annie," Julia said. "You're on this, right?"

"I'm there," she said.

That night she got on a plane, no longer tracking whether she ought to be asleep or awake. In California the car delivered her to a hotel, where she took a bubble bath, then ordered room service. Outside, the sun glared over a tangled mass of highways. Her interview wasn't until the next day, and she had hours to enjoy herself on someone else's money. So she went swimming at the hotel pool, then took another long bath. She remembered Hilary, when she first came to stay, gulping down donuts and any other food in the apartment. In retrospect, her appetite was surely fueled by pregnancy, but she also seemed to believe in eating while the eating was good, like a feral cat. Anne felt the same way about creature comforts. When luxury was available, she would gorge herself.

Then she pulled out the script that had been waiting for her when she checked in. She read it through and started rehearsing her lines. Low expectations or not, she wasn't going to sabotage herself. She'd work with what she had. She remembered Julia's parting words. "You may not be the best or the prettiest, but you don't have to be," she'd said. "You only need to seduce one person at a time."

Her appointment was at ten, on a studio lot. When she arrived, two people were waiting—Michael Linker, her fan from the play, and a woman he introduced as Diane. The office was both lavish and uncomfortable, designed to put newcomers at a disadvantage. Michael sat on a white Lucite desk, lounging in jeans and a crisp white shirt. Diane leaned back against a windowsill piled high with scripts. Anne was given an entire white leather couch to herself, into the depths of which she sank gracelessly, looking up at them.

"Thanks so much for coming in," Michael said.

"Yes, thank you," Diane echoed, smiling broadly. "We're so happy you could make the trip. Michael's been raving about you ever since he got back from the Hamptons, and finally I just couldn't stand it anymore and told myself, I have to see this girl!"

"You were incredible in that play," Michael said. "You ruled the stage, and that final scene was, my God, so heartbreaking."

"And Michael's not easy to impress," Diane said. "I hardly ever hear him gush like that."

This was clearly a lie. It was their job to gush. Anne crossed her legs, trapped in the couch, and kept smiling. "Thanks. You guys are *so* nice."

"It's our pleasure, really," Diane said. She had long, dirty-blond hair and wide-set, strangely vibrant blue eyes. Anne wondered if they were colored contacts. She was having a little trouble concentrating. Ordinarily she worked best one-on-one, responding to cues from the person in front of her; with two people, though, each broadcasting a distinct sexual energy, she couldn't quite figure out how to play the situation.

"Okay, my dear," Michael said. "Enough shameless flattery. Are you relaxed? Let's talk about the story. Then let's hear you work with it."

The character was an abused woman who triumphs against the odds and finds love again. In the scene Anne had been given, she confronts her cold, unremorseful husband, the abuser, with anger, tears, and recriminations.

Now sitting behind his desk, Michael was reading the husband's part. Diane had pulled up a chair beside him and was fiddling with her nails.

Anne figured she knew this much: When sex is there at the beginning, it's still there at the end. Even a woman who hates you still wants you to think she's beautiful, desirable, so great that you never should've treated her so badly, never should've let her go. So she played the scene as sexy as she could make it.

When she was done, Diane muttered something under her breath, but Anne couldn't hear what it was.

"Fabulous," Michael said routinely. "Could you just give us a minute, darling?"

"Sure." She stood outside in the hallway, breathing a bit heavily, adrenalized and a little turned on. An old boyfriend, a medical-school dropout, had told her that when he needed to calm down during sex, he used the images of diseased skin from his dermatology textbook. Pustules, rashes, oozing sores. Of course, after he told her this, during sex she was always thinking about him thinking about skin diseases, and pretty soon she was too turned off to see him again. But she kept the technique. After running through the images in her mind, she felt more nauseated than anything else.

The door opened and Diane smiled at her, blue eyes glowing. "Let's go down the hall and see if the camera loves you as much as we do, okay?"

She went through the scene again, this time with an actor Michael brought out without explaining who he was. Anne didn't recognize him. When they were done, he unbuckled his belt, peeked down his pants, and said, "Scared the shit out of you, didn't she, buddy?" Then he laughed and left the room, patting Michael on the shoulder. Anne could have turned this remark over endlessly in her mind, but didn't. Her mother had once told her that whoever cares the least has the greatest advantage. It wasn't a motto she herself had been very good at putting into practice. But Anne was.

And it must have worked, because months passed before she went back to New York. She let her apartment languish there, unpaid—it wasn't her name on the lease, and the furniture was worthless, so who cared?—as a new life in L.A. grew up around her.

She was cast in the pilot and had read-throughs with the actor playing her husband—not the one from the original audition, but a kindly type who brought a charming snakiness to the role that was significantly more disturbing. As she studied the script, she realized that what she'd thought was a starring role was in fact a small, supporting one. How had she gotten this impression? Had they actually lied to her or simply let her believe something that wasn't true?

The main character was a man who had partnered with her husband in a business deal whose crookedness extended to the top echelons of a major corporation and, from there, to the government. Her job was to be beautiful and damaged—at one point she was taken hostage—and in most of her scenes she had no lines, because she'd been gagged.

Diane found her a place to stay, a tiny mother-in-law cottage on some producer's estate. It had a sweet little yard clustered with cactus and blooming plants, fuchsia petals leaning gaudy and lovely against the stucco walls. Beyond the garden was the mansion where the producer lived, a Spanish-style villa with a red tiled roof. Diane also leased her a car and gave her an advance on her salary. She was almost impossibly helpful, and from this Anne could only deduce that Diane thought she was going places. When she told Julia what was happening, a tightness stole into her agent's voice that she recognized as the palpable fear that Anne would screw it all up. This fear was justified. The easier things came to her, the more worthless they felt, and the more she was tempted to cast them aside.

But she liked Diane. She could be catty and obnoxious and she talked shit about Michael behind his back. She told Anne that her little cottage was hideous and had to be redecorated as bluntly as she had told her that her ass was saggy and she needed to join a gym.

"I don't do gyms," Anne said.

"Honey, this is L.A.," Diane said. "You don't have a choice."

They compromised by jogging together on the beach, a picture of California living so cinematic that Anne had a hard time keeping a straight face. Fortunately, Diane was extremely fit and the pace she set forced Anne to breathe hard, straight face or not. Afterward she made Anne order an egg-white omelet, paid the check, then drove her home. She didn't introduce her to anybody else, and for the first two weeks she was the only person Anne knew in town.

At home, she read and reread the script. She sat on a patio chair in the garden wearing a broad-brimmed hat, letting the sun play on her legs. Other than that, she had nothing to do. Sometimes she got in the car and drove around aimlessly, along the city's wide avenues where no one was on foot, so unlike New York. She never thought about what would happen next; she lived in the bubble of the present moment, waiting, waiting.

On Monday of her third week, Michael called to say that the funding couldn't be secured and the project was dead. "Fortunately for you, my darling child, you'll get snapped up by somebody else before you can even turn around. Some of these other assholes are going to be in real trouble."

After he hung up, Anne called Julia, who said, "What did you do?"

"It wasn't me. The whole deal fell through."

Julia sighed. "I guess you better come home."

"Will they pay for my ticket back?"

"Please," Julia said.

That night Diane showed up with two bottles of rosé, which they drank while sitting on the plastic lawn furniture in Anne's living room.

On the third glass, Diane burst into tears. "I'm just so fucking tired," she said, her blond hair shining in the dark.

In front of them, the windows of the producer's villa glowed with light, though nobody ever seemed to be at home. The lights were on timers that went off and on at the same time every day. There were alarm systems, pesticide warning signs, gardeners, and maids, but no one who actually seemed to live there.

"What happens now?" she asked Diane, who shrugged, her usually erect posture collapsing under the wine.

"We all hustle and find something else to do. You'll do great, you just have to get out there. You've got so much fucking charisma it's ridiculous. I, on the other hand, will get fired, probably tomorrow."

"You will? Why?"

"Because this is the third project I've had fall apart on me. Three strikes, you're out. Like baseball and jail."

"But what are you going to do?"

Diane snorted. "Look for another job, I guess, where I can get fucked over by a fresh set of faces."

Something about her transparent made-up toughness reminded Anne of Hilary, and she sighed.

Diane looked up, laughing. "Look at how pathetic we are. It's terrible. Let's go out or something."

"I don't have any money," Anne said.

"Oh, shut up. You know I'll pay."

In addition to paying, she drove. She took Anne to a club where they did shots of tequila and danced and flirted with a couple of guys Diane introduced to Anne, though she couldn't tell if Diane actually knew them or had just started talking to them on her way back from the bathroom. They were cute, surfers in suits with wavy hair and blinding teeth. Too pretty to have sex with, Anne thought.

They'd expect all kinds of gratitude and wouldn't do any of the work. But flirting was fine, and so was dancing and drinking. She threw her body into it, letting her muscles flow and her thinking stop. It was three in the morning when they got back into the car. Diane was talking a mile a minute—maybe she did some coke in the bathroom?— about how she might go down to Baja and just chill for a few weeks, get her head clear, maybe work on this screenplay she had an idea for, or meet a Mexican guy and get laid and drink tequila on the beach, did Anne want to come? Diane's voice was ringing in her ears like an annoying phone, and she was on autopilot herself, so she used her usual trick to get someone to shut up, which was to lean over and kiss her. It wasn't the first time she had ever kissed a woman, but it had been a while.

Diane tasted like lip gloss and alcohol.

"Oh, wow," she said. "Wow."

Instead of driving home they went to a nearby hotel. It was expensive, and Diane paid. The bed had the nicest sheets Anne had ever felt. She ran her hands through Diane's hair. She was a beautiful thing, Diane, scrubbed and shiny and soft. Anne felt like she was stroking a puppy, a feeling made stronger by how little the other woman weighed and the soft whimpering sounds she was making. It didn't exactly feel like sex—not the sex that Anne was used to—but it felt good, at least until they passed out.

When Anne woke up, she was alone. She had danced off a lot of the alcohol and felt better than she would have expected. She took a long shower, and when she came out Diane was back, wearing a hard-to-read smile.

"I went for a walk," she said. "My head was killing me. I ordered breakfast for us. How do you feel?"

"Better after the shower," Anne said.

"I'll take one too."

While the water was running, room service came, everything under silver lids, like in a movie. With food in her Anne felt sleepy again.

"You can stay until noon if you want," Diane said. "I guess I should get changed for work. They'll expect me to be at the office so they can kick me out on my ass, those bastards."

She slid out of her robe, revealing her smooth, pretty body, then stood behind Anne and ran her hands down inside her terrycloth. Anne surprised herself by arching her back in response, a need rising up that she hadn't known was there. They went back to bed, this time sober, and neither of them left the hotel until noon.

Diane did get fired, but she didn't go to Mexico. Instead, she moved Anne into her little house on a winding side street in Los Feliz. Anne liked the neighborhood, which felt cluttered and cozy. Wide-set bungalows with deep, shady porches and slanted roofs were set back from the street, and in the yards there were tangles of spiky desert cacti. They took walks, Diane pointing out the California plants to her, eucalyptus, yucca, bougainvillea, the words like a new language on Anne's tongue. Sometimes they hiked in Griffith Park, the city spread out beneath them, clothed in smog. Anne went on auditions and took meetings, and Diane went out for lunches and consultations and took meetings. Everybody in L.A. was taking meetings. When Anne drove around the city now and witnessed its sunny leisure—people dawdling beneath umbrellas, sipping smoothies on the beach—she understood that these weren't vacation days or tourist pastimes, they were all meetings. After her own appointments, she would join Diane and sometimes her personal trainer, who would run them through an exhausting sequence of repetitions. Anne was in better shape than she'd ever been and she felt great. Inextricable from this were her evenings in bed with Diane, their thin, muscled bodies wrestling and twirling in what felt at times like another session with the trainer, at other times something more serious and important, a real *meeting*.

Diane was the first person who ever ran her fingers over the delicate white scar tissue, barely raised now, on her torso, from when she used to cut herself. She shivered as Diane's index finger traced this old map across her abdomen, replaced then by her mouth and cool tongue. Diane looked up at her. "If they need to," she said, "they can cover these with makeup."

Anne took a meeting with a friend of Diane's, a producer named Adam. He wasn't handsome, but like everybody else she met in L.A., he'd been exercised and tooth-whitened to the point where he seemed like he was. He was developing a pilot about sexy spies and thought she might fit the bill. After lunch, he said, "I have a script you could look over, but I left it at my house. Why don't we just swing past there, and I'll give it to you. Do you have time?"

She did. They had a drink in his living room and kept talking about the pilot. His house was full of modular white furniture and bulbous, fluorescent lamps. Then she asked him how he got started in the business—a question that in L.A. always led to a lengthy answer—so she could have a little time to think.

"It's a cliché at this point to say that the industry chews you up and spits you out, right? For actresses, of course, it's worse than anybody else. I mean, this isn't news to you, I'm sure," he said as they went into the bedroom; he was nominally giving her a tour of the house. "But I've been smart enough to navigate it pretty well so far. I'm not one of those fucks who's looking for one good hit and then wants to buy some mansion in the Hollywood Hills and retire. Those people are pussies, if you ask me. This game is about risk. About gambling your whole life. Don't you think?"

"I wouldn't know," Anne said. "I just got here."

"Yeah, spare me the I-just-got-to-town routine," Adam said. "You're an operator, same as me. We're like computers running the same program. Let's see your body."

"Just see it?" she said.

"For now," he said, and checked his watch. He was lying across his bed, a low futon with a black bedspread. Off to the side, in the bathroom, Anne saw a matching black sink, black shelves, and black towels. Diane's flowery red shower curtain flashed in her mind, not out of guilt but as a reward, what she'd get back to after she was done with the business at hand.

She expected him to take off his clothes, but he didn't. Instead he circled her, patting, groping, murmuring to himself. "How old are you?" he said at one point.

"How old do I look?" she answered, as Diane had advised her to.

"Too close to thirty for comfort."

"Oh, come on," she said. "Don't bother trying to make me feel bad."

Adam smiled. "I like you." His hands were on her breasts.

"If you say so," she said.

Back at Diane's she took a shower, not because she felt dirty but because she was tired, the same as anyone after a long day at work. When she came out, Diane was cooking dinner. Anne poured herself a glass of wine, and they kissed. It was the closest she had ever been to a domestic life, and it was only three weeks old.

"So how did it go with Adam? Did he give you a naked evaluation?"

"You knew about that?"

"He always does it. I'm sorry I didn't warn you, but he doesn't like it when people are tipped off. I know he's a creep, Annie, but he's a successful creep. If it went well, which I know it must have because you're gorgeous, he'll get you in somewhere."

Anne studied her as she flaked salmon into a bowl of salad. Feeling a swell of warmth, she put her arms around Diane and rested her head on her shoulder. They were around the same height, the same weight. The comfort of a double. "He's a freak," she said. "He didn't even want to have sex. Just to grope and look."

Diane laughed, gently disengaged herself, and carried the salad to the table. "You sound offended."

"It was a power play. It wasn't about getting laid. It was about making me feel like shit."

"Well, obviously."

"You think I should be grateful for the opportunity."

"I think, let's hope it works."

While eating, they talked about the screenplay Diane was writing, a black comedy about a woman manipulator, an *All About Eve* for the present day.

"Totally unsellable," Diane said. "The market doesn't like black comedies, and it doesn't like vehicles for women, but what the hell? Now's the time to take a chance."

Anne half listened to this jumble of wishes, paying more attention to Diane's body as it rustled and slid across from her. That night, lying in bed with their legs tangled together, she repeated the words *let's hope* to herself. She had a loose, sweet feeling in her body, the sense of a future she might be able to hold on to, and of the risks associated with that future—of landing a job or not, of being with Diane in this strange constellation of sex and friendship without knowing exactly what it meant. It was the feeling of knowing nothing this good could last, of getting away with it for now, for as long as she possibly could. *Let's hope.*

A week later, she got a phone call from Adam.

"It's Mr. Feeler-Upper," he said cheerfully. "I want you for my pilot. You're the sexy one. You'll show some skin, but not too much. It's a family show."

Anne rubbed her forehead. Some part of her that distantly remembered her theatrical career was giving her a headache.

Adam was still talking, giving her instructions on where to go and when. "This is the biggest thing that's ever happened to you," he said, "so get ready." Then he hung up.

When she turned around, Diane had her arms outstretched. "I knew it," she said, her eyes warm and bright. "This is it. The big time."

Anne accepted the hug, but *the big time* puzzled her. Did Diane really talk like this? Did she actually *believe* it? She felt the first separation yawn between them, like a candle snuffing itself out. But then Diane kissed her neck, and she lit up again.

One thing you had to give the television people: they knew what they were doing in the looks department. Techniques and materials had been refined. They were working at the cutting edge. They did her hair, her clothes, her makeup, her skin tone, and she looked like a different person, unrecognizable to herself, a transformation that brought her nothing but pleasure. She looked beautiful, if more generic; she could've been any one of the millions of shiny-haired L.A. girls.

Firmly, dictatorially, Adam took over her life, telling her what to wear both on the set and off it, cultivating her soon-to-be celebrity life. "Holistic oversight," he called it, and made appointments with a dentist, a dermatologist, a nutritionist.

"You're welcome," he said, though she hadn't thanked him. "I'm all about details."

Once filming started, Diane sometimes came to the set to watch. The first scenes were shot at night, on bone-dry streets that had been hosed down to look like the rain-slickened avenues of New York. She had always loved rehearsals, going over the same lines again and again, each time locating some new modulation or nuance; she and the other actors would argue over blocking and interpretation, over the meaning of a line, or even a word, for hours. But the repetitions of television were entirely different. The mechanics were so elaborate that no one paid any attention to what she said or how she said it; it was all about the camera tracking and how she looked in front of a tree or a stop sign. Over and over she walked out of a building, stood in the street, and looked confused. One, two, three steps, look confused. This went on for five hours, then a break.

Her character was a college student whose father was killed by some evil spies in a case of mistaken identity, so she became a spy herself in order to track them down. In the meantime, as a cover, she worked as a photographer, a job that enabled her to travel to exotic locations and walk around with a camera around her neck, its straps framing her breasts, staring poutily into the distance. Each episode was supposed to focus on a different "photo assignment," which usually involved her flirting with a man who either turned out to be no good or, if he was good, died.

Now that he'd cast her, Adam took no more interest in her body. Neither did the director, a happily married father of three who often played with his kids during breaks. The only ones who did pay attention to her body were the professionals who tended to it, the hair and makeup people, who were all women and gay men. It felt safe but sexless. Anne had always needed chemistry—the glint in the other person's eye, the tactical, pheromonal equation—but now her only partner was the camera, and she felt like she was floating in space, unwanted and untethered. She heard herself delivering lines with a cardboard flatness that, coming from another actor's mouth, she would have cringed at. But nobody noticed, or else they simply didn't care.

The hours were irregular and insane. Sometimes she was out all night and other times she needed to be on set at five in the morning. She had to work out enough to keep her stomach flat but not so much that her breasts got smaller. Some days she barely saw Diane, or else she was at home all afternoon lounging on the couch, doing her nails, while Diane, annoyed, tried to work on her script. When Anne tried to get back on her good side—sex being her strategy—Diane would push her away and sigh, saying, "It's not always about that, Annie. I need you to support me on this."

"Support you how?"

"Read the draft. Tell me what you think."

"But I don't know anything about character arcs and whatever," Anne said. "I'm just a puppet." She mimed as if her arms were held up by invisible strings. "I'm a marionette."

"You just think it's too much work," Diane said.

Anne started to protest, but they both knew it was true. "I'm not much of a reader," she said.

"It's a *script*. You're an actor. Come on."

So Anne read it, and it was terrible. Diane, so sophisticated and well educated, turned out to be a clumsy, fumbling, primitive writer. Without a doubt, producing was exactly the right job for her, not writing. Her script was corny, the dialogue boring, and the characters unsympathetic, with nothing redeemable or exciting about them. It had all the flaws of a commercial movie and none of its virtues.

Of course, Diane walked into the room right as Anne turned the final page. Sidling up to the fridge, not making eye contact as she poured herself some iced jasmine tea, she was so transparent, so endearing.

Without thinking, Anne said, "I love you."

Diane came over, set her glass down, and put her arms around Anne. "But not the script."

"God, no."

Diane snorted. "I can't believe you won't even pretend to like it."

Anne was surprised. How could she? Didn't somebody this smart know when a script was bad? She felt wetness on her shoulder, and realized Diane was crying. "Do *you* like it?"

"That's not the point," Diane said, wiping her nose on the sleeve of Anne's T-shirt. "The point is, if you love me, you should support me."

"By saying the script's good when it isn't? What would that accomplish?"

"When you love someone," Diane said, her lips trembling, "you don't tell them their script sucks. You give them some *notes*. You point to a particular detail that you do like. You say, I think it's got *potential* but it's not quite there yet. That's what you say if you aren't some robot or a person who was raised in a *barn*."

"I'm sorry," Anne said, taking her hand, but Diane left the house and didn't come back that night and this was their first fight, ever.

It upset her more than she would've anticipated. She felt off-balance, almost nauseated, and couldn't sleep, and the next day the makeup girl tutted and shook her head at the dark circles under her eyes. This made her mad at Diane, so instead of going back to her place after they stopped shooting, she went back to her own. She had been spending so much time at Diane's that she'd practically forgotten she still had the little cottage. She had no stuff there anymore, not even a toothbrush, and compared to Diane's house it was barren. The hulking villa loomed over her cottage, its emptiness both sterile and ominous. There was life in Los Feliz, people walking their dogs, crowding the parking lot at Trader Joe's, chatting and drinking tea under the umbrellas at the Alcove Café. Anne missed all of this, and Diane most of all, and in the cottage she felt shabby and exiled.

They made up two days later. Anne invented some positive comments on the script, and Diane admitted that she was better at cajoling work out of others than doing it herself. They drank a bottle of wine, then went to bed and found each other again, newly tender. The fight had given texture to their relationship: they had admitted how much they cared, and now things were deeper, stranger, stronger.

Giving up on the script, Diane got a job at an independent production company, and they took a weekend trip to Palm Springs to celebrate. At a restaurant one night, a woman who knew Diane approached their table to say hello, and Diane said, "This is my girlfriend," and Anne realized that it was true. She was surprised—not about being with a woman, or even about being a girlfriend. The surprising part was how much she liked it.

Shooting wrapped a week later, and now the long pause began as the pilot was edited and presented to the network. In the meantime, Anne became what Diane called "a kept woman." She had signed a contract that forbade her from working elsewhere until a decision was reached on the show. She worked, instead, on being Diane's girlfriend. Every day she asked her about her job, the minor details and ongoing disputes. Diane's work stories were the world's most boring soap opera, but Anne never let on how she felt. As always, once she started playing a part, she started *being* the part, finding aspects of herself that she hadn't known were there. She could grow into it, even things that were really a stretch, like knowing which of Diane's two bosses she was talking about; they were both named Jim, and Diane never mentioned their last names, differentiating between them only by tone—one Jim she liked, the other she despised.

Anne was good at this, and Diane responded like a plant to careful tending. She almost immediately got a promotion and gave her the credit for it, though Anne couldn't remember giving her any advice; in fact she rarely did, instead just parroting back Diane's own opinions.

In the middle of all this, on a Tuesday night, Adam called and invited her out to dinner. "Just you," he said. "Tell Di it's a work thing."

Diane said, "Is he going to feel your tits again?"

"Hopefully not at the restaurant."

"At least be discreet."

"Hey," Anne said, "whatever it takes to get ahead."

Diane punched her arm lightly, then held her close. "Be careful," she said.

At an expensive Italian restaurant on Melrose, Adam ordered

champagne, poured it, *sniffed* it, so obviously and pathetically milking the suspense that Anne could barely keep from rolling her eyes. Obviously the pilot had been picked up.

He raised his glass and nodded for her to do the same. "Congratulations, beautiful," he said. "They chose us."

They chose *me*, she wanted to say, but didn't. "That's amazing," she said. "I can't believe it."

Adam narrowed his eyes. "I expected more squealing, maybe a mad dash around the restaurant, shots at the bar. What's wrong with you?"

Anne played the dumbfounded ingénue. "I think it hasn't sunk in yet," she said. "I can't even believe it. When will it run?"

"Well, hold on," he said. "There are still more hoops to get through."

This discussion took them through appetizers and the first bottle of champagne. By the second, they were both drunk. When Adam ordered dessert, she knew another announcement was coming.

"I'm sure you know what's next," he said over flourless chocolate cake. "It's time for you to get out of your thing with Diane."

"What? Why should I do that?"

"Until the pilot got picked up, nobody cared, but once you're on the air, they're going to be taking pictures of you at the grocery store. I know what you're thinking, this is the twenty-first century, but trust me on this. I don't want to see 'Anne Hardwick and gal pal at Starbucks' in *Life & Style* magazine. You're a sex symbol on this show. A *straight* sex symbol. Also, any embarrassing trips you need to take, any doctor's appointments, any purchases you don't want people to know about, now is the time."

"But I'm not . . . " She had been about to say "gay," then realized how idiotic it sounded. She had no idea how she could explain, in a phrase or two, that this was just about her and one particular person, that it was strange and unexpected and highly specific.

"You're not Jodie Foster, is what you're not," Adam said. "Time to deal."

Diane was waiting up, and from the look on her face it was clear she'd already guessed what had happened. Anne stood in the living room in her celebration dress, the most expensive she'd ever owned. To dissolve the relationship explicitly would require a more direct conversation than they had ever had about starting it. Diane started crying, and Anne couldn't listen to that, not right now.

"Let's just go to bed," she said.

Diane nodded, looking relieved. She gave a lopsided smile, then took Anne by the hand and led her to bed. They didn't do anything, just lay there holding hands, not talking.

In the morning, Diane was firm and calm, everything Anne could've wanted her to be, and she hated her for it. Diane handed her a cup of coffee and said, "If I were Adam, I'd want the same thing. They've made an investment in you, and they don't like risks. That's how the business works. Why don't you take the first shower?"

When Anne came out of the bathroom wrapped in a towel, her clothes were packed in a suitcase by the door and Diane was laying out an outfit for her on the bed. Anne looked at her and said, "You're sure about this?"

Diane shrugged wordlessly. Anne felt a slight sense of relief—that they'd agreed, that there'd be no scenes. "Okay, then," was all she said. They didn't even kiss good-bye.

Back at the cottage, Anne burst into racking sobs and wound up hunched over the toilet, throwing up, Diane's coffee bitter in her throat. Wrecked, she crawled under the covers and woke up an hour later, her skin parched and itchy. Trying to distract herself, she poured body lotion on her legs, arms, stomach. One thing led to another and she made herself come, thinking about Diane touching her, and then she cried again.

She joined a gym and got Adam to hire her a personal trainer, who put her on a diet so restricted and confusing that she spent most of her time shopping for the peculiar ingredients; the rest of the time, low blood sugar made her feel too weak to think clearly about anything, even Diane. One day at the gym, she was drinking a shot of wheatgrass at the juice bar when a guy said, "Hey, you don't look so good."

"Then why are you talking to me?" she said.

"I didn't mean to insult you," he said. "It just looks like you worked out a little too hard. You look like you could use a steak."

Anne picked up her bag and slid off her stool. As she did, she almost fainted; spots crossed her vision, and she had to lean against the counter for balance. The guy grabbed her arm, his muscles rippling. He was wearing a blue T-shirt and Adidas sweatpants and she said, "Yeah, I probably need some meat," which made him smile.

Two hours later they were back at her place, in bed. There was so much she had forgotten—the roughness and heft of a man, his smell and force. She never even asked him his name.

So began a period of sleeping around, of dates in restaurants, of men in bars. A dentist, a studio executive, a chef, another studio executive, a Pilates instructor, and the original gym guy, whom she ran into at the juice bar from time to time. She finally learned his name—Neal—and got him to take her to a restaurant where she and Diane used to go, whose food she missed, and then back to the cottage. They were dozing in bed around eleven when somebody started banging on the door.

It was Diane, and she was weeping and drunk. "You cunt," she said.

"What are you doing here?"

"Fuck you. I'm here to call you a whore."

Neal, hearing voices, came out wearing boxers and holding his cell phone. Anne wondered if he was going to call the police, or ask Diane if she wanted a steak. A good protein source was his answer to everything.

"Well, now you have," Anne said. "So I guess you can go."

"You're a coldhearted bitch," Diane said. "You had to fucking sleep with guys from *my office*. I had to hear about this in meetings. You couldn't at least do me the decency of whoring outside the entertainment industry?"

"Everybody out here works in the entertainment industry," Anne said.

"I don't," Neal said.

"Who the fuck are you?" Diane said.

"I'm Neal."

"Sorry," Anne said. "Diane, Neal."

"Is this your boyfriend? Do you already have a boyfriend?"

"Is this your girlfriend?" said Neal, an edge of interest in his voice.

It was too much. Anne started laughing—it was hysterical laughter, not genuine, but the only person who knew her well enough to recognize this was Diane, and she was lost to her now.

Diane was sobbing. She reeked of alcohol and perfume. Anne could picture it perfectly: she had taken a bath, drunk a bottle of wine, trying to soothe herself, and wound up in a fit instead. Only the image of Diane's naked body, slick with soap, enabled Anne to stop laughing and calm down.

"Diane," she said gently. "Go home."

Sometimes at night her skin ached for Diane, and the only cure for this was to have somebody else in bed with her. Hence Neal became a regular. They worked out and slept together a few days a week. It wasn't a relationship; it was exercise. Neal bought her gifts: a notebook so she could write down what she ate every day, a heart-rate monitor, a juicer. It didn't seem to bother him that she bought him nothing in return. But when his parents came to town, he wanted her to meet them. She would have understood if he'd said that he wanted them to *see* her, to show her off. But he actually wanted them to meet so that she could get to know him better.

"No, thanks," she said.

"Man," he said, "you really are this cold. My friends thought I was making it up."

"You've never complained before."

"I should've listened to that Diane. Are you, like, autistic? My friends said you were the perfect woman. Sex and a workout partner without any obligations. But that's, like, weird." When he got worked up, Neal sounded like a teenage girl.

"If it really means a lot to you," she said half-heartedly, "I'll go to dinner."

"No, that's okay," he said. "I don't want to put you out."

This, for them, was a long conversation. He wasn't much of a talker, just a teddy bear of physical perfection, something to hold in the night. She'd thought he might be the ideal man, but he was letting her down now. He went around the apartment gathering up the juicer, the heart-rate monitor, the pedometer watch. She understood; it was expensive stuff, he could sell it or use it himself. He wasn't made of money.

Standing in the doorway, he said, "You aren't even upset, are you?"

"I'm not sure why you think I should be."

"The thing is, if you never get upset over anything, doesn't that mean you just don't give a shit?"

Anne looked at him, glad they'd never tried having conversations before. "I guess so."

"And if you never mourn for anything you lose, doesn't that mean that nothing in your life's worth anything?"

Anne raised her chin. "Life insights from the gym guy," she said. "Workout for your soul along with your body and mind."

"Okay, you mock." He touched her cheek. "I'm not Diane; I'm not so heartbroken. But I'm not spending much longer around you, either. I don't want to turn into a robot. You take care. Don't forget to eat your protein."

With those last romantic words, it was over.

In her mind, she mocked him relentlessly. But what he said about mourning she knew to be true, because she was alone and thinking about Diane, and about Hilary's baby being born without her even knowing where or when. *Eat your protein.* Didn't he know she'd been trying? She wanted to eat protein, eat muscles and blood, even her own heart, until nothing, not a single ounce, was left.

The night the pilot aired, she watched it with fifty people at the director's house in the Hollywood Hills. Anne stood outside until the last possible moment, bumming cigarettes from one of her costars, then someone opened the plate-glass doors, said it was starting, and dragged her inside.

To her the pilot looked embarrassing and lame, like a high-school talent show. The pulsing techno music of the theme, the way her mouth pursed in puzzlement as she stared into the distance. Watching this, she ran her tongue over her lips, lush and protuberant from chemical injections, and turned away. It felt like she was masturbating in front of the whole room.

She went back outside, ignoring everyone's encouraging shouts. For the first time she started wondering about the future. They had filmed three episodes and had a contract for ten more, though she'd been cautioned that the network could pull the plug at any moment. By now she had heard this so often that she assumed that's what would happen. The idea that it wouldn't—that this was her life now—felt even more frightening than failure.

Julia was calling all the time these days, but Anne had a new L.A. agent, Molly Senak, who kept sending her scripts for movies she could shoot once the season was over. The parts were always the hooker who dies, the girlfriend who walks away in the early scenes, the cheating temptation for the flawed hero. "Places to shine in small ways," Molly called them, the building blocks of a certain kind of career.

She missed New York—not the life itself so much as its familiar sense of difficulty and want. And more often than she would have imagined, she also found herself thinking about even more distant times in Montreal. Her father she refused to think about, but her mother sometimes wafted into her thoughts, along with memories of their house, her old room, even her therapist, who she realized now was the closest thing she'd had to a friend back then. Trying to boost her confidence, Grace had once told her to pretend she was a star, that she was all grown up with the life of her dreams. She wondered if any of them would see the show. If they'd be proud.

She left the party fifteen minutes after the director turned off his enormous TV and broke out the champagne. Back at the cottage, she listened to the message Diane had left, stiffly congratulating her. She felt an agonizing twist of pity and longing at the sound of her voice, but set it aside. She set it aside every day, and each time it was easier, more automatic, less twisting.

⚬⚬⚬

Reviews were bad; ratings were good. She filmed the new episodes, working sixteen-hour days, and perfected the art of the sudden nap; at any moment she'd lie down on the couch in her dressing room and drop off. She was sleeping one day when a PA knocked on the door and came in. She was a twenty-year-old UCLA dropout, timid and lithe. Anne couldn't remember her name.

"I'm sorry to bother you," she said.

Anne yawned. "What is it?"

"There's a call for you," she said, "that got forwarded from the production office." She held out a phone. "I wasn't sure what to do, but this woman's been calling, first the network and then the producers. She's very resourceful, and really pushy. On the one hand it's probably a crazy person but I just thought, what if it's not? What if she's telling the truth and I didn't tell you? I hope you aren't mad."

Anne stared at her blankly and took the phone without giving it much thought.

"I'm really sorry," the PA said. "It's just, you know, I wasn't sure what to do. She says she's your sister."

"I don't have a sister," Anne said. She weighed the phone in her hand, then hung up.

A week later the girl came by Anne's trailer again and stood in front of her so long that she had to say something, if only out of impatience.

"I haven't seen you for a while," she said. "Everything okay?"

The PA's face wrinkled. "I've been here. I think you just didn't see me."

Anne rolled her eyes. "I'm self-involved, but I'm not *blind*."

The PA nodded, apparently taking this as a statement of fact instead of the joke Anne had intended. Then someone swooped in to reapply her makeup, blocking the girl from view, but Anne heard her say, "Anyway, I'm *really, really* sorry."

"For what?"

"I brought you this," the PA said, producing a manila envelope from her messenger bag and handing it to her.

Anne stared at it, having no idea what it was.

"It's your fan mail," the girl said. Her walkie-talkie crackled and she turned to leave.

As the stylist kept working, Anne glanced at the letters. It was her first fan mail ever: young girls, middle-aged women, boys asking her to their proms, convicts, men promising they'd leave their wives in a heartbeat if she'd meet them for a drink, they really felt like there was some kind of special connection there, two hearts that could beat as one. If you wanted to feel optimistic about the human race, fan letters to a TV star were not the place to start. She flipped through the stack, not thinking she was looking for anything in particular, until she saw it. A letter postmarked Utica, New York, with Anne's name written in the bubbly, curly penmanship of a teenage girl.

She thought that waiting to read it would make the letter seem too important. Better to read it as quickly as possible, then throw it away.

She saw the words *Annie, we need money* before she panicked and crumpled it up. Even though she had stopped reading, words kept throwing themselves at her: *television* and *please* and *need* and *baby,* each one giving her a strong, unpleasant, sickening sensation. How could she have taken in so much of the letter when all she wanted to do was get rid of it?

"Sweetie, do you want a Xanax?" the stylist said. "Please try not to cry, it'll be hell on your makeup."

Two more weeks of twenty-hour days, all workouts and hunger, tanning and fittings. She was stretched into a new shape, her skin and muscles reconfigured, cut from new cloth. At night she dreamt of cheeseburgers and banana splits. She had never had trouble keeping her weight down, but this was a whole new discipline, and she embraced it. She didn't even have to try to forget the phone call and letter; her body was too busy forgetting everything for her.

She made friends with the PA, who sometimes came over after work with some Zone meals for dinner. They'd watch movies, and several times the PA slept over on the couch in the living room. Her name was Lauren, but Anne still thought of her as the PA. It comforted her to wake up and see her there; Anne would make coffee and bring her a cup, happy to do at least one thing in her day for somebody else.

So she was surprised and a little annoyed one afternoon when the girl brought her a phone and said her sister was on hold.

"Please," Anne said. She was wearing a leather bustier and five-inch stiletto heels and could barely move. "I thought I told you."

"She keeps calling," the PA said. "I know you said you don't have a sister, but this woman . . . To be honest, Anne, the producers kind of want to know what's up. They're wondering if something's, like, weird. That the media might get a hold of? No judgment or pressure or anything. They totally understand that everybody has, you know, some family strangeness. But here they'd just like to know the particulars."

At this, Anne's eyes narrowed. "Give me the phone," she said, then held it to her ear. There was breathing on the other end, and she felt like she was going to be sick when she heard a long, gentle sigh, like a sheet settling on a bed. "Hello?" she said.

There was no answer, just another sigh. It was like getting a crank call from a ghost.

"Well, talk to me if you're going to call," she said.

What came through the line was the sound of weeping, and this was so unexpected, so shocking, that she dropped the phone on the ground. "Whoops," she said to the PA.

The girl instantly picked up the phone and held it to her ear.

From her expression Anne could tell that the call was still connected. "Damn," she said under her breath, and held out her hand.

"Annie," Hilary said all in a rush. "Please don't hang up. I saw you on television, and we need help."

Anne's stomach twisted uneasily. "What's going on?"

"Alan lost his job and then the baby got sick and we don't have insurance, and now the hospital says we owe thousands of dollars, and our parents don't have any money either."

"Where are you?"

"We're at home, we're still right here."

"You'll figure it out," Anne said, remembering the day in her apartment when Hilary's uncle revealed all the lies Hilary had told, how

Anne had heard nothing from her when the baby was born. Words came back to her from the long-ago past, not her mother's hysterical voice but Grace's calm, soothing, maddenly therapeutic one. *You can be anything you want to be. You don't have to be like them.* "Don't call here again," she said, handing the phone to the PA, who took it back with an expressionless nod and went off to get her some coffee.

In New York, it was late fall. In the year she'd been gone she'd been back only once, for upfronts when the show was picked up, the visit a blur of luncheons and parties with press and execs, questions about how much was she like the character she played and did she enjoy the romantic scenes with the handsome guest star and did she have a boyfriend in real life and was he jealous. Each night she'd return to her room and tumble into bed, too tired even to watch TV, then she'd get up the next morning to face more of the same. She had barely been outside in the three days it lasted, and before she knew it she was leaving the hotel for the airport, hardly having set foot on a sidewalk or sat in a cab or seen anything of New York at all.

This time was different, the city colder and drabber than she remembered, void of the color that gave every day in California a sense of health and possibility. She was in town for some meetings and a magazine photo shoot, but she had a few hours to kill. Leaving her Midtown hotel, she walked south in a daze, not planning her route, trying only to avoid the worst of the crowds. She had always liked the big department stores on Fifth Avenue; they reminded her of old movies and the wholesome glamour of an easier time. Gradually she moved east, then south, past Union Square, not even tracking how many blocks she'd walked, and then she looked up and realized that she was staring at the windows of her old apartment.

Had she really allowed a grubby teenage runaway and her pimply, construction-worker boyfriend to live in her apartment and sleep in her bed? It felt like someone else's life.

People were walking in and out of the building, all strangers, not a single one of the old ladies who'd once clustered there. Maybe the landlord had succeeded in replacing them all with higher-paying tenants, or had sold the building. There was no movement in the windows of her apartment. There was nothing to see.

The day was brisk, winter skidding leaves off trees, and she wasn't dressed warmly enough. She wrapped her sweater around herself and walked on. Down the block, a baby was wailing miserably, and she saw the mother pushing a stroller toward her. For moment, she had the insane thought that it was Hilary; but this woman was older and looked wealthy, bundled in a cashmere scarf, her long hair a cascade of glossy curls. The baby had a big round head that rolled from side to side. The wind had whipped his cheeks to a rosy red, like children in old picture books. Jowly and fat, with a cascade of chins, he was a little clown in a big white suit. As they passed Anne, the baby stopped crying and stared at her, and she looked back into his bright blue eyes.

Farther down the block, he started crying again, and the mother took him out of the stroller and held him to her chest, kissing the top of his head. Anne studied the scene for a moment, thinking how strange it was that Hilary would be doing these same things—as if she'd stepped across a threshold into another country, and Anne couldn't imagine what it was like to live there. Rarely, if ever, did she think about those weeks when she herself had been pregnant, or imagine how old that child would be now if she had decided to keep it. She remembered feeling no physical or emotional change back then, only the sheer sensation of panic, like a bird trapped in a house, flapping her wings in frenzy and desperation.

It all seemed so accidental, how lives were invented and chosen. A child enters the world. A child exits the world. Both for almost no reason at all.

Of the events leading to the pregnancy she thought even less. She had been hanging around at the Faubourg after school, doing homework and drinking coffee to avoid going home to her bickering parents. She used to tell them that she was at a friend's or studying at the library or seeing Grace. In truth, all she wanted was this hour or two by herself, to drink bitter coffee and bum a cigarette from some guy and inhale until she could feel the smoke burning her lungs.

Then she'd go into the washroom, her head buzzing from the caffeine and nicotine, and press those small, precise cuts into her skin. She called it surgery. She'd swipe a finger through the drops and lick the blood; the taste of it was like knowing herself, a confirmation that she existed. Then she'd go back out into the shopping center, feeling a little sticky, a little dirty. It was a trespass on the otherwise pristine routines of her life.

On one such day she came back out and cadged a cigarette off a French guy who was reading *La Presse* and drinking an *allongé* in the food court. He was old, wearing a suit, and had touches of gray at his temples, appraising her breasts with an old man's smile.

"*Qu'est-ce que tu fais dans les toilettes?*" he said.

"Sorry." She shook her head as if she didn't understand the question, although she did. He had been holding the cigarette out to her but now took it away, folding his arms with it clasped in his fist. She put her hand on her hip. Her coat was open and her school uniform visible beneath it, and she could see him looking at her pleated skirt, her wool tights. The schoolgirl thing was such a cliché. They all went for it.

"What you do in the bathrooms for so long?" he said. "You were in there a long time."

"Makeup," she said, licking her lips as he stared at her, hard. Suddenly, before she could react, he reached out and lifted up her shirt, then dropped it. In days to come she would wonder how he knew to look there, where the most recent cuts ran in three parallel lines to the left of her belly button. The square of paper towel she had pressed against them fell to the floor. His eyes flickered, and she knew that the blood excited him, even more than the wool skirt and the white button-down and her being sixteen. Before he had been playing, but now he was serious. He wanted something.

He stood up. He wasn't much taller than she was, but he was older, a man, and his voice held authority. "Come with me," he said. "I want to show you something."

He led her upstairs and down a hallway into a part of the concourse that was under construction, where the shops hadn't yet been opened, the area empty and dark. She was still wondering what it was he'd show her—drugs, she hoped, wanting to try something new—when suddenly his mouth was on hers and his hand was under her shirt scratching the cuts and adding new ones, the other one pressing her shoulders against the wall. Then he pulled down her tights and unbuckled his pants and suddenly he was inside her.

He never covered her mouth, nor did she call out for help. She wasn't sure, later, if she had even said no. It all happened so fast. She was a girl who did her homework, who pleased her parents, who wrote thank-you notes. She had no practice in refusal.

He groaned into her shoulder and it was over. Without looking at her, he buckled his pants and walked away. Her tights were still around her knees, and her legs wobbled as she pulled them up. After he was gone, she realized he hadn't even given her the cigarette.

She never told anyone, wanting the secret to be contained and buried. Later, she did tell her therapist she was pregnant. A quiet, brown-haired woman with circles under her eyes, Grace wore earth-toned sweaters and simple silver jewelry, and Anne found it impossible to imagine that she had ever had sex, or done anything bad, in her entire life. As soon as Anne told her, she regretted it. Her eyes turning moony with sympathy and concern, the therapist wanted to understand and to help. Sixteen years old, shaking with hate, trapped at home with her hopelessly unhappy parents, Anne knew that nothing Grace said could help her. In some respects, her life since then had been a repudiation of the whole idea of help, a big fuck-you to it.

Anne now thought of that time and the incident at the Faubourg without anger. It was years ago, and whatever injuries she'd suffered had long since healed over. It wasn't an excuse for the person she'd become, just another memory; but it was the first time she had learned to walk away.

Being in New York made her L.A. life feel made up, unreal, and now that she was here, she felt no loyalty to California. She spent the day walking around her old neighborhood, looking in store windows, people-watching. The Midtown hotel seemed like a bad mirage, nothing that had anything to do with her. She was eating egg rolls at

Panda Kitchen when she finally checked her cell phone. There were seventeen new messages, all from various people she hadn't attended to, about the events and appointments she had blown off. Five were from Adam, asking her to call him as soon as she could. She deleted these without even listening all the way through, and cutting him off mid-sentence gave her no small amount of satisfaction. The last was from Julia, confirming their dinner tonight. Anne texted her that she wouldn't be able to make it.

She licked the salty residue of the egg rolls off her fingers. She had a photo shoot in the morning and knew she'd get in trouble; too much salt made her lids puffy and gave her skin a creped quality. But maybe she wouldn't do the photo shoot. Maybe, she thought with a smile, she wouldn't go back at all.

She didn't return to the hotel until midnight, and she threw a blanket over the blinking red voice-mail button on the phone and went to sleep. In the morning, she took a cab down to Tribeca for her photo shoot, where her late arrival earned her a cursory, halfhearted scolding from the publicist. They were used to this kind of thing. They dressed her up in a variety of outfits—a spy, an executive, a nurse, and the president of the United States, if the president were very young and a little bit slutty.

The lights beat hot on her face and people were yelling instructions and a woman kept oiling her cleavage, then dusting it with sparkly powder.

Amid the hubbub she became aware, after a while, that Adam was standing in the back, watching with a lazy, proprietary interest. An hour later, he came up as she was removing the many layers of makeup. Her fake eyelashes felt exoskeletal, and she peered at him through their spiky, bristled edges. Outside of L.A. his posturing looked even more ridiculous, his tan incongruous, his teeth strangely uniform, plastic.

"That was hot," he said. "You're going to do fine."

"Why are you here?"

"The show's going off the air," he said. "It underperformed."

He had arranged his features into an expression not of concern or reassurance, or even of a readiness to listen and explain, but of complete neutrality. *Don't blame me*, it said. *You're on your own.*

"So that's it?" she said.

He put a hand on her bare shoulder. "I should've canceled the shoot, but there's this little fucker at the magazine that I've been waiting to get back at for years. So now they'll have to eat the cost. I'm glad you showed up. I thought maybe you were on a bender or something."

"I don't do that," Anne said mechanically. She was out of her pinstriped miniskirt now and slipping on her jeans.

"No, you're a wholesome girl," Adam said. "Good luck."

She cabbed it back to the hotel, where her room had been tidied, her clothes folded, the toiletries replaced. She took a long bath, her skin pruning. When she got out, her cell phone was beeping. There were two messages: the first from Julia, who almost sounded like she was crying. She was sorry about the news, she said, but while she understood that Anne might be upset, the time to get back on the horse was now. It was the most sympathy Anne had ever heard from her, and she was surprised. The second message was from Hilary—there was no doubting the tears in *her* voice—begging for Anne to call back.

She deleted Julia's message and listened to Hilary's again. The baby was making noises in the background, and she thought about the baby she'd seen on the street outside her apartment, staring back at her, curious and unafraid. But Hilary's baby was in a small town that Anne couldn't picture and would never see.

Suddenly she was crying too, the short, dry sobs shaking her all over, her body shivering involuntarily. There was no one to go to or run away from. What had Neal said—that if you have nothing to mourn, then nothing in your life's worth anything?

She was dangling at the end of her particular tether.

She spent an hour like that in the dark, sterile room, and she felt dismantled. Ended.

Okay, she finally thought. Okay.

So everything was over, the short wild ride. She called her landlord in L.A., broke her lease, and told him to sell whatever was left, which wasn't much. She decided that today she would do one good thing. She rooted around in her purse and wrote out a check to Hilary for the entire amount she'd earned from the TV show, more money than she'd made in her entire life and far more, she was sure, than Hilary had ever imagined. She put the check in an envelope, added the address in Utica, and left it with the concierge to mail.

When she checked out, she was carrying a single bag that was no bigger than the one she had had when she first got to New York. Rinsed of all her trappings, she felt lighthearted and at ease. For years she had been escaping into one life after another, and this wasn't the time to stop. People like Hilary and Alan were only temporary runaways. They would always go home; they belonged to the place they came from. Other people were destined to keep leaving, over and over again.

ELEVEN

Montreal, 1996

GRACE DEBATED FOR DAYS whether to even make the trip. What did she expect? She turned it over in her mind, picturing the best- and worst-case scenarios. Eventually she decided to go, because at least she would stop thinking about it and be reckoning with something real.

Tug had never talked much about his hometown or his life there. When Grace spoke of her childhood, which came up naturally every now and again, he'd nod and listen but only rarely reciprocated with stories of his own. Looking back, she understood that this elusiveness had been part of his appeal; he withheld himself, and kept her wanting more.

Knowing this didn't mean she had stopped feeling that way.

At the funeral, she had stayed in the back and watched his parents—well-dressed, quiet-looking people, his mother in glasses, his father balding, slightly stooped—navigate the service. They didn't know who she was, or even that she existed, and she wasn't about to introduce herself then. Perhaps this wasn't an appropriate time either, but she couldn't help wanting to go.

The drive to Brantford wound through farm country, with silver silos and red barns and cows here and there. The day was gray and drizzly. Grace felt a tightening in her chest, her heart seized by the dreary prettiness of the landscape. She crossed from Quebec into Ontario, the farms neat and well tended, the fruit trees black in the rain. Things Tug would never see again.

Feeling sick, she stopped at a gas station and let her stomach empty itself out, as if some interior part of her wanted to escape. Afterward, she sat in the car with the wipers on, their rhythmic sweep soothing her. It was Saturday. There was nowhere she had to be.

Tug's parents were listed in the phone book, and she pulled up in front of a two-story house, red brick with black shutters, as well kept as the farms she'd passed. His father was a retired chemist; his mother had never worked outside the home. In the years Tug had been abroad, they had always stayed in Brantford, rarely traveling. "They never wanted to see the world," Tug once said, and the disapproval in his voice rang clear. Now that she'd arrived, Grace was tempted to turn around and drive back to Montreal. Maybe all she'd wanted was to see the childhood home of a man she'd loved, to know that it still existed, some remnant of him in the world.

A woman in a yellow rain slicker walked her dog past the car, frowning in the few seconds she looked at Grace. It wasn't the kind of neighborhood where you could just sit in a car without attracting notice. Everybody here must know everybody else, and which cars they drove. Still, she didn't move. In the warmth of her car, an exhaustion came over her that was strangely close to contentment. Was this enough? Had she already gotten what she'd come for? She turned on the radio, leaned back in her seat, and closed her eyes. The CBC was playing opera, and a woman's voice tripped light and high through an aria Grace didn't recognize.

She could sleep here a few minutes, she thought, before going home.

The sound of a door closing made her open her eyes. And there was Tug's mother, a little old lady stepping down the cobbled pathway that led from the house to the street. Wearing a dark red raincoat, her head bent against the rain, she was clutching her purse to her stomach as if she, too, felt sick. She was heading for the maroon Honda that Grace had parked behind, but with her head down and the rain starting to fall harder, she wasn't likely to notice her sitting there. Then the front door opened again and another woman came out—this one blond, pretty, and much younger—and Grace's stomach bucked again. She had seen Marcie at the funeral service too.

As if she could hear Grace's thoughts, Marcie glanced down the street at her car. Barely seeming to register the rain, she looked right at Grace, her expression indecipherable. All Grace could think was how pretty she was.

When the wipers swished, clearing the windshield, Marcie's eyes met Grace's, and she stepped off the path, walked over to the car, and knocked on the driver's-side window. And Grace—feeling as though this were a dream—rolled it down.

"I recognize you," Marcie said. "You were at the service."

Grace nodded, her tongue gummy and thick. Marcie was waiting for her to say something, her eyebrows knitted.

Swallowing, Grace said, "I was a friend of Tug's."

Marcie grimaced. "I'll bet," she said.

It wasn't what Grace was expecting. "Excuse me?" she said.

The other woman glanced at Tug's mother's car; the engine was on, the taillights glowing red in the rain. When she looked back at Grace, she shrugged in a strangely airy way. "You know," she said, "my husband had a lot of friends."

Grace didn't know what this meant, and didn't want to, either. "I see," she said softly.

"Oh, do you?" Marcie was still standing there bent over, her head down at Grace's level, a position that couldn't possibly have been comfortable. Her cheeks were flushed. Rain was dripping into the car. "That's good," she went on. "I'm so glad you see."

Grace flushed now herself. In her grief over Tug, in her need to see where he came from and trace his roots in the world, she had forgotten that those roots were, of course, planted in other people. "I'm sorry to have troubled you," she said.

"Right," Marcie said.

Grace wondered what she was doing here, and where she was going with Tug's mother. Tug had told her that when the marriage had fallen apart she'd gone to live with her parents in Hudson.

"I'll be going," Grace said.

"So soon?" said Marcie. "We just met."

"What?" Grace said.

"Did you come from Montreal?"

"Yes."

"Why?"

Grace had no idea how to answer. All she felt was embarrassment and regret. The woman's voice was taut with anger, and her eyes burned feverishly. She kept staring at some spot just to the right of Grace. It was as if she knew that Tug had once sat in the passenger seat, slumped against the door.

"I think I'd better go," Grace said, waiting for Marcie to step back so she could roll up the window and back away. But instead, Marcie moved her head even closer, and Grace could see that her eyes were ringed with dark circles or maybe smeared mascara. In front of them, the taillights on the other car faded, and Tug's mother got out and walked over.

Marcie straightened up. "Joy," she said with a bright, false smile, "this woman is a friend of Tug's."

Grace was mortified. She hadn't really planned what she might say to Tug's parents—if anything—but whatever fantasy existed in her head, this wasn't it. A sick feeling washed over her like the sudden onset of flu, and she clenched her abdominal muscles and prayed to be delivered from this moment. As the older woman bent down, her face next to Marcie's, Grace turned her head and retched onto the passenger seat.

"Oh, dear," said Tug's mother. "You'd better come in."

Fifteen minutes later she was sitting on the sofa in Tug's childhood home, cradling a cup of tea in her hands while three strangers sat around her in postures of fake repose. It was pouring outside, the rain loudly lashing the windows, and Grace was nauseous and hot. No one spoke. Tug's father, a tall, rangy man with short-cropped white hair, kept glancing longingly toward the den, where an afternoon hockey game was playing on TV, the sound of the crowd rising and ebbing in the background.

Grace looked around the room. She couldn't imagine Tug sitting on this furniture or running through this room as a child. The couches were dark pink and flowered, and white vases sprouting plastic flowers sat on doilies on the side tables. Everything smelled of Lysol.

One night, in bed, Grace had told Tug about her divorce, and about how Mitch had moved his things out of their apartment so quickly and thoroughly that she'd felt like she was being robbed. When she saw his frantic packing she resorted to stealing a few small things from his boxes—a photograph of him as a child, a teapot that had belonged to his mother—just so she wouldn't feel like the entire world they'd built together was disintegrating completely. And then he put his stuff in storage and went off to the Arctic, leaving no phone or contact information, and she felt doubly bereft: both divorced and abandoned. Tug had shrugged. "When you realize you're in the wrong place," he'd said, "it makes sense to get out."

His mother now peered at her. "Are you sure you wouldn't like some aspirin?"

"No, thank you," Grace said.

The politeness was epidemic. At least with Tug's parents. Marcie sat in an armchair and glowered, her legs crossed tightly.

Grace had already apologized several times, and now sat with her head swimming, wishing she had stayed at home. "Do you have any saltines?" she said.

"Let me check, dear," Tug's mother said. She practically ran into the kitchen, delighted to have a mission, and Grace could hear her opening and closing cupboards. Joy was a short, round woman with kindly green eyes. Tug resembled her more than his father—the same curly hair, the same sloped shoulders. Amid the nausea, another physical pang coursed through Grace's chest. She missed his body, the warmth of his arm flung over her in sleep, the smell of his hair and skin.

Joy came back with a plate of Peek Freans cookies fanned decoratively on a plate. "Will this do?" she said. "I'm afraid we don't have any crackers."

"Perfect," Grace said. "I'm so sorry about this."

"We told you to stop saying that," Tug's father said gently. For all his kindness he was also appraising her, keeping his distance, much as Tug always had. He waited while she slowly ate a cookie, forcing it down. "So," he said once she'd finished, "how did you know him?"

Grace bowed her head. Of course she would tell them everything; that was the price of being here. "I met him skiing one day, on the mountain. We became . . . friends."

Marcie sighed, a long, sad whistle.

Tug's mother ignored her. She was sitting very straight in her chair, her hands cupped together in her lap. Her dignity was immense; so was her pain. "My son was very fond of skiing," she said.

"Yes," Grace said. "We went a few times later, too. This winter."

"You were with him," Joy said slowly. "This winter."

"Yes," Grace said again.

At this Tug's mother and Marcie exchanged a look.

Grace was deeply at sea, lacking any footing in the conversation, and wished desperately that she hadn't come. She blamed Tug for not telling her much about his family, for being so mysterious, for being gone. Yet seeing his parents in front of her, the crazy quilt of features that had combined to produce him, was for a moment like having him in the room, and she was glad of that.

"Well, now we know," Marcie said.

She wasn't speaking to Grace, who answered anyway. "Know what?"

Marcie's gaze was a slicing blade. "Where my husband was before he died," she said.

In the silence following this remark, Grace sat perfectly still on the sofa, as if this might lessen her emotional exposure. But she couldn't stop herself from eyeing the front door, trying to plan her exit. What had she wanted from all this? Not a confrontation with his family. She'd had so little of Tug, his presence in her life had been so glancing, that maybe she just wanted a picture of him as a child. Some tiny memento like that. She was like a beggar at this house, panhandling for loose change.

Just then a clicking sound came down the hallway and the Dachshund she had met that first night came ambling into the room, blinking his eyes drowsily. He made straight for Grace's lap and settled himself there, just as he had in Tug's apartment, and Grace began to cry quietly, small unstoppable tears.

"Oh, dear," Joy said again.

"Sparky, come here," Marcie said sharply.

The Dachshund slowly abandoned Grace's lap and padded over to his owner.

Was Marcie living here? Grace felt she had no right to ask any questions. With an internal shrug, she let go of everything, including whatever dignity she had left. "I'm sorry I came here," she said. "I didn't mean to bother you. I just . . . "

She could feel Marcie's eyes on her, their almost palpable heat.

"I don't know anybody else who knew him," she said.

When she looked up, Tug's mother was crying. There was so much pain in the room, and so little to say about it.

"So you thought you'd come rub my face in it, is that it?" Marcie said, her voice raspy with anger.

"Marcie," Tug's father said.

"Come on, Will. She shows up here looking for sympathy? The *girlfriend*? What am I supposed to do, give her a hug?"

"Let's just stay calm," Joy said, smiling weakly.

Grace couldn't imagine that he had come from this place, the sad-eyed man of the world she'd known; his cynicism, his lust to see the world, his practicality, all of it seemed totally alien to this house of doilies and chintz. Which, she supposed, was as good an explanation as any of how people became who they were. In reaction to the homes where they were raised.

"When you came and wanted to spend time here, Marcie," Tug's father said, "we didn't question it."

Marcie's eyes flashed around the room. "Are you comparing me to her?"

"Let's have some more tea," Joy said.

Shaking her head, Grace stood up. With a couple of cookies in her stomach she felt better, stronger, finally able to take command of the situation. "I'll leave now," she said, then turned to Marcie and looked her, with some difficulty, in the eye. "I'm so sorry," she said.

She walked to the front door and opened it, but then Joy was beside her, putting a small, almost weightless hand on her arm. "Please," she said. "Tell me how it was, at the end."

It turned out that there were things all of them wanted to know, gaps they all needed to fill. Though of course no one could fill the greatest gap, that of Tug's absence from their present and future lives. Still, thinking they could tell one another something useful, they forged a tentative alliance. Joy made a pot of tea, Grace thinking that there was comfort in rituals, in places set at the table, the tinkle of china and spoons. Then quietness stole into the room, and everyone took a deep breath.

Except Marcie, who looked at her in-laws as if they were traitors and left the room, taking the dog with her.

Tug's father brought out a bottle of whiskey and poured a slug into his tea. His wife didn't scold him. He tipped the bottle in Grace's direction, but she declined. There was a secret lying inside her, only a few weeks old. Would she tell them? She didn't know. She lifted a filigreed teacup to her lips and drank.

At first, Joy did most of the talking. Something in her seemed to have been released—whether by the tea, or by Grace's presence, or by Marcie's absence. As the three of them sat around the dining-room table, she spoke for almost ten minutes, an undammed flood of reminiscences that, Grace could tell, kept him alive for her.

"Johnny always had his eye on faraway places," she said, "even as a child."

For a moment Grace was disoriented, being used to his nickname, which had seemed so fully to suit him, his thoughts and memories always tugging him somewhere else. But of course he had been given a Christian name, had been a little kid, here in this very house, with these parents.

"He always loved maps. And books about pirates, and space travel, and India. His head was full of different facts, things I couldn't hardly keep track of. I'd be in the kitchen working and he'd come in and tell me these stories about all the places he'd read about, and it was amazing, like he'd been there himself."

Grace couldn't help reaching across the table to touch her hand. But Joy didn't meet her eyes, and her hand was cool and inert; she didn't want to be touched. Flushing, Grace put her hand back in her lap and kept her eyes on the tablecloth. It felt like a prayer circle, like grace before a meal.

"His sister was always different. She was a little Suzy Homemaker, playing with her Easy-Bake Oven. She never wanted to leave home, not even to go to school. Her favorite thing was to help me cook dinner and then set the table. Mind you, Johnny was good around the house too. They both were. I always said I was lucky with my children." At this point her voice broke slightly, but she swallowed and composed herself. "It's been hard on Marcie," she said.

Grace didn't look up.

"When they lost the baby she was just heartbroken," Joy said. "Her parents are good people, but they want her to move on and start thinking about the future. She came to stay with us for a little while, until she gets her feet back under her. You know, it's brought us all together, I think, going through this."

Grace would never have considered, at any point in her marriage, moving in with her mother-in-law; then again, she had never experienced any of this. For a moment she remembered playing cards and drinking tea with Mitch's mother, a thought that made her grimace and smile at the same time. And then Joy's words resounded in her mind. *When they lost the baby.* Tug hadn't told her anything about that.

"I know my son wasn't perfect," Joy went on, as if to twist the world even further off-kilter. "Marcie says he strayed more than once. But he helped so many people. He was a good person, a truly good person, I know he was."

Grace sat knitting her fingers together. She had half a stranger inside her.

Joy was still talking, the words coming slowly and evenly, dripping like an IV into Grace's veins, regular and numbing. She was talking about having seen Tug and Marcie together a month or so ago, when he came to visit and they all had dinner. She knew he wasn't happy—he had seen so much and worked so hard—but he was talking about switching careers, maybe going to law school.

He was in this room, Grace thought, maybe sitting in this exact chair. Shivering, she reached across the table for the whiskey and poured some into her tea. Tug's father nodded at her imperceptibly. Under different circumstances, she thought, they would have liked each other. Or maybe his silence just reminded her of Tug's, and thus felt familiar.

The whiskey warmed her and settled her stomach.

Joy was looking at her, her eyes pale, watery, and unfocused. "Please, tell me about him."

Grace paused a long while. "He was unhappy," she finally said. "He couldn't shake the things he'd seen."

Tug's mother nodded, and Grace could see her shifting the blame over to those things and the places where he'd seen them, making compartments for this blame, cabinets in which to store it away. But even as she watched the process unfold, Grace began doubting herself. She didn't know if Rwanda had anything to do with it. The darkness that had led to his death might have been inside him all along; it could have been what sent him abroad in the first place, along with his restlessness, his sparks of anger, his desire to escape. It seemed as though he had always felt hemmed in.

"Was he planning . . . ," she said. His parents waited for her to finish, her father's elbows propped on the white tablecloth. "Was he coming back here?" Back to Marcie, she meant, but wasn't sure if they understood.

They looked at her, both of them aged, stooped, the skin on their faces wrinkled and loose, as if the events of the past few weeks had weighted them physically, pulled them toward the ground. Tug's father shrugged. "You know as much as we do."

It seemed a terrible thought. All three of them knowing so little about him.

Sitting at this table, Grace realized that she had come because she hoped it might help her to decide what to do about the baby. But now she saw that his parents had no answers; they had as many questions as she did.

So many patients wanted her—or somebody, anybody—to make their choices for them, partly to absolve themselves of any blame. She always told them that no one else could live their lives for them, that they had to take ownership, and they were never pleased to hear it. What was worse than having to take responsibility for everything you did or felt or said? For the way your actions radiated out to change not just your own life, but those of the people around you? She understood fully now how hard it was to follow her own advice.

And Marcie. Grace ached for her, and for her sake truly wished she hadn't come. And to say that she was pregnant—that was impossible, even if she decided to keep the baby. It would cause everyone so much more pain, and introduce endless complications. To keep the secret was terrible, yes, but to share it was even worse. She thought of what Tug had said about life in the "comfortable nations." This house was a comfortable nation, she thought, or at least it wanted to be, to safeguard its borders and tend to its citizens. She shouldn't disturb it any further.

"I'm sorry," she said for what seemed like the hundredth time. "I'm sorry I came here. I didn't mean to intrude." Her voice trailed off, as if noting its own insincerity. Obviously intruding had been the entire purpose of her visit, but Tug's parents were too polite to point this out. Silent Canadians.

Her heart throbbed for them, for the loss they had to bear, so much deeper and harder than her own. "I didn't know Tug very well, or for very long," she said, her voice gathering strength as she went on. "We were just friends. I'm a therapist, and he talked to me a little about his problems."

Joy sat with her head bowed, as though receiving a benediction or a blow.

Grace was determined to make it the former. "He talked so much about you," she said. "And Marcie. All of you. How much you had given him over the years. He felt terrible that everything he'd been through kept him apart from you."

His mother sniffled.

"He loved you so much," Grace went on. "He told me that often."

Neither of them spoke, and she wondered if they would ever speak again. She stood up, but then Joy did too, throwing her arms around her with surprising speed and force. She was short and frail and it felt like being hugged by a sick child.

Grace spoke through tears into her short gray hair. "I'm sorry I couldn't help him."

She put her arms around Joy's shoulders, a tentative, constrained hug. She had told what comforting lies she could, and she didn't regret it. If anything, sad as she was, she felt closer than she ever had to Tug, who had told so many lies. The notion that he could go on, survive, find some happiness in the world—this was the biggest lie of all, not because it was outlandish or fake, but because it had been so possible and so close to coming true.

When she left a few minutes later, the rain had stopped and the sky was pearled and gray. She was holding a box of cookies that Joy had insisted she take—a memento she never would've imagined bringing home. As she got into the car she looked back at the house, where most of the curtains were drawn. But on the second floor a window was open and a lamp was shining, and she could see Marcie pacing back and forth with her hands in her hair.

Grace felt utterly alone. Having isolated herself within the miniature universe she and Tug had created together, so intent on rescuing him, she had almost forgotten how to live in the actual world. Now that he was gone, to emerge from that experience felt like waking from a drugged sleep.

Behind the steering wheel with the engine running and the heater on, she shivered not from the cold but from a sense of possibility, of the enormity that lay ahead. She knew she would have the child of a person she had loved for just a few months. Despite her pain and sorrow, it somehow felt like exactly what she'd always wanted—for her life to change in a way she couldn't foresee. She said a silent farewell to Tug's family and drove off into the future, and the unknown.

TWELVE

❦ ❦ ❦

Montreal, 2006

AS THE FALL went on, Mitch's work life settled into a routine that was, if not exactly easy, then comfortably regimented. Group-therapy meetings took up Monday, Wednesday, and Friday; Tuesdays and Thursdays he devoted to paperwork and individual counseling. It was the one-on-one sessions that spooked him most. With just one other person in the room, the narrowness of the equation struck him as dangerous and potentially explosive: eyes either glancing away from his or boring into him with pain or anger. It was simply too intense. To cut down on these, he volunteered to take on every administrative task he could instead, from grants and project management to a review of hospital procedures. At lunchtime, he'd close the door to his office and eat a sandwich he'd brought from home while listening to sports radio. Hockey season was starting and he let the predictions and opinions wash over him, defensive pairings and forward lines, who was being called up or traded, gambling scandals, injuries. Sometimes he even took notes, picking and discarding players for his fantasy team. When people knocked and came in, they often saw him scribbling away and frowning in concentration, and he let them think he was absorbed in work.

One weekend he went to visit Malcolm in Mississauga. His brother and Cindy lived in a messy, rowdy house in the suburbs, where they managed the chaos by constantly adding to it. Three children, two cats, and a dog; video games, toy pianos, televisions. To their menagerie they had recently added a rabbit, who sat in a cage in the living room, cowering inside an empty tissue box, though the children kept trying to tempt it out with carrots and celery and once, in an unattended moment, a hamburger.

"I know you like hamburgers, but Snowball doesn't," Cindy explained soothingly to her sobbing daughter after throwing the meat away. "It's just not his thing."

Malcolm was laughing. "Snowball was at school," he told Mitch, "but he's allergic to the fluorescent lights in the classroom or something. So we're foster-parenting him, I suppose. Out of the frying pan and into the fire."

From a skinny, spastic boy Malcolm had grown into a round-bellied, amiable, balding man with a moustache and a constant smile. Being around him relaxed Mitch when nothing else would. On his visits to the house he felt like just one more happy addition, inconspicuous but loved, with little demanded of him, much like the rabbit. It didn't matter that he slept on the couch or, when he woke up in the morning with a burning sensation in his leg, found a Transformer action figure wedged under his thigh, or that Emily, the youngest, threw up on him in the backyard after a game of tag they were all playing got a little too rough. The children beat up on him, included him in their games, and left him alone when he said he was tired. The place was dirty and hectic and he could disappear into it, losing track even of himself, like he couldn't anywhere else.

He didn't know how Malcolm had managed to become such a good father without having a model for it, nor did he know how he and Cindy still managed to laugh at each other's jokes and argue cheerfully about whose turn it was to cook or do the dishes. Malcolm wasn't an especially successful engineer; he had made it to a certain level and hadn't been promoted further in years. He wasn't a particularly good cook, either, or hilarious or even all that hardworking. Cindy complained that he was disorganized, useless at home repairs, and not very good with money. He wasn't good about asking Mitch questions about how things were going. His sole talent, one he'd had since childhood, was the best imaginable, and it had surrounded him his entire life, flexible, capacious, grown to embrace his wife, their family, their house, and, when he was around, even his brother. He had the gift of being happy.

It was always a shock for Mitch, after leaving those crowded confines, to find himself back in his quiet apartment in Westmount. He could hear his downstairs neighbors, a gay couple, entertaining a group of friends to gales of laughter.

The future he was looking at was without color, without noise. Hopelessly quiet. He spent the night awake, unable to shut out the silence that had taken over his life.

And so he was alone. To combat this solitude he had but few weapons: his job, his routine, and, increasingly, Grace and Sarah. October became November and he continued to help them as best he could. Grace's cast had been removed and she was walking again, though she still winced at times and there was a stiffness in her movements, in the hunch of her shoulders, that made her look older than she was. Four days a week she went to rehab and returned home exhausted, close to tears, even though, as she told Mitch, most of the time she was lying down while the trainer pushed her legs in one direction and then another, working on her mobility. "You wouldn't think it would hurt so much, but it does," she said. "By the end of it I want to throttle this poor nice woman who's just trying to help me. It's like when Sarah was born and I told the doctors I hated them."

"You hated the doctors? Why?" Sarah called. She was in the other room but had the smart child's habit of listening closely at inconvenient times.

Grace grimaced. "I didn't *really* hate them," she said. "I just thought I did."

Sarah came into the kitchen, where Grace and Mitch were sitting at the table, with a drawing dangling from her hand. Her forehead was creased with concern. "Because it hurt when I was born?"

"It hurt a little at first," Grace said carefully, "but then it didn't. And then you came out, and I was so happy." She drew her close and wrapped her in a hug. Sarah buckled her arms around her mother's waist, squeezing hard, and Mitch saw Grace clench her teeth in pain. She kissed Sarah's head and said, "Now go back to your drawing. Don't you have homework to do?"

"I finished it," Sarah said, and left the kitchen, her troubles apparently forgotten.

Mitch brought Grace a glass of water and a couple of Tylenols, knowing her well enough to tell when she needed some. There was an extra weariness to her face, as if her head weighed too much for her neck, and her eyes grew blurry and vague.

"Thank you," she said.

Mitch had stopped coming around as much, since now she could do almost everything herself. But he continued to run a few errands, adding their usual weekly groceries to his, stopping by to change lightbulbs, take out the trash, fix the shower rod, things she wasn't up to yet. He had grown used to the shape and purpose these activities gave to his days, and he looked forward to Sarah's happy greeting and his chats with Grace. By this point he wasn't sure if he was helping or being helped, or whether the distinction even mattered. He and Grace were casual together, having slipped into a practical, easygoing friendship. Eventually she wouldn't need his assistance at all, and he didn't know if they would continue to be part of each other's lives.

One day, Azra was coming up the steps as he was leaving the apartment. He had last seen her in mid-September, back when Grace was utterly prone.

"Hey!" he said, and gave her a quick hug, only noticing as he drew back that her expression was less friendly than quizzical.

"Hi," she said. "What are you doing here?"

"What do you mean?"

She looked flustered. "Nothing, I guess. You're still helping out? That's nice." It was a poor recovery; obviously she found his presence unexpected and strange.

"Well, not all the time or anything," he answered lamely, wondering, even as he spoke, why he was acting like it was something to be ashamed of. "Grace hasn't mentioned it?"

"No," Azra said, "she hasn't."

Together they absorbed the implications of this remark. The only way he could think to end the awkward pause was to tell her he had to be going.

Back at the apartment, he resolved not to call or visit Grace unless she specifically asked him to, and felt a flush of shame whose source he couldn't explain. Should he feel bad for having been there in a time of need?

But it turned out he couldn't keep the resolution. He enjoyed the time he spent with the two of them, and he and Grace were getting along well. There was no reason, he told himself, that they couldn't be friends. The following weekend, he called her up and proposed various plans for an afternoon outing. This was what Martine would have expected: an exhibit at the museum, or a new children's movie, or he could teach them how to fly a kite. He had researched the possibilities beforehand.

Grace sounded touched but puzzled. "That seems pretty ambitious," she said. "We're more like not-goers. Not-doers. Sometimes we go to the park."

This took him aback. "So what do you usually do on the weekends? Or used to, I mean, before the accident."

Every child he knew—and this included his niece and nephews—faced a battery of activities and playdates on Saturdays and Sundays. They started playing competitive sports before they were five, and their lives were enriched by music lessons and art classes as soon as they could walk. For Grace to buck the trend so completely was not, he thought, quite like her. Then again, maybe he didn't really know what she was like.

"Not much," she said. "Why don't you come over?"

So he did. Grace sat on the couch, as she had throughout her recovery, surrounded by a disassembled newspaper, some unanswered mail, a mug of tea, and a half-eaten sandwich on a plate. Sarah lay in front of her on the carpet, working on a jigsaw puzzle, her long blond hair in two braids. In the kitchen, talk-radio voices debated some issue, though Grace didn't seem to be listening.

She offered him a cup of tea, a snack, maybe a book—should he have thought to bring one himself?—all of which he declined. Instead he sat opposite the two of them in an armchair, with the front section of *The Globe and Mail* in his lap. He was thinking that this was the most feminine scene he had ever witnessed in his life. Maybe his mother would have liked to have a Saturday like this, instead of taking him and Malcolm to the park and watching them beat each other over the head with sticks.

The atmosphere felt so serene that he was surprised to notice Grace staring worriedly at her daughter. He knew she was still concerned that the accident had marked her psychologically, but if this were so, the damage was subtle and well concealed. Sarah was lying on her stomach, wearing blue jeans and a white sweatshirt, her legs kicked up in the air. She had pushed her puzzle aside and was reading a book, propping her chin on her hands, her eyes so close to the pages that they were almost crossing. Mitch waited for Grace to scold her—his mother certainly would have—but she didn't.

"What's *institutionalized*?" Sarah asked. It was clearly an adult book, and Mitch wondered if she should've been reading it.

Grace, however, seemed unfazed. "What's the context?"

"The girl was *institutionalized* against her will, and she stayed under doctors' supervision for five years."

"Okay," Grace said. "So if it was against her will, what does that imply?"

"That someone else put her somewhere."

"Good. And if there are doctors there?"

"That the somewhere is like a hospital?"

"Excellent. To be institutionalized is to be placed in a facility, often a hospital, when you can't care for yourself."

"My father was institutionalized."

Mitch looked up. It was the first time he had heard the father mentioned.

"No, he wasn't, Sarah. He was never institutionalized."

"But he was sick."

"That's right. He was sick, and he died."

"In a hospital."

"In a—oh, I see what you mean." Grace's tone was very calm. If the subject upset her, she didn't show it. "Usually, to be institutionalized means in a mental-health facility or a prison, something like that."

"And my father wasn't in any of those."

"No, honey," Grace said, "he wasn't."

Sarah went back to her book. Grace looked up and her eyes skated over Mitch's. The expression on her face was one he had seen before: part guilt, part pain, part unidentifiable something else. As if she were listening to some inner voice, some call that no one else could hear.

A few minutes later, tiring of the book, Sarah asked Mitch to play with her. Flattered, he got down on his knees, but she shook her head and led him into her room. Holding his hand, she showed him around and explained everything in great detail: her dolls, her schoolbooks, her winter clothes, her summer clothes. She had a collection of seashells she had brought back from a holiday in Prince Edward Island, and another of barrettes that she'd been adding to, she told him very seriously, "her entire life." She held out a piggy bank and asked him to guess how much it weighed.

"Heavy," he said. "Maybe five pounds."

"Lots of money in there," she said airily. "I've been putting it away for a rainy day."

"Very responsible of you."

"I'm mature for my age," she said. "My teacher told Grace. I wasn't supposed to hear, but I did."

This was an affectation, he knew, calling her mother by her name, to tell him she was grown up. Was this childish flirting? Certainly it made him uncomfortable. His niece, Emily, was a tomboy, and his nephews were hooligans who cared only about hockey and wrestling. A simple fake-out punch to the gut was all it took to get the ball rolling with those three. It was like playing with a bunch of puppies, all laughter and flung-out limbs. Sarah was a different animal altogether.

"Here," she said, "look at this."

On her tiptoes, she pulled a shoebox off a shelf, then sat down on her bed and balanced it on her lap. He sat down next to her, and she opened it with a ceremonial gesture that made clear it was the most important thing in the room.

"What's this?"

"This," she whispered, "is the rainy day."

He couldn't tell, at first, what it was; it looked like a box of lit-ter and dirt, with some paper envelopes and tiny, shriveled objects nested in tissue.

She took things out one by one and placed them in his hand. "These are seeds for forget-me-nots. These are seeds for daisies. This is a tulip bulb. This is an iris. This is freesia. This is clematis."

"You've got a whole flower garden in here."

"No. These are just the seeds and bulbs," she said impatiently. "I save my allowance and buy them from a catalog. Next spring we're going to plant them in the back. We were going to do it last year but I didn't have enough money yet. Since my birthday I have enough. And there's more in the bank. In the summer we can get live plants."

His hands were overflowing with bulbs and envelopes. She put the box in his lap, and he started placing them carefully back inside.

Then she jumped up off the bed and opened a photo album. "This is what it's going to look like," she said, her voice hushed to a stage whisper. "The secret garden."

There were no photographs inside, just pages cut from magazines, construction-paper drawings, collages, seed catalogs with prices cir-cled. Each page was an explosion of yellow and purple and pink. She had all the names memorized; she wanted to put the daisies next to the irises and the daffodils. She had arranged the garden a thousand times in her mind, she explained, as she flipped the pages for him.

"How did you get so interested in flowers?" he said.

She cocked her head. He thought she was seriously considering how to answer, but it turned out that she was just deciding to ignore the question. After going through all the pages, she put the album away, took the shoebox from him, and replaced it carefully on the shelf.

Then she came back to the bed and scrunched herself up against the wall, with a pillow in her lap. "This is the story," she said. "There's a girl, and her parents die, and she has to go live in a big house that belongs to her uncle. But he's not there. And she finds the key to a secret garden in the back of the house, and she unlocks it and makes all the flowers grow again. And there's a crippled boy named Colin, and she brings him outside and he learns to walk and the uncle comes back and everybody's happy and it's all because of the garden."

"So that's why you want to have a garden too?" Mitch said.

Sarah shrugged. "It's just a notion of mine," she said.

She came out with these words, these shrugging, adult phrases so out of sync with her age. He supposed it was because she read so much. But it gave her a quality of otherness that, despite her cute blond looks and her obvious intelligence, wasn't exactly charming. Both she and Grace were a little internal, and together they seemed a closed circle, walled off from everybody else. A secret garden. It made him want to pull them out of the apartment and into the world, make them laugh and run around. Help them be messier. Sillier.

"Think fast!" he said, and grabbed the pillow from her lap.

She reached for it, laughing, craning her arms to get to where he held it, up behind his head. "Give it back!"

"You have to come get it," he said, holding it higher.

She was bouncing on her bed now, reaching around him, shrieking with laughter and excitement, the seeds and bulbs forgotten now. At last she crawled over his lap, and he let her grab the pillow and hit him over the head with it.

"Oh, you got me," he said. "You're too fast."

"That's true," she said modestly, and smiled. "I'm *extremely* fast." Then she jumped off the bed and ran out of the room.

An hour or so later, bundling themselves into jackets and hats, they went off to the park. Sarah almost immediately ran into a friend and went off to the swing set with her. But instead of playing on it, they each sat down in a swing and fell deep into conversation.

Grace watched them, her hands stuck deep in her pockets. "They're already adolescent at ten," she said. "God help me."

The other mother, a young woman with long curly hair and dangly earrings, nodded vigorously. "It's only going to get worse, too," she said. "She's asking me for makeup."

"Oh, no," Grace said.

The two of them went back and forth, trading dark forecasts about the future, while their girls gossiped together not fifty feet away. The wind picked up. Mitch stared longingly at a group of guys playing Frisbee at the other end of the park. There seemed no reason why all this static talking had to take place outside. Women, he thought.

Everyone else in the park was on the move: people throwing sticks for their dogs, toddlers careening around wildly while their parents chased after them, couples with their hands in each other's pockets. A Peruvian band was unpacking their flutes and drums. Despite the clouds, the atmosphere was festive and happy.

An extremely pretty young woman walked by. She was under-dressed for the weather, wearing jeans and a sweater, no hat, and her long blond hair was flapping around her like a flag. High-heeled boots gave her walk a sexy, rolling sway. She passed them with a glance, but Mitch didn't think much of it, other than to note her beauty. But then she turned around and came back toward them. Mitch ran his hand through his hair before he could stop himself. She obviously wasn't looking at him—he was old enough to be her father—but her attention was blatant.

The young woman was staring at Grace. As she got closer, Mitch thought she looked familiar, though so faintly that he couldn't have said where he knew her from. Grace barely noticed. Her eyes flickered over the girl, pausing uncertainly for a second, and then she turned back to her friend. They were discussing how to introduce new foods to kids who were picky eaters.

"I try to tell her it's good for her," Grace was saying, "but she doesn't want to listen."

The young woman walked by, making no secret of her staring, then crossed the street and was gone.

The three of them headed back to the apartment.

"God, it's great to be able to walk," Grace said, smiling. She stretched her hands out on either side, reveling in her health. Her pinched posture was uncurling, her shoulders squared, and the wind had reddened her cheeks. Mitch could still see the memory of pain in the shadows under her eyes, in the care she took when stepping off the sidewalk; it colored the happiness she was feeling, gave it form and weight. She and Sarah were holding hands.

His thoughts shifted to Martine and Mathieu, and then, reluctantly, to Thomasie. He had been doing his best not to think about any of these people, and spending time with Grace and Sarah had helped to distract him, but of course they were always there, alert soldiers standing forever at attention in the back of his mind. He looked at Sarah and thought that the life Grace was giving her was, despite its recent rockiness and the lack of a father, bright and secure, and it was impossible not to contrast this with the wan, difficult lives of others he had known whom he had abandoned or been abandoned by.

All these presences and absences. A child enters the world; a child exits the world. He felt heavy with responsibility and regret.

Sometimes he hated himself simply because he was alive when others were not, and he wanted to wipe out the memories of every patient he'd had, every problem he'd caused or heard about or failed to alleviate. Other times he thought he would never forget any of these things and that it was important not to, perhaps the most important task of his life. Witnessing the pain of others is the very least you can do in this world. It's how you know that when your own turn comes, someone will be there with you.

Sarah was telling her mother a story about a magician who flew all around the world, making waterfalls stop, making trees grow. He couldn't tell whether it was from a book she'd read or a movie she'd seen or if she'd made it up herself. She was a fanciful girl who didn't seem to always distinguish between fiction and reality; perhaps Grace indulged her too much in this.

Back at the apartment, Grace ordered a pizza and asked Mitch if he wanted to stay. He shook his head. Sarah had gone off into her room.

The two of them were alone. Though they had spent a fair number of hours together over the past few months, today was somehow different, more awkward, probably because he hadn't come over to help; he had just *come over*. The whole time, at the apartment and the park, he had felt distant from the two of them, a separate entity, a hanger-on. He guessed that their time together had reached its logical end; their lives would go on, on divergent tracks, as they had already done for so many years.

Grace was puttering around the kitchen, putting dishes away, wiping down the counters. She had accepted his help so silently, so willingly, then hid it from Azra. She'd taken what was expedient and left the rest. The only thing he'd wanted out of the situation was not to feel ashamed of what he was doing, but now he did, and that was Grace's fault. He stood there silently fuming.

Sensing his mood, Grace turned around and leaned back against the counter, wiping her hands on a dish towel. "Azra told me she ran into you the other day," she said.

"Yes, outside. I didn't realize my coming around was a secret, Grace."

She was courteous enough to blush. "It's not." She crossed her arms. "She just didn't understand."

"She was the one who asked me to help in the first place."

"To bring in the mail, water the plants. She thought it was weird that you'd be so involved."

"It's not *that* weird, Grace. I mean, yes, a little. But not impossibly weird, or I wouldn't have done it."

"I know," she said. "Of course. But Azra worries about me, when it comes to men. She thinks I live too much in the past already."

"This is about Sarah's dad, I guess?"

That same faraway expression stole over her face.

"Don't say it's a long story," he said.

She laughed. "It's not that long. I really threw myself overboard when I met him. I wanted that feeling, whether or not it was real. The feeling of totally giving yourself over to something. Of not looking back."

"And then what?"

Tears were glimmering in her eyes. "Now I can hardly remember his face," she said. "I grieve for that."

He reached out for her hand, his right clasping her left, like some secret reverse handshake. "I'm sorry," he said.

She nodded and withdrew it, the heat of her palm lingering for a second in his. "Maybe you shouldn't come around so much."

"Okay," he said, and then: "That's it?"

She didn't answer, and they stood there in the kitchen. It had been a strange collision, this time they'd had together. He wondered when or if they'd see each other again. Somehow the word *good-bye* seemed too final, so he didn't say it, and neither did she.

In the nights to come Mitch lost the ability to sleep. He watched old movies in the middle of the night, spent hours with the Weather Channel. He went to work and got through the group-therapy sessions on autopilot; he listened intensely to the participants' stories but forgot them immediately; when writing up his notes he couldn't remember much of what they'd said, and his scrawled observations seemed like the thoughts of a stranger. He called no one. He ran five miles a day, his skin flooded with warmth against the increasingly cold air. In November, a freezing rainstorm encased the leafless trees in ice, the salt on sidewalks crunching beneath his feet. The Habs lost to the Maple Leafs. His fantasy picks were a shambles.

He didn't take up drinking; he didn't miss a day of work. He wasn't even sure that other people could see the numbness inside him, the mechanical nature of his commitment to his own life.

There came a time when, without quite noticing at first, he was sleeping through the night. The running helped, and so did work. He wouldn't have said that his spirits, for lack of anything else to do, were rising; he wouldn't have wanted to admit that. He would have said that he came from a family where each person had a talent. Their mother's was to take care of them. Malcolm's was to be happy. His was to let things go.

When the card came in the mail, a thick white envelope with a Christmas-tree stamp, he recognized Grace's handwriting with a mix of pleasure, guilt, and regret. She had always loved holidays, every one of them—she gave gifts at Valentine's Day, Easter, even Memorial Day—and none more than Christmas. She started shopping in September, stashing the presents under her bed. Mitch smiled, thinking of it now. *We're doing great*, the card said. *Thanks again for your help this year. Love to your family, Grace and Sarah.* The card was a picture of the two of them in red sweaters, a blond head and a dark one smiling at the camera. Grace's eyes were lined and tired, but she looked less frazzled; with her arms around her daughter, she seemed purposeful and amused.

Love to your family, he read again.

He called her, and when she picked up the phone she sounded breathless.

"Oh, Mitch," she said. "This time of year is always so crazy, isn't it?"

It was the day before Christmas Eve. He had the following week off, and would spend Christmas itself with Malcolm and his family, returning the next day. It wasn't, for him, an especially hectic season, but he knew that for others it was.

"Thanks for the card," he said. "How's everything?"

"We're getting by. Leaving tomorrow for Christmas in Vancouver. I don't know what possessed me to travel. It seemed like a good idea at the time."

"Vancouver will be nice," he said. "Warm."

"I'm sure it'll be great once we get there. Now I have ten thousand things to get before we go, and no sitter for Sarah. The usual insanity."

Mitch paused, but only for a second. "Can I help?" he said.

He thought this might provoke an awkward moment, but Grace seized upon the offer.

"That would be *amazing*," she said. "Can you come by in an hour and pick us up? My car's having issues, by the way. It's that kind of holiday season."

"You got it," Mitch said.

He put on his coat, grabbed his wallet and keys, and turned off the lights, finding himself humming. He could have stopped to tidy things up in his apartment before leaving, but he didn't have to. Everything was already in order. He didn't have a single thing to arrange.

He drove them downtown, heading along Sainte-Catherine so Sarah could see the Christmas displays at Ogilvy's, and parked in a lot on de Maisonneuve. As they walked, the winter air bit their cheeks and noses. He followed Grace and Sarah into the stone church facade at Promenades Cathédrale, descending down the long escalators into the underground city. The neon-lit stores stretched endlessly, each a riot of shoppers, the air hot and close. From every store blasted a new carol. *Christmas is coming*, the Payolas sang wearily, *it's been a long year.* Roving packs of teenagers were jostling around the kiosks. One of them, a boy, almost knocked Sarah over and when Mitch yelled at him he spun instantly away, muttering something. "It's okay," Grace said, "let it go."

Sarah waded through the crowds with her coat unzipped, pointing at the decorations, the gaudy trees, the robot snowman waving his arms and nodding his head, the children lined up to see Santa. After a while she started to get cranky, so Mitch took her to the food court for some ice cream while Grace ran around picking up various purchases.

"What do you think?" she asked Mitch when she came back with a sweater for her uncle. He suspected the man would prefer not to receive a sweater at all, but didn't say so. He felt a headache coming on and related more to Sarah's exhaustion—the girl was listing sideways, trawling her plastic spoon through a pool of chocolate sauce—than to Grace's stress over choosing the right present.

"Listen," she said, folding the sweater back into its bag. She sat down across from him and put her arms around Sarah, who leaned against her. "I'm sorry about how we left things."

"It's okay, Grace. You were right. It was weird."

She smiled at him. Her coat was open and beneath it she was wearing jeans and an old McGill sweatshirt. She still moved slowly, stepping gingerly as though she were wearing high heels instead of solid, fur-lined, rubber-soled boots. Despite this lingering air of fragility, though, she looked good. Her eyes were bright, her cheeks flushed, and her long hair fell to her shoulders in smooth waves.

"So how are you?" she said.

"I'm good," he said.

"Are you going to Mississauga for Christmas?"

"Sure. I have to teach Malcolm's kids new bad habits for 2007."

Grace cocked her head. "I'm glad. You're alone too much, I think."
He let this pass.

"I feel like I never thanked you enough for helping me out."

"You thanked me plenty," he said.

When they exited the stores, the day had fled and the streetlights picked out sparkles on the icy sidewalks. The three of them hurried to the car, backs hunched against the cold, the adults laden with presents they stuffed into the trunk. Mitch turned the heat on high, and within a few blocks Sarah fell asleep in the back, her face practically hidden by her hat and hood.

He drove west on Sherbrooke toward Grace's neighborhood. Beyond the McGill campus, the rounded shadow of the mountain hulked on the horizon with its illuminated cross. Grace turned the dial to a classical music station, and the soft ripples of a piano concerto filled the car. They didn't talk. Her face was turned away and she was looking out the window, which grew opaque with condensation. Like a child, she pulled off one of her gloves and with her fingertip wrote some illegible letters on it, then wiped it all away with the flat of her hand and put the glove back on. He kept taking his eyes off the road to glance at her, wondering at her silence, so notable after her animation in the mall. She was probably exhausted too. Drawn to the sight of her strong, thin frame in the passenger seat, her burgundy-colored hat, her dark hair spilling out from underneath, he felt a flicker of unaccustomed energy shiver across his skin. He'd missed her.

Ten minutes later, he pulled up to her apartment building and parked. Sarah was still asleep in the back.

Grace rubbed her eyes, then turned to him. "You saved my life today," she said. "Thank you so much."

"It was nothing," Mitch said.

"No, it wasn't." She leaned over and kissed him on the cheek, an ex-wife's kiss, friendly, sexless.

Yet something in it washed over him and he found himself holding her hand, their gloved fingers intertwined. He could just barely detect the contours of her hand beneath the leather and fleece, its muscles and heat. "I'm glad you're doing better," he said.

Grace nodded, her eyes grave and tender in the shadowy interior. Whatever she heard in his voice must have registered on her, because she squeezed his hand. She seemed to know exactly what he needed, and he couldn't figure out how, unless maybe this was *her* talent. She got out of the car and gathered her daughter in her arms. Mitch opened the trunk, unloaded the many gifts, and stood there in the street, the handles of the shopping bags cutting into his gloves, waiting.

She smiled at him in the winter dark, and then invited him inside.

ACKNOWLEDGMENTS

I'm grateful to Lafayette College, which provided me with a year-long leave from teaching during which I completed an early draft of this book, and where my colleagues have been unfailingly supportive of my work. I began the first chapter while at the MacDowell Colony, and was lucky enough to write later chapters during residencies at Djerassi and the Château de Lavigny—all beautiful places whose nurturing of artists is invaluable. Many friends and family members offered perceptive comments on different drafts, including Joyce Hinnefeld, Don Lee, Ginny Wiehardt, my brother, and my parents. Jenny Boyar contributed helpful research on therapy and acting. Thanks to Liette Chamberland, Yves and Christine Cormier, Ann Devoe, and Diane Robinson for their assistance with French dialogue and Montreal details. My grade two teacher, Grace Tugwell, encouraged my creativity as a child, and I have taken the liberty of borrowing her name (though nothing else) for my characters.

My editor, Gary Fisketjon, has taught me more about writing than I can say. Amy Williams somehow manages to be a wonderful, trusted agent and an even better friend. Lastly, I'd like to thank Stephen Rodrick for reading the book, for making me laugh, and for the future.

A NOTE ABOUT THE AUTHOR

Alix Ohlin is the author of *The Missing Person,* a novel, and *Baby-lon and Other Stories.* Her work has appeared in *Best American Short Stories, Best New American Voices,* and on NPR's *Selected Shorts.* Born and raised in Montreal, she teaches at Lafayette College and in the Warren Wilson MFA Program for Writers.

A NOTE ON THE TYPE

The text of this book was set in Loire, a typeface designed in 1996 by Jean Lochu (b. 1939). An old-style font, Loire was issued in 2001 by Monotype Imaging.

PRINTED AND BOUND BY
Berryville Graphics, Berryville, Virginia

DESIGNED BY
Claudia Martinez